BLOODY CREEK MURDER

BY

Susan Clayton-Goldner

Tirgearr Publishing

Published by Tirgearr Publishing
Ireland
www.tirgearrpublishing.com

ISBN 978-1-910234-52-5

A CIP catalogue record for this book is
available from the British Library.

10 9 8 7 6 5 4 3 2 1

DEDICATION

For my writing friends, Martha Miller, Jane Sutherland, Marjorie Reynolds and Susan Domingos. My life is enriched by your friendships, support and unconditional love.

ACKNOWLEDGEMENTS

A novel never makes it into a reader's hands without help from many others. I owe thanks to the people who helped me along the way. To my husband, Andreas, and my children David and Bonnie. To my beta readers, Marjorie Reynolds, Randy Troyer, Jude Bunner, Susan Domingos, Shirley Reynolds, Cathy Geha, and John Karam. A special thanks to my early reviewers who read the book and posted their reviews on Goodreads and Amazon. Your continued support means everything to me.

As always, I want to thank James N. Frey—my mentor for two and a half decades. He is always just an email away if I run into a wall or need advice or help with plot.

My sincere gratitude to my editor, Lucy Felthouse for her careful readings, Elle Rossi for her incredible cover designs, and Tirgearr Publishing, the best small press in the world, for believing in me.

Finally, a special thanks to Nichole Ferrari Hamm for my author photo.

Before you embark on a journey of revenge,
Dig two graves.
– Confucius

CHAPTER ONE

Ten-year-old Holden Houseman was no stranger to death. His mother died from pancreatic cancer when he was five. But until Monday, he had no idea how fast a siren could shatter the pine-scented silence. How, in the space of a heartbeat, a boy could stop believing in miracles. Or the way the solid ground he'd once believed would remain forever could slip so quickly from beneath his feet.

Holden and Tommy Bradshaw had been next-door neighbors and friends for as long as either of them could remember. They spent long hours discussing their plans to become astronauts—built rocket ships from Legos and visualized themselves hurtling through outer space, as weightless as helium balloons.

On school days, they did their homework together at the Bradshaws' kitchen table. They ate snacks that Jung-Su, Tommy's Korean housekeeper and former nanny, had prepared, then held wrestling matches in his treehouse, hoping to one day compete on the team at Mountain View High School. Holden's father, Carl, once held the Oregon State High School Championship in his weight class. Holden knew his dad hoped his only child would follow in his footsteps.

Monday afternoon, around 5:30 p.m., as they'd exited Tommy's treehouse and were about to start down the wooden ramp, Holden did a surprise, single-leg takedown. Just once, he wanted to pin Tommy and win their match. When Tommy stumbled onto the platform surrounding the treehouse, the two of them wrestled, about twenty feet in the air. The sun was hanging low in the western sky and cast a soft, golden glow on the wooden platform and in the treetops of the smaller pines and maples below them.

Tommy, the larger of the two boys, did a reversal, flipped Holden onto his back and pinned him easily, then laughed. "You don't know who you're messin' with, my man."

Holden fought the urge to punch him. It wasn't fair. Tommy always won.

"Don't worry." Tommy released his hold. "Once you're wrestlin' in your own weight class, you'll be a superstar."

Disappointed and a little pissed off, Holden turned his body toward the structure, not wanting his friend, who was always so nice, to read the jealousy on his face.

It all happened in slow motion.

Tommy must have momentarily forgotten they weren't inside the treehouse and rolled in the other direction.

Holden scrambled to his feet and reached for Tommy's arm, but it was too late.

Tommy tumbled off the platform. He let out a surprised gasp, then seemed to hang suspended in midair for a moment before landing, with a sickening thud, on one of the stakes in the wrought-iron fence surrounding the tree.

Heart hammering in his throat, Holden raced down the curved ramp circling the tree and stood beneath Tommy, looking up at his pale face. The fence post was lodged in his chest. His lips were trembling, and blood trickled down the post, pooling on the pine needles on the ground beneath him. Tommy moaned.

"I'm sorry," Holden said. "I didn't mean…I just wanted to surprise you…to win for once in my life. Are you okay?"

Tommy stared straight at Holden for an instant, opened his mouth as if to say something, but before he could get the words out, his eyes dimmed—some of the usual bright blue shine disappeared. But his chest still moved in and out. He was breathing.

Holden closed his hands into fists and rocked from one foot

to the other, waiting for an answer he knew wouldn't come. He thought about Miss Blair, Tommy's mother, who was already unhappy for reasons he only glimpsed in the silences at the Bradshaw dinner table whenever Holden spent the night.

The muscles in Tommy's right shoulder twitched beneath his pale, green T-shirt.

A drop of blood fell onto Holden's hand. He checked again for movement of Tommy's chest. It moved, slowly, in and out. "You're gonna be okay. Don't worry, I'm gonna get some help."

And when Tommy didn't say anything, Holden raced through the woods like a blind person, stumbling over his own limbs. The treehouse was situated a little closer to Holden's house, and he needed to call 911. As he ran, he tried to scream for help, to make enough noise to be heard, but his voice came out strangled.

He muttered, "Tommy will be okay. Miracles happen. I see 'em on television all the time when doctors shock hearts back into beating again. Everything'll be okay. Tommy's mouth opened. His shoulder twitched. His chest moved in and out. That must mean he's still alive. I'm gonna get help."

But Holden's body didn't believe his words, and when he came out of the woods, he couldn't see his own backyard because of the tears streaming down his face. He could smell the sharp and bitter scent of marigolds as he raced by the flowerbed they kept planted in memory of his dead mother. He glanced at the fat, little laughing Buddha his mom had set up in the center before she died. If only he hadn't taken Tommy down, the fall wouldn't have happened. This was his fault. He used his open palms to wipe his cheeks, then fumbled for the key in his pocket. He finally managed, despite the way his hand shook, to get it into the keyhole and open the back door.

Once he stepped into the kitchen, it was so quiet he could hear the ticking of the clock on the back of the stove. 5:35 p.m. His father should be home any minute. *Just wait*, he told himself. His dad would know what to do. When the ice machine dropped its cubes into the plastic freezer bin, Holden's entire body jumped.

He raced for the telephone, picked it up and dialed 911.

"Do you have a medical emergency?"

Holden was unable to move any words out of his mouth. What was wrong with him? Tommy needed help.

"Do you need emergency medical assistance?"

"My…my…my…" He stuttered, tried again, but the words wouldn't come.

"I'm sorry, but I can't understand you." The operator grew impatient. "What is the nature of your emergency?"

"P…p…please. You have to help him." Holden dropped the phone. It dangled by its curled plastic cord.

It seemed like hours but was only seconds before he heard the sound of the garage door rising. Holden stood, waiting, and the moment the door into the kitchen opened, he raced into the safety of his father's arms.

His father cradled him for a moment. "What's wrong, son?"

He clutched his dad around the waist, his hands locking behind his father's back. Holden was comforted by the smell of the starch and detergent the laundry always used on his dad's dress shirts, the cedar scent of the aftershave he splashed on his cheeks each morning.

After a moment, his dad unclenched Holden's hands and grabbed him by the shoulders. "You're scaring me. Are you hurt?"

Holden put his hand to his mouth and bit down hard across his index and middle fingers, wanting to feel the pain. When he released his hand, teeth marks indented his skin. His mouth opened and closed like a fish. "No…Not me…I don't…know… It's all my fault," he said between sobs.

His father shook his shoulders. "You have to tell me what happened."

"Tommy and me…we were wrestlin' on the platform instead of inside the treehouse like we usually do. I did that single-leg takedown you showed me. Tommy…he fell off, and…he…he landed on one of those pointy fence posts."

Tommy's father had the fence installed after cougars were seen in the woods behind their houses.

His father flinched. "Did the fence post tear his skin? Do you think he needs stitches?"

4

Holden said nothing.

"Answer me, son. Is Tommy okay? Did he get up after he fell?"

Holden pulled back, tears carving a river down his face. He looked up at his father. "Tommy didn't fall all the way to the ground. The fence post…it got stuck inside him." He pointed to the left side of his chest, over his heart. "Right here."

His father squeezed his eyes shut for an instant like he didn't want to imagine the scene Holden's words painted. When he opened them again, he stared hard at Holden. "Did you call 911?"

"Yes. But I…I couldn't talk about what happened. The words wouldn't come out. I was too scared. Will I have to go to jail?"

His dad's hand trembled as he picked up the telephone. At that moment, they heard the wail of sirens.

His dad stood up real straight, and he clutched the back of Holden's head, pulling him in hard against his chest for another moment that Holden wanted to last forever, to feel the protection of that hand on the back of his neck for the rest of his life. "Either Jung-Su phoned for an ambulance or they traced your call. It's going to be okay now, son."

It felt good, being held so tight he couldn't possibly hurt anyone or anything. With his ear pressed against his father's chest, Holden heard his dad's heart beating fast.

When his dad let him go, Holden ran to the window as an ambulance, followed by a fire truck, pulled into their driveway, wheels screeching through the silence.

His father raced outside and pointed toward Tommy's treehouse, then returned to the house and spoke to Holden. "I'm going to see if there is anything I can do to help. You stay here. Don't let anyone inside and don't answer the phone."

After his father left, Holden paced back and forth across the kitchen until he finally collapsed on the hardwood floor. He drew his legs up, leaned back against the dishwasher, and pushed his head into his knees. He stayed that way for a long time. He really didn't know how to pray. But he kept telling himself the men in the ambulance would know what to do. They'd patch Tommy up and make his eyes shine bright again.

There was never a time when he'd wished harder for a mother. Someone to put her arms around him and tell him it wasn't his fault and that everything would be okay.

He couldn't help it; he cried for a long time, not loudly, which was what he wanted to do but soft, the tears dripping down his cheeks and onto the front of his white school shirt. His mind kept going to a place he didn't want it to go. To scenes he never wanted to imagine. Like his friend hanging from the fence stake. What if Tommy died? He pinched the skin on his arm hard to stop the imagining. If he didn't let himself think the word, he wouldn't have to face everything it meant.

Across the room, on the back of the stove, the clock ticked away the minutes and time passed, unbroken by Holden and his father's nightly routine. A simple dinner. Their usual chess games. The hot chocolate they drank after Holden's shower. A chapter from *Tom Sawyer* they read together before bed.

It grew dark, but Holden didn't bother to turn on the lights or get up from the floor. When he finally heard the sound of his own name, it took him a moment to understand, to raise himself back to his feet.

Light flooded the kitchen. Holden wiped his face on his shirt sleeve and stumbled into his father's arms. He tried to swallow, but his tongue felt too thick. Finally, the question came out. "Is Tommy gonna be okay?"

After hugging him close for a second, his father held him by the shoulders at arm's length. The look on his dad's face was so pinched, his eyes swollen, red and filled with sadness, it frightened Holden even more.

"Listen to me, son. I'm sorry, but Tommy didn't make it. I followed the ambulance to the hospital. Jung-Su rode inside with him. But he was already dead when they arrived. The doctor in the emergency room said he didn't think Tommy suffered for long."

Holden jerked away, clamped his eyes shut and heard the sound of Tommy's gasp and the awful thud again before his eyes went funny.

His father gave his shoulders a gentle shake. "It's not your fault, son. It was an accident. A terrible accident."

The words wouldn't sink in. Holden didn't think he could possibly survive to grow up and become an adult, that he could ever bear the weight of this thing in his heart that already hurt so much. He opened his eyes.

"Does Miss Blair know?" Holden loved Tommy's mother and often wished she was his mother, too. Now, she would hate him forever.

"Not yet. Jung-Su called Tommy's parents. They're on their way to the hospital. I came home because I didn't want to leave you here all by yourself any longer."

"Where's Tommy now?"

His father let go of Holden's shoulders, and the boy watched him struggle to find a way to tell the truth. They were always honest with each other. "His body is in the emergency room, or maybe it's been moved to another location in the hospital. After his parents arrive, I imagine it will be sent either to the medical examiner or to a local funeral home."

"Will I ever see him again?" Holden didn't go to church, but he knew enough about religion from friends who did to wonder if Tommy's soul might have taken flight. If he might be hurtling somewhere in outer space, living the life the two of them had once dreamed of.

"I need to say something to you, son. And I want you to listen very carefully. This is important." Lines of worry furrowed his father's brow. "The police sometimes investigate fatal accidents. They may come here, or even to your school, to talk to you because you were the last person to see Tommy alive. The officers might not understand this was a tragic accident. Did Jung-Su see you leave?"

"No. She was still in the kitchen." The treehouse wasn't visible from the Bradshaws' house. "She didn't come down to call Tommy for dinner yet."

"Good. If the police come, I want you to say Tommy was fine and still inside his treehouse when you left. Tell them you heard him cry out, ran back, saw what had happened, then raced home to call 911. That you were so scared you couldn't get all the words out. Tell them your dad heard the sirens and knew they'd traced the call and sent an ambulance. Say I made you stay inside while I went to see what was going on next door. I want you to say that to Mr. and Mrs. Bradshaw, too. And Jung-Su, if she asks you."

"But that's a lie, Dad." His voice wavered. "You told me to always tell the truth. That I wouldn't get in trouble if I did."

"I know, son. But this is one of those times when that rule doesn't apply. It's my job as your dad to protect you. I know Tommy was your best friend. I know how much you loved him, and would never do anything to hurt him. But the police don't know that."

"You mean they might think I hurt Tommy on purpose?"

His father's eyes were cast down at the hardwood floor. "Let's not take that chance, okay, son?"

Holden stared at his father, then ran down the hallway and into his bedroom, slamming the door behind him. Telling the truth had always been a steadfast rule in their household. His dad said he'd never get in trouble with him as long as he was true to himself and always told the truth.

Tommy was dead.

And the truth was he should never have done that maneuver to trip Tommy. Even if Holden had won the match, what he'd done was against the rules—considered cheating. Holden had no one to blame but himself and his selfish wish to beat Tommy, just once. His dad must feel the same way. Otherwise, he wouldn't have told Holden to break the rule and lie about what happened.

Still lost in the surprise of what he'd done, Holden stood at his bedroom window, somehow outside himself, and watched from another place, adrift in the moments and decisions leading up to Tommy's death—decisions that he already understood would shape the rest of his life.

Outside the window, on the koi pond in front of their house, the moon and stars were reflected on the water's dark surface as if even the sky had been turned upside down.

* * *

"I don't want to go," Holden said. "What if I see Tommy dead and start crying? What if I can't stop?"

His dad stared at him but didn't respond.

For a moment, Holden wondered if he'd heard him.

"That tie is all wrong for a funeral." His father pulled a black and gray striped clip-on from the bottom dresser drawer in Holden's bedroom. "How about you wear this one."

Even though Miss Blair liked red, Holden ripped off the red tie and clipped on the one his father had chosen.

"You won't have to see his body, son. Tommy was cremated, and this is a celebration of his life. His mom wanted to hold it in the woods near his treehouse—because it was Tommy's favorite place. You were his best friend. Other classmates are attending. It will look bad if you aren't there."

"But if I see the treehouse again, I'll remember everything and what if…" Holden shifted his weight from one foot to the other.

His father knelt in front of him, his brow furrowed. He put his hands on Holden's shoulders and stared directly into his eyes like he always did when he told Holden something important. "All you need to remember is you were nowhere near that treehouse when Tommy Bradshaw fell."

Holden pressed his fists into the sides of his head. His whole body went rigid. He'd wear the darn baby clip-on tie. But lying to Miss Blair, someone he loved, was wrong. She deserved the truth, and he planned to tell it.

Still, he was nervous. He had never been to a celebration of life. He couldn't understand why anyone would celebrate a life that only lasted ten years. But this was Tommy, his best friend, and after what happened, Holden knew he'd never forgive himself if he didn't attend.

"Come on, son." Holden's father urged him across their backyard and towards the familiar woods behind Tommy's house and the haunting sound of a harp playing *Amazing Grace* in the distance. "We don't want to be late."

Holden kept putting one foot in front of the other like his

dad told him, and soon they were standing in front of Tommy's treehouse. Sections of the wrought-iron fence surrounding it were draped with red and white roses. Holden's gaze landed and wouldn't let go of the one spike where Tommy had hung.

His dad nudged him past the fence to where caterers had set up ten rows of white chairs in front of a table, draped with a black cloth. A vase-like container sat on top with Tommy's ashes inside. Holden tried to imagine Tommy's body changed into ashes. Were they like the ones they swept from their fireplace? A huge, framed photo of Tommy in his Scout uniform, fourteen badges on his sash, sat next to the vase. Holden only had twelve. In the photo, Tommy's smile was so big it looked like Christmas morning. The light had caught in his blue eyes and made them shine. His sandy-colored hair was a little longer than usual and curled over the top of his ears. Tommy always hated them, the way they stuck out a little further than most kids' ears did.

Holden memorized every detail of the photograph, then swallowed and looked away.

Lights had been strung in the trees and on the top of the fence. A woman sitting next to the big leaf maple played church songs on a harp. She had blonde hair and was dressed all in white like an angel.

Friends of the Bradshaws and kids from their class at Sand Creek Elementary School had erected a memorial in front of the fence surrounding the treehouse. Holden added the Lego docking station he'd built, then stood with his head down, beside his father.

His dad bent and whispered in his ear, "Remember what I told you."

Holden pushed him away, still angry for the lie his father insisted upon. When he spotted Miss Blair, Tommy's mother, her face streaked with tears, her eye sockets dark, Holden escaped his father's grip and raced over to her. He planned to tell her the truth. If he wanted to grow up to be a good man, he needed to take responsibility for his actions. That's what his dad always told him. At least it was what he used to say.

After Holden wrapped his arms around Miss Blair's waist, he

buried his head in the soft and slippery fabric of her blouse. It smelled like flowers.

She stumbled, nearly lost her balance.

Her skirt was black velvet, and it felt so soft beneath his fingertips. She held him close for a moment, rubbing his back, but didn't say anything. Her touch pierced something inside him. More than anything, he wanted to tell her the truth—to tell her he was sorry. Wanted her to know how much he'd loved Tommy, how he hadn't meant… He opened his mouth to speak, but the words wouldn't come. What if she hated him? What if she'd never wrap her arms around him again? What if he lost her forever the way he'd lost *his* mother?

His father gently took him by the arm and led him away from Miss Blair and into a seat in the second row. They sat, side by side, his father's arm draped over his shoulders until the minister finished his eulogy and gave the signal for Holden and the other nine kids from Tommy's class to step forward. They huddled together in front of the gate into the treehouse area, held their battery-powered candles, and recited the Lord's Prayer.

Afterward, the preacher said a blessing and food was served. The other kids from his class climbed the ramp into the treehouse, but Holden stayed close to his father. He never wanted to step inside that place again.

Later that night, in the safety of his own room and unable to sleep, Holden remembered the truth he'd never be able to forget.

CHAPTER TWO

Friday, May 4, 2001

Detective Winston Radhauser lunged the roan stallion in the round pen on his family's ranch in Ashland, Oregon—a thirty-two-acre paradise they'd named Graceland. Ashland was a Renaissance village set in the foothills of the Siskiyou mountains. It was most renowned for its diversity and its world-class Shakespeare Festival. The picturesque university town had surroundings so beautiful, visitors often called it God's Country. After nearly a decade, Radhauser and his family called it home.

The bay stallion, Ameer, the Arabic name for prince, was a lean, spirited Arabian about fifteen hands high with four white feet and a blaze. Radhauser wanted to prove he'd learned a few things about horse training. He planned to saddle break the horse for Gracie. Ever since the cancer, diagnosed during her pregnancy with Jonathan, he was a bit over-protective of his wife and couldn't imagine his world without Gracie and the kids. She'd come through chemo and radiation like the trooper she was. All signs pointed to a complete recovery. Still, he knew how fast his world could change, and he wasn't about to let his guard down again.

At first, Ameer had reared and kicked until he worked up a sweat. But over the last few weeks, the stallion became accustomed to the halter and bridle and had even allowed the saddle blanket to stay on his back for an extended period of time.

Radhauser stopped lunging and draped the blanket over the subdued horse, added the saddle, then carefully tightened the cinch. The air around them was tinged with the smell of alfalfa from the dozens of bales he'd stored in the alcove behind the arena.

With the coat of molasses he'd put on the bit, the horse took it without a fight. He led Ameer over to the fence surrounding the pen, then climbed up the rails until he was higher than the saddle.

"Are you gonna ride him now, Daddy?" His six-year-old daughter, Lizzie, sat on the fence beside her mother. Just like Gracie, she wore a pair of denim jeans, red cowgirl boots, and a short-sleeved, red T-shirt with the Arabian Horse Association logo, a black sculptured horse head, on the front.

Outside the round pen, seventeen-month-old Jonathan sat playing with bristle blocks in a playpen set up under the shade of a big leaf maple tree.

"I suggest you lunge him with the saddle on for another ten minutes or so." Gracie smiled and gave him one of her looks that said, *Listen up. I know more about this than you.*

Radhauser ignored her advice and slowly lowered himself into the saddle until his full weight was resting on it. But before he was firmly seated or could grab the saddle horn, Ameer reared and bucked. With his ears pinned back, he snorted and jerked his head, his black mane flying. His front legs lashed out, and his dark eyes were wide open like he'd been spooked.

The detective was tossed backward off the smooth leather saddle and landed with a thud on the sandy floor.

Gracie laughed.

Radhauser let out a sigh, stood and brushed off the seat of his jeans while Ameer bolted in circles around the fence line of the pen. His pride hurt more than his body.

"Better stick to what you know," Gracie said. "You're not exactly Bill Shoemaker."

Shoemaker was one hell of a rider—an old-time jockey who held the world record of most professional wins for twenty-nine years. "I'm a foot and a half taller than he was and about a hundred pounds heavier. It puts me at a slight disadvantage."

She gave him a knowing look. "Believing yourself invincible can be a handicap."

"Daddy fell off the horse." Lizzie covered her mouth and giggled. It came out in little bubbles, like water starting to boil.

Gracie slipped from the fence and walked slowly toward Ameer. "It's okay, boy. You're okay now."

At the sound of her voice, the horse's ears shot forward and he whinnied a greeting. Gracie Radhauser, the horse whisperer, took a carrot out of her back pocket.

Ameer moved closer to her. While he nibbled, she removed the bit and bridle, replaced it with a halter and led him around the pen.

When she passed Lizzie, still sitting on the fence, she squeezed the little girl's leg. "Maybe Daddy needs a little more training."

Lizzie giggled again—a sound Radhauser loved more than any other.

Even Jonathan got in on the fun. He scrambled to his feet, stood in his playpen, and clapped his hands. "Daddy go boom."

As if on cue, Radhauser's cell phone rang. He answered, relieved to discover it was his new partner, Maxine McBride.

"I know you're on vacation. But any possibility you can help me out? Officer Corbin just called. He's at a house over on Sand Creek Road. The husband suspects his wife committed suicide because of the recent death of their ten-year-old son, Tommy. But Corbin isn't so sure and wants us to check things out. He thinks we may have a murder case. From what I understand, it isn't pretty. The victim is Blair Bradshaw. Apparently, she's an actress with the Shakespeare Festival."

"Nothing I'd rather do." Radhauser wrote down the address and gate code. "Meet you there in ten minutes. And call Heron. You know how he likes to investigate the scene himself."

Gracie continued to work Ameer, but glanced up at Radhauser and smiled. "Looks like you've been saved by the bell."

He lifted his hands, palm side up. "What can I say? Murder calls. So, I'm off to do something I'm actually good at. But you be careful. That's a stubborn one."

She gave him a gratuitous smile. "Don't worry. Ameer has met his match in me."

14

And Radhauser knew she was right. Gracie was a far more skilled horse trainer than he'd ever be.

His daughter, always the diplomat, grinned. "You're good at being my daddy."

He ruffled her dark hair, releasing the smell of apple shampoo and sunshine. "Thanks, Lizzie girl. That makes me feel a lot better."

* * *

After driving through the open, arched, wrought-iron gates and continuing down a long, asphalt driveway lined with sweet-scented, pink-flowering cherry trees, Radhauser parked his Crown Vic behind an ambulance and two police cruisers and got out of his car.

The Bradshaw house was a cedar A-frame with a stone foundation. Two sprawling wings jutted out on either side. Massive stone chimneys rose on both ends of the central area. He looked around, wondering if a neighbor could have witnessed something, but could only see the driveway of one other house. The Bradshaw property must be at least five acres.

All this beauty juxtaposed against what Radhauser knew awaited him. His knowledge of Franklin Bradshaw was mostly by his reputation and the few times the detective had testified against a client Bradshaw represented. The man was a tiger shark. Probably the best and most expensive criminal defense attorney in Jackson County. Cops called him "the lawyer most likely to free the guilty."

And though he disliked Bradshaw for professional reasons, Radhauser couldn't help but think about the dark and rutted road Franklin Bradshaw would have to travel now. A journey Radhauser wouldn't wish on his worst enemy. No one knew better than he did the pain involved in losing both your wife and son. All Bradshaw's wealth and beautiful surroundings hadn't made him immune.

The pain might lessen over time, but it never disappeared. Sometimes it awakened Radhauser in the middle of the night, twisting through his stomach into his chest until his heart drummed and he felt like he couldn't take another breath. When

15

it happened, he'd lie there in the dark, praying it would go away. He'd try to force it from his mind and remember something happy the three of them had done together—not the images of Laura and Lucas' broken bodies on steel gurneys in the hospital morgue.

Gracie thought memory was a gift from God, but Radhauser knew it for the nightmare it could be. Then one day, you woke up and realized that grief was now a permanent part of you.

Radhauser followed the sound of voices, inched his way around to the back of the house. A kidney-shaped swimming pool sparkled in the sunlight and gave off a faint hint of chlorine.

He stood for a moment, imagining Tommy Bradshaw doing a cannonball off the side of that pool. In slow motion, Radhauser saw the ten-year-old draw his knees up to his chest, clamp his arms around them and jump. Now Bradshaw's wife was dead, too. Yes, the attorney's life would change in silent ways he'd never dreamed possible. Radhauser shook his head to clear his thoughts and reminded himself he was here as a detective, not a grief counselor.

As always, he moved slowly, taking in everything—noticing anything that might turn out to be evidence. The sounds led him down a worn path into the woods where Officer Corbin was cordoning off the scene with yellow crime-scene tape.

Radhauser greeted the officers, two of whom were combing the grounds for evidence, then slipped his notebook from his inside pocket and made a quick sketch of the area. He removed his camera from his backpack. Even though forensics would take photos, he liked to snap his own—from a distance first in order to get an overview of the entire crime scene.

In a clearing in the woods, an elaborate treehouse, constructed like a miniature of the family A-frame, was set on a platform between two thick branches about halfway to the top of an old, massive oak tree. A three-foot-wide wooden ramp led up to the house, circling the tree a few times before reaching the top. It reminded Radhauser of a castle's drawbridge—the wooden posts about four feet apart and draped with heavy rope.

A six-foot-high fence of black, wrought-iron spikes that came to arrowhead-like points, set about two feet apart with a matching

16

wire mesh between them. The fence surrounded a twenty-foot square area around the oak tree, planted with grass as thick as any golf course. Behind the treehouse, dense woods nestled against the foothills of the Siskiyou Mountains, a perfect backdrop.

It was a warm spring day, seasoned with the scent of wildflowers and pine sap. Purple lupine, miniature sunflowers, and hot pink shooting stars blanketed sunlit areas of the woods. Below him, water cascaded over rocks as the bright sun melted the remains of their mountain snows into Sand Creek. Radhauser paused a moment to listen. Again, he was struck by the beauty—an idyllic setting for a boy and his treehouse, and not one where you'd expect to find a horrific, double tragedy.

In an approximately three-by-ten-foot area in front of the fence, on either side of the gate, mourners had left stuffed animals, cards, books, flowers, battery-powered candles and hand-painted signs in child-like script. *We love you, Tommy. I'll miss you, Tommy.* One of the kids had constructed a Lego space station. A poster board held messages from the entire fifth-grade class at Sand Creek Elementary.

Tucked in front of the shrine lay the body of a woman Radhauser presumed was their victim, Blair Bradshaw. She was stretched out, wearing an ankle-length, black velvet skirt and black silk, short-sleeved satin blouse with a single strand of pearls. An empty red wine bottle sat upright beside her left elbow.

He shifted his gaze to the treehouse for a few moments, remembering the photograph he'd seen in the *Medford Tribune* early in the week. Tommy Bradshaw was the ten-year-old boy who, according to news reports, had fallen from his treehouse and landed on the spiked fence.

The article claimed Tommy's parents had installed the fence because there'd been cougar sightings in the area and Tommy and his friends often had sleepovers in the treehouse. Neither parent was home when the accident occurred. The housekeeper found Tommy when he failed to respond after being called for dinner. According to the article, one of the spikes punctured his heart, and he was DOA at Ashland Hospital.

This irony wasn't lost on Radhauser. Had there been no fence, the boy might have had the wind knocked out of him, or broken bones. A fence designed to protect Tommy had killed him instead.

A wave of nausea passed over him the way it always did when he came face to face with a child's death. But he couldn't think about that now. The police had ruled Tommy's death an accident. Radhauser was here to find out what happened to the boy's mother. He sucked in a breath, slipped on his latex gloves, then proceeded slowly toward the crime scene, making a large circle around the treehouse.

A creek flowed over rocks behind the structure. He stood on the bank and glanced down at the water. Something that looked like blood pooled on one of the rocks. Another boulder held a partial bloody shoeprint. Radhauser inched down the bank and photographed the blood. The print looked as if it had been made by an athletic shoe of some type. He guessed it to be a size ten or eleven. In the shallow water, a syringe was caught between two rocks. In case it might be related, he photographed it, picked it up and let the water drain, then dropped the syringe into an evidence bag. He labeled it with the date and location found, then tucked the bag into his jacket pocket.

As he wrote *May 4*, a feeling of dread washed over him. It was the tenth anniversary of the kidnapping of three-month-old Ryan Patterson—Radhauser's first big case after he and Gracie moved to Ashland. The baby was never found. Every year, on the anniversary of the kidnapping, Sean and Holly Patterson stopped by Radhauser's office to see if anything new had developed. As if this day wasn't bad enough, he suspected he'd have to face the Pattersons.

After he climbed back up the bank, he bent and separated some small piles of dried leaves and pine needles with his gloved finger. They were clumped together with something that could be blood. Again, he bagged and labeled. It was then he spotted drag marks someone had tried to cover with forest debris. The marks led from the top of the creek bank to the fence where the memorial was set up. Radhauser photographed everything. It appeared to him the victim had been killed behind the treehouse, near the creek bank, then dragged into the flowers and other memorabilia left for her son.

Finally, he lifted the yellow tape, ducked under it and stepped over to Officer Corbin. "I don't want anyone who isn't official anywhere near this crime scene. The scene is larger than you originally thought. Cordon off the area behind the treehouse, the creek bank, and the section of the creek with the bloody footprint on the rock. After that, I want you to stand guard. Nobody goes in or out of the area unless authorized by me. Understand? No press. And no statements yet. Nobody says a word."

Blair Bradshaw appeared to be in her mid to late thirties with long, streaked, blonde hair and a slender figure. Her makeup was smeared, mascara stained her cheeks. He took a close-up photo of the bottle and its label. Pinot Noir from the *Robertson Vineyard* in the Applegate Valley.

The victim's eyes were closed, and a pair of black, three-inch heels were set, side by side, against the fence. After photographing them, Radhauser picked them up. The shoes looked new, the narrow heels showed no evidence of wear, but the backs were scuffed, further indication the victim had been dragged through the woods. He replaced the shoes against the fence.

Both her skirt and blouse were arranged neatly, her hands folded over her chest like someone had carefully staged the scene. But why? What was the murderer trying to tell them? Did he or she feel remorse? Pity because of the victim's dead son?

He photographed the body from several different angles, then bent to examine it more closely. He could smell the blood—salt and copper with the rankness of a butcher shop.

Areas of the velvet on her skirt were stained and stiff. Was it blood? Her feet and nylon stockings were caked with something that looked like dried blood. Where did it come from? Had she been raped?

When a pair of polished cordovan loafers attached to some huge feet and long legs appeared beside him, Radhauser looked up. The Medical Examiner, Doctor Steven Heron, wore his usual blue/gray lab coat and matching apron. He pulled a pair of latex gloves from his apron pocket and slipped them on. He shook his head. "Just when I thought I'd seen it all."

The ME was a strange man who resembled the Great Blue Heron, often seen roaming the banks of the Rogue River or raiding koi ponds, enough to earn him the nickname, *Blue*. It was mostly because of his slender frame, his long neck and the way his head seemed to arrive in a room before the rest of his body. But when it came to forensics, this ME was unparalleled. Heron placed his aluminum case on the ground near the fence and crouched beside Radhauser.

"I'm not one hundred percent certain, but from the looks of the blood over there," Radhauser pointed to an area near the creek bank. "And from the drag marks and blood I found in the pine needles, the scuffs on the back of her shoes, I'd say we have a murder."

"Don't be so hasty, cowboy. We both know suicide victims can stage a scene to look like a murder."

"That's right. And murderers, in an attempt to hide what they've done, can stage one to look like suicide," Radhauser said. "I'd bet my best boots on murder. But I have no idea what kind of weapon was used. Unless it was the syringe I found wedged between two rocks in the creek. But that wouldn't account for the blood." He took the evidence bag out of his pocket and handed it to Heron who studied it for a moment, then dropped it into his larger evidence collection box.

"Let's have a look at her." Heron knelt beside the victim and lifted her eyelids. Her eyes were bright blue and clear. "No sign of petechia."

Radhauser knew petechia were pinpoint hemorrhages in the eyes, always present when a victim was suffocated. He removed her pearls, tucked them into an evidence bag, labeled it, and added them to the box.

Heron examined her neck. "No bruising around the neck leads me to believe she wasn't strangled."

"Judging from the blood on her feet and stockings, either rape or a botched abortion is a definite possibility," Radhauser said.

Heron used a pair of tweezers to lift two hairs from Blair Bradshaw's skirt, carefully placing them into evidence bags. Then he gently raised the skirt. "I'm sorry I have to do this," he said to the victim.

Others might find it odd, but Radhauser admired the respect his friend showed for the dead. Her slip and underwear were intact but covered in blood. There were small pools of blood in her groin area.

When Heron wiped it away, he discovered two-inch incisions on both her left and right groin—cut through her pantyhose.

"Her femoral arteries have been severed."

A streak of horror shot up Radhauser's back, as real as a lightning strike. The hair on his forearms lifted.

"There's your cause of death," Heron said. "She would have bled out in a matter of minutes. Given that her pantyhose are on pretty straight, it's unlikely she was sexually assaulted. But once she's on the table, I'll check for semen and vaginal tears. Could you help me turn her over?"

Radhauser and Heron gently rolled the body over onto its stomach. The velvet on the back of her skirt was crushed, nearly threadbare in places, pine needles, and other forest debris embedded in the fibers. The back of her pantyhose, at her calves, were also shredded.

"I can't imagine she sliced herself at the top of the creek bank, then dragged her own body over here," Radhauser said. The scene looked too perfect—almost like it had been staged. The wounds being self-administered wouldn't explain the blood and shoe print he'd found on the rocks near the creek. He glanced at the pair of black heels lined neatly against the fence. No way that shoe print belonged to the vic.

Radhauser stood and turned to the two-man forensic team, dressed in white hooded coveralls, who'd been working the scene.

"Any special instructions?" one of them asked.

"Photograph everything. Including each item in the memorial. Dust them for prints. Check to see if the victim placed a note in the memorial. Pay close attention to the shoes and wine bottle.

Take swatches. Bag her hands and feet. And check the blood and footprint on the rocks in the creek. Don't miss a damn thing. Search the area in a wide radius for a cutting instrument the victim could have used to slice herself, then tossed. Rake the area and sift through what you find. If this turns out to be a murder, the whole community will be in an uproar."

"I haven't ruled out suicide," Heron said.

"She couldn't have committed suicide without a weapon. So far, I haven't found anything that could account for two severed femoral arteries."

The ME leaned in a little closer. "Be patient. Give forensics time to search. I'll know a lot more after I get her on the table. Once I clean her up, I'll be able to determine if the wounds could have been self-inflicted."

"Come on, Heron. You know she didn't scoot through the woods on her butt after she'd sliced her femorals. Not to mention arranging herself so precisely in the memorial. Why can't you just accept she was murdered?"

Heron's Adam's apple bobbed—a sure sign he was annoyed. "Because that's not the way I do things. And you know it."

Radhauser knew it all right. Heron spent long hours in his autopsy suite, laboriously measuring and weighing every organ, taking extensive notes. It was probably what made him good at what he did. There was no way Radhauser could be a forensic pathologist. He was far too impatient for answers.

He decided to change the subject for a moment, stared up at the treehouse and wondered if there could be a connection between Blair's death and the death of her son. "Did you do an autopsy on the Bradshaw boy?"

"No. But I did talk to the ER doctor who pronounced him. He had no reason to believe it was anything other than accidental. The boy was clean, healthy, and well-nourished. No record of multiple ER visits, old fractures, or any other evidence of abuse."

"Did anything strike you as odd about the accident? The boy was ten years old, not a toddler who might trip over his own feet and fall."

Heron thought for a moment. "Bizarre accidents happen. But his father found the way Tommy landed on the spike a bit suspicious. I've testified for him in court a few times, so he asked me to take a look. I adjusted the dummy to seventy-five pounds and four feet, eight inches, the same weight and height as the boy, and carried out a couple experiments."

Radhauser wasn't surprised. Heron left nothing to chance, and not much escaped him either. "And what did that tell you?"

"I determined it could have been an accident, but the victim wasn't standing when it occurred. After I placed the dummy flat on its back and rolled it off the platform, it landed on one of the fence spikes. There were no witnesses, so we'll never know for sure what happened."

"Have your thoughts about it changed now that his mother is dead, too?" Radhauser looked over at Heron, saw the weight of the question pulling his shoulders down.

Heron exhaled a long burst of air. "Yes. I think you should take another look. Maybe there is someone who thought his or her life would be better without Blair and Tommy Bradshaw."

Radhauser thought about that and, of course, the first person who came to mind was the husband and father.

Maxine McBride, his partner, spotted Radhauser and hurried over. A beam of sunlight caught the gold in her left earring and gleamed. Maxine was a small woman who couldn't weigh more than a hundred and ten pounds and stood less than five feet, four inches tall. She kept her light brown hair streaked with blonde and short as a young boy. But the gold rattlesnake earrings she always wore, their bodies coiled around her earlobes, warned suspects and other officers not to underestimate her competence. Maxine was one of the best police officers Radhauser had ever encountered. He was pleased when Captain Murphy took his recommendation to promote her to detective and make her Radhauser's new partner.

"Forensics estimate she died sometime between ten and midnight," she said. "Heron may be able to narrow it down even more."

"I requested they do a thorough search of the area for a cutting tool that might have been used to slash her femoral arteries. If we don't find one, that pretty much rules out suicide. Looks like we've got ourselves a murder case."

She jerked her head toward a man who paced in front of a cluster of Madrone trees, just outside the crime scene. "That's her husband. He was the first one to find the victim. I figured you'd want to question him yourself. His name is Franklin Bradshaw. He's a lawyer with Bradshaw, Foster & Meyer, in Medford."

Radhauser waited inside the crime scene tape while Heron finished his external examination, bagged her hands and feet, then lifted her body onto a gurney. She wore a diamond watch on her left wrist. Radhauser removed it and slipped it into an evidence bag. They could eliminate robbery as a motive.

The two of them wheeled her through the woods to the ME's van parked in the Bradshaws' driveway. "You know how fast things go cold," Radhauser said. "I'm going to investigate the way I would if you'd already ruled it a murder."

Heron smiled. "Call me surprised."

Once Blair Bradshaw was loaded into the van, Heron turned back to Radhauser. "Stop by my office on your way home tonight. I'll be working late. I suspect I'll have a preliminary report for you by 6 p.m. or so."

CHAPTER THREE

When Radhauser approached, Franklin Bradshaw stopped pacing the worn path between two enormous pine trees and slipped his left hand into his pants' pocket, lawyer style. He was dressed for work in an expensive charcoal-gray suit, pale blue dress shirt, and wingtips polished to a high shine. In Radhauser's judgment, they looked to be about a ten or eleven—just the right size to have made that bloody footprint on the rock. Bradshaw's dark hair was gelled into place. From a distance, he looked like a male model, but up close, he had the veined nose of a heavy drinker. He smelled like British Sterling with a hint of sweet, metabolizing alcohol seeping through his skin.

If he recognized Radhauser from the times he'd testified against one of Bradshaw's clients in court, he gave no indication.

Radhauser tipped the brim of his Stetson, showed his badge, then offered his hand. "I'm Detective Winston Radhauser with the Ashland Police Department, and I'll be investigating your wife's death. I'm very sorry for your loss, Mr. Bradshaw."

After shaking Radhauser's hand, Bradshaw leaned against the smooth trunk of a Madrone tree and lowered his head. "Loss," he mumbled. "Such a minuscule word. First, my son and now my wife." His frayed voice had a hollowness to it as if the sound had traveled through an empty tunnel.

Radhauser gave him a moment to compose himself. No one understood better than he did how hard it was to comprehend the enormity of something this devastating. Like cancer, grief was carnivorous and fed on its victims whether they fought it or not. But he had a job to do, and he couldn't let his sympathy get in the

25

way. "Would you be more comfortable if we talked in the house?"

He glanced at Radhauser's cowboy boots, a bit muddy from his climb down the creek bank, then over at the crime scene Corbin had taped off. "Here in the woods is fine. What difference does it make?"

"Can you tell me what happened?"

Bradshaw shoved both hands into his pockets. "I think it's more than apparent. My wife killed herself. Blair was depressed over the death of our little boy. Tommy was her life." He shrugged, his face a mask of pain at the mention of his son. "What else do you need to know?"

"Your wife's femoral arteries were severed. And whatever was used to sever them is nowhere near the body. It doesn't take a genius to conclude that suicide wasn't the cause."

Bradshaw took his hands out of his pockets and raised them to cover his face. "Her femoral arteries?" After a moment, he lowered his trembling hands and shook his head, but didn't meet Radhauser's gaze. "That's horrible, but it doesn't rule out suicide. Blair was an actress and always went for the scenes with the most drama."

It was a strange thing to say at a time like this, and his use of the past tense so soon after his wife's death didn't escape Radhauser. "I don't believe her wounds were self-inflicted."

"Are you saying she was murdered? Who would murder Blair?" Bradshaw clutched his chest like a man about to have a heart attack. He backed up a few steps.

The gestures seemed slightly melodramatic to Radhauser, especially for the usually calm and collected Franklin Bradshaw. "We won't know for certain until after her autopsy results are available."

"I think you're wrong," Bradshaw said. "Blair is…was a popular Shakespearean actress—well-loved in Ashland and beyond. I can't imagine anyone wanting her dead."

Popular people were rarely loved by everyone. Someone hated Blair Bradshaw enough to kill her in a brutal and personal way. Radhauser suspected that person wasn't a stranger. "Do you have a life insurance policy for your wife?"

Bradshaw frowned. "Of course I do. Don't think for a minute I'm unaware of where you're going with this. It's always the husband, right?"

"No," Radhauser said. "It isn't. But I'd be remiss if I didn't question you. Would you mind telling me the beneficiary and the amount of the policy?"

"I'm the beneficiary, obviously. Just as she's the beneficiary of *my* policy." The look he shot at Radhauser held a dart inside it.

"I'm merely doing my job, Mr. Bradshaw."

"My wife's policy is for $500,000. We took it out when she got pregnant with Tommy. It was her idea. I wasn't making the kind of money I do now, and she wanted to be sure I could afford help with the baby if something happened to her. Look around you, Detective." He gestured toward the big house, the manicured grounds, the swimming pool. A treehouse that probably cost as much as a Porsche. His hands were shaking so hard he pressed them against his pant legs. "Does it look like I need the money?"

No. It didn't. But it was clear to Radhauser this man needed something else. A drink. "Did your wife stay out in the woods alone after the service ended?"

Bradshaw's face clouded over. "When I left, her brother, Jason, was with her. Everyone else had gone. I went back up to the house to pay the caterers. Blair said Jason wanted to talk to her alone."

"Was she close to her brother?"

He laughed, a bitter sound. "Hardly. I didn't know he existed until a few weeks ago. When her father found out he didn't have long to live, he called Blair. Apparently, the old man wanted to see his daughter again before he died."

What kind of marriage did the Bradshaws have? Radhauser couldn't imagine not knowing Gracie had a sibling or never having met her mother. "Did she go visit him?"

"Yes. And a week later, we heard from his attorney she was in the will. When I questioned her about her father and brother, Blair claimed she was so young when her father left and took the baby with him that she'd forgotten she had a brother. Imagine that." Bradshaw paused and rolled his eyes like that was the most ridiculous thing he'd ever heard. "After the divorce, Jason lived with their father. Blair stayed with their mother. When we first met, she told me her parents were dead, and she never wanted to talk about them. Turns out her father, though dying now, was very much alive then."

Two gray squirrels scurried up the trunk of a big leaf maple. Both Radhauser and Bradshaw turned toward the sound of them chirping. The air smelled of wood smoke and pine sap.

"I haven't checked in with the hospital yet today, but as far as I know, he hasn't died yet. But it's just a matter of days. From what I understand, he's under hospice care now."

"How about her mother?"

"I have no idea," Bradshaw said. "She could be alive and living in the Hollywood Hills for all I know."

"Given the fact they hadn't seen each other in decades, did you think it was odd her brother showed up at the memorial?"

Bradshaw's smile appeared forced. "I thought it kind of him to offer his support."

His answer surprised Radhauser. "Do you happen to know how the will was set up in the case of Blair's death before her father's?"

"I didn't see the actual document. Blair was pretty close-mouthed about it. But, as you no doubt know, inheritance isn't joint marital property. It belongs solely to the one who inherits unless the will states that in the event of the primary beneficiary's death, proceeds will go to a surviving spouse or child."

"Is her father's estate a sizeable one?"

"All I know is it includes a house and a vineyard in the Applegate Valley." His face turned ashen. "Oh, my God. You don't think Jason…?"

It was too early for Radhauser to focus in on any one suspect, but Jason was definitely in the running. "At this point, it appears he was the last known person to see her alive. You can bet I'll be talking to him. Do you have an address?"

"Somewhere out on Route 238 near Applegate."

"Did you see Jason leave last night?"

"I saw his taillights as he pulled out of the driveway. It was about 10 p.m." Bradshaw pulled up a monogrammed cuff and checked his Rolex. Again, his hands quivered. "I'm exhausted. Can we finish up here?"

The man saw her brother leave, but was unconcerned for his wife when she failed to return. Radhauser tried not to groan. "When your wife didn't come back to the house after her brother left, weren't you worried?"

"In truth, I didn't think anything of it. Blair and I don't... didn't...have the kind of marriage that attached us at the hip. Blair was always a bit aloof. I assumed she needed time alone— to feel close to..." He stopped and swallowed hard, then took a handkerchief from his breast pocket. The initials *FAB* were embroidered in the corner. He blew his nose. "You see...our son loved that treehouse. I had it built for his ninth birthday. I should have hired a structural engineer, should have put a railing..."

The pain on his face when he talked about his son was genuine and one with which Radhauser could easily identify. "About what time did the other mourners leave?"

Again, Bradshaw checked his watch, as if he had an important date. "This is getting ridiculous. What difference does it make when everyone left?"

"Just answer the question."

Bradshaw picked up a pine cone and tossed it back and forth in his hands. "Between 9 and 9:30. It was a school night, and some of the mourners were Tommy's friends. Their parents wanted to get their kids to bed. Have I answered all your questions?"

"No."

"I've been standing here for hours, and I need to use the bathroom," Bradshaw said. "Besides that, I have some calls to make."

"I'm happy to wait while you go up to the house and do your personal business." He was tempted to say, *pour yourself another drink*. "But the phone calls can wait until we're finished."

Bradshaw sighed, rocked back and forth on his feet for a moment, then tossed the pine cone into the woods and hurried toward his house.

Less than five minutes later, he returned. He'd tried to disguise the smell of fresh whiskey on his breath with something menthol. "Look, I know how important the first twenty-four hours in a murder investigation can be. Things go cold fast. So, why don't you get out there and investigate someone who might have actually killed Blair?"

Radhauser's patience was wearing thin. "I won't try to tell you how to do your job if you don't tell me how to do mine. Bear with me a little longer, Mr. Bradshaw. This won't take more than another five or ten minutes. Do you know why she was out in the woods so late last night?"

Bradshaw threw his hands up into the air. They were steadier now. "It's been a traumatic few days for both of us. For God's sake, Detective Radhauser. Do you have any idea what it feels like to have your child die before you do?" He met Radhauser's gaze for the first time since they'd shaken hands. Bradshaw's brown eyes were bloodshot.

Radhauser pushed the memory of his wife and son on the steel gurneys aside and looked away, but not before he'd noticed Bradshaw had made no reference to Blair.

"We spread our son's ashes and had the memorial by his treehouse last night. I tried to convince Blair to use a more formal venue, but she insisted there wasn't any church or cemetery anywhere in the world that could hold her grief. When she said Tommy would want it that way, I changed my mind. And maybe she was right. So many of his friends came."

He told Radhauser how the caterers had hung lights in the trees and set up tables of food. That Tommy's classmates and friends held battery-powered candles and said The Lord's Prayer. The man who didn't have time to talk, had calls to make, rambled on now like he was nervous, or trying to hide something. Either that or he'd practiced his speech like it was one of his closing arguments.

"It was a beautiful and moving service. Everyone said so."

"I'll need a list of attendees," Radhauser said.

"Those people were our closest friends. They wouldn't hurt Blair. But the funeral home provided a guest book. Ask our housekeeper, Jung-Su. She'll know where it is."

Radhauser jotted notes. Based on the extent of rigor, the ME estimated the victim had been dead for at least eight hours. "When it got really late and she still hadn't come back to the house, why didn't you go check on her?"

"God knows, I should have. But I must have fallen asleep. I don't know. I drank too much at the memorial. I...I..." Again, he put his hands over his face.

Radhauser thought about the empty wine bottle beside the body. "How about your wife? Was she a heavy drinker?"

"Not usually. Sometimes a glass of wine or two. But after Tommy...well, who could blame her?"

"When did you start to look for her?"

"I already told all of this to Officer Corbin. He wrote everything down. Can't you check his notes and allow me some alone time to grieve?" He sighed.

"The sooner you answer my questions, the sooner you can make those phone calls and have time alone. When did you start looking for her?"

Bradshaw released another long sigh. "Not until this morning. I woke up later than usual, and she wasn't in bed. I showered and dressed for work, thinking she'd gotten up early and gone downstairs for coffee. But when I looked in the kitchen, Blair wasn't there either. I called out her name, and she didn't answer."

"And then what?"

He told Radhauser he'd questioned Jung-Su and when she hadn't seen Blair, he called her cell phone, and it rang in the dining room.

"I'll need to have our lab take a look at that phone. I'll return it when I'm finished."

He stared at Radhauser for a moment, as if trying to see inside his head. "Jung-Su can give it to you."

"When I couldn't find my wife in the house, I went outside to the treehouse, thinking she might have spent the night there. I thought maybe Blair had decided to sleep in Tommy's bed as a way to feel close to him."

Radhauser understood. He'd slept in Lucas' bed for weeks after the automobile accident that killed him. No one had mentioned how time slowed down with tragedy, and each minute became painful—excruciating to merely exist in a world without his son.

"About what time did you find her?"

"Look, I know the husband is always the first suspect you have to eliminate. And I'm confident you will eliminate me because I had nothing to do with Blair's death. I'll answer all your questions later. But now I have to get to work."

"Work?" Radhauser said. "Really? Your wife was just murdered, and you're going to work?"

"I understand how it must look to you. But I've been home since Tommy died, hoping it might help Blair. But now that she's gone, too, I don't have anything except my work. Am I supposed to stay here and relive this nightmare over and over?"

In spite of the sympathy he felt, Radhauser remained firm. "As you know, I can get a warrant and force you to come down to the station to answer my questions. Now, what time did you find your wife, Mr. Bradshaw?"

"Around 8 a.m. She was lying among the flowers and candles. She looked almost peaceful."

"What did you do?"

"At first I thought she'd gotten drunk and fallen asleep. I called out her name. When she failed to answer, I moved closer. I could smell the blood. And there were flies crawling on her. I checked for a pulse, and when I couldn't find one, I panicked because I didn't have my cell phone. I ran back to the house and called 911. I knew she was distraught over Tommy, so I made the logical assumption she'd killed herself."

"Did you move or disturb the body in any way?"

"No, I just tried to shoo the flies away and put two fingers over her carotid."

Radhauser gave him a sideways glance. "Before Tommy's accident, was your wife behaving strangely? Or did she seem to be worried about something or someone?"

"She had the locks changed and a more sophisticated security system installed about a month ago. And didn't mention it to me beforehand. When I came home from work, she handed me a new set of keys. She said there'd been a series of burglaries in the neighborhood."

Radhauser made a note to check police records to determine if this allegation was true.

"Do you or your wife have any enemies? Someone with a grudge against either one of you?"

Bradshaw thought for a moment. "It's so hard for me to believe someone did this to her. Who? Why? Under the circumstances, suicide still seems logical to me. Maybe you didn't find a weapon because she threw it into the woods or the creek."

"The absence of the weapon is not the only reason I suspect she was murdered. The ME is very thorough, and I'm sure he'll confirm my suspicions."

"What other evidence do you have?"

"You, of all people, know I need that kept confidential until I have a suspect. Did Blair have a best friend?"

"Most of her friends are theater people. She's pretty close to her understudy." He paused and appeared startled, the way he would if he'd just thought of something. "I guess she'll get the leads now. A young woman named Diamond DeLorenzo." He shrugged. "Obviously a stage name."

Radhauser jotted the name in his notebook. People had murdered for less than a leading role. "Anyone who might have a grudge against you?"

"In my line of work, enemies are a given."

From his own experience in the courtroom with Bradshaw's cross-examinations, Radhauser had no trouble believing that statement. "Make a list for me."

"It will probably be long." He gave Radhauser a cynical smile. "You might even be on it."

So, the arrogant ass recognized him, after all. "I don't care how long it is. We'll check each one out and see if they have an alibi for the time Blair was killed."

"I don't understand why we can't wrap this up. Officer Corbin took copious notes. I told him everything I know."

"I'm the kind of detective who needs to ask his own questions."

"Fine," Bradshaw said, more than a trace of impatience in his voice. "And I'm the kind of attorney who needs to satisfy his obligations to his clients. I already got a continuance so I could be home with my wife this entire week, but the trial is rescheduled to begin Monday morning. Jury selection is today. Do you know how much work goes into preparing a criminal defense?"

There was something almost predatory about the way Bradshaw's gaze fell on Radhauser. Something the detective had noticed in other criminal defense attorneys. They were always looking for something, waiting to find an entrance to the one place inside someone's head where they didn't belong.

"And do you have any idea how much work goes into a murder investigation? I suspect someone else could handle both the jury selection and the trial for you. Or under the circumstances, I'm sure a judge would grant another continuance."

Radhauser had arrested the man Bradshaw was about to represent, and the detective had no doubt about the man's guilt. But Radhauser had done his part, the rest was up to the DA.

"The trial has been delayed long enough. I have an innocent client imprisoned for a crime he didn't commit. Selecting the right jury can mean the difference between life and death in a murder trial." Bradshaw crossed his arms over his chest.

Odd, Radhauser thought, how much crime existed in the world and how few people imprisoned for them ever admitted to any guilt.

"Did your wife blame you for your son's death?"

Bradshaw took a step back—a flash of real sadness in his eyes. "She didn't have to. I blamed myself."

He put his hand on Bradshaw's shoulder. He had sympathy for the man one moment and disgust at his arrogance the next. "Okay. Just one more question and then you're free to go. But I'm sure I'll have more questions later."

"I have a trial. I'm not going anywhere."

"Did you find it odd that Blair never mentioned her brother to you?"

"No."

"Why is that, Mr. Bradshaw?"

"I don't know. Blair was like that."

"Like what, Mr. Bradshaw?"

He sighed as if exasperated by the question. "Different."

"Different in what way?"

"Lots of ways."

"She was your wife. I suspect you knew her as well or better than anyone."

Bradshaw glared at Radhauser for a long moment, contempt darkening his stare. "You're dead wrong. I didn't know her. And I suspect no one else did, either. But I'll tell you something about my wife," he said, a bite in his voice. "She was a woman who loved her secrets. Secrets were power. Secrets were better than sex. Secrets, I firmly believe, were Blair's drug of choice."

If Blair Bradshaw had something to tell him from the grave, it was clear Radhauser would have to work hard to hear it.

They exchanged business cards. "Let me know if you remember anything else," Radhauser said. "Anything at all."

Bradshaw stuck out his hand like he was sealing a business deal.

Radhauser shook it, then tucked the business card into his blazer pocket.

Before leaving the scene to forensics, he wanted to take a closer look at the treehouse. He took the narrow, rope-lined ramp onto the wooden platform, about four feet wide, that formed a square around the entire house. He stood for a moment, looking down at the stakes on the fence. It wasn't hard to imagine how a small child could fall and land on one of them. But a ten-year-old seemed less likely. Once again, he wondered if there could be some connection between the two deaths.

He opened the door and stepped inside. The walls were painted sky blue. One of them held a shelf of sports trophies, an assortment of framed photographs of Little League and soccer teams, a Boy Scout troop camping on the Oregon coast in Brookings. In one of the photos, a smiling boy, with his father's good looks and a sprinkling of freckles across his nose, held up a stick with a roasted marshmallow on its tip. His arm was wrapped around the shoulders of a smaller, dark-haired boy. They wore their Scout uniforms and stood in front of a roaring campfire.

Radhauser swallowed and turned his back to the photo gallery.

On the other side of the twelve-by-twelve-foot room, two bunks were built into a wall paneled in knotty pine. Each held a bookcase filled with *The Hardy Boys* mysteries. It was easy to imagine Tommy and a best friend giggling, holding farting contests and whispering long into the night.

Outside the window, a gray squirrel made a chattering sound as it leaped from one branch to another. Clear, mote-swirling light seeped in through the glass and landed in golden squares on the neatly made and empty bunk beds.

CHAPTER FOUR

*Y*ou don't grow up planning to murder another human being.
Especially if that person is someone you're supposed to admire,
maybe even love. And you didn't return to the woods last night because
you wanted her dead. Another chance at reconciliation and the desire
to make her understand what you needed from her was the reason you
came back. You intended to be reasonable and patient—to reestablish
your relationship and transform it into something extraordinary.

What does it take to turn an intelligent, law-abiding individual
into a murderer? FBI profilers believe they can unravel the mind of a
killer through childhood traits. Were you a bed wetter? Male? Female?
A preteen who set fires between the hedges? Were you a child who
strangled the neighbor's cat or mutilated stray dogs just to watch them
suffer and bleed? Were you the victim of sexual, emotional, or physical
abuse?

Of course, you're not prepared to answer any of those questions,
at least not now. And you don't anticipate being caught. No one ever
does. But you do understand that if you are apprehended, the truth
will be known soon enough.

In the meantime, you'll tell them something about yourself, but not
much. When you were a child, you loved cats and dogs and wanted one
more than anything in the world. Despite your desire, you never had
a pet of your own. But you did chase and catch lizards. You studied
their colorful and slithering bodies in the sunlight, even petted them a
little, before you sliced them wide open with your makeshift scalpel. A
curious kid, interested in biology, you wanted to cut out and identify
their pretty little organs. You were a fast thinker, even then and told
your foster father, Mr. Higgins, when he caught you in the act, that

you wanted to be a heart surgeon and were practicing your craft.

"More likely a serial killer," he'd muttered, as he grabbed you by the ear and led you straight home. Eventually, you chose a different career path. But you never lost your knack with the blade.

You have to give him credit, though. Turns out Mr. Walter S. Higgins may have had the rare gift of prophecy.

* * *

Radhauser sat at the teak table in the Bradshaws' kitchen breakfast nook. He hoped to get information from their housekeeper that might lead him to a viable suspect. The kitchen was painted a soft yellow and lit by skylights. A huge window sill over the sink held a half dozen plants, most of them herbs. It was, by far, the largest kitchen Radhauser had ever seen. The cabinets were a rich cherry-wood, the counters granite, and the appliances were all restaurant grade, stainless steel, and gleaming. Even the floor, also made from wide planks of cherry, was polished to a high shine. It was the kind of kitchen he imagined a gourmet chef dreamed about.

On the other side of the room, Jung-Su, a short and slender Asian woman in her mid to late fifties, puttered around, pulling mugs from the cabinet, setting out cream and sugar while brewing a fresh pot of coffee in an elaborate machine. She wore a pale green uniform with a matching apron. Her shoes were white, like the ones nurses often wear, and her black hair pinned into a bun at the nape of her neck. After pouring a rich-smelling cup for both of them, she sat across the table from Radhauser.

"I no believe this happen." She wrung her hands. "Miss Blair such good woman. She love Tommy so much. And she very sad. But I no think she…she kill herself."

"I don't think she did either." Radhauser took a sip of the coffee, hot and black the way he liked it.

Her dark eyes widened like she'd just been slapped. "But Mr. Franklin. He say she is dead."

"She is. The medical examiner will soon confirm that she was murdered. My job is to find out who killed Mrs. Bradshaw and why."

Her gaze fixed on him like two hot beams. "You say someone

kill her? She murdered? You wrong. Miss Blair very nice person. No one would hurt her."

"Someone did, Jung-Su, and I'm hoping you may be able to help me find out who."

"I no like so much talking to police." There was a fearful catch in her voice. "And my English. It not so good. Miss Blair and Mr. Franklin, they take care of me."

"Your English is quite good," Radhauser said, trying to find a way to make her feel more at ease with him. "Do you live here full time?"

"Yes. Before, I have one-room apartment in Medford, but after Tommy come, I here all time."

"Are you married? Do you have a family of your own?"

She closed her eyes for a moment and took a deep breath. "My family in Seoul. Two boy and one girl. I send money to help them. But they no can come here yet." She shifted in her chair.

The thought passed through Radhauser's mind that Jung-Su might be illegal. He'd read that Asians were now outranking Hispanics in illegal immigration. Was she afraid of deportation? Was that why she was reluctant to talk to the police? "I'm only here to investigate Miss Blair's death. I'm not with Immigration, and I'm not here to hurt you in any way."

She looked at him for a long time as if trying to decide if she could trust him. "I lie. Tell Mr. Franklin I have green card."

Radhauser nodded. "I understand. I hope your family will be able to join you someday. But right now, you want to find out what happened to Miss Blair, don't you?"

She raised an eyebrow, her worried gaze on the herbs in the window sill above the sink. "Yes, I want this."

"Answering my questions will help me find whoever hurt her."

"I no can lose my job."

"I will do my best to protect you." He didn't want to mislead her, couldn't promise to keep what she said confidential. It might be information they'd need to help convict the person responsible for Blair's death. And Jung-Su might be called to testify.

She stared into her coffee cup and wouldn't meet his gaze.

"It's okay, Jung-Su. You can trust me."

"I know nothing. I only work here. Cook. Clean. Take care of Tommy." At the mention of his name, her eyes puddled. She grabbed a Kleenex and wiped the tears. "Sorry. I no understand why he fall. Tommy and Holden. They tell jokes and play in treehouse. Nobody ever fall."

"Was Holden with Tommy on the day the accident happened?"

"Yes. Like every day, I make them snack after school. They do homework here at kitchen table." She patted the wood surface. "Then they go to treehouse. But when I call Tommy for dinner Monday night, he no come. I go to woods." She stopped and put her hands over her eyes like she was seeing it all over again. "Tommy on fence. Blood all over his shirt. Dripping down fence. And Holden, he gone."

"What time was that?"

"5:30. Same every night."

Did this mean Holden had left earlier than 5:30? Maybe there was more to the accident than originally thought. "Do Tommy and Holden ever fight?"

She grimaced and shot him a disapproving look. "Why you ask that? Holden never hurt Tommy." She bit her bottom lip. "They good friends. Like brothers. They wrestle, but only in fun."

"Do you know where Holden lives?"

"He live next door. His mother, she is dead. He live with father. I watch him after school until time Mr. Houseman come home from work."

"Does his father pick him up here at night?"

"Sometimes. Mostly Holden know when 5:30 come and he go home. If he no there when father gets home, Mr. Houseman, he call. Or he walk here. Sometime he call to say he work late and ask can Holden have dinner here."

"What can you tell me about the Bradshaws' marriage? Would you say it was a good one? Were they happy?"

She cocked her head like she was unsure what he meant or what she should say. "Why you ask me that?"

"These are just routine questions. I can ask you here, or I can take you to the police station and ask you there."

Her eyes widened. "I no go to police. I talk here."

He repeated his question.

"I think so. Why not? They have beautiful house. Good jobs. Plenty money." She bounced her right foot against the hardwood floor and looked away, then continued without making eye contact. "They happy. But now, Tommy gone. Miss Blair say her world go black. She tell me she surprise earth no stop turning. She very sad. Me, too."

"Before Tommy's accident, did they spend much time together? Go on vacations? Out to dinner?"

She looked tired, with a hint of loneliness in her eyes. "They busy. Mr. Franklin work long hours. Miss Blair, she is very good actress. Does theater shows many nights. Home after Mr. Bradshaw and Tommy in bed. Sometimes Mr. Franklin work so late, he sleep at office."

Radhauser made a note. In his experience, most men who claimed to sleep at their office were doing more than working late. "Has anything strange happened lately that you're aware of? Maybe a visitor you've never seen before? Someone you noticed hanging around the house who doesn't belong here? Or was Mrs. Bradshaw worried about anything?"

Jung-Su clenched her eyes shut again and seemed to be fighting against her fear. "I no think I should talk to you."

"Listen. There is no way I want to do this, but I can have you arrested for failure to cooperate in a murder investigation."

When she opened her eyes, he could see the fear in them. "About a month ago." She paused, tried to find the words. "Miss Blair very upset. She tell me call locksmith, change door locks and add new ones on back and front door. Then men come. They paste sticker in every window. If I no careful, I set off alarm and police come."

Radhauser had noticed the sign planted in the ground near the front gate. *Beware. This property is protected by Superior Security Systems.* "Did she tell you why?"

"No. But she scared. Woman call Tuesday night after Tommy

died. Tell me she think she is Tommy's grandmother. I say not true. Miss Blair mother dead. Mr. Franklin mother dead, too. Miss Blair take phone from me. Tell woman no call here anymore. Then Miss Blair tell me this woman, she is crazy. Miss Blair's mother dead for years. I must hang up if crazy woman call again." She ran her hands through her hair.

"But didn't this call come after she had the security system put in?"

"Maybe this woman call other time when I grocery shop and Miss Blair answer."

"Do you know where this woman who claimed to be her mother lives?"

"I know nothing."

"How about her brother? Have you met Jason?"

"I meet him last night. First time. He bring wine from his vineyard into kitchen. Say it is for memorial."

Radhauser thought about the empty wine bottle from *Robertson Vineyard*. It shouldn't be too hard to find Jason.

"Did either of her parents ever visit their grandson?"

She shook her head so fast the bun at the nape of her neck quivered. "Never. Until she call, I think both mother and father, they dead. But father call, too. He very sick and want to see Miss Blair."

He couldn't imagine what would make a grown woman pretend both her parents were dead. "Did she visit him?"

"In hospital. After she come home, I hear her tell Mr. Franklin that her father leave something to both her and her brother."

This all confirmed what Bradshaw had told him. Radhauser made a note to look into Blair's family situation. Her brother might not be happy to share his inheritance with a sister he hadn't seen for years.

"Did Mr. Franklin get angry with Miss Blair?"

She gripped the arms of her chair hard enough to bleach her knuckles and lowered her voice to a whisper. "I not know what you mean." Her bottom lip trembled. "Miss Blair always nice to me. I... But I don't know if Mr. Franklin, he keep me here without

Tommy." She cradled her head in her hands.

"Mr. Bradshaw works long hours. I suspect he'll still need you to keep the household running."

Jung-Su looked up at him. Silent tears dripped from her eyes. "Mr. Franklin. He say he need no one."

In an attempt to encourage her to keep talking, Radhauser told Jung-Su what happened to his first wife and son—the loneliness and grief that nearly consumed him for a year afterward. About the way his time at home had stretched out into something that moved so slowly, he'd found it almost impossible to bear. Then he told her how he'd finally met Gracie and now had Lizzie and Jonathan.

She watched him intently while he talked. "I happy for you. But Mr. Franklin, he is not like you."

"What do you mean?"

"I tell you truth. Maybe Miss Blair and Mr. Franklin not so happy." Her voice changed, deepened slightly, and the aura of caution and fear seemed to disappear. "He stay late at office, not come home much. When he here, he look like he counting minutes till he goes back to work. He like this, even on weekend. Sometimes, Miss Blair, she talk to me. She think maybe he…"

Radhauser mentally filled in the words the housekeeper was reluctant to say. Blair thought her husband was having an affair. "Do you know if Mr. Bradshaw left the house after the memorial ended and he'd paid the caterers?"

She stared at the door into the garage for a moment before her gaze darted back to Radhauser, then landed on the tabletop.

"It's important that you tell me everything you know."

"I for sure lose my job if I talk too much."

"Please. I know you want to help me get justice for Miss Blair. I'll do my best to keep your name out of any discussions I have with Mr. Bradshaw."

She cocked her head to one side and studied him for another minute. "You no tell Mr. Franklin I say, but I hear garage door open around 11 p.m. My bedroom wall back up to garage. Door makes loud noise like train. I look out window, Mr. Franklin…he

43

drive somewhere. Maybe he go to his office."

So, the tiger shark lied about his whereabouts last night. "Did you hear him return?"

"Yes. It still dark outside. But I awake wondering what happen to me now with Tommy gone. Clock say 5 a.m."

This would explain why he didn't check on his wife during the night. "Did he take a shower after the memorial, before he left at 11?"

She wrapped her arms around her middle, her dark eyes wide and unblinking. "You no think he hurt Miss Blair?"

At this point, Radhauser wasn't willing to share his opinion of Franklin Bradshaw. "Did he shower after the memorial?"

"No. When he go, he still dressed in suit he wear at memorial."

Franklin Bradshaw had six hours to account for and a lie he needed to explain. Could he have parked on the street, reentered the woods, murdered his wife, then gone somewhere to clean himself up?

"I need the guest book from the memorial. Along with Miss Blair's cell phone."

She stood. "Miss Blair keep guest book with her last night. Must be in woods still. But I get you phone."

"Do you know if Holden went to school today?"

"Mr. Houseman, he ask me to watch him after school until he make other arrangement. I say I no mind watch Holden. He good boy." Jung-Su hurried out of the room and returned a moment later with the cell phone.

Once he found the guest book, he'd have a better idea who attended the memorial. Someone must have seen something that could lead him to a viable suspect. He'd do his best to leave Jung-Su's name out of it when he paid another visit to Franklin Bradshaw and confronted him with his lies.

* * *

Radhauser found the guest book tucked among the flowers, candles, and stuffed animals in the shrine friends and family members had left for Tommy. Before leaving, Radhauser cornered McBride who was still working the crime scene. "I'm going to go over to the hospital and talk to the ER doc who saw Tommy. Then I'll interview the victim's brother. Do you have waders with you?"

She smiled. The sun hit the rattlesnake earring in her left lobe, and the serpent's rhinestone eyes gleamed in the sunlight. "In my trunk, just like you taught me."

"Good. Search the creek for a razor blade, a scalpel, or Exacto knife. Anything that might have been used to slice her femoral arteries. Forensics is combing the immediate area, but our killer may have tossed the weapon as he or she was leaving. In which case it might be somewhere further down the creek."

"Sure thing, boss."

He handed her the phone and guest book. "After that I want you to take these to the station, see if you can find telephone numbers and call everyone. Ask them their relationship to the deceased and what time they left the memorial. And if they saw anything or anyone who seemed suspicious or out of place—like they didn't belong there. Have the lab check the cell phone. See if there are any calls she may have deleted that seem suspect. Make a list. Look at texts, too. Flag anything that looks odd to you."

"I'm on it," she said.

"Good. I'll check back with you after I've talked to Heron. I'll need to re-interview the husband. Seems he lied about his whereabouts after the memorial last night."

"I've got that surprise birthday party for my mother tonight. Would you rather I cancel?"

"No," he replied. "You've been planning it for months. If you're gone when I get back to the office, I'll catch up with you in the morning. I know it's Saturday, but…"

She smiled. "Thanks. Don't worry. I'll be in early. I was never much for Saturday morning cartoons."

Radhauser laughed. "Don't let Lizzie hear you say that."

* * *

As always, Radhauser got that queasy feeling in his stomach as soon as he pulled into the hospital parking lot. He'd stopped believing it would ever go away—that visceral memory of the night his first wife and son were killed.

45

More than a decade had passed, and their ghosts didn't visit nearly as often as they once had. But somehow, hospital emergency rooms always caused them to reappear. He swallowed the golf-ball-sized lump that had lodged in his throat and parked his Crown Vic. After grabbing his backpack, he jogged across the asphalt, through the double glass doors, and up to the desk.

He introduced himself to the dark-haired, fresh-faced nurse. Despite his phobia about emergency rooms, he'd been in this hospital enough times to be on a first-name basis with many of the nurses, but this one was new to him. Radhauser told her he was investigating a murder case and would like to speak to Doctor Landenberg. Perspiration gathered on the back of his neck, and there was a slight tremble in his hands.

She folded her arms across her chest. "Take a seat, and I'll let you know when he's free."

Radhauser tipped his Stetson, then headed for one of the vinyl chairs in the waiting room. He sat, pressed his palms together, and wedged them between his thighs to stop the shaking.

Five minutes later, Doctor Landenberg appeared. "Nice to see you again, Detective Radhauser." The Abe Lincoln lookalike, without the beard, was wearing his usual green hospital scrubs with a stethoscope dangling on his chest like a necklace. He'd aged since the last time Radhauser had seen him—his dark hair streaked with even more gray. He was as tall as Radhauser, around six feet three inches, and his face was ruddy and in need of a shave. He looked like a man who'd worked through the night.

Landenberg led Radhauser into a conference room that held a loveseat, a small round table, and two chairs. He closed the door, then nodded toward the loveseat.

Radhauser sat, took off his Stetson.

"You caught me just before I go off duty. What can I do for you?" His voice was thick with fatigue.

"I wanted to talk with you about Thomas Bradshaw, the ten-year-old boy who was brought in last Monday night after being impaled on a spiked fence."

Landenberg pulled a chair from under the table and turned

it to face Radhauser. The doctor looked like he'd rather get a colonoscopy than talk to a detective about a dead kid. "The DOA? Such a bizarre accident."

"I was called to the scene this morning," Radhauser said. "Franklin and Blair Bradshaw held a memorial service for their son last night in the woods by his treehouse. His mother was found dead in front of the shrine his classmates left. At this point, I believe she was murdered. And that has made me question if there could be some connection to her son's death."

Landenberg clamped his thick hands on his knees and leaned forward as if it hurt to even imagine the scene. "Are you sure it was murder? I have to be honest with you, Detective. I've never seen a better candidate for suicide. That poor woman was hysterical. She insisted on seeing her son's wound. When she did, she collapsed, dropped to her knees on the floor and howled. It was one of the worst sounds I've ever heard. It took both her husband and me to get her back on her feet and into a chair. We did some blood work that turned out to be normal. But I wrote her a prescription for valium. I wanted to admit her, but she was adamant she wanted to go home."

Though Radhauser had no real basis for the feeling, Landenberg's words and his slight southern accent gave off a sense of confidence that this physician was someone who both cared about his patients and could be trusted to tell it the way he saw it.

"Based on the evidence we found at the scene, we're pretty sure she was murdered. I can't be one hundred percent certain of anything until Doctor Heron finishes with his autopsy. But, for now, I'm investigating it as a murder."

"I understand." Doctor Landenberg's Adam's apple bobbed.

"Just one more question. In your estimation, is there any possibility Tommy Bradshaw's death was no accident?"

The physician rested his big chin in his cupped hand like it had grown too heavy to hold up. He told Radhauser there was nothing to make him suspect abuse —no old bruises or evidence of healed fractures. That it was Tommy Bradshaw's first visit to the ER. "From what I understand, there were no witnesses to the fall.

To me, that means anything is possible, Detective Radhauser. But who'd want to murder a ten-year-old boy?"

CHAPTER FIVE

On the drive to the *Robertson Vineyard*, Radhauser reviewed what he knew so far. The Bradshaw marriage had some flaws. Franklin sometimes spent the night in his office—or claimed he did. He had an insurance policy on his wife for half a million dollars. In addition to the money, he'd have even more to gain from his wife's death if it turned out he was having an affair or was actually in love with someone else. Though from what Jung-Su had told him, he doubted Bradshaw's ability to love anyone more than himself. The man had failed to mention he'd left his house after the memorial ended. Where was he last night between 11 p.m. and 5 a.m.?

Of course, he may have been working late, pulling an all-nighter in preparation for Monday's trial. He certainly seemed obsessed with doing everything he could for his client. A half million dollars in life insurance was a fortune to most people, but Franklin Bradshaw claimed he didn't need the money. From every appearance, he was right. Good criminal defense attorneys were well paid. Most people would spend their life savings if they believed it would prevent their loved one being imprisoned.

Blair's brother also had a motive. In all probability, the half of their father's estate that would have fallen to Blair would now stay in the hands of Jason Robertson. People have murdered for far less than a family vineyard.

As he drove down Main Street in the historic town of Jacksonville, he passed the Belle Union Saloon. Brick storefronts along the main road hadn't changed in more than a century. It was an old gold mining town in the mid eighteen hundreds and was now a favorite spot for both tourists and locals.

Once through town, the road narrowed onto Route 238, and the Applegate Valley opened its lush, green arms. Though it was once home to cattle and horse ranches, this area was now Southern Oregon's wine country. A different type of gold. New vineyards cropped up all through the valley—little sticks closely spaced, each encased in a plastic tube to protect the new plants.

He didn't like Franklin Bradshaw very much. But he reminded himself the man had just lost both his wife and son. Radhauser hadn't been the most cooperative or congenial person either after getting that kind of news. Everyone handles grief in their own way. Bradshaw claimed he drank too much at his son's memorial. Maybe he went to a bar, and the bartender could provide him with an alibi. Either way, Radhauser intended to find out.

As he crossed the narrow, two-lane bridge, the Applegate River glinted through the trees. He took a moment to admire the log lodge and restaurant that sat on its banks. He'd have to bring Gracie to dinner here.

An arched, wrought-iron gate with the words *Robertson Vineyard* in gold leaf across the top marked the entrance. The gate was decorated with golden grape clusters. It was open, and Radhauser drove through. On both sides of the narrow driveway, vines grew on the hillsides in straight and perfect rows. Many of them were in bloom with tiny, green flower clusters that by September would become the coveted black pinot noir grapes that grew so well in this valley.

He parked in front of a rustic yet modern tasting room constructed of cedar, glass, and old fieldstone. It occupied about a quarter-acre of thick, green lawn. Deep and overflowing flowerbeds of shasta daisies, marigolds, and white, wave petunias were planted along the front of the structure, on either side of the entry. A hundred yards or so to the left, a freshly painted and modest bungalow was offset by an equally lush lawn with mulched flowerbeds. Jason Robertson and his father were men who cared about appearances and took good care of their property.

As Radhauser exited his car, a man and his border collie

stepped outside. The man wore a pair of pale blue coveralls with *Robertson Vineyard* embroidered over the pocket above a cluster of dark grapes. He was small in stature, not more than five feet nine with closely-shorn curly brown hair and the kind of handshake you could feel in every bone of your body. Along with his goatee and mustache, he wore a black beret, and if it was meant to make him look like a Frenchman, it succeeded.

"Welcome," he said. "I'm Jason Robertson. This is my friend, Molly." He patted the dog's head. "It's not my usual day for tasting, but I'd be happy to pour you a glass." He smiled, a wide and very likable one, his teeth white and even with a small gap between the front two incisors. It was the kind of smile that made you smile back, even when they didn't come easily to you.

Molly remained by his side. The dog was both well-behaved and groomed, her rust and white-colored coat clean, recently brushed and gleaming in the sunlight.

Radhauser tipped the brim of his Stetson and introduced himself. "I'm here to ask you a few questions about your sister, Blair Bradshaw."

Jason took a step back. "Has something happened to her?"

Radhauser said nothing but thought it a little odd that should be Jason's first assumption. He didn't want to break the news of her death until he had a chance to learn what he could about Jason Robertson before his guard went up.

Jason twisted his watch band. "Did her bastard husband beat her up?"

"Nothing like that," Radhauser said. "But you've aroused my curiosity. Does Franklin Bradshaw have a history of spousal abuse?"

"I was out of line," Jason said. "I know almost nothing about the man. He was civil enough when I met him at the memorial."

Radhauser looked him dead in the eyes. "Then why would you ask that question and call him a bastard?"

Jason shifted his gaze to the flowerbed. "Don't mind me. My ex-wife always accused me of jumping to conclusions without all the facts."

"You must have had some reason for saying that."

"Who knows how a man will react when he finds out his wife is leaving him? But as far as my sister is concerned, I'm not sure I can tell you much. I only met her a few weeks ago. Is she in some kind of trouble?"

"Nothing like that. Is there somewhere we can sit and talk?"

"Of course. Tasting rooms are designed for relaxing, sipping, and conversation." He turned to Molly. "You stay here. I'll be back soon."

The dog gave him a longing look, but remained outside the door.

Radhauser followed Jason into the sun-filled space. He could smell the fermenting wine that was undoubtedly housed in wooden barrels behind the tasting room.

Jason cupped his right hand around his ear. "Listen." His blue eyes brightened.

Radhauser stood very still. In the silence, he heard a slight hissing and bubbling sound.

"That's the carbon monoxide being released through the crust of the grape skins." Jason took a deep breath. "Robert Louis Stevenson said it best: '*Wine is bottled poetry.*'"

This was a man in love with his vineyard. And probably one who didn't want to share it with a sister he barely knew.

Radhauser glanced at Jason's feet. He wore a pair of lace-up leather work boots, his feet about the right size to belong to the person who'd left the bloody footprint on the rock.

Jason stepped behind a bar and before Radhauser could stop him, poured two glasses, then nodded toward a small, round table near one of the front windows looking out on the flowerbeds.

Radhauser sat.

After setting the glasses on the table, Jason pulled out the chair across from Radhauser, settled into it and stretched out his legs, like a cat roosting on a sun-drenched windowsill. Without saying a word, he picked up his glass by the stem and angled it, examining the color against the white linen tablecloth as if he were inspecting a precious ruby for its clarity. He leaned back in his chair and twisted his wrist, forcing the wine high up on the sides, then plunged his nose into the glass.

Radhauser was tempted to laugh at the theatrics. Maybe acting was something that ran in the Robertson family. But Radhauser was more of a Sam Adams Boston Lager man. He didn't know much about wine. And though Gracie had dragged him to a couple of local vineyards, he would never willingly attend a wine tasting.

Apparently satisfied with the bouquet, Jason took a sip and held it in his mouth for a few seconds before swallowing. "I like my Pinot Noir with a little flesh on its bones." He set his glass on the table and nodded toward the generously-filled glass in front of Radhauser. "Aren't you going to try it?"

"I'm on duty right now. I make it a policy never to drink when I am."

Jason lifted his hands, palm side up. "Good for you. I guess that means there's more for me. Can I get you something else? A cup of coffee? I have some sparkling water in the refrigerator."

"No, thank you. I'm fine."

"I don't know what I can tell you about a sister I didn't know I had. I hope she didn't drive anywhere last night after the memorial. She was way too drunk to get behind the wheel. Blair wasn't in some kind of accident, was she?"

"No. She wasn't involved in a motor vehicle mishap."

Jason shifted in his seat. "Then why are you here?"

"I believe I already answered that question. I'm here to ask about your sister. You say you just met her. I understand your parents were divorced but didn't you remember Blair from childhood?"

"I was two when our parents split." He stared at his hands. "I think Blair was four or five. Once she discovered I existed, she claimed to have some vague memory of a crib in her bedroom."

"Do you know anything about your mother? Your sister claimed she was dead. But the housekeeper told me a woman telephoned after Tommy Bradshaw's fatal accident, claiming to be his grandmother."

Jason laughed, and his gaze met Radhauser's. "If what my

father told me is true, our mother could very well be dead. He said she was a drug addict. From what I understand, they're often dead before they reach forty. Dad said the court gave him full custody of me."

Why would the father be granted custody of one child and not the other? "But not your sister?"

His easy smile disappeared. "Our parents didn't go through the courts to establish custody. Blair told me she stayed with our mother because she believed the woman needed her more. But I think she was just saving face. Dad cried when he told me about the will. He said that at the time of the divorce, he didn't think he could take care of two kids, especially a little girl. I know now that he always felt guilty for leaving her with our mother. That's why he wanted her to inherit." Jason shook his head as if he still couldn't believe it. "The man never once mentioned I had a sister, and I didn't even know her name until he showed me his will. He told me he hired a private investigator to find Meadow."

"It must have been quite a shock."

Jason stiffened. "That's putting it mildly. My father, who claimed to be of sound mind, planned to leave half the vineyard and everything else he owned to a sister I didn't know existed." Resentment dripped from his every word.

"How do you feel about that?" The answer to his question was obvious, but Radhauser wanted to watch Jason's reaction.

He winced, and a tide of something bitter washed over his face. "About how you'd expect, I guess. I grew up here in this valley. I've worked this land since I was big enough to hold a rake and shovel. This vineyard means everything to me. I talked to Blair about allowing me to make payments and slowly buy her out. But oh no. That's not good enough. She's demanding I sell it as soon after Dad's death as possible and split the proceeds with her. It's out of my hands. I've got a realtor coming on Monday to give me an appraisal."

His consistent use of the present tense when talking about his sister didn't escape Radhauser. But from everything he'd observed, Jason Robertson was a fastidious and careful man. If he'd killed his sister, he would have planned for this interview, maybe even practiced using the present tense. "That must really sting."

He opened his mouth to speak, then closed it. "It breaks my heart," he finally said, then took another sip of his wine. "From the looks of her mansion, gardener and live-in housekeeper, it doesn't seem to me like she needs the money. And I told her so." His voice turned as wintry as his eyes. "But she claimed her marriage was going south. That her husband could be a real asshole. She suspected he was involved with another woman. She didn't want to put her son through a nasty divorce or a court battle over settlement and child support. Blair needed the money from the vineyard so she and Tommy could start over."

"Did she give you a timeline for the separation and divorce?"

He furrowed his brow. "After school let out for the summer. Of course, who knows what she'll do now that Tommy's dead? She's pretty broken. But you never know, sometimes a tragedy brings people closer. What's this really all about, Detective? Why the interest in my sister's bad marriage? And my woeful tale about losing my family vineyard?"

As much as Radhauser always dreaded delivering this message, it was time. "I have something I need to tell you."

Robertson shifted in his chair. "Is it bad news?"

"It depends," Radhauser said. "Under the circumstances, you might consider it good news."

"Well…I don't know what could be worse than what Blair told me about selling my vineyard."

Maybe what Radhauser was about to say wasn't news to Jason Robertson at all. "Blair Bradshaw was found dead in the woods this morning. Her husband discovered her about 8 a.m. She was lying on the ground just outside the shrine the school children had made for Tommy."

The shock on his face seemed genuine, but Radhauser had run into some good actors in his line of work.

The look he aimed at Radhauser held more than a little disgust. "I resent your thinking I might find my sister's death good news."

Radhauser didn't respond. They sat together in silence for a couple minutes in the slatted beam of light that shone through the tasting room window.

"Was it suicide?" Jason finally asked.

"I should have a definitive cause of death later. But at this point, we don't think her wounds were self-inflicted."

"Wounds? Was she shot?"

"No."

Jason cocked his head, his eyes narrowing. "Are you sure it wasn't suicide? She was pretty depressed last night. Like I already told you, drinking way too much to boot. I shouldn't have brought that case of wine."

Had he murdered his sister, tried to make it look like suicide, then left the wine bottle upright beside her body as a subtle way of reclaiming his vineyard?

A look of confusion spread over Jason's face. "Did she cut her wrists?"

Was it confusion, or a ruse? He seemed like an intelligent and educated man. "I'll know more after the ME completes his autopsy and toxicological studies."

"Oh my God," Jason said, his cheeks flushing. "Toxicological studies. Do you think Blair was using drugs? Or are you thinking our drug-addled mother might be involved in this?"

Radhauser hadn't mentioned the syringe. Was he trying to divert attention away from himself? "I don't know. But I plan to track her down and talk to her."

"Blair didn't have it easy. She told me she grew up out in Wildwood, but left as soon as she was old enough to make her own money. Do you know Wildwood?"

"No," Radhauser said. "I've never been there. Never even heard of it."

"It's a small town out by Redwood Highway on the way to the coast. It lives up to its name. Lots of counter-culture people live there. Some artists, too. Many of them potters." He paused and shrugged. "Or potheads. Maybe you should try there."

"What was her maiden name?"

"My father never talks about her. But my birth certificate lists my mother's name as Sunflower—no last name if you can believe that. She named me Raven, but my father changed it after he gave up the hippy life and decided to grow grapes. Blair changed her name, too."

"Do you have any idea what her birth name was?"

He gave Radhauser a long, searching look. "No. I asked her the first time we met, but she wouldn't tell me. You can bet it was something like Daffodil or Waterlily. If she didn't keep the Robertson last name, she probably grew up without one. It wouldn't be uncommon in Wildwood."

Radhauser made a few notes. "Did anyone at her son's memorial seem out of place?"

"No." Again, Jason twisted the watch on his left wrist. A Timex, not the Rolex his brother-in-law wore. "But it would have been hard for me to tell since all of them were strangers to me."

"So why did you attend?"

"A couple reasons. One, I thought it was the right thing to do. But I was also hoping to talk to Blair afterward. Now that Tommy was no longer alive, I thought maybe she'd fight her husband for what was legally hers without worrying about putting her son in the middle. I thought she might reconsider and give me the option to make payments and eventually buy her out. I was hoping we could come up with some compromise so I wouldn't have to sell the vineyard."

"And did you ask her?"

"Yes. We talked for a few minutes after everyone else left. I even suggested she could move into the house with me. It has three bedrooms. That maybe we could run the vineyard together."

"Did she agree?"

His expression grew pensive. "She said she'd think about it. But I suspect she was only humoring me."

"We have reason to believe you were the last person to see your sister alive."

He blew out a long breath. "That can't be true. If she was murdered, someone else was the last person to see her. You can't think I...I'm a gentle man, Detective Radhauser. I grow prize-winning grapes."

"Where were you between 10 p.m. and 12:30 p.m. on Thursday night?"

Something inside Jason Robertson seemed to collapse slightly as if the air had been sucked from his lungs. When he lifted the wine glass meant for Radhauser, his hand trembled. "I left the memorial around 10 p.m. I came home right after Blair and I talked. Must have been 10:30 or so when I got here. I took Molly out for a quick walk, called the hospital to check on dad at around 11 p.m. and then again about midnight or so. He was having a rough night. Then I went to bed."

"Can anyone support that claim?"

"Not unless the hospital keeps a record of calls from a patient's family. I live alone now that my father is in hospice." He settled his gaze on Radhauser briefly, then drew it away. A movement often associated with guilt.

"Is there a neighbor who may have seen you return last night? Or out walking the dog?"

"The vineyard is fifty acres. No neighbors are close enough to know if I'm home or not. So, if you're looking for an alibi, I don't have one. But maybe I do need an attorney."

"You're certainly entitled to have one present, but at this point, I'm merely gathering information. Asking questions of everyone who knew your sister or was present at the memorial. I'd also like to speak to your father. Can you tell me where to find him?"

Jason's breath caught. "Jesus, Radhauser. I told you he's in the hospital under hospice care. He could die at any minute. You can't possibly suspect him."

"I don't. I just want to talk to him about your mother. He may have some idea where I could find her. Which hospital is he in?"

He folded his hands in front of him. "Medford Memorial. But go early. They increase his morphine around 8 p.m. so he can sleep. Once they do that, he isn't likely to tell you much. Please don't tell him about my sister or his grandson. I'd like to spare him that anguish."

"Is that where Blair visited him?"

"Yes. I took her. I waited in the cafeteria while she and Dad talked. But he was much more lucid then. Hard to believe that was less than three weeks ago. Pancreatic cancer goes fast."

"What happens to Blair's part of the inheritance if she is deceased? Does it pass to her husband?"

"No. My dad didn't set it up that way." The words came out strangled and far too soft. He stared at Radhauser, clearly disturbed by the question. He studied the detective like he was attempting to read his mind, to discover what evidence against him it might hold. "I might as well tell you because I know it won't be hard for you to discover this on your own. With her only child dead, too, it reverts back to me."

Silence hung between them.

Jason broke it. "You have to believe me. In most ways, I was actually happy to learn I had a sister, especially with my father about to pass away. You can't think I'd…" He trailed off. "I've never hurt anyone in my life. Why would I start now?"

"I'd say getting to keep your vineyard would be reason enough."

The tendons in Jason's neck corded. "Are you suggesting I'm a suspect in her murder?"

"Thank you for being honest," Radhauser said. "You saved me some valuable time. At this stage in the investigation, everyone who had something to gain by her death is a suspect."

CHAPTER SIX

It was nearly 5 p.m. when Radhauser arrived at the ME's office in Central Point. Assuming Heron was still in the autopsy room, Radhauser bypassed his office and headed down the hallway, through a set of swinging steel doors labeled *Morgue*, then another six yards to the single door with a brass sign that said *Autopsy Suite*.

As always, he stepped into the little alcove, then took off his Stetson and hung it from the hook above the metal cart stacked with disposable gowns, masks, rubber gloves, and shoe protectors. He grabbed a green gown and face mask, then pulled shoe protectors and latex gloves from the boxes provided. He put on the garb, then headed into the actual autopsy room. White tiles stretched from floor to ceiling. The bright fluorescent light buzzed above him.

At his stainless-steel table, Heron stitched the usual Y-shaped incision he'd cut in Blair Bradshaw's torso. Classical music played in the background—this time Vivaldi's *Pachelbel Canon in D Major*. Radhauser had always been more of a country music fan, but he had to admit Heron had reeducated him a bit and he always looked forward to the ME's selection.

Heron stood beside the gleaming steel cart that held his surgical instruments—as clean and organized as any hospital surgical suite. He kept a very clean morgue, but it was hard to disguise odors like stomach and bowel contents.

Heron tied off his last stitch. His sutures were always as careful, small, and neat as a plastic surgeon repairing a young girl's face. He turned to Radhauser. "You're early. But I can tell you one thing with absolute certainty—Blair Bradshaw was murdered."

"Was it the severed femoral arteries that killed her?"

"Yes. And you were right. Her wounds weren't self-inflicted. The angle and depth of the cuts indicate the razor entered near the groin and was pulled downward toward the thigh—not the other way around." He used his hand to indicate the way a person would self-inflict this kind of wound, entering at the thigh and cutting upward into the groin. "And there were no shallow hesitation cuts. We usually see them, especially with women, when a victim tries to slash her own wrists, for example."

"Did you find anything under her nails?"

"Nothing obvious. I've sent what scrapings I could get to the lab."

"Was she raped?"

"Absolutely not. There was no evidence of semen or any bruising or tears in the vaginal or rectal area. Her pantyhose was on straight and intact, except for the shredded backs of the legs and the two slashes in the groin. There was no intracranial bleeding or skull fracture to indicate she was struck over the head. Based on the preliminary toxicological results, I suspect that by the time our murderer slashed her groin, she was pretty well unconscious."

"What do you think about my theory she was murdered behind the treehouse, near the creek bank, then dragged to the memorial where her husband found her?"

"I say you nailed it, cowboy. As we noticed at the scene, there were pine needles stuck in the back of her skirt, hose, and blouse. I found pieces of leaves and other forest debris in her hair. The blood you discovered in the pine needles and on the footprint on the rock were a match for our victim. She had some faint bruises on her wrists, I suspect from the murderer's hands as he or she dragged her through the woods." He paused and looked Radhauser in the eyes. "And what would that bruising indicate?"

There was nothing the ME loved more than to quiz Radhauser, who was eager to learn and almost always went along with it. "It tells us she was still alive while being dragged."

Heron smiled. "Excellent. Before long, you can conduct your own post mortems and won't even need me. The faintness of the bruising would lead me to believe she was near death when she was being dragged. Most of her blood had been exsanguinated."

"Do you think a woman could have committed this crime?"

"I'd say it was possible. Blair Bradshaw only weighed a hundred and ten pounds."

"Any usable prints on her shoes?"

"Wiped clean."

"How about the wine bottle?"

"Clean as the proverbial whistle."

"Got a theory on a murder weapon?"

"From the depth of the wounds, I'd say it was a single-edged razor blade. Maybe a box cutter or one of those utility or razor knives used to trim carpet and wallpaper. But it could have also been a surgeon's scalpel."

"Wouldn't she have screamed bloody murder and kicked for all she was worth if someone tried to slash her groin? She was obviously subdued or restrained somehow." Radhauser thought about the empty wine bottle again. "What was her blood alcohol level?"

"It was 0.24. High enough to make someone of her size very submissive, if not comatose, but there's something else." Heron beckoned with his index finger for the detective to move closer.

Radhauser stepped over to the autopsy table, knowing he was about to receive another lesson in forensic pathology.

"Check this out." Heron held a magnifying glass to the inside bend in her elbow. "See those three puncture marks?"

"I do."

"Notice the slight bruising around the injection sites. Best I can determine, either the victim or someone else, maybe your murderer, administered a shot of heroin shortly before she died. Unless she had blood drawn recently, she was injected two other times. Probably a couple days earlier."

Radhauser remembered what Doctor Landenberg had told him. "I spoke with the ER doc, who examined her son. He said she collapsed and the hospital did some blood work. Do you think the punctures were made by the syringe I found in the creek?"

"Hard to match a needle, but there were still minute traces of heroin in the syringe. Between the heroin, the high level of alcohol in her blood and also the presence of valium, it was enough to render her pretty helpless," Heron said. "But the therapeutic level of valium leads me to believe it was prescribed by her physician after her son's unfortunate death."

Radhauser told him what he'd learned from Doctor Landenberg, about his prescribed 5mg of valium. "Do you believe the heroin was administered by our murderer?"

"Impossible to say. But considering where you found the discarded syringe, it could have been the murderer who tossed it into the creek. Especially if the victim has no history of drug abuse. Only three puncture marks is not your typical user. Especially since you can account for at least one other one. It may have taken the hospital phlebotomist two tries to find the vein."

"Did you search her body for other injection sites?"

Heron gave him a look that said, *Do you think I'm stupid?* "Of course. Even between her fingers and toes. I found nothing. But the murder definitely looks personal. Like someone who knew the victim and was enraged with her, but cared enough after it was over to feel some remorse and arrange her body in the flowers and mementos for her son."

Radhauser agreed. "The three Rs. Rage. Revenge. And finally, remorse. What's your estimate on time of death?"

"Given her stomach contents, liver temperature, and the level of rigor, I'd say she died sometime between 11:00 p.m. and 12:30 a.m. Lividity would indicate she'd been flat on her back for at least eight to ten hours."

Radhauser thought about the victim's husband leaving the house at 11 p.m. And then her brother and how Blair's death ensured he'd inherit the *Robertson Vineyard*. "Could it be as early as 10 p.m.?"

"Yes. I could definitely be off by an hour on either side."

"Did forensics find anything else?"

"Not much. Your murderer wore gloves and was careful. I've sent the hairs from the victim's skirt off for DNA analysis. I put a rush on them, but it may still be a few days before we get any results. The lab is working on the shoe print, trying to get a size and make. But I suspect it will be a common brand you can buy at Walmart."

One thing was certain, a criminal defense attorney would know to be careful and not leave any usable evidence. "Wouldn't you say chances are the hairs are from people who attended the memorial?"

"I would, but there's more." When Heron smiled his characteristic slow smile that spread across his face and deepened the dimple on his left cheek, Radhauser knew the ME had saved the best for last.

"Spill it. I'm going to need all the help I can get with this one."

"Well, there are two more things. First off, your killer took a souvenir. He whacked a clump of hair from the back of her head. I suspect using the same razor-type instrument he used to slash her femorals."

Radhauser thought for a moment. "I'd say that confirms this was personal. If robbery was the motive, the killer would have taken her pearls and that diamond watch she was wearing."

Heron nodded. "You're right. He left her a souvenir as well." He pulled an evidence bag from his apron pocket and handed it to Radhauser. "When I removed her clothing, I found this."

Radhauser turned the bag over in his hands. It contained an antique, sterling silver baby rattle about three inches long with hearts on both ends—the perfect size for a newborn's hand. The hearts were engraved with an ornate pattern—like something from the Victorian era. There were some words, none of them legible, except *a mother's love.*

"See those tiny white specks in the pattern?" Heron asked. "It's silver polish. I'd say our victim, the murderer, or someone else cleaned and shined this rattle pretty recently."

"Maybe it belonged to her son, Tommy." Without thinking, Radhauser fingered the Western belt buckle he always wore. "It might have comforted her in some way. Something to help her get through his memorial." He swallowed back the little lump of sorrow that seemed to reside permanently at the base of his throat.

"Perhaps," Heron said, more than a hint of doubt in his voice. "Or maybe it was a family heirloom. But I found it inside her bra, superglued to her left breast, right over her heart. When even acetone wouldn't work to loosen it, I had to surgically remove it from her body."

"Any prints?"

"Not a one."

It was an odd thing for a grieving mother to do. It seemed unlikely she'd wipe the rattle clean of her prints. But grief was never predictable. She may have worn latex gloves to avoid getting glue on her hands. The loss of a child left a person desolate and vulnerable to something equivalent of phantom-limb syndrome. Pain where there was no visible cause. Pain generated by the nothingness their loved ones left behind.

Radhauser would check with Jung-Su and Franklin Bradshaw, see if either of them recognized the rattle. "Still not very much to go on."

Heron dropped his hand on Radhauser's shoulder. "Chin up, cowboy. I've seen you solve murders with less."

CHAPTER SEVEN

Radhauser rang the bell on a brick house about half the size of the Bradshaws', but twice as big as the one he and Gracie shared. He wanted to talk to Holden Houseman, Tommy Bradshaw's friend, to try to determine if there was more to Tommy's death than an unfortunate accident.

A man who appeared to be about thirty-five answered. He wore a pair of khaki Dockers and a polo shirt with dark brown trim around the collar and sleeves. His feet were bare and looked about the right size to belong to the person who made the bloody shoe print. His blond hair was neatly combed with enough gel to make it appear wet. He looked like a preppy, over-aged college boy.

"Are you Mr. Houseman?"

He cocked his head. "I'm Carl Houseman. And who might you be?" A trace of suspicion laced his voice.

"I'm Detective Radhauser from the Ashland Police Department." He showed his badge. "I wonder if I might come inside and talk with you for a few minutes."

He took a small step back, and a flash of something that looked like fear crossed his face. "What's this about?"

"I'm investigating a case."

"I thought they'd ruled Tommy Bradshaw's death an accident?"

"There's been another death in the neighborhood."

Houseman's mouth dropped open. "In this neighborhood? A death that requires a police investigation? You have to be kidding."

"I wouldn't joke about death," Radhauser said. "But speaking of this neighborhood, have you heard anything about a series of burglaries that took place about a month ago?"

"Absolutely not. I'd know because I'm the president of our neighborhood watch group."

So, if there'd been no robberies in the neighborhood, why did Blair Bradshaw have that elaborate security system installed and lie to her husband? Who or what was she so frightened of? He made a mental note to check with the installers. Maybe she said something during the installation that might lead him to a suspect. "May I come inside?"

Houseman stepped aside so Radhauser could enter, then led him through the entryway into a nicely furnished living room, with wide-planked, cherry-wood floors, a white leather sectional, two matching recliners and a television with a screen the size of a small movie theater. Magazines lay scattered about, and a Lego spaceship, halfway into the building process, was set up on the coffee table along with a half-eaten bowl of popcorn and two mugs that looked like they'd held hot chocolate with melted marshmallows on top. A house where a father lived alone with his son. Though they probably had a cleaning person, it was easy to tell no woman lived full-time in this household.

Radhauser took off his Stetson, sat in one of the recliners, placed the hat crown-down on the end table, and looked around. The entire wall above the fireplace was filled with photos of a young boy growing up—many of them included his father and Tommy Bradshaw. A framed 8x10 pictured Tommy, Holden and his dad riding horseback among the Saguaros in the Arizona Desert.

For an instant, Radhauser's mind flashed on his son, Lucas, and the way they'd once rode together in the desert wash behind their house in Tucson. He pushed the memory aside and looked at another photograph of Houseman sitting with two boys in front of a roaring campfire. He was wearing a Scout uniform and had an arm draped over each boy's shoulders—obviously their Boy Scout leader. Radhauser shifted his gaze to another photo of the three of them frolicking in the backyard swimming pool behind Tommy's house.

Holden was smiling in all the photographs. Nothing new about that. Most people smiled when they had their pictures taken, but the smiles in these photos were genuine. Holden Houseman was a handsome and happy kid, so radiant it was as if he were spun from light.

Another wall held professionally-framed and matted artwork, obviously done by a child. In addition to being happy, it appeared Holden was well-loved and nurtured by his father.

Studying the photos above the fireplace for a moment, Radhauser wondered, once again, what his life would have been like had Lucas survived the car accident and Laura had not. He shook his head to clear the image. And he counted himself the luckiest man alive because Gracie, Lizzie, and now Jonathan had come into his life.

Houseman took a seat on the sofa across the room, putting as much distance between them as possible. "Are you going to tell me who died?"

"Your next door neighbor, Blair Bradshaw."

A look of horror shot across his features, and he grimaced as if in pain. He planted his elbows on his knees, clasped his hands in front of his mouth and blew on them, like a person who'd been out in the cold. "When I saw her at the memorial, I was afraid of this. She took her own life, didn't she?"

"What did you see at the memorial that made you suspect she might hurt herself?"

"I'm not one to talk badly about the dead."

"These are special circumstances, Mr. Houseman. Now, please. Why were you so concerned?"

"Her drinking for one thing. Blair wasn't a heavy drinker. She seemed to be almost in a trance. Maybe it was the valium. She told me the doctor prescribed it. Or the combination. But she was distant and very far from herself last night."

"She'd just lost her son, Mr. Houseman. Wouldn't you expect her to be changed?"

"Of course, but Blair wasn't the type who showed emotion easily. She was out of control and, well, almost paranoid. I tried to talk to her to express my condolences, but her gaze kept darting around the crowd like she was searching for someone. And she had a fearful look on her face."

"Do you have any idea who she might have been looking for?"

"None. I should have stayed longer. But it was a school night, and I wanted to get Holden, he's my son, into bed. If I'd waited, maybe I could have talked to Blair, maybe prevented her…" He trailed off.

"She didn't commit suicide, Mr. Houseman. I just came from the medical examiner's office. He ruled the death a homicide."

He jerked his head back. "*Murder?* Oh, my God. Who would want to hurt Blair? This is terrible. Do you think she was afraid someone was after her last night? And that's why she seemed so overly vigilant?"

"That's what I'm trying to find out. She was your neighbor and the mother of your son's best friend. I don't think you want her killer to get away with it. Is there anything else you can tell me about last night, Mr. Houseman, before I talk with Holden?"

Houseman's spine grew rigid at the sound of his son's name. "There is no question she was distraught over Tommy. That pompous jackass she married…" He stared at Radhauser silently for a moment. "I shouldn't have said that. No one knows how they'll behave when something like that happens. If I lost Holden…" Again, he stopped himself short. "But what does her death have to do with me?"

"You obviously cared about her." *Maybe a little too much.* "The two of you were friends. You're her next-door neighbor. You attended the memorial. Your son spent his afternoons at the Bradshaw house. Seems to me you'd want to help us find out what really happened."

Houseman sighed, long and low. "You're right. I'm sorry. Ask me anything you want."

"Where were you between 11 p.m. and 12:30 a.m. last night?"

"Right here with my son. You can't think I had anything to do with Blair's murder. I cared about her. A hell of a lot more than that so-called husband of hers."

"These are routine questions, Mr. Houseman. I'll be asking

them of anyone who knew Mrs. Bradshaw. At the beginning of a murder investigation, almost everyone who is close to the victim is a person of interest. Can someone verify you were here all night?"

"Only Holden. He fell asleep around ten."

"Why do you dislike Franklin Bradshaw?"

"Because he's an arrogant SOB who doesn't deserve someone as kind and generous as Blair. He loves his reputation and his legal practice more than his wife and son."

"It's hard for any of us to know what's in another person's heart." Radhauser handed him a business card. "Call me if you think of anything else. Or if you remember anyone who didn't look like they belonged at the memorial. But in the meantime, I'd like to talk to your son about the evening of Tommy Bradshaw's accident."

Houseman stood and backed away with his hands raised. "Holden had already left and was on his way home when the accident occurred. He heard Tommy cry out and ran back. When he saw what had happened, he tried to call 911 from here." He returned to his seat, knotted his hands in his lap. Drops of sweat did relay races down his forehead.

What was he so nervous about? "I need to speak with your son, Mr. Houseman. See if he saw anyone or anything in the woods that might be suspicious. Like maybe someone lurking around."

"He's in his room. Holden's been pretty upset since it happened. He and Tommy had been best friends since they met in preschool. I think seeing Blair so distraught last night was almost too much for him. Every time she cried, so did Holden. I don't know how I can tell him Blair is dead, too." He looked at Radhauser as if waiting for an answer.

For a moment, Radhauser said nothing. "Holden will find out soon enough. Probably better if he hears it from his dad. But why do you think he was so affected by her grief last night?"

"She's been a great friend to us, like a mother to him." He stopped short like he was trying to decide whether to say more. "You see, Holden's mother died when he was five. Cancer. Seeing Blair crying...well...suffice it to say I had to drag him away from her side or he would have clung to her through the entire memorial. He would have spent the night sitting beside her and holding her hand if I'd allowed it."

"Sounds like you were both pretty close to Mrs. Bradshaw."

Houseman wiped a line of sweat from his upper lip. "What are you implying?"

"I'm merely making an observation."

"Because of our circumstances, we're thrown together pretty often. Blair helps a lot with Holden. Franklin's rarely home. I try to pick up some of the slack for Tommy. I mean, I did. He was a great kid. Franklin has no idea what he missed by not being more involved in his son's life."

From everything he could see, both in the photographs above the fireplace mantel and those hanging in the treehouse, Houseman played an active role in Holden's life. Maybe a little too active. But that probably couldn't be avoided for a single parent. Again, Radhauser's thoughts leapt to his late son. How overprotective would he be with Lucas if Laura had died in that car accident and their son had continued to live? "From your observations, despite your feelings about Franklin, was the Bradshaw marriage a happy one?"

"On the surface. I mean, they put on a good act when other people were around. But, if you ask me, Blair deserved better." Houseman shrugged, then smiled and held his hands up, empty, holding no answers. "But who am I to judge?"

His window looked out on the Bradshaws' driveway. He could have easily seen Franklin leave the house. Could Houseman have returned to the memorial after everyone else left? It would have been a quick walk through the woods undetected once Holden had fallen asleep. Did Carl Houseman confess his feelings to Blair Bradshaw? Had she rejected him?

"Were you aware she planned to leave her husband?"

He tilted his head and stared at Radhauser for a moment. "Not really," he said, no hint of shock in his voice. "But I could tell she was unhappy with how much time Franklin spent, or claimed to spend, at the office."

"Did you know Mrs. Bradshaw had a brother?"

"She told me about Jason recently, but we didn't meet until last night at the memorial. He seemed like a nice enough guy."

"What did she tell you?"

"That she hadn't seen him since he was a toddler. That she was surprised when she learned her father planned to leave his vineyard to both her and her brother. Blair said she'd never been there. But she thought it ironic that she'd been drinking their pinot noir for years."

"I appreciate your help, Mr. Houseman. And now I'd really like to speak with Holden."

"He's just a little boy. Don't you think he's been through enough?"

"I have young children at home, and I promise you I'll do my best not to upset him. If you won't allow me to question him here, I can get a warrant and bring him down to the police station. I suspect that would be a far more traumatic experience."

Houseman's gaze shot over to Radhauser and hardened. "What do you want with him?"

"I want to hear what he has to say about the afternoon his best friend died."

Houseman gave Radhauser a hot glare of such withering disapproval that the temperature in the room must have heated by ten degrees. Without saying another word, he stood, turned, and headed down a narrow hallway.

* * *

Holden sat at his desk, working on one of the complicated Lego spaceships both he and Tommy had saved money from their allowances to buy. The two boys had been racing to see which one of them would finish first. Now Tommy was gone, Holden wanted to build his ship and present it to Blair as a gift for her upcoming birthday. She'd been so sad at the memorial, he hoped his gift might cheer her up.

He heard his father tap on his door but ignored him. Holden had been angry ever since his dad refused to let him spend the night in Tommy's treehouse with Blair after the service.

Besides, his dad's incessant questions about his day at school, who he sat with at lunch, and whether he was making any new friends were more than he could handle right now. All he wanted was to be left alone to work on his gift for Blair.

His dad knocked again, louder this time, then opened the door. "Hey, buddy," he said, stepping over to the desk to admire the ship. "That looks amazing."

"Thanks. I want to give it to Miss Blair for her birthday."

The color drained from his father's face, and it took a moment before he spoke. "There's a police detective here who wants to talk to you about Tommy's accident."

Holden drew his shoulders in toward his chin. His whole body felt cold. Before he could stop himself, he shivered. "I have to go to the bathroom." He stood and tried to make his legs move.

His father grabbed his wrist, wrapped his thumb and forefinger around it like a handcuff. "There's nothing to be afraid of. Just tell him what we talked about. Tommy was fine and still in the treehouse when you left. You didn't know anything was wrong until you heard him call out."

"I'm not afraid," he lied. "I just have to pee." He twisted himself free, then headed toward the small bathroom set between his bedroom and his father's study. He closed and locked the door, then splashed water on his cheeks, dried it off and combed his hair. As he brushed his teeth, he stared at the face in the mirror. Was it the face of a liar? The face of a boy who killed his best friend?

A minute or so later, Holden returned, sat at the desk, and knotted his hands in his lap. "I don't want to talk to him."

His dad reached for his hands and gently unknotted them. "I don't think you have a choice, son. Come on, let's get it over with."

Holden jerked his hands away.

His father tried again, this time jiggling Holden's shoulder.

He kept his gaze on the floor, refusing to look at his dad. "Do I have to?"

His father squatted down in front of him like he was a soccer coach or something. "Yes. But I think you'll only have to talk to him once. I'll be by your side the entire time. Just remember what we talked about. As soon as you answer his questions, you can come back here and work on the ship. Or we can play a game of chess. How does that sound?"

Holden took a deep breath, then stood and followed his father out into the hallway. He felt dizzy, the way he did when he first got off a roller coaster like the ground was moving a little underneath his feet. Nothing seemed black and white anymore. This time the virtues of truth his dad used to preach might get him in big trouble.

He'd practiced the speech his father had prepared for him, but he wasn't at all sure he was going to recite it. What Holden Houseman did know was that he was scared—scared right down to the middle of his bones.

CHAPTER EIGHT

Carl Houseman returned to the living room about five minutes later, Holden beside him.

The boy was thin and small for his age, about four-feet six or so, and wore a sleeveless, slightly oversized Oregon Ducks T-shirt, a pair of black gym shorts, and high-top sneakers. One of his shoelaces was untied and made a slapping sound against the hardwood floor. Though it was only May, his skin was nut brown as if he'd spent a lot of time in the sun. His hair was a rich mahogany color with a hint of red, and he wore it cut in a Dutch-boy bob. With his dark, thickly-lashed eyes, and delicate features, Holden Houseman was one beautiful boy.

"This is my son, Holden," Houseman said, his hand resting on the boy's head. "Holden, this is Detective Radhauser."

Radhauser stood and offered his hand. "It's very nice to meet you, Holden."

Holden hesitated, then shook Radhauser's hand.

Houseman nudged his son toward the sofa. "Detective Radhauser wants to ask you a couple of questions about the night Tommy got hurt."

Holden shoved his hands in his pockets but made no effort to sit. His somber features didn't hold a trace of the genuinely happy boy in the photographs.

"I understand you and Tommy were best friends for a long time," Radhauser said.

"Practically our whole lives." Holden darted his gaze away from Radhauser and back to his father. Was he looking for approval?

There was no way Radhauser would get the truth out of this

boy with Mr. Houseman in the room. "I'd like to talk to Holden alone."

Houseman draped his arm over Holden's shoulders and pulled him a little closer. "Not on your life."

"Sometimes, kids are more comfortable talking if their parents aren't in the room."

"I know my rights." Houseman's face reddened. "And I have the right to stay with my son."

"If he's being questioned as a suspect in police custody, you do. But this is just routine, and the law doesn't require parental consent or their presence for me to talk to a minor."

"Then I want my attorney here," Houseman said. "And until he gets here, I'm not leaving."

"Why do you feel so strongly about being here?"

"Because I've heard of situations where a child is coaxed into admitting to something he didn't do."

"But your son isn't accused of anything."

Holden took a step back, raked his trembling right hand through his hair.

Houseman's arm dropped to his side.

"Okay, then," Radhauser said, realizing Houseman wasn't about to give in. "Why don't we all sit down?"

The boy sat on the sofa beside his father.

Radhauser returned to the chair across from them.

"I understand you were with Tommy last Monday night when the accident occurred."

Holden grimaced. "We were together after every school day. Jung-Su watched me, too."

"What did the two of you usually do together?" Radhauser tried to put the boy at ease by asking routine questions.

"We came home on the school bus. Jung-Su gave us a snack. We did our homework. Then we mostly goofed around in Tommy's treehouse until my dad came home."

Houseman gripped his son's thigh. "But you weren't there when the accident occurred, right, Holden? You left before Tommy fell, remember?"

Holden scrunched up his face and jerked away from his father, slipping his right hand back into his pocket. The red imprint of his father's fingers lingered on the boy's bare leg. "Isn't that right, Holden?"

"I don't know," he said. "Stop askin' me so many questions." He lowered his head.

"Mr. Houseman. I think this would go a lot better and faster if you left the room. I can and will get a warrant if you fail to cooperate."

"It's okay, Dad. I want to talk to him by myself."

Houseman opened his mouth, then closed it again. He looked down at his bare feet, then stood in front of his son, his back to Radhauser. "Just tell the detective the truth like we talked about, okay, son? You didn't do anything wrong, and you don't have anything to be frightened about."

The boy said nothing.

Houseman turned to Radhauser. "You better not upset him." His voice was so low and flat, it was hard to tell if the man had a pulse.

Once Houseman left the room, Radhauser stood and moved closer to the sofa. He knelt in front of Holden and gently lifted the boy's chin with his fingertip. "Your dad's right. There's nothing to be afraid of. I'm just trying to find out what really happened to your friend."

Holden's eyes were wide, white visible around the dark irises. He seemed to draw back into himself and bit his bottom lip. "Everybody knows what happened. He died. Tommy fell into that stupid fence post. And the pointy stake, it….it…went through his heart." He jerked his hands out of his pockets and hid them under his oversized shirt as if they were shameful things.

"Yes. I do know that. But I'd like you to tell me how it happened. What made him fall? You're not in trouble. You won't be, even if you *were* there when Tommy fell."

Holden said nothing.

"I had a little boy, just a few years older than you are—and I know how accidents can happen." Radhauser pushed a shock of

77

Holden's hair from his eyes in an attempt to calm him. His hair smelled like little boy sweat and pine-scented shampoo. He had a cowlick that stuck up in the back. It looked like a small flame that had caught the light from the window behind the sofa.

"What happened to your little boy?" Holden's breath held the faint scent of toothpaste.

Radhauser puffed out his cheeks, released the air slowly. "Lucas died." He was stunned, as always, at how the words just came out. *Lucas died.* Like any other sentence. *Lucas wanted to be a rodeo rider. Lucas won the belt buckle I always wear. I loved my son more than life.* "He was killed in a car accident. And so was my wife."

"My mom died when I was little." Holden's bottom lip trembled. "I was like five or something. But I still remember her. I won't ever forget." His body seemed to cave in on itself.

"I know, and I'm really sorry. Your dad said Tommy's mom is like another mother to you."

"Yeah. She's always nice to me. If I spend the night, she tucks me in, just like with Tommy. My dad's really nice, and he does all kinds of things with me, but I want to be like everyone else who has a mother. With Miss Blair, I feel…I don't know…like a regular kid…like her love gets inside me and makes everything all right." He paused like he was trying to think of other things she did for him. "She even brings cupcakes to school when it's my birthday. That's why I couldn't…" He kept his gaze cast down at the floor, refusing to look at Radhauser. "Even though Tommy died…I mean…I still want Miss Blair to be like my mom. I want her to love me." He told Radhauser about the Lego spaceship he was building for her birthday.

Radhauser froze. Should he tell Holden about Blair's death? Or let him continue to believe that she would be there bringing cupcakes to school, standing in for his mother? No, he decided. Not now. Breaking that kind of news to a boy was his father's job.

"It's okay, Holden. You can tell me the truth. Tommy's mom will never have to know."

Holden glanced toward the hallway where he'd last seen his father. "How about my dad? Will you have to tell him?"

"I suspect he already knows the truth."

He lowered his voice to a whisper. "Yeah. But does he have to know I told you?"

Radhauser gave him a sad smile. "Your dad won't hear it from me. You can decide if you want to tell him for yourself."

He stared at Radhauser for a moment, his dark eyes big and watery. "Tommy and me. We were wrestling like we always did, except we were doing it on that wooden walkway that goes around the treehouse, not inside the big room like normal. We weren't mad or nothin', but then it just happened. I rolled toward the doorway into the treehouse, and he must have rolled the other way. He fell and landed on the fence. I should have run to Jung-Su for help. But my house was closer, and I was scared I'd get blamed—that everyone would hate me. That Miss Blair...I tried to call 911, but I couldn't talk. Maybe Tommy would be okay if only I..." He started to sob.

Radhauser sat on the sofa beside Holden and wrapped his arm around the boy's shoulder. Holden pushed his face into Radhauser's chest, and he cupped his hand around the back of the boy's head the way he did with his own two children when they cried.

Holden's crying increased, and his shoulders shook. He allowed Radhauser to hold him for a moment before pulling away. He looked up, his face red and swollen, his nose running. Tears clung to his eyelashes and caused them to clump. "Are you gonna take me to jail now?"

Radhauser swallowed the lump in his throat. He took a clean handkerchief from his blazer pocket and handed it to Holden. "No way. You're a very brave boy for telling me the truth. It was an accident. Nobody's fault. Even if you'd run for help the second it happened, it wouldn't have changed anything."

"How do you know that?"

"Because I talked to the doctor who saw Tommy at the hospital. There was nothing you or anyone could have done to save him."

The boy wiped his eyes, blew his nose, handed the handkerchief back, then looked Radhauser square in the face. "Are you sure?"

"I'm positive. But I know how you feel. I used to think I could have done something to change what happened to my wife and son."

"Were you driving the car that hurt them?"

"No. I wasn't even with them. I was working on a case."

Holden dug at his eyes with his fists. "It was an accident. It wasn't your fault so you couldn't change anything."

"That's right, Holden. The only thing people like you and me can do now is go on, remember the people we loved, and live the best and most honest lives we can. I think that's what Tommy would want for his best friend."

* * *

About ten minutes after Holden told the truth to Detective Radhauser, his father tapped on his door again.

"It's okay, Dad. Come on in."

Holden was lying on his bed, reading *The Hardy Boys* book, *The Secret of Red Arrow* he and Tommy had started the last time they spent the night together. He couldn't really concentrate and kept reading the same paragraph over and over. After saving his place with a Star Wars bookmark, he set the book on his nightstand and glanced up at his dad.

His father sat on the side of the bed. He looked stressed, his eyes red as if he might have been crying, too.

"Is everything okay, Dad?"

His dad nodded but said nothing.

"It's okay. I'm not in any trouble. Detective Radhauser was real nice. It wasn't hard to talk to him. He told me he had a little boy who got killed in a car accident. He said he thought it was his fault because he didn't go with his wife and son that night."

His father studied him for a moment as if trying to see inside his brain. "You told him the truth, didn't you?"

"Please don't be mad."

"I'm not mad, son. You did what you thought was right. I was wrong when I told you to lie. I was scared and didn't want anything to hurt you ever again." A single tear rolled down his father's cheek before he hunched over like Holden did when he had a stomachache.

"What's wrong, Dad?"

"I don't know how to begin to tell you this. And wish I didn't have to, but I don't want you to learn about this on the news or from anyone else."

Holden's heart thumped inside his ears. "Did Detective Radhauser lie? Am I in bad trouble?"

"No, son. But I'm afraid I have some more sad news."

Holden sat, pushed his back against the maple headboard of his bottom bunk. "What is it?"

"It's about Miss Blair." His father's voice was barely more than a whisper.

Holden clenched his hands into fists. "Does she know what really happened? Does she hate me?"

His dad sucked in a breath and let it out real slow. "She died last night after the memorial."

Holden scrambled off the bed and onto his feet. Had Miss Blair killed herself because she couldn't face her life without Tommy? He planted his hands on his hips. "Tell me the truth. Was it because of me? Because of what I did to Tommy?"

His father grabbed him around the waist and pulled him onto his lap.

He felt stupid, being held like a baby, but it also felt kind of good. For a moment, neither of them said anything.

"Absolutely not, Holden," his dad finally said. "What happened to Tommy was an accident. He rolled off the platform. Miss Blair knew that. This is going to be hard to hear, but Detective Radhauser and the medical examiner who studied the scene and her body think someone hurt her."

Holden buried his head in his father's shoulder like he used to as a little boy. "But she was so nice. Why would anyone want to hurt her?" he said, then sobbed until his shoulders shook, sobbed until he believed no more sound could come out of him.

After a few minutes, Holden said, "I'm tired, Dad. I think I want to go to sleep now."

His dad slipped off his shoes and socks, then tucked him into bed still wearing his shorts and Oregon Ducks shirt. "We'll skip the shower tonight, buddy. Tomorrow is Saturday. Maybe we can go to the Science Museum. Would you like that?"

Holden didn't respond.

As soon as his father left the room, and Holden heard the sound of the shower turn on, he slipped out of bed. He pulled a pair of cowboy boots over his bare feet, then picked up the Lego spaceship and hurled it against the wall. It broke into what seemed like a hundred small chunks.

Once he started, he couldn't stop. With the heel of his boot, he stomped the plastic pieces, over and over, until his right leg ached. The cockpit soared across the room and dented the wallboard.

When his rage was spent, he picked up the pieces and dumped them into the trash, then sat on the side of his bed and buried his face in his hands. He hated himself so much.

And he wished, for just one more day, he could live in a world where Tommy and Miss Blair were still alive.

In a world where he hadn't done anything bad.

CHAPTER NINE

A second visit to the hospital in one day was almost more than Radhauser could tolerate. He stepped over to the information booth. An older woman wearing a pink smock glanced up at him. Her eyes, the green of spring grass, were big behind magnifying, horn-rimmed glasses. "How may I help you?"

"I'm here to see a Mr. Robertson. I understand he's in hospice care."

"Our hospice beds are on the third floor." She entered something into the computer, then scanned the screen. "There we go. Landon Robertson. Room 308."

Radhauser took the stairs two at a time. He checked in at the desk and signed the visitor log. After standing in the doorway for a moment to allow his eyes to adjust to the dim light in the room, he stepped inside.

"Jason, is that you?" Robertson's voice was faint.

"No. I'm not your son, Mr. Robertson. But do you mind if I turn on the light?"

"Suit yourself. I'm in no position to stop you."

Radhauser flipped on the overhead light and moved closer to the bed. "I'm Detective Radhauser from the Ashland Police Department, and I'm hoping I can ask you a few questions, Mr. Robertson. Are you up to it?"

The skin around his blue eyes was red, and large, brown crescents of weariness hung beneath them. Though he was probably in his mid to late fifties, he appeared much older. His face looked as if it were hung with weights, everything pulled down slightly. He'd lost all his hair, and his body was as thin as a concentration camp survivor, his collar bone sharp and visible through his pale blue hospital gown. "It's a little late to arrest me for the heist I pulled at the K-mart when I was six. Two packs of Wrigley's Spearmint as I recall."

Radhauser smiled. He instantly liked the man and found it amazing he could be so close to death and still maintain a sense of humor. "I'm here to grant you a stay of execution."

When Robertson tried to sit up in bed, he grimaced. "I'm afraid it's a little late for that."

Radhauser could see the depth of the man's pain and knew beyond doubt that this man's world had shrunk to the dark, pulsing nucleus of impending death. All that had mattered to him before no longer did. "You don't have to sit up."

His gaze fixed on Radhauser, but his voice was barely more than a whisper. "Joking aside, why would a detective need to talk to me? I'm dying, for Christ sake. If I committed some crime other than leaving my daughter to be brought up by a drug addict and the chewing gum robbery, it's too late to arrest me now. I'd never make it to trial."

"I'm here about your daughter, Blair Bradshaw."

Robertson stared at Radhauser brokenly, his tone even softer now, almost mournful. "She's a lovely young woman." His eyes grew watery. "I did her wrong."

At that moment, Radhauser decided not to tell him about her death. Maybe the poor man could die in peace, having met his beautiful daughter and believing both his children were reunited.

A nurse stepped into the room. "I'm here with your morphine, Mr. Robertson. Are you in a lot of pain?"

He nodded.

"Please, could you hold off for a moment?" Radhauser introduced himself. "I have a few questions for Mr. Robertson, and I need him to be as coherent as possible."

"I'm more concerned with his comfort than your questions, Detective Radhauser. We always increase his morphine at night."

"I'm only asking for five minutes."

"It's okay, Norma. I want to talk to him. It's about my daughter."

Norma shot Radhauser a look hot enough to light a candle. "I'll be back in five minutes."

Radhauser pulled a chair as close as possible to the bed. "I'm trying to help her find her mother," he lied. "And I wondered if you might know where I should start looking."

He gave Radhauser a puzzled look. "She didn't say a word to me about that."

"Maybe she changed her mind after seeing her father."

"Wildwood." The effort of talking was already beginning to take its toll on the man. He breathed with exaggerated force, rhythmically, like a pant. "Last…place…I saw Sunny."

"Do you remember the address?"

"PO Box."

Without the slightest warning, a wrenching sob broke from him. It seemed to come from an unexpected depth, a sob that all but gutted him.

Radhauser grabbed a tissue from the bedside table and handed it to him.

He blew his nose. "She was a beautiful…little girl. Sunny and I, we named her…Meadowlark."

Radhauser leaned in a little to hear him better.

"But I always called her Meadow." He dropped his head forward then brought it back against the pillow so hard that the force rattled the bed. "I should have taken her with me. She and her brother…They should have grown up together."

"Do you know if Sunny kept the Robertson name after you divorced?"

"Never took it. Kept her maiden name. Finney."

Radhauser made a note. "Do you think she raised Meadow as a Finney?"

"Maybe."

"Do you remember anything else about Sunny?"

"She would…never…cut her hair. Claimed it sapped her strength. It got so long. Used to drag…on the floor." He was breathing in short gasps now, loud and furiously, like a diver gearing up for a frightening plunge. "Probably gray as steel…by now."

"I'm going to let you get some rest." Radhauser lightly touched the man's shoulder. "Thank you for your help."

He grabbed Radhauser's wrist and whispered. "Tell Meadow… I'm sorry I…I never met my grandson."

"He's a really cute kid." Radhauser honored Jason's wish by talking about him in the present tense. "Blair knows your regrets. She's already forgiven you."

"That's good," Robertson whispered. "Really good. And thanks…for the stay of execution…on the gum theft. I'd hate… to spend my…final hours in the…slammer."

Radhauser tiptoed from the room, saying a silent prayer that Landon Robertson would depart this life without ever knowing his daughter and grandson were dead.

*　*　*

It was nearly 8 p.m., and the darkness descended as Radhauser drove back toward his office. He thought about Holden Houseman and the accident that took Tommy Bradshaw's life. They were just a couple of kids horsing around like boys do. Telling the truth to Franklin Bradshaw wouldn't bring his son or his wife back. The fact that they were friends and neighbors could only hurt Holden more than the guilt he already carried. It was difficult enough for a grown man to comprehend the enormous absence in such a loss—a void where there was supposed to be someone you loved.

The first time Radhauser laughed after Laura and Lucas died, he'd clamped his hand over his mouth as if the sound that bubbled out of him proved his disloyalty to them both. It didn't matter that he knew his wife and son would want him to be happy and enjoy what was left of his life. He'd still felt like he was betraying their memory.

Yes, there was a long and painful road ahead of Franklin Bradshaw and Holden Houseman. And that poor boy's father had to tell his son that he'd lost his other mother as well.

Radhauser parked in his usual spot near the Plaza and hurried across the lot to the station, relieved there were no reporters waiting for him. It wouldn't be long before they learned of the bizarre murder of the wife of Medford's most prominent criminal defense attorney. Once that happened, Radhauser's life would become a nightmare of questions, demands, and accusations.

After a quick wave to Hazel Hornby, their administrative assistant, he headed down the hall.

"Wait a minute," she called after him.

Radhauser stopped and turned back.

"The Pattersons were here," she said. "I told them you'd probably be back this evening. "They're having dinner at the Greenleaf and said they'd check again when they finished."

"I'll be here for at least another couple hours," he said, though he dreaded seeing the hope on their faces and having to tell them after another year had passed, no progress had been made. Ten years and they still held onto faith their son would be found alive.

Each year on Ryan's birthday, they bought and wrapped an age-appropriate gift for him. Holly baked and decorated a birthday cake, and they sang happy birthday to their son before blowing out the candles. They kept his bedroom prepared, redecorating it as the years passed—replacing the crib with a toddler bed, the teddy bear wallpaper with race cars. The year Ryan would have turned six and started school, they added bunk beds and a desk. When Holly told Radhauser this, every word had punctured his flesh like a dart.

For years after the kidnapping, Radhauser would call police stations in a three-state radius, asking about their unidentified baby boys, then toddlers, then school-aged children. The baby and child John Does. He'd ask if the boy had a birthmark just above his left nipple, shaped like Africa. He'd shown photographs, first the infant pictures the Pattersons had provided, then artist renderings of what the child might look like as he aged.

Later, he'd used FBI age progression software to generate likenesses—wanting one of the unidentified missing children to be Ryan on the one hand, and terrified one of them would be on the other. But mostly Radhauser wanted him to be found—even if he had to tell Holly and Sean their boy had been dead for years. Because he knew what they seemed not to understand. Even if by some stroke of pure luck, they found Ryan alive, the kid would likely be damaged goods. No longer the boy he might have been.

After every yearly visit, even though the case was stone cold, he'd remove the file from his bottom drawer and reread everything. By now, he knew the circumstances of Ryan's disappearance by heart.

Holly Patterson, a surgical nurse at Rogue Valley Medical Center, had returned to work when Ryan was six weeks old. On the day he disappeared, Ryan's nanny phoned in sick. With surgeries scheduled, Holly became desperate and called her sixteen-year-old niece, Tiffany. Mountain View High School had parent/teacher conferences that day, so Tiffany agreed to sit for Ryan. But when one of the most popular boys in her school, seventeen-year-old Taylor Mullens, phoned and wanted to go to the mall, she couldn't resist.

According to the hysterical teenager, the baby fell asleep in his stroller. Tiffany parked it in the corner of the food court. While she and Taylor stood in line to order their cheeseburgers, fries, and chocolate milkshakes, an unknown woman apparently stepped up to the stroller and silently pushed it out of the food court, down the center of the mall and through the main doors to the parking lot.

After studying the security tapes for hours, Radhauser believed cameras had picked up her exit, but the face of the woman pushing the stroller was downcast, grainy and unidentifiable. Ryan had vanished. No one who might be able to give a description had suspected anything. There was nothing strange about a woman pushing a stroller across the mall parking lot. Given the crowds at the food court that day, the investigating officer believed the kidnapper had driven away long before Tiffany realized the baby was gone and reported him missing.

Now, Radhauser hurried down the hallway to Murphy's office, trying not to think about how depressing police work could be. And the sense of failure that always overcame him after Holly and Sean Patterson paid their yearly visit.

Radhauser's baby, Jonathan, had changed so much in the seventeen months since his birth. If he'd been taken away from them at three months old, would he and Gracie even recognize their son if they passed him on the street? Maybe the Pattersons needed to believe Ryan would be found. Perhaps it was the only thing that grounded them and made it possible to go on living. He tried to force thoughts of the Pattersons from his mind and focused on the murder case.

Radhauser stood in the doorway. Captain Murphy looked up from behind his desk where he stood, packing his briefcase. "You got a suspect for me yet?" He looked a little forlorn in his brown suit, with his recent mustache and melancholy eyes. Murphy's hairline had receded and what hair was left had grown thin, except for two thick strips of grey hair on either side. His forehead was smooth and as shiny as the hood of a new car.

Radhauser filled his captain in on what he'd learned so far in the Bradshaw case, the suspects he'd interviewed and the fact that McBride was checking on the attendees at the memorial and reviewing texts and phone calls. "I still need to talk to the victim's understudy at the Shakespeare Festival. I hope to arrange that for tomorrow."

"What about the husband?"

"I did an initial interview with Franklin Bradshaw."

Murphy scowled. "That pompous prick over in Medford who loves to free the guilty?"

"One and the same. Arrogant as they come."

"How much insurance does he have on his wife?"

"I asked. At first, he wouldn't say, but he finally admitted it was half a mil. Said it was his wife's idea when she got pregnant with their son. From the looks of his house, the man doesn't need money."

"Then find out if he's getting any on the side." Murphy took a deep breath; the way people do when their thoughts turn to the past.

About a year ago, his wife, Naomi, had an affair, then left him for a man Murphy had once considered a friend.

"It's part of my plan," Radhauser said.

"Good." Murphy closed his briefcase. "Find me a viable suspect before the press gets hold of this." He slapped Radhauser on the back and left the room. This was the thing he hated most about his boss—the way he was more interested in obtaining a suspect than in the long hours of investigative work it often took to discover the real perpetrator.

As Radhauser returned to his office, Hazel led Holly and Sean Patterson down the hallway. Sean's dark hair had a few more grays at the temples, but Holly looked the same, as delicate and striking as the first time Radhauser had met her. She was about five-feet, four inches, and slender with olive skin and walnut-colored hair. But the most memorable thing about her was her smile and the way her dark, thickly-lashed eyes danced under the fluorescent light.

"Holly and Sean." He shook Sean's hand and accepted a hug from Holly. "It's nice to see you." He led them into his office. "Would you like to sit down?" Radhauser indicated the two vinyl chairs he kept in front of his desk.

"No, thanks," Sean said. "I'm sure you're busy. But you know why we're here." He reached for his wife's hand. "Have there been any new developments in Ryan's case?" Before Radhauser could respond, Sean let go of his wife's hand, wrapped his arm around her waist and pulled her close, waiting for Radhauser's response. Neither of them took their gaze off his face—that God-awful hope lighting their eyes.

All cadets in the police academy are advised never to make a promise to a victim's family they may not be able to keep. Even so, Radhauser had told the Pattersons he would not stop looking for their son until Ryan was either found or his body laid to rest. It was a promise he planned to keep. But each year when the Pattersons visited his office, the full gravity of that pledge welled up around him.

For a moment, the silence was knotted. It was almost like Sean and Holly stood naked in front of him as if he was witnessing something between these two parents that was as intimate as lovemaking. "I'm so sorry." Radhauser struggled to maintain his composure as shame, pity, and remorse entered him. "But we've found nothing new."

He looked out the window behind his desk to see if the predicted rain had manifested. But the hard, moonless night had turned the glass into a mirror. His own face was the last thing in the world Radhauser wanted to see right now. "I haven't forgotten Ryan." The truth was he would never forget that case and how it had haunted his sleep for months. "I keep the file in my bottom drawer. But I don't have to read it anymore. I know it by heart."

"You think we're crazy to keep hoping, don't you?" Holly said, her gaze still riveted on him. "You think our son is dead." There was fear on her face and in her posture now.

Radhauser drew in a deep breath. He understood, perhaps better than many, that fear settled in your chest and seeped its way through your skin into muscle and bone. It settled in the soul and sucked all joy out of life. The beauty and the pleasure. But not the hope. Somehow hope found a way to resist the fear and live on. Maybe it was their hope that made the next intake of breath possible, the next step forward. A way of rebellion against what their logic told them. A way to keep living. That tiny act of rebellion was everything to them, even if it was simply to stay alive.

"I'm his mother," she said. "I'd feel it in my soul. Believe me, I'd know if my only child were dead."

CHAPTER TEN

For a few moments after the Pattersons left, Radhauser sat at his desk with his head in his hands. Knots tightened the back of his neck. He massaged them for a few moments, then stood and printed the photos he'd taken at the crime scene. There was nothing for him to do at this point except follow through with his murder investigation. Hopefully, it would eventually lead him to a viable suspect. He pinned the photos to his corkboard under the heading, *Crime Scene.*

Afterward, he printed DMV photos of Jason Robertson, Franklin Bradshaw, Carl Houseman, and Diamond DeLorenzo. He tacked them under the heading, *Persons of Interest.* He added a question mark with the words *Bradshaw's lover* to his list—at this point, it was only an assumption, based on what Jung-Su had told him. He was unable to find a photo for Sunflower Finney. Perhaps the woman, like so many in the small mountain towns in Southern Oregon, didn't have a driver's license.

It wasn't much, but it was a start.

On the white side of the case board, Radhauser made a list of persons of interest he still needed to interview. Sunny Finney and Diamond DeLorenzo. The artistic director at the Oregon Shakespeare Festival.

Once he had more information, he'd re-interview Franklin Bradshaw, confront him with the fact that he'd left his house at 11 p.m. and not returned until 5 a.m. He'd also talk to some of his colleagues at the law offices.

Jason Robertson aroused some suspicion with no alibi and his bitterness over the prospect of sharing the family vineyard.

92

Hopefully, McBride had come up with something from the cell phone and memorial guest book.

It was after 10 p.m. when Radhauser returned home. He parked the car under the overhang of the barn, then made his nightly walk through the center aisle to greet the horses, stopping in front of each stall as he always did to scratch their necks and offer a handful of sweet feed with molasses.

Too tired to jog down the driveway toward his house, he walked. Gravel crunched beneath his boots. Overhead, the moon was hidden behind a low bank of clouds and light from the stars seemed to thicken and gather like smoke. As he neared their ranch house, a warm golden glow burning in their bedroom window told him Gracie had waited up for him.

He locked his gun and holster into the cabinet in the mudroom, then tiptoed down the hallway to check on his kids. Lizzie lay crosswise across her bed, her comforter kicked to the floor. After picking her up and placing her back on her pillow, he pulled the comforter up to her neck and kissed her on the cheek, then stood for a moment, watching her sleep.

Jonathan slept, as he always did, with his knees tucked under his chest, his diapered butt straight up. He thought about Sean and Holly Patterson as he touched the baby's head, his golden-brown hair impossibly soft, then hurried into the bedroom he shared with Gracie.

Just out of the shower, his wife stood inside their bathroom doorway, a towel wrapped around her. "Long day?"

"Don't ask."

"It's May fourth," she said. "Did the Pattersons stop by?"

"I'm afraid so. And, as usual, I had nothing to give them."

"I'm sorry." She tilted her head and held his gaze. "But I missed you."

Radhauser smiled. "Oh yeah. How much?"

She dropped the towel. "About this much."

* * *

It's three a.m. on Saturday morning, and you can't sleep. Blair Bradshaw's demise made the late-night news. The medical examiner is calling it a murder. Not that you're surprised. But you keep wondering if you made a mistake by not leaving the razor beside her body. If you'd done that, the police might have concluded it was suicide, and you wouldn't have to keep looking over your shoulder. You thought about it but ultimately decided to rinse off the blade and its wooden holder in the creek and put it in your pocket. So, you guess maybe, at least at that moment, you wanted it to be known that someone murdered the successful and self-assured wife, mother and Shakespearean actress. The selfish woman who'd dished out more than her share of heartache and deserved exactly what she received.

Other than the mini lights caterers had hung in the trees, it was dark in the woods last night, so you can't be certain, but you don't think you left any evidence at the scene that could possibly lead them to you. You're too smart for that. You caught her injecting her arm with some drug—probably heroin from the bizarre way she behaved. You tossed her syringe into the creek on purpose—thinking it might lead police to suspect her drug-addled mother. And you wore latex gloves, so you're positive you didn't leave any prints—even if you were in the system, which you're not. Blair had been far too drunk and high to put up a fight, so you're sure they'll discover none of your DNA under her perfectly-manicured fingernails.

In spite of all that, something is bothering you. Last night, as you left the scene, it seemed as if the trees had eyes and were watching. You know that sounds paranoid. And there's more. Now, each time you hear a siren, you break out in a cold sweat. You always believed in the law. You still do. Aristotle had it right when he said, 'at his best, man is the noblest of all animals; separated from law and justice he is the worst.'

Undoubtedly, killing Blair Bradshaw was you at your worst. It was the first crime you've ever committed. But you can't help wondering if it will be your last. You've read some criminal psychology books that say people can get addicted to killing as easily as they can to cigarettes, drugs, or alcohol. Perhaps your childhood propensity for dissection will rear its murderous head again. Maybe old Mr. Higgins was correct in his prediction for your future.

Truthfully, you're not sure if you regret killing Blair. What choice did you really have? You tried to convince her to give you another chance, tried to make her understand what was most important to you, but she refused to listen, even after Tommy died and you believed she might be more open to your proposal.

Signing that name as the last entry in the guest book was brilliant. Not to mention the baby rattle you glued over her heart. Whacking off a lock of her hair was clever too, wouldn't you say? Something that might confuse Detective Winston Radhauser of the Ashland Police Department.

A little puzzle that will be challenging, if not impossible, for our homicide detective to solve.

* * *

When Radhauser awakened, it was just after dawn. Outside the bedroom window, the first hints of sunrise came through the trees in broad, orange, and yellow bands. He tiptoed into the bathroom, then showered and shaved before Gracie or his children awakened. After leaving a note on the kitchen table for his wife, he headed to his office. It wasn't so much that he was expected to show up on the weekend as it was his obsession to get a murder case solved as rapidly as possible. Evidence grew cold quickly, and the faster he moved, the more likely he'd find Blair Bradshaw's killer.

He arrived just as the morning brightened around him. He opened the door to the smell of freshly-brewed coffee and McBride at her desk. Radhauser was surprised, but shouldn't have been. His new partner was as obsessive as he when it came to a murder case. "Did you have any luck finding a weapon in the creek?"

She looked up at him, disappointment in her gaze. "I'm afraid not. Forensics raked the entire area around the treehouse and along the creek banks a good fifty feet on either side of where you found the blood and drag marks. If it was there, one of us would have found it. So, I don't see how Blair Bradshaw's death could possibly be suicide."

He told her what Heron had discovered about the direction of the cuts in her groin. "It would have been pretty awkward, if not impossible, for her to manage that, especially with the level of drugs and alcohol in her system."

"I've got that list of attendees at the Bradshaw memorial," she said. "I phoned all of them. Everyone who signed the guest book claimed to be either friends of the Bradshaws, colleagues at the law firm, other actresses and actors at the Shakespeare Festival, or the parents of Tommy's classmates and friends. And none of them noticed anything out of the ordinary." She raised her right eyebrow, an indication that she'd saved the best for last. "But something did strike me as strange. The last signature in the guest book was someone named Auden F. Bradshaw. The ink was different from the other signatures. I can't find a telephone listing for him anywhere in a sixty-mile radius of Ashland. No DMV record either."

"Auden's not a very common first name. Did you check to see if anyone by that name had a sheet?"

"No luck there either. I phoned Mr. Bradshaw's office to check with him but got a recording. I forgot it was Saturday."

"Easy to do in our line of work," Radhauser said.

"I already called his house, too, thinking Auden might be his brother, but Mr. Bradshaw was unavailable. His housekeeper said she didn't recognize the name and that, as far as she knows, Bradshaw is an only child. She said she'd have him phone me back, but so far he hasn't."

"That's okay. I plan to track him down and pay a visit later today. I'll take the memorial book with me. Anything suspicious on the cell phone?"

She shook her head and handed him the book. "The lab didn't find anything Mrs. Bradshaw had deleted that raised a flag. Her texts were mostly from the Shakespeare Theater office, a woman named Diamond DeLorenzo, or her husband. There were a couple from her brother, Jason, about the vineyard and their father's declining health."

"Damn," Radhauser said. "I was hoping for more. DeLorenzo was the victim's understudy." He took the bag holding the baby rattle from his backpack and handed it to McBride. "Heron found it glued to Blair Bradshaw's left breast."

McBride studied it for a moment. "It looks old," she said.

"Much too old to have belonged to her ten-year-old son."

"I thought so, too. But maybe it's a family heirloom."

"What seems odd is that she would glue it to her breast," McBride said. "Hard to imagine a woman like Blair Bradshaw doing something like that unless she was planning to take her own life. Since we know she didn't, that would indicate the murderer put it there, but why?"

"You could be right, but it could also have been her grief," Radhauser said. "No rhyme or reason to it. Maybe it did belong to Tommy."

"I'll do a little research," she said. "See if I can date the rattle, but even if it is old, it still won't tell us she didn't glue it there herself."

"Use this." He handed her the photograph he'd taken of the rattle. "I want to see if the housekeeper recognizes it. She's been with Franklin and Blair Bradshaw since before Tommy's birth."

After examining it carefully, McBride returned the rattle to him.

"While you're researching, I'm headed over to Superior Security. If I get there before 8 a.m., I might be able to talk with whoever installed the Bradshaws' system. Maybe our victim said something that might help us understand who she was afraid of and why."

"Oh, that reminds me. I checked to see if there were any reported break-ins, either robbery or burglary, in the Bradshaw neighborhood. It's a low crime area where most of the properties are gated and protected by security systems. Nothing reported in the last two years—not even any vandalism."

He remembered what Carl Houseman had told him about being the president of the neighborhood watch. "I suspected as much."

"Call me if you need anything else."

"I'd like you to interview the artistic director at the Shakespeare Festival and see if any company members had a beef with Blair."

"Anything I can do to help, boss."

"After I talk with whoever installed the Bradshaw system, I plan to track down Franklin Bradshaw." He told McBride what he'd learned from Jung-Su about Bradshaw leaving the house at 11 p.m. and not returning until the following morning. "I need to get some answers as to his whereabouts at the time his wife was murdered."

CHAPTER ELEVEN

Radhauser got out of his car in the parking lot of Superior Security on Airport Road. The air was spiked with the smell of newly-cut grass, and a leaf-blower hummed somewhere behind the building. Since the lights were on inside, he tried the door, and it opened.

When the bell indicating a customer had entered rang, a young, red-haired woman looked up from behind the counter. She was barely more than a teenager, with a sprinkling of cinnamon-colored freckles across her nose. Her brown shirt had the words Superior Security embroidered in tan over the pocket, and her name tag read *Sheila Thomas*.

"You're an early bird," she said with a smile. "How can I help you?"

Radhauser took off his Stetson and introduced himself, then explained he was working on a case involving a woman for whom they'd recently installed a system.

Her blue eyes grew wide. "Oh, my God. Did someone break into her house? Did one of our systems malfunction?"

"My visit has nothing to do with a fault in your system. I'd just like to speak with whoever installed it."

"Are you interested in having one installed in your own home, Detective Radhauser? We can set up an appointment to have someone come by and give you an estimate."

"No," he said. "All I want today is to talk to the person or persons who installed a system at the Bradshaw house on Sand Creek Road in Ashland."

"I'm not authorized to let you do that," she said. "In my job training, they told me I should maintain confidentiality. Our clients may not want information released about their homes or systems."

"I'm not here to get information about a system. I'm here to talk to the men who installed it in case my victim said something that might be helpful in my investigation. I can come back with a warrant if you make that necessary."

"Your victim? Is someone dead? Do you mean a warrant for you to arrest one of our installers?" There was more than a hint of fear in her voice.

He laughed. "No, I mean a warrant to get the installer to speak with me. As far as I know, Superior Security and its employees are guilty of nothing."

"Okay," she said. "Could you give me the name of the client again?"

"Blair and Franklin Bradshaw. They have a big house over on Sand Creek Road near Ashland."

She opened a file cabinet drawer, searched for a few seconds, then pulled out a manila folder. "The guys are out back loading the equipment for today's installations. Can you wait for just a moment?" Sheila gestured toward a puke-green vinyl chair in the small waiting room.

Radhauser sat while she hurried down a hallway and out what he assumed was the back door onto the loading dock.

A few moments later, she returned with a tall and very slender man who looked to be in his thirties. He wore a larger version of Sheila's brown T-shirt, khaki slacks and a pair of lace-up work boots.

"This is Ernie Glosser," she said. "He installed the Bradshaw system."

The man had dark eyes, a black crewcut with long sideburns and an easy smile with teeth straight and white enough to do toothpaste commercials.

Radhauser stood, introduced himself, and offered his hand.

After shaking it, Ernie suggested they talk in the breakroom. "It's more private there."

Radhauser followed him down a narrow hallway into a room with a brick-patterned linoleum floor and walls painted lemon yellow. It smelled like pepperoni pizza. The room held a round table and six chairs along with a refrigerator, coffee maker, and an assortment of coffee mugs and, no surprise, a cardboard box from Domino's Pizza.

"You want a cup of coffee?" Ernie smiled. "But I'll warn you ahead of time, man, it ain't exactly Starbucks quality."

When Radhauser declined, Ernie took a seat at the table, and Radhauser pulled out the chair across from him and sat.

"I'm a law-abiding citizen with a wife and two kids. I ain't never been arrested for nothin'. So, what do you need from me, Detective Radhauser?"

He explained his mission. "I don't have any great leads at this point, except that the victim was terrified of something or someone. And I thought she might have said something to you. Was she present when you installed the system?"

There was a moment of silence and the air in the breakroom chilled. "We got training on not to talk about our clients or what type of installations they bought." He folded his hands on the tabletop. Thin quarter moons of grease outlined the tips of his fingernails. It was something Radhauser admired whenever he saw it—something that said this person works hard for a living.

"This is a criminal investigation, Mr. Glosser, and what you were trained to do isn't really pertinent under the circumstances. I can come back with a warrant. Or I can have you come down to the police station in Ashland if you prefer."

"Saturdays are busy. I've got installations scheduled for today."

"Then I suggest we get this done as quickly as possible."

"What kind of criminal investigation?"

"Murder."

Ernie shifted in his chair. "Murder?" He jammed his hands under his armpits as if to protect himself. "You can't think I had anything to do with no murder." He grabbed a pack of Marlboro Lights from his breast pocket, lit one up, then sucked in a big drag and blew it out.

Radhauser had given up smoking over a decade ago, and like many converts, he preferred not to be around smokers. His aversion must have shown on his face.

"It's okay," Ernie said. "We're allowed to smoke in the breakroom." He nodded toward the ashtray on the table. "I'm a little nervous. I never talked to a detective about a murder before."

"You've nothing to worry about, Mr. Glosser. Our conversation is entirely private. I don't suspect you of anything. I'm merely trying to shed some light on my case by talking to anyone who may have information about Mrs. Bradshaw. Someone murdered her, and I think that someone was the reason she had the security system installed in the first place."

"What do you want to know?"

He repeated the question. "Was Mrs. Bradshaw present at the installation?"

Ernie put out the cigarette, leaned forward, and his words seemed to rush from his mouth. "Are you kidding? She never left my side, watched every move I made. If you want to know the truth, it was a little bit nerve wracking. Even followed me out to the truck when I needed another tool or something. She was nice enough but had more questions than my four-year-old kid. That chick seemed close to the edge, man, a woman about to explode and barely in control."

"Anything at all, you can tell me might help."

"It was a beautiful place, I remember that much."

"Did she say anything about what she was afraid of?"

"Only that she wanted to make sure no one could get inside the house unless she invited them. She had me install new locks and keyed deadbolts. She was very concerned about broken windows and how fast security could get to her house in the event the alarm went off."

"What did you tell her?"

"Given the location—place is out in the boonies, man—I said it shouldn't be more than ten minutes before we could have someone there. She freaked out. Gave me a run-down on everything that could happen in ten minutes. This chick was afraid of her own shadow and was shaking like a wet cat. Said ten minutes was way too long. And then she asked if putting bars on the windows and glass parts of the doors would keep anyone from getting in. When I told her iron bars would certainly make it a lot harder, she looked me straight in the face. 'Then do it. I don't care what it costs.'"

There'd been no bars on the windows and doors when Radhauser talked to Jung-Su. "When did you install the system?"

He opened the manila folder and scanned an order form. "April tenth. Almost a month ago."

"And what day did she place the order?"

Again, Ernie scanned his form. "One week before we installed. That would make it April third."

So whatever terrified Blair Bradford probably happened on April third or shortly before. Radhauser made a note of the dates. "There were no bars on the windows when I was there yesterday."

"I did all the measurements on the tenth after I completed the alarm installation, but before I could call the guy who makes the grates, her husband canceled the order. The dude, some big shot lawyer, said she was being ridiculous, and he wasn't going to have his son grow up inside a prison."

Radhauser pushed his chair away from the table and stood. "Thank you for your time, Mr. Glosser. You've been very helpful."

They shook hands.

"I hope you find whoever killed her. She was scared out of her wits, and at the time, I figured she was some kind of paranoid sicko or something." A flush crept over Ernie's cheeks. "But now it seems like the poor woman had good reason to be afraid of her shadow."

* * *

Jung-Su answered the door. When she spotted Radhauser, she straightened her back. After wiping her forehead, where the sweat was already gathering, she opened her mouth to speak, then closed it. "Mr. Franklin…he say…" She clenched her eyes shut and seemed to bite back on something bitter. "He say he my boss and I no spcak to you. Or he fire me."

"Mr. Bradshaw has no right to tell you who you can and can't speak to."

She opened her eyes.

"Besides, I came to talk to him. Is he home?"

"No, he say he have trial to prepare. Be gone all day. For me no worry about dinner."

"May I come inside for a moment?"

She stretched her arms across the door frame as if to prevent him from entering. "Mr. Franklin, he say—"

"Okay. You don't have to let me in. But I may return with a warrant and then you won't have a choice. I plan to head over to Mr. Bradshaw's office, but before I go, I need your help." He pulled the rattle from his pocket. "Did this belong to Tommy as a baby?"

"He no have baby rattle like that one. Only plastic or rubber. This one too heavy for baby. Might hurt himself."

"Are you sure? I need you to look at this very carefully."

With a trembling hand, she took the rattle and studied it for a moment before handing it back. "No. Miss Blair, she no like silver. She allergic to the polish and break out in hives. When Tommy born, she asked me return all baby gifts that were silver."

There were traces of silver polish on the rattle. Pretty unlikely a woman allergic to polish would glue that silver rattle to her own breast.

"Could it have been a rattle that belonged to Mr. Bradshaw or Miss Blair when they were babies?"

Jung-Su smoothed her hair with her right hand. "I no think so. I clean every room, and I never see this rattle before."

One more thing. He pulled out the memorial book and showed her the last signature. "Does this look like Blair's handwriting?"

"I no think so. But you ask Mr. Franklin. He know better than I do."

"Thank you, Jung-Su. You don't have to be afraid of me. What you say to me is strictly confidential. I'm not here to do you any harm, I just want to get to the truth about what happened to Miss Blair."

"You good man," she said. "I can tell."

CHAPTER TWELVE

The law offices of Bradshaw, Foster, and Meyer were located in a renovated Craftsman-style house on South Oakdale, near the municipal court. It was painted a pale shade of yellow with black shutters and a wide porch with pots of colorful purple petunias and pungent-smelling yellow marigolds hanging between the stone pillars. The house set on a small lot, perfectly landscaped with a pink flowering dogwood in the middle of the lush, green yard. The wide porch, with its plank floor painted sage, held a wicker swing and matching chairs with a table between them. A setup designed to make someone comfortable, like they'd just stepped onto the porch of a house featured in *Southern Living Magazine* for a glass of lemonade.

Radhauser rang the bell.

A moment later, a young woman appeared at the door. She wore a pair of tattered jeans and a black T-shirt with the words *Attitude Is All I Got* scrawled across the front in hot pink. A few strands of her dark hair had come loose from the cotton bandana she'd wrapped around her head. The stray hairs hung in moist ringlets on her forehead and cheeks. She wore no makeup, and her forehead glistened with sweat.

He introduced himself and showed his badge. "And what's your name?"

"Millie," she said. "Millie Peterson."

"Nice to meet you, Millie. I'm here to see Franklin Bradshaw. I understand he's working today."

"I'm the cleaning lady," she said. "And there's no one here but me. You could check with one of the partners, Lucinda Foster.

105

They've been working a lot of overtime on a case together." She wiggled her eyebrows and smiled. "If you know what I mean."

"What time do you come to work?"

"I work from 10 p.m. until 2 a.m. Monday through Thursday. And half day on Saturday. I clean for two other law offices as well. You'd be surprised how messy lawyers can be."

"Has Mr. Bradshaw been working a lot of late nights this week?"

"As far as I know, he's been off all week. The offices have been empty when I got here at night. I'm sure you heard about his son." She grimaced. "What a terrible, terrible thing for Mr. and Mrs. Bradshaw."

"And you're sure Mr. Bradshaw wasn't here when you arrived on Thursday night."

"That was the night of his son's memorial. No way he would have been here working."

"Any possibility you could save me the time of looking it up and give me Lucinda Foster's home address?"

"I'd do most anything for a handsome cowboy." She shifted her gaze to the wedding ring on his left hand. "Even a married one." She returned a moment later with an address on Glenview Drive in Ashland. "Don't tell them you got it from me."

Radhauser smiled. "Don't worry. Confidentiality is my trademark."

* * *

The house on Glenview was a Queen Anne, painted pale yellow with Wedgewood blue rickrack and shutters. He parked his Crown Vic on the street and hurried up the front walk. Like most houses in this coveted area of Ashland, the yard was neatly groomed, the lawn edged and the flowerbeds planted and mulched with fragrant pine bark.

He rang the bell.

After what seemed like an inordinately long time, a tall and slender woman answered. She wore an exercise outfit, a sleeveless white T-shirt, red pants with a white stripe down the side and a pair of expensive running shoes to match. Her blonde hair was pulled back into a ponytail, and her forehead glistened with sweat. "I'm Detective Radhauser with the Ashland Police Department. I'm looking for Franklin Bradshaw. Is he here?" He showed his badge.

Her forehead furrowed. "Lucinda Foster," she said. "And yes. He's here. I just got back from my run. We're working a capital case together. The trial starts on Monday."

"Do you always run before you work?"

"I go to Lithia Park most early mornings. The solitude and the running help me think. I love the way the earth absorbs the sound of my footsteps, and I can barely hear myself passing through the trees."

Bradshaw appeared behind her. Unlike Ms. Foster, he was dressed in khakis and a polo shirt and looked fresh, as if he'd just shaved and stepped out of the shower. Obviously, he hadn't been running. "What brings you here, Detective Radhauser? And more importantly, how did you know I'd be here?"

"I'm a detective. When you weren't home or in your office, and aware of the big case you have on Monday, one of your partner's homes seemed a logical starting place."

"What do you want with me now? I missed almost an entire week of work, and we've got a lot to accomplish this morning."

"I understand," Radhauser said. "But I'd like to ask you a few questions before you begin. Would you please come out to my car?"

The veins in Bradshaw's neck corded. "Oh, for Christ sake. You can ask me in front of Lucinda. I don't have secrets from her."

"I'd rather talk with you alone. I can take you to my office if you prefer. But talking in my car will get you back to work much quicker."

He let out a long sigh like this was one of the most irritating things that had ever happened to him. "Lucinda. You go ahead and get started on the depositions. I'll work on the discovery. And the DA's inculpatory evidence when I finish with this idiot detective."

Once Bradshaw was settled into the passenger seat, Radhauser began. "My partner took a look at the sign-in book from your son's memorial. In fact, she called everyone in the book except the final entry. Auden F. Bradshaw. She couldn't find any listing for him. Do you have any idea who that person might be?"

"None." He tugged at the neck of his shirt. "I'm an only child, as were my father and grandfather. Besides, I knew every person at that memorial, and none of them was named Auden."

"Does the name mean anything to you?"

"Nothing except it was the last name of a famous poet, W. H. Auden. He was born in the early nineteen hundreds and was best known for his political, left-wing writing. He won a Pulitzer in 1947 for his long poem, *The Age of Anxiety*."

The man was smart and well-rounded in his knowledge, but there was still something about him Radhauser didn't trust.

"If that's all you wanted to know," Bradshaw said. "I'd like to get back to work now."

"Not so fast. You told me you drank too much at the memorial for your son and fell asleep early—leading me to believe you slept in your own bed at your own house. But now I've discovered that wasn't true. You left your house around 11 p.m. and didn't return until 5 a.m. on Friday—the morning you allegedly found your wife dead in the woods."

"There is no allegedly about it." He sucked in a breath and let it out slowly. "I found my wife dead in the woods around 8 a.m. And who told you I left my house?"

Radhauser needed to be careful, he didn't want to incriminate Jung-Su or cause any friction between her and her employer. "The who doesn't matter. Suffice it to say, I have an eye witness who saw your car turn out of your driveway Thursday night around eleven and return again at 5 a.m. the following morning."

"Carl Houseman needs to mind his own business."

Radhauser didn't bother correcting Bradshaw's assumption. The last thing he wanted to do was cost Jung-Su her job. "Well, now it's my business. The ME puts the time of death for your wife at sometime between 11 p.m. and 12:30 a.m. Where were you during that time?"

"I was working on the case. I couldn't sleep. It looked like Blair was going to spend the night in the treehouse and I understood her need to do that. I was behind on my trial preparation because of taking the week off to be with my wife. So, I went into my office, where I'd have access to my law library, made a pot of coffee and worked all night."

"Can anyone verify you were there? Maybe a night watchman or cleaning person?"

"I was there alone. But Lucinda probably knew I was working."

Radhauser tapped his index finger against the steering wheel. "And why didn't you tell me that during my first round of questions?"

"You didn't ask. Besides, I know how you detectives think. You always suspect the husband first. And I didn't want you to think I was out having an affair. Or that I had any reason to want my wife dead."

"Better I think you an adulterer than a murderer, wouldn't you say? And now you've lied to me, you've moved up my suspect list in your wife's death."

"I don't care what you think. And I don't give a damn about your list. I had nothing to do with Blair's death. Believe me, you'll have a hard time proving I did."

Radhauser pulled the rattle from his inside pocket. "Have you ever seen this before, Mr. Bradshaw?"

Bradshaw took it, studied it for a moment, then handed it back. "Never. Why would a baby rattle be significant?"

"The ME found it glued to your wife's left breast—over her heart. Are you sure it didn't belong to Tommy?"

"Positive. Blair didn't have any sterling silver in the house. She was allergic to the polish. It made her break out in hives. Now, can I get back to work?"

"Could it have been something left over from yours or Blair's childhood?"

"No. Neither of us saved anything."

He showed Bradshaw the last signature in the memorial book. "Do you recognize this handwriting? Could Blair have written it?"

"Not unless she was deliberately trying to disguise her handwriting. Now may I go?" He reached for the door handle.

Radhauser hit the lock button. "Not so fast."

"What the hell are you doing? This is false imprisonment."

"I need to see your cell phone." Radhauser couldn't risk Bradshaw texting Lucinda and asking her to claim he was at the office. He was, after all, the senior partner. That might make her willing to lie for him.

"It's inside on the dining room table. That's where we work."

Radhauser unlocked the car door. "Good. You wait here. Or take a little walk if you don't want to be falsely imprisoned. I'll be right back."

Bradshaw threw his hands into the air. "Who do you think you are telling me what I can and can't do?"

"You're a criminal defense attorney, Mr. Bradshaw. You know how this works. When someone lies in a murder investigation, he automatically becomes a suspect. I'm trying to cut you a break here. I could arrest you, take you in for suspicion of your wife's murder. Slap on the handcuffs and haul you over to Ashland Holding for at least twenty-four hours. But I'm trying to get you back to work on your trial preparation. So, I suggest you wait here. I'll be right back."

The look on Bradshaw's face could have melted candle wax.

When Radhauser reached the front door, Lucinda was already standing in the doorway. "What's going on?"

"As you probably know, Blair Bradshaw was found dead yesterday morning. After performing the autopsy, the ME is calling it a homicide."

"A homicide? Oh, my God. But you can't think Franklin had anything to do with it. They'd just lost their only son. Franklin works way too much, but he loves his family."

"Were you present at the memorial for Tommy Bradshaw on Thursday night?"

She rested her right hand over her chest. "No. And I felt a bit bad about it. I sent a flower arrangement. But I didn't know Tommy or Blair all that well, and Franklin said not to worry about it."

If she and Franklin were having an affair, Lucinda Foster might have reason to avoid being in Blair's presence at the memorial, and she might have reason to want her dead. "I'm asking this question of everyone I interview. Can you account for your whereabouts between 11 p.m. and 12:30 a.m. on Thursday?"

"Yes." There was no hesitation in her voice. "I had tickets to see *The Tempest* Thursday night in the Bowmer with a girlfriend from law school. She lives down in California. We'd been planning it for months. The two of us had dinner at the Renaissance beforehand. The play let out around 10 p.m. We stayed for the backstage talk with the actors, then had a glass of wine at that little bar outside the theater. We got home around midnight. She left just before 8 a.m. yesterday to head back to San Francisco."

"Would you mind giving me your friend's name and phone number?"

"Of course." She wrote down a name with a San Francisco area code and phone number on a post-it and handed it to Radhauser. "It's a seven-hour drive, so you probably won't be able to reach her until later this afternoon. Hold on a moment," she said, then rummaged through the purse she'd left on her kitchen desk. "I still have our ticket stubs." She handed them to him.

The stubs looked legitimate, and he had every reason to believe Lucinda was exactly where she said she'd been. "Do you know if Mr. Bradshaw worked at the office on Thursday night?"

"I doubt it," she said. "I took my friend by to show her my office at about 11 or 11:30 p.m. The cleaning crew had already left, and everything was locked up tight. Besides, it was the night of his son's memorial. I don't suspect he felt like working after that."

Radhauser hurried outside and opened the car door. "You're under arrest for suspicion of murder in the death of Blair Bradshaw."

Bradshaw's face had lost its smugness and turned a bluish shade of gray.

"You have the right to remain silent…"

He stared hard at Radhauser. "Oh, for God's sake, I'm a

criminal defense attorney. I know my rights."

"Then you also know I'm required to read them to you." Radhauser finished reciting the Miranda rights. "Anything you can and do say can be held against you in a court of law…"

"You're making a huge mistake, Radhauser. And I'll have your badge for it."

"I sincerely doubt that. You lied to me twice. That makes you a suspect. Your partner brought her friend to the office between 11 and 11:30 p.m. after attending a play at the Shakespeare Festival Thursday night. She said it was dark and locked up tight when she got there."

"I can explain." Bradshaw closed his eyes.

"Explain what? That you thought because she's a junior partner, your second chair in a big murder trial, that she would automatically lie for you?"

He continued to shake his head, eyes still closed. When he finally opened them, his voice was softer and more conciliatory. "No. I meant that I can explain why I lied."

"You'll get your chance."

CHAPTER THIRTEEN

Radhauser and McBride stood in the hallway outside Interrogation Room 2 and watched Franklin Bradshaw through the one-way glass. He paced across the small, windowless room, occasionally stopping to look at himself in the one-way mirror on the wall facing the hallway, his anger and frustration easily visible on his face.

"I found out some things about the baby rattle," McBride said. "It was made by Tiffany in the late eighteen hundreds. If you look carefully, you can still read their insignia."

"Pretty swanky." Radhauser pulled it out of his pocket. And sure enough, the engraving *T & Co* was still visible on the side.

"Apparently it was a popular baby gift for the rich at the turn of the century."

"Interesting information. But how and why did it end up glued to Blair Bradshaw's left breast?"

"I suspect you could pick one up cheap at a garage or estate sale," McBride said. "Especially if it were tarnished. But it obviously meant something to our murderer—if he or she was the one who glued it to Blair Bradshaw's breast. The question is what?"

Radhauser slipped the rattle back into his pocket. He hoped to visit Sunflower Finney later today and find out if it meant anything to her. But for now, he had Franklin Bradshaw to deal with.

The interrogation room contained only a 3x4 foot table with a tape recorder and box of Kleenex on top of it along with three metal chairs, their seats upholstered in green vinyl. Radhauser told his partner about the way Bradshaw had lied about his whereabouts and claimed to be working at his office but was not there when his partner brought a friend by at 11:30.

"Let's see if we can find out where he spent the night on Thursday. He's an arrogant man, and pretty angry with me, but he might be more willing to talk to you. So, you take the lead on this one."

"Sure thing, boss."

"If he has an alibi that checks out, we'll let him go. I don't think he'd leave town. He's got a murder case that starts on Monday, and he won't miss it. That trial might be an incentive to finally get the truth out of him."

Radhauser opened the door and entered, McBride at his heels.

Bradshaw stopped pacing and glared at them, nervously twisting the Rolex on his left wrist. "Don't think I'm not on to your tactics. Leaving me alone to stew in this hell-hole."

"Have a seat, Mr. Bradshaw." He introduced Detective McBride.

Bradshaw sat. "I demand to know what evidence you have in your possession that would indicate I did anything to harm my wife."

McBride and Radhauser ignored his demand, pulled out the two chairs across from him, and sat. Radhauser set a tablet and pen on the table in front of himself. For a few moments, no one said a word.

"Just for your information, Mr. Bradshaw," McBride said. "We don't make a habit of granting a murder suspect's demands. Lying to the police constitutes evidence."

His eyes widened. "Suspect? Why do you insist on labeling me a suspect when I had nothing to do with my wife's death?" His shrill voice gave away his fear. "And I'm absolutely certain you don't have one iota of inculpatory evidence against me. How could you when none exists?"

"I'll be taping this interview." Radhauser turned on the tape recorder and dictated. "This is the interrogation of Franklin Bradshaw, husband of Blair Bradshaw, who was murdered between the hours of 11:00 p.m. on Thursday, May 3 an d 12:30 a.m. on Friday, May 4. The date is Saturday, May 5, 2001. We are in

Interrogation Room 2 of the Ashland Police Department. Present are Detectives Radhauser and McBride along with the suspect, Franklin Bradshaw."

Bradshaw held his hands up like a man about to be robbed. "Is recording all this really necessary? I can clear up any misunderstandings."

"Recording interviews is procedure. And, as you know, it protects you as well as the police department." Radhauser leaned forward and pushed the recorder a little closer to Bradshaw. "Would you state your full name, age, occupation, and place of employment."

"Franklin Paul Bradshaw. I'm forty-two years old, an attorney and the senior partner in the Medford law firm of Bradshaw, Foster, and Meyer. Look, I'd like to clear this up quickly so I can get back to work. You already know I have a big case on Monday."

McBride studied him for one long moment, her gaze, like a telephoto lens, didn't miss a thing. "There's nothing we'd rather do, Mr. Bradshaw. Why don't you begin by telling us where you went on Thursday night around 11 p.m.? And let's aim for the truth this time."

"Look, I realize I should have been more forthcoming from the beginning. But I'm human and was merely trying to protect someone I care about."

"With no disrespect intended, Mr. Bradshaw," McBride shot him a venomous look befitting her rattlesnake earrings, "Who protected your wife that night?"

Bradshaw was obviously taken aback by the question. Or was it the look McBride gave him? He hung his head for a moment, then lifted it and met McBride's gaze. "I'm ashamed to say no one did. And I'll have to live with that. I cared about Blair. I'm not the one who hurt her." His voice was choked with emotion.

"Oh," McBride drew out the word. "Is that so? I suspect you hurt her plenty, Mr. Bradshaw. But go ahead. Tell us the name of the other woman you spent the night with. The woman for whom you left your grieving wife after she'd just endured your ten-year-old son's memorial service. That hardly constitutes a nomination for husband of the year."

A flush spread across Bradshaw's cheeks. He stared at her silently for a moment, and Radhauser expected him to yell back some sarcastic reply, but instead, something seemed to unravel deep within him. Maybe the man had a conscience, after all.

"You've got me all wrong, Detective McBride. I can understand why." His eyes narrowed like someone trying to bring a blurred image into focus—perhaps the image of a better husband and father. "But you know nothing about my relationship with my wife. She wasn't an easy woman. Even so, the truth is, I'd do anything to have a second chance with Blair and Tommy. Don't you think I know that if I'd only gone back to the woods after paying the caterers, things might have turned out differently? If I'd taken Blair into my arms and held her, if only for a moment. If I'd told her we could spend the night together in the bunk beds in Tommy's treehouse that maybe, just maybe, she'd still be alive?"

McBride didn't seem moved by his confession and list of hypothetical questions. "So where did you go instead of comforting your wife and spending the night in your son's treehouse, Mr. Bradshaw?"

The man was silent for a long moment, then cleared his throat. "I'm not proud of this. But I've been involved in a relationship with one of the paralegals in our office for nearly a year now."

McBride cocked her head. "By relationship, do you mean extramarital affair?"

He nodded.

She tapped her finger on the tabletop, an indication of her impatience. "Speak up for the recorder, Mr. Bradshaw."

"Yes," he said. "I was having an extramarital affair."

"Does this paralegal have a name?" McBride slid Radhauser's tablet closer, picked up the pen, and made a note.

Bradshaw's shoulders curled inward. "She's very young, her family is quite religious, and I don't intend to involve her in a scandal."

McBride stared at him, bullets in her gaze. "I'm shocked. The choices we make in our lives have a way of showing others who we are, Mr. Bradshaw. And I don't much like the man I see right now."

Detective McBride, who'd divorced her cheating husband five years ago, had a way of going for the jugular. She was almost as good as a criminal defense lawyer at taking words, twisting them around and aiming them right back at the suspect who'd uttered them. Some people used bullets to wound. McBride used words.

Bradshaw met her gaze for a moment before he looked away. "Yes, I engaged in the affair while I was married. I'm ashamed of the way I betrayed my wife's trust. I can only hope and pray that Blair didn't know."

"Oh, she knew, all right." Even though she'd already hit her mark, McBride kept firing. "The wife always knows."

Radhauser was tempted to tell Bradshaw what Jason had said about Blair planning to leave him, and that was the reason she needed the money from the sale of the vineyard. But he decided to keep that information to himself for now. McBride was doing a fine job of knocking Franklin Bradshaw off his self-erected pedestal.

"Now," McBride said. "I suspect you already know we're going to take you over to Holding and have you booked unless you provide us with an alibi for the night your wife was murdered. So, what's this paralegal's name?"

Bradshaw was visibly sweating now. He grabbed a Kleenex from the box on the table and swiped his forehead. "If I give that to you, would you please go easy on her when you verify my alibi and make sure she's alone? Her roommate tends to be judgmental. And she works part-time for the firm, too. The last thing I need is her sounding off her pious mouth. Sonya's so young, and I don't want to do anything that might ruin her life."

"Maybe you should have thought about that before you had the affair. She's what, twenty years younger than you are?" McBride liked the direct approach.

In fact, it was the approach Radhauser also employed when conducting most of his interrogations. He wasn't a detective who liked to play games.

Bradshaw dropped the tissue into the wastebasket beside the table. "Twenty-two years younger, to be exact. But yes, Detective

McBride, I should have thought about that, and a lot of other things, like putting a railing around the platform on my son's treehouse. Look, I know they weren't my finest hours, but having sex with another woman doesn't make me a murderer."

"I'm not reassured." McBride gave him a slow and humorless smile. "In truth, another woman has been the motive for countless wife murderers."

Bradshaw speared his hand through his thick hair, revealing some gray at the roots and standing it on end. He turned to Radhauser. "Does she ever let up? And I thought you were the pit bull."

If he'd liked the man better, Radhauser might have laughed. The pit bull and the rattlesnake. Perfect partners. "Let's have your paralegal's full name."

"Sonya Clifford. She lives in Medford over on Oakdale. Her roommate, Rebekeh, is an international flight attendant and travels during the two weeks every month she isn't working for us."

"How convenient for you." McBride made no effort to hide her contempt.

"Is there an address and phone number where I can reach her?" Radhauser asked.

Bradshaw gave him both from memory.

Radhauser stood. "I'll be right back."

"Am I free to go now?" Bradshaw asked. "It's almost noon, and I've wasted the entire morning here."

"Not until I confirm your alibi. McBride can get you a cup of coffee or a sandwich if you're hungry."

"No, thanks," he said.

Radhauser left the room, purposely allowing the door to slam behind him, hard and unforgiving as a slap.

His desktop was cluttered with crime scene photos and notes he'd made on the Bradshaw case. He felt a pang of guilt when he spotted the Ryan Patterson kidnapping case folder and tucked it back into his bottom drawer. The entire office smelled like oranges, from the peelings he'd left in his trashcan last night. He gathered up the crime scene photos and notes and put them into a manila folder he placed on the credenza behind his desk. He picked up the receiver and placed the call.

The phone rang five times before a woman answered.

"Are you Sonya Clifford, a law clerk with Bradshaw, Foster, and Meyer?"

"Yes. Who is this?"

He told her. "I need to talk with you for a few moments. Would you mind coming into the Ashland Police Department? We're on the Plaza, across from Pivorotto's Toy Pavilion and the Greenleaf Restaurant, near the entrance to Lithia Park. It's a white building."

"I know where you are," she said. "I can be there in fifteen minutes. But would you mind telling me what this is all about?"

"Your name came up in a case I've been working."

"My name? How in the world would my name be involved in a police investigation? Am I in some kind of trouble?" Her voice wavered.

"Not at all," he said. "I just need you to verify something for me."

"Can't I do it over the phone?"

Radhauser knew it was far easier to lie over the phone than face-to-face with a detective at the police station. "I prefer to talk with you in person." And he didn't mind leaving Franklin Bradshaw to simmer in his own deceptive juices a while longer.

CHAPTER FOURTEEN

Radhauser took off his denim jacket and draped it over the back of his chair, watching Sonya Clifford as he did. Her hair was the first thing he noticed about her. It was long, black and glossy, and she had a nervous habit of gathering it with her right hand and pulling it forward. She then twisted it into a thick and shining rope over one shoulder. Sonya wore a pair of washed-out blue jeans with ragged tears at the knees and a hot pink T-shirt with a yin-yang symbol on the front. She was about five feet six and athletic-looking with eyes that were deep blue, and wide. They made her look even younger than her twenty years.

"Have a seat," he said, nodding toward a chair.

She sat, appearing more than a little frightened as she fidgeted in the seat in front of Radhauser's desk.

He gave her what he hoped was a reassuring smile. "I know you're wondering why I asked you here."

"Yes, sir. I am."

"Can you tell me where you were between 11 p.m. and 5 a.m. on Thursday night?"

"I was home."

"Can anyone verify that?"

She tapped her fingernails against the arm of her chair. "My roommate was out of town, and I had a friend over to spend the night. My friend came over Thursday night and didn't leave until early yesterday morning."

"Does that friend have a name?"

"I'd rather not say." She looked at him as if checking for a reaction, but he said nothing. "Do I have to give you a name? I

120

don't want to get anyone in trouble."

"If it's the person I have in mind, he'll be in much more trouble if you don't give me his name."

"I don't know what's going on here. Am I under arrest or something?" Sonya crossed her arms, her lips a tight seam on her pale face.

"No. But I do need to know who spent the night at your house on Thursday. Not answering the question isn't an option, Miss Clifford."

She let out a heavy sigh. "It's someone I work with."

"I need a name."

"Will my parents have to find out? They're born-again Christians. My roommate, too, and she wouldn't be able to stop herself from trying to save my sinning soul. She works part-time with me, and the whole firm would know about it."

"Not unless you tell them."

She looked around the room like she was searching for an escape route. "It was my boss, Franklin Bradshaw."

Radhauser locked his gaze on her face. "What time did he arrive at your house?"

"It was late. Around 11:15."

"Thank you," Radhauser said. "That wasn't so hard, was it?"

She appeared to think for a moment. "I don't know. I have a lot of shame about what we've been doing. Frank being married and all. But why are you asking me about him? Is he all right? Is he in some kind of trouble?"

He might as well tell her. One of the local news stations had already called Murphy for a statement. It would be in tonight's paper for sure. "His wife, Blair Bradshaw, was murdered Thursday night or early Friday morning."

Her eyes widened into large blue pools. "Murdered? You can't think I had anything to do with it. I may have called her a couple times. But I never even met her."

"What was the nature of your calls?"

"I'd rather not say."

"You weren't a suspect when I called you in here, but unless you cooperate fully with the investigation, you're about to become one."

"I'm not proud of this," she said. "But I wanted her to leave Franklin. I wasn't sure he would do it on his own."

"What are you trying to say?"

"I told her about us."

"And how did she react?"

"She laughed and told me I wasn't his first. And that as far as she was concerned, I could have him."

His respect for Blair Bradshaw just elevated a notch.

"Did you threaten her in any way?"

"No. I just thought she should know about us, especially…." She stopped short.

"Can you verify the alibi that Franklin Bradshaw provided? Was he with you from 11:15 p.m. on Thursday night until early Friday morning?"

"Alibi?" She jerked back in her chair, then curled her hands over her abdomen.

It was a protective gesture he'd seen his wife, Gracie, often make during both her pregnancies. Could Sonya Clifford be pregnant with Franklin Bradshaw's child? He thought about the baby rattle glued to Blair's breast. What was the killer trying to say? Could it have been Sonya? Could she have used the rattle to announce her pregnancy?

"So," she said. "I assume Frank already told you about us and that's how you got my name. Are you saying he's a suspect in his wife's murder?"

"Early in any investigation, we always look at the people closest to the victim. When Mr. Bradshaw arrived at your house, what was he wearing?"

She folded her arms across her chest. "A dark suit and white dress shirt. Except for his having taken off the tie, he was still dressed for the memorial they held for his son, Tommy. You know about what happened to him, right?" She cringed as if conjuring up a vision of the boy impaled on the iron stake.

"I do. But right now, we need to focus on Franklin Bradshaw.

What type of shoes was he wearing?"

"His usual. Those dressy shoes lawyers wear. The ones with the perforations in them. I think they're called wingtips."

"Did you notice anything different about him?"

"You mean other than the fact he was brokenhearted about his son? He loved that little boy so much."

"Did you notice any blood on his clothing or hands?"

Her eyes turned to stone for an instant. "Absolutely not."

"Did he ask to use the bathroom, or shower as soon as he arrived?"

"No. I fixed him a drink, and he told me about the memorial and how impressed he was with Tommy's friends and the way they'd read the Lord's Prayer with candles lighting their faces. He kept asking why? *Why Tommy? He never hurt anyone. He was such a good kid.* He was drinking a lot more than usual. And then he broke down. I'd never seen him cry before. It was awful. I didn't know what to do. How to help him."

For the second time since he'd met Franklin Bradshaw, Radhauser softened toward him a little. He knew something Bradshaw didn't. His questions would never be answered, but with time, he might find a way to live with them.

It would have been impossible for whoever murdered Blair Bradshaw to escape without blood on their body, clothing, and shoes. When a femoral artery was slashed, blood erupted like a geyser from the wound. Could Bradshaw have washed it off in the stream, had another suit jacket and pair of shoes in his car? But that didn't make sense either. It would take about fifteen minutes to drive from Bradshaw's Ashland home to Sonya's place in Medford. And the shoe print on the rocks had tread, not the smooth sole of a wingtip.

Jung-Su said Franklin left the house at about 11 p.m. Blair's body was carefully arranged in the memorial—the scene set. If both Jung-Su and Sonya were telling the truth, Franklin Bradshaw could not have murdered his wife.

But what if Sonya was pregnant and the two of them concocted a murder—agreeing ahead of time to alibi each other? He thought about that for a moment, but Sonya was just a kid, pretty much without guile. She'd even admitted to the telephone calls to Blair. Radhauser was pretty good at spotting lies. In his gut, he believed she was telling him the truth. But that didn't mean he couldn't be wrong. Had she glued the baby rattle over Blair's heart to announce her own pregnancy and justify what they'd done?

"And he was with you the entire night?"

"Yes. I made a pot of coffee around 2 a.m., and we sat in the kitchen and talked until just before dawn when he left. He said he didn't want Blair to wake up and find him gone. I know this may be hard for you to believe, but Frank cared about Blair. The last thing either of us wanted was to see her hurt."

He pulled the rattle from his pocket, took it out of the evidence bag, and handed it to Sonya.

"Have you ever seen this baby rattle before?"

She bit her bottom lip. "Never. Why would I?"

Radhauser took a deep breath and followed his hunch. "This is going to seem like a very personal question, and you don't have to answer it if you don't want to, but are you pregnant?"

She stared at him in disbelief for a moment, then dropped her gaze and burst into tears.

Radhauser handed her a tissue. "Does Mr. Bradshaw know?"

"Not yet." Sonya dabbed at her eyes. "I found out for sure about two weeks ago. I was going to tell him the day Tommy died, but…" She paused and took a deep breath. "You see, I wanted to wait until he'd had time to grieve for Tommy. I wanted Frank to be happy about our baby. You think I should tell him, don't you?"

Radhauser said nothing.

"I know what you're thinking," she said. "But the heart…it wants what it wants, no matter how many times you tell yourself it's wrong." Sonya lowered her head into her arms and sobbed.

Radhauser stood and moved the Kleenex box on his desk a little closer to her chair. "Take as long as you need. I'm going to tell Mr. Bradshaw he's free to go."

She lifted her head from her arms, her face blotchy, black lines of mascara running down both cheeks. "You mean Frank is here?"

"He's in one of our interrogation rooms."

She put her hands over her face. "I'll tell him soon, I promise. But I can't let him see me like this."

Radhauser stepped over to the doorway. "He'll be leaving in a few minutes. I'll close the door and give you some privacy.

* * *

Radhauser dragged himself back down the hallway to Interrogation Room 2. He stood in front of the window for a moment, watching Bradshaw who sat at the table with his head in his hands—almost a mirror image of his young lover.

To leave no stone unturned, Radhauser planned to see if he could get independent corroboration of Bradshaw's alibi by talking to Sonya Clifford's neighbors. After that, he hoped to get access to the Bradshaw house. He needed to have a better grasp on Blair. Who was she, and what did she value? Maybe he'd find some clues, maybe find out who or what she was so afraid of. Or uncover a secret that might lead him to her killer.

But, at this point, there wasn't enough evidence for Radhauser to obtain a search warrant. With any luck, Bradshaw might cooperate if Radhauser could make him believe he had nothing to lose.

After opening the interrogation room door, Radhauser conveyed the message he'd hoped he wouldn't have to deliver. "You're free to go, Mr. Bradshaw. Sonya Clifford verified your alibi."

Bradshaw stood.

Radhauser waited for an angry and sarcastic, *I told you so.*

"Thank you, Detective Radhauser. For working so diligently to find Blair's killer. I'm sorry I lied in the beginning. I don't have any good excuse. Except that the events of the last week in my life hit me like a tsunami. First my son…" When his voice cracked, he paused for a moment. "And then Blair. Our relationship wasn't perfect, but I cared about her, and she was a wonderful mother to our son." Again, his voice broke. Either he was an amazing actor, or he felt some genuine loss at the death of his wife.

Radhauser understood because he'd once been washed away by his grief. And he didn't have the same level of guilt that must be consuming Franklin Bradshaw. Yes, Radhauser had refused to accompany his wife and son to the horse show. He'd chosen work over his family. But at least he wasn't living a dual life.

Despite the man's lack of judgment in impregnating a girl young enough to be his daughter, Radhauser wanted to offer some words of consolation. But what would they be? How could he help this man come to grips with the loss of his wife and son when Radhauser hadn't been able to help himself? Even after all these years, he couldn't imagine a future where the deaths of his first wife and son no longer ripped him apart inside.

Bradshaw wasn't finished. "It's human nature, I guess. The need to move to higher ground while a person still can. Admitting to an affair with a twenty-year-old wasn't going to get me there. I'm sorry." He stuck out his right hand—the epitome of cooperation. "No hard feelings?"

Radhauser shook the outstretched hand. "None on your part either, I hope. I was just doing my job."

"I know," Bradshaw said. "And from what I've seen so far, you're damned good at what you do."

Excellent, Radhauser thought. His plan was working. Though he hadn't yet cleared Bradshaw as a suspect, he'd let him think that he had in order to get what he needed. "I'm still going to need your help, and I'm hoping you'll cooperate now that you've been cleared."

"Of course," he said. "Whatever you need."

"I'd like to take a look at Blair's bedroom and the rest of your house, Mr. Bradshaw. I know it might feel intrusive, but doing this helps me get a feel for the victim. Helps me know who she was and what she valued. The more I know about Blair, the more likely I am to find her killer. I can get a warrant if necessary, but I'm hoping you'll give me your permission."

"Head on over whenever you like. I'll call Lucinda and tell her to pack all the case files up and bring them to my house. We can work there just as easily."

The last thing Radhauser wanted was to have Bradshaw following him around the house, watching his every move.

Radhauser was the type of detective who worked best alone. "It might be Monday before I can make it there," he said, knowing Bradshaw's trial started on Monday. "I've got several other things to do first."

"Fine," Bradshaw said. "Whenever you like. I'll be in court on Monday, but I'll tell Jung-Su to give you free run of the house. Look at whatever you need to. I've got nothing more to hide."

"Do you need Detective McBride to give you a lift back to your partner's house or your own?"

He shot Radhauser a look that said, *no way in hell am I going anywhere with her.* "I'm sure she has better things to do. If you let me borrow your phone, I'll call a cab."

CHAPTER FIFTEEN

Without her knowing it, Radhauser followed Sonya Clifford back to her house on Oakdale and waited until she'd entered her garage and closed the door. He parked his Crown Vic in front of the neighbor's house and walked up to the door. It was an old and beautifully-restored bungalow, painted sage green with rust-colored shutters.

An elderly woman answered. She had tight gray curls and watery blue eyes behind her wire-rimmed glasses. The yellow housedress she wore was printed with cornflower-blue daisies on the collar, cuffs, and hem. It reminded Radhauser of a dress his grandmother often wore.

He introduced himself and showed her his badge.

She looked him over from Stetson to cowboy boots, then took a step back and quickly broke eye contact, a frightened look on her face. "You don't look like a detective."

"Well, ma'am," he said. "I'm not sure I know how a detective is supposed to look, but I am one. I guarantee it. Now, what's your name?"

"I'm Gladys Simmons. Is something wrong? Did someone rob that 7-Eleven again? Is there a criminal loose in the neighborhood?"

"No. Nothing for you to be afraid of, Mrs. Simmons. I was hoping I might talk to you for a few moments."

"What about?"

"It's about your neighbor, Sonya Clifford."

"Has something happened to her?" She shook her head. "No, that can't be. She must be okay. I just saw her car pull into her garage."

"Do you watch out for her?"

128

"I try to. She's so young, and her roommate isn't home much."

"May I come inside?"

She hesitated, her brow creasing. "I live alone, and I don't usually allow strangers inside my house."

"I'm a police officer, ma'am. I'm not going to hurt you."

"Well, okay, I guess." She opened the screen door. "And you can call me Gladys."

He took off his Stetson and stepped directly into her living room. It was a light-filled, cheerful place with big windows on three walls, hardwood floors and comfortable-looking furniture—an overstuffed sectional and two side chairs. More than half a dozen free-standing teak bookcases. One of the windows looked out on Sonya Clifford's driveway.

Radhauser sat on one of the side chairs and set his hat on his lap.

Gladys took the sofa across from him, pulled a lace handkerchief from her pocket and twisted it in her hands. "Is Sonya in some kind of trouble?"

"No, I don't think so. But she provided an alibi for someone and because she cares about this person—maybe enough to lie for him—I need to confirm it with someone else."

"Oh, no. I was afraid of something like this. Is she involved with someone bad? Like a murderer? Or the mafia?"

Radhauser was taken aback. "Why would you think that?"

"It's the fancy car that's always parked in her driveway. But only when Rebekah, that's her roommate, is out of town. I sneaked out one night with a flashlight, and I saw it was a Jaguar. Only rich people and those mafia guys can afford cars like that. And he always has on one of those fancy, shiny suits like gangsters wear. Please, don't tell me someone murdered her, attached some cinder blocks to her body, and dropped it into the Rogue River."

Either Gladys knew something he didn't, or she'd obviously watched too many episodes of *The Sopranos*.

"Was that fancy car parked in her driveway on Thursday night?"

"She told me it was her uncle. That he had business in Ashland twice a month and needed a place to stay. But I didn't believe a word of it. If that was the case, why wasn't the car in her driveway every night during those two weeks? Mark my words, that girl has herself a lover. A dangerous one. I've seen him closeup enough to know, he's old enough to be her father. Makes me sick inside. I plan to tell Rebekah when she comes home next week. She's a God-fearing young woman. Maybe she can talk some sense into Sonya."

"Gladys, I need you to think hard. Was the Jaguar in her driveway on Thursday night?"

"I don't have to think hard. I keep a notebook." She stood and moved over to a small drop-leaf desk and pulled out the top drawer and retrieved a hot-pink notebook not unlike the one Radhauser carried in his jacket pocket. Except his was black.

She flipped through the pages, then clucked her tongue against the roof of her mouth. "Just as I suspected. Thursday, May 4. Jaguar arrived at 11:15 p.m. Still there at 1 a.m. when I got up to go to the bathroom. Gone at 6 a.m. when I made my coffee and had my morning constitutional."

"Is there any way they could have left in Sonya's car?"

"Not without him moving his car out of the way. It's only a one-car garage and driveway."

"Would you have heard him if he did?"

"I hear everything," she said. "My audiologist said I've got the hearing of a twenty-year-old. I guess I'm what you might call a one-woman surveillance team."

Radhauser stood. "Thanks so much, Gladys. That's all I needed to know."

"Do you think I should tell her roommate?"

"I think you should let Sonya do that herself."

* * *

The trip out to Wildwood took a little over an hour through densely forested areas. Radhauser had been unable to get an address for Sunflower Finney. He hoped to find a local post office and see if the postmaster might be able to help him. When he spotted the sign for Wildwood, he veered off the main road and traveled down a paved country road that narrowed into a mostly gravel lane, barely big enough for two cars to pass each other.

Small wooden structures, hardly sturdy enough to be called cabins, dotted the hillsides along with an assortment of single-wide trailers, abandoned railway cars, and rusted-out motorhomes.

When he passed the Wildwood Grange and came to what looked like the center of town, he stopped the car and got out in front of a country store with a wooden porch stretched across the front. A single gas pump was set in the middle of the parking lot. The asphalt was riddled with cracks, and crabgrass burst through the openings in bright green tufts. Tall yellow grasses in the surrounding fields shimmered and tossed in the brisk afternoon wind while big, puffy clouds with gray, rain-filled bottoms bloomed in the sky.

Radhauser's boots made a hollow sound as he walked across the planked wooden porch floor. Painted in black letters across the front door were the words *Wildwood General Store, Established in 1902.* Radhauser pulled the door open and stepped inside.

The floor was just like the porch, wide planks of unfinished wood. Shelves were also wooden and filled with just about everything you'd expect, from cases of wilted produce to boxes of crackers, cereal, canned soup, and spaghetti sauce. A refrigerated section held dairy products and a large selection of beer. Wine bottles covered an entire wall near the front to the left of the checkout counter.

Four wooden benches surrounded a pot belly stove set in the center of the room. They housed an assortment of old men with beards, sixties hairdos, some braided or tied in a ponytail. Others wore it straggly and hanging over their shoulders. The men were either dressed in bib overalls with long underwear underneath or sleeveless T-shirts and baggy jeans held up by wide elastic suspenders. It had been a while since Radhauser had seen so much sagging flesh in one room.

In unison, the men stiffened when Radhauser entered, all gazes on him, like wolves on high alert. The room smelled like sweat, too-ripe apples, beer, and chewing tobacco.

Radhauser braced himself. "Can anyone tell me where the post office is located?"

One of the old-timers looked at him like he'd just dropped in from outer space, then leaned forward and spat a stream of brown snuff into a tarnished brass spittoon beside the stove. It made a dull, plopping sound as it landed. "It's right behind the store. Same place as it's been for ninety years. You blind or somethin'?"

"Not blind. Just new to these parts." Radhauser tried to country up his speech a little, an attempt to fit in.

The old man crossed his arms over his chest. "Well, just so you know, we ain't crazy 'bout strangers here in Wildwood. 'Specially someone who looks like he could be a cop or some government fool workin' for the Internal Ripoff Service. State your business and get out."

So much for fitting in. Radhauser decided it was in his best interest not to admit being a detective. "I'm looking for someone who used to live here. I'm hoping she still does."

A man with ratty gray hair and caterpillar eyebrows stood and took a step toward Radhauser. "In case you haven't heard, most folks out here in Wildwood ain't too fond of the US Government. Or the police department either."

"Do I look like a police officer?"

"You look like a city slicker tryin' to pretend he's a cowboy. What is it you want with that person who used to live here and might still?"

Instinctively, Radhauser stiffened. "I just want to talk. I have some news about her daughter."

"Good news or bad news?"

He tried not to react to the small gray rat that scurried into a hole in the floorboards, its tail slithering behind it like a snake. Radhauser's toes curled in his boots, but no one else seemed to notice. "I guess that depends on how she felt about her daughter."

The old man with the eyebrows studied Radhauser like he was an insect trapped under a magnifying glass. "This person got a name? I been here my whole life. Was borned in the same house I live in now, like lots a' folks in these parts. I know most everybody who lives in Wildwood. And I got a nose for people who don't belong, too." He stared at Radhauser and wrinkled his veined nose as if he'd smelled something unpleasant.

Radhauser met the man's gaze head-on. "Then maybe you'll know who I'm looking for. She used to go by the name of Sunflower. Maybe Sunflower Finney."

The man laughed. "Sunny is crazier than a loon at midnight during the full moon. As far as anybody 'round here knows, she ain't seen her daughter in a whole bunch of years." He paused and put his index finger under his chin. "Come to think of it, it's probably more than that now. Meadow hightailed it out of Wildwood soon as she could. I don't even think she finished high school."

Radhauser tried again. "You know what they say about time. Sometimes it heals old wounds. Maybe Sunny would want to hear news about her daughter."

Caterpillar Eyebrows sat on the bench beside his cronies. "Sunny smokes a fair amount of weed, and she's been known to use the harder stuff, too. I wouldn't be a bit surprised if ole Sunny don't even remember she had a daughter."

"I'd really like to talk to her if you can tell me where I can find her."

"She ain't lost. Lives over on West Fork just like she always did. On the right-hand side of the road. Little two-bedroom place at the edge of the river. Long driveway with lots of potholes. The mailbox has yeller sunflowers painted all over it. You can't miss it. They're faded, but you can still tell what they are."

"Can you point me in the direction of West Fork?"

He pointed a gnarled finger to his right. "Go on down the road a' piece to the stop sign, just past the school and turn left. West Fork's your first right. Just follow the river."

Outside, the wind picked up, and big drops of rain peppered the rusted awning over the porch.

Eyebrows stood and followed Radhauser to the door. "If you got one a' them bulletproof vests, you might wanna put it on. Sunny's got a shotgun, and she knows how to use it."

"Thanks for the warning. You fellas have a great evening." Radhauser stepped outside, grateful for some fresh air. It had turned dusky, the sky still molten at the edges.

CHAPTER SIXTEEN

Once inside his car, he turned on his windshield wipers and headed toward West Fork Road and a mailbox painted with sunflowers.

He found it easily, and the Crown Vic bounced up the long drive, splattering muddy water up over the car doors and onto the windshield and side windows. Eyebrows wasn't joking when he said the driveway was rutted with potholes.

Radhauser stopped in front of a wooden structure that looked more like a shack than it did a home. In the gray light he could make out a shadowy form about a hundred yards behind the house, coming up the shallow rise he assumed rose up from the west fork of the Wildwood River. He sat in the car as she moved closer.

The rain had decreased to a fine mist, and in a moment of bravery or insanity, Radhauser stepped out of the car. He stood beside the driver's side door and waited for her to reach him.

She held a dead possum in one hand and a shotgun in the other. Her wide face was seamed, spotted with age marks and deep lines. The face of a woman who'd spent a lot of time in the sun, though her skin tone was more gray than tanned. She looked like she was seventy-five or eighty, not the sixty or less Radhauser figured her to be. Her hair, just as her ex-husband had remembered, hung all the way to the ground and dragged in the mud behind her as she walked. It was gray and stringy. Even from a distance, Radhauser could smell her, bitter and salty with more than a hint of urine.

To his surprise, she smiled when she spotted him and gave him the peace sign. One of her front teeth was broken, another missing. Could this really be the mother of the beautiful and sophisticated actress, Blair Bradshaw, and the handsome vineyard owner, Jason Robertson? He thought about Landon Robertson, who'd seemed like an intelligent and educated man—one who'd grown award-winning grapes and built a successful vineyard. What had he once seen in Sunflower Finney?

"You lost your way, mister? My driveway don't lead nowhere but here." Her voice was raspy, a smoker's voice gone to rust.

"No, ma'am. I'm looking for Sunflower Finney." He glanced at the shotgun. "The men down at the Wildwood Store told me to wear a bulletproof vest. You don't aim to shoot me, do you?"

She laughed and raised the gun for a second, before lowering it again. "I have my reputation to live up to, so I might have to fire a round or two." Her blue eyes twinkled with likable mischief. "But I'll try my best to miss."

Radhauser smiled back at her. "I understand how important it is to maintain one's reputation, but I hope you won't aim too carefully at the messenger. I have some news about your daughter."

She raised her left eyebrow. "I ain't got no daughter anymore. She made that clear when I tried to talk to her last week. Selfish bitch. I just wanted to offer my condolences about her son." She paused and shook her head. "Here all this time I had me a ten-year-old grandson, and I didn't even know until I heard on the news he was dead. What kind of daughter treats her own flesh and blood like that?"

"I wonder if you'd be willing to talk to me for a few minutes."

"I don't know. I'm pretty busy right now." She held up the possum. "I need to get this guy cleaned and in the pot. I'm making up a stew for my neighbor lady. She ain't been well lately."

"It's about your daughter."

"I done told you. If it's about Meadow, I ain't got nothin' to say."

"I'm afraid I have some bad news."

"Why should I care?"

"Maybe you won't, but I thought you had the right to know. Your daughter was murdered on Thursday night, just after a memorial service for her son."

What little color Sunny had drained from her face, leaving an even grayer pallor. For a moment she said nothing. "I'm not surprised," she finally uttered, but it was clear she was shocked. "That bitch needed some lessons in how to treat people. But then I shoulda' expected her to behave the way she did. Meadow always did think she was better than everyone else around these parts. When I learned she was in hoity-toity Ashland, I wasn't one bit surprised."

"Could we sit down somewhere and talk for a few minutes?"

"Long as it ain't about Meadow." She headed up to her house, dropped the rifle and the possum onto a small bench on the porch and sat on one of the rickety rocking chairs. Her hair fell around her, blanketing the wooden floor like a long gray cloak that had been dragged through the mud.

He climbed the three cinderblock steps, pulled up another chair, and sat beside her. "My name is Winston Radhauser. I'm a detective with the Ashland Police Department. I'm trying to find out who killed your daughter and why."

"If she treated everyone the way she treated me, I expect you'll have yourself a long list to choose from."

"I can tell she hurt you deeply, Sunny. I'm really sorry that happened to you." Maybe if he took her side, she'd be more willing to open up.

She rocked back and forth in her chair but said nothing.

"Can you tell me where you were between 10 p.m. and 12:30 a.m. on Thursday, May 3 and Friday, May 4?"

"I didn't kill Meadow. If I was gonna kill her, I'd a' done it when she was fifteen. Selfish, lyin' little bitch. I was right here during them times you mentioned."

"Is there anyone who can verify that?"

"I told you I didn't kill her. Ain't my word good enough for you?"

"Don't take offense, Sunny. This is just routine. It's the way we detectives eliminate people from our suspect list. I had to ask her husband and her next-door neighbor the same things."

"Do I look like I've got me a live-in boyfriend? Them days

are over. I live alone now. I don't have a driver's license or a car."
She pointed to a makeshift lean-to beside a small outbuilding.
It housed a rusty and mud-caked ATV. "That's my all-terrain
vehicle. I use it to get back and forth to the general store for my
groceries. Otherwise, I don't go nowhere I can't use my own two
feet to get to."

"So you've never been to Ashland?"

"Never. It's a little high-brow for the likes a' me."

"Would you mind telling me how you found your daughter? It
couldn't have been easy since she changed her name and obviously
didn't want to be found."

"It weren't all that hard. An old friend of mine seen her in a
play in Ashland. Her daughter, who was a friend of Meadow's
from high school, took her mother to the play for her birthday.
Some daughters don't disown their mother just because they ain't
educated or dress fancy. My old friend come over the very next
day and told me she seen Meadow acting in the play. That her
name was Blair Bradshaw now and she was married to some rich,
fancy-ass attorney. So, I knew where she was for a couple years.
But I never bothered her 'til I heard about little Tommy dying."

"When did you call her?"

"On Tuesday, after I heard it on the news. If she was anything
like she was as a teenager, she weren't the best mother in the world.
But then I expect neither was I. One thing I do know is what
it feels like to lose a son. I felt so sorry for her. I was fixin' to
apologize for throwing her out. I thought maybe…we might…"
She paused and shook her head, sadness in her gaze. "So, I used
the phone down at the store, and I called her up. I shoulda' known
better. It's time for you to go now." She stood. "I got work to do."

"And that's the first and only time you've talked to your
daughter since she left Wildwood?"

"Yes."

Blair had the security system installed a good month before
Tommy's death. Whatever she was terrified of, it wasn't her
mother. Looked like he'd just hit another dead end.

"I spoke to your son." Radhauser attempted to keep her talking.

"He grows grapes out in the Applegate Valley and makes wine from them. He seems like a nice man."

She dropped back down onto her chair. Her face lit up, and she gave him another partially-toothless smile before the questions tumbled out. "You saw my baby? You saw Raven? You talked to him? Is he all right?"

"He seemed fine. His name is Jason now, and yes, I talked to him yesterday."

"Does he have any babies? Did he make me a grandma?"

"As far as I know, he's unmarried, and I don't think he has children. But he's not that old. There's still time."

"Do you think he might be willing to talk to me?"

Radhauser swallowed, tried to imagine what it would be like to be estranged from Lizzie and Jonathan. "I don't think you'd have anything to lose by trying."

"His father took him away from me when he was only two. Me and Landon came here right out of school. It was the sixties. We were flower children who met up in Haight-Ashbury. We come up here from San Francisco and bought this piece of land in 1967. It was the summer of love, and Meadow was a toddler. But after Raven was born, Landon said he outgrew being a hippie. He wanted another kind of life for his son. Raven probably doesn't even remember his mama. God only knows what Landon told him about me."

"Please," Radhauser said. "Would you answer one more question for me? I'm going to be in a lot of trouble with my boss if I don't solve this case." He pulled out the evidence bag containing the baby rattle and handed it to Sunny. "Have you ever seen this before? Could it have belonged to Meadow when she was a baby?"

Sunny studied it for a long time, and Radhauser thought he saw a flash of recognition on her face. "When you polish them up, these old-timey rattles look pretty good, don't they? Where'd you get it?"

"It was left on Blair's body." He waited, hoping she might shed some light on the rattle. How would she know it had been polished? Had she seen it before when it was tarnished? Had she found it at a garage or estate sale?

Instinctively, Radhauser knew in order to find the person who murdered Blair Bradshaw, he'd need to know the reason behind that rattle.

She rocked a little faster, obviously agitated, then waved him away with her left hand. "My trigger finger's startin' to itch. I think you best be leavin' now."

"But you didn't answer my question," Radhauser said.

"Have you looked around this place? Meadow never owned nothin' that fancy until long after she left here." Sunny handed the rattle back to him. Without another word she picked up the possum and rifle, then stepped inside her house and closed the door behind her.

CHAPTER SEVENTEEN

Diamond DeLorenzo was a striking brunette with deep blue, heavily-lashed eyes that gave Radhauser the sense she could gaze inside him and didn't like what she saw there. She wore a floor-length charcoal dress with a red underskirt and low-cut bodice with a hint of red lace covering some of her ample cleavage. "I've got a dress rehearsal in twenty minutes. I hope you can make this quick."

In the small dressing room at the back of the Bowmer theater, Diamond sat on a stool in front of a mirror surrounded by light bulbs. The room was windowless and smelled like baby powder. Racks of ornate costumes, shoes, wigs, and jewelry lined the walls.

Radhauser pulled over a small chair. "You're probably aware that your fellow actress, Blair Bradshaw, was murdered on Thursday night."

"I am," Diamond said. "And the whole company is in shock. Especially me. I'm filling in for her playing Miranda in *The Tempest* and Blanche in *A Streetcar Named Desire*. That's quite a load for someone new like me."

"How well did you know Blair?"

"I was her understudy and knew her pretty well. I admired her work and wanted to be like her."

"Looks like you'll get your chance."

She tapped her fingers on the dressing table. "What's that supposed to mean? I didn't wish her dead, Detective Radhauser, so I could have her parts. Besides, I was here, standing in for her in the role of Miranda in *The Tempest* the night of her son's memorial. That's why I couldn't attend. And we're required to stay afterward for the audience/actor talks."

"I know you didn't kill her, Diamond. But I still wanted to talk to you to see if you know anyone who might have wanted her dead. Someone who might have benefited from her death? Or someone who might have threatened her or been jealous over her success."

"Blair was popular with the other company members. As far as I know, she didn't have any enemies, at least not here."

"Did she seem upset or more nervous than usual lately?"

"She missed rehearsal one day about a month ago because she was having a security system installed in her house and she wanted to be there. Blair claimed there'd been some break-ins around her neighborhood, but I didn't believe her."

"Why not?"

"It's the way she said it—like she was terrified. She said something else that day that struck me as strange. Something about the way you can never escape your own past. How it always comes back to haunt you."

Was she talking about the call from her mother? But that didn't make sense. They'd already established that Blair had the security system put in weeks before that call. Sunny was off-the-bell-curve eccentric, but she didn't seem dangerous. She seemed more hurt by Blair's rejection than she was angry. With only a rusted-out ATV for transportation, how would she have managed to get from Wildwood to Ashland?

Could it have been the visit with her father? But, if what Jason told him was true, that didn't make sense either. Her father giving her half the vineyard should have made her happy. It gave her the money she needed to leave her husband. So, who and where was this person from her past who frightened her enough to install a state-of-the-art security system?

* * *

Monday morning, around 9 a.m., and before anything else got in his way, Radhauser decided to take advantage of Franklin Bradshaw's change of heart and visit the house he'd shared with Tommy and Blair. His car windows were open, and as he pulled into their driveway, the clean smell of pine sap swept in from the forest, and a dark, brooding sky hung over the house, threatening rain.

His cell phone rang. He picked it up.

"I need to talk to you right away." Heron sounded breathless.

"Can't it wait? I'm in the middle of a murder investigation."

"No. This can't wait. Come by my office. Now."

Radhauser glanced at his watch. "Can't you just tell me over the phone? I'm about to search Bradshaw's place. His trial starts today, and I want to do it when he isn't home to follow me around."

Heron blew out a breath, loud enough for Radhauser to hear. "This is way too important. We need to talk face-to-face."

"Okay, you win."

Twenty minutes later, Radhauser burst through the door to Heron's office. As always, it was tidy, well-lit, and smelled of gingerbread from the candle he often burned on the credenza behind his big, walnut desk. This was a pleasant change from the odors of the autopsy suite. "This better be good. I'm in the middle of the Bradshaw investigation, and I don't have time for one of your pop quizzes on forensics." He smiled to let Heron know he was joking. In truth, he enjoyed bantering with this brilliant, if a bit peculiar, man.

Heron stared at him over the top of his glasses. "It is good. Very good, in fact. Why don't you sit yourself down? I don't want you fainting from the shock of what I'm about to reveal."

Radhauser took a seat in front of Heron's desk, his Stetson in his lap. "What is so crucial and important you couldn't tell me over the phone?" He tapped his cowboy boot against the carpeted floor.

"It's not that I couldn't tell you on the telephone, it's that I wanted to see your reaction." Heron leaned forward in his chair, a wide grin on his face. "I know how much that case has haunted you over the last decade."

Radhauser cocked his head, confused. "What case?"

"That baby...the one who was kidnapped from the food court at the Rogue Valley Mall right after you moved to Ashland."

As if it had wings, Radhauser's right hand flew to his chest.

"Ryan Patterson? Are you talking about the infant, Ryan Patterson, who disappeared on May 4, 1991?" His voice seemed to have raised an entire octave.

"One and the same." Heron removed his glasses and rubbed the space between his eyes as if he were tired.

The skin on the back of Radhauser's neck tingled. "I worked on that case for years. What could you possibly find that I haven't?"

Heron's dark eyes twinkled under the fluorescent light. "Have I taught you nothing about the magical powers of forensic science?"

"You've taught me plenty, but come on, Heron, I don't have all day. Get to the point."

"The point is…I've come very close to finding your missing boy. At least I know he's alive and most likely lives here in Ashland and was a friend of your murder victim's son, Tommy Bradshaw."

Radhauser's pulse jumped into his temple and hammered. "How could you possibly know that?"

Heron cleaned his glasses with a tissue, then returned them to his face. "Remember the two hairs we found on Blair Bradshaw's skirt? The ones I sent out for DNA?"

"Of course, I remember. But what's that got to do with Ryan Patterson?"

"Turns out, plenty. I got the results back an hour ago. I ran them through our database, and one of them was a perfect match for your kidnapped boy."

For a moment, Radhauser was too stunned to speak. "For Ryan Patterson? How can that be? Are you sure?"

"One hundred percent," Heron said. "DNA doesn't lie."

This almost never happened. Either kidnapped kids were found within the first couple days, or they were never found. At least not still breathing. Radhauser had given up all hope that Ryan Patterson would be found alive.

"Could the hair have belonged to Tommy?"

"Not unless the Bradshaws kidnapped him. But I had the same thought, so I sent one of Tommy's hairs for analysis, too. It didn't match either of the hairs on her skirt."

"I can't believe it. That means Ryan must have attended the

memorial. And most likely goes to Sand Creek Elementary School. That's practically in the Patterson's backyard. Practically in my own."

How could it be that after all this time, the boy he'd spent years searching for, the boy whose parents had paid Radhauser a visit on the anniversary of his kidnapping for ten years, was living in Ashland the entire time?

Some part of Radhauser wanted to rush over to the Pattersons' house and give Holly and Sean the news they'd waited more than ten years to hear. But another part wanted to wait until he'd met Ryan—until he understood what the child had endured during the last decade. Until he had a better understanding of what happened and why. Until he could prepare the Pattersons for what most likely lay ahead of them. He had to move slowly and cautiously.

After a decade of working together, Heron was pretty good at reading Radhauser's mind. "I know this is going to be tricky to handle, cowboy. But his parents have a right to know their boy is still alive and, in all likelihood, living right here in Ashland."

"Is there any, even slight, possibility this could be a mistake?"

"None," Heron said. "The DNA from that hair came from Ryan Patterson. There is no doubt."

"But could it have gotten onto Blair Bradshaw's skirt some other way?"

"The hair I sent for analysis wasn't the hair of a three-month-old. You get me some DNA samples of every male child who attended the memorial, and I'll try to put a rush on them. Looks like you'll have their boy back by the end of the week."

Radhauser leaned forward, his hands on his knees. "I need your advice. Would you inform the Pattersons now, or wait until we're absolutely sure and actually have the boy in protective custody?"

"I'll leave that one up to you. But think about what you'd want if it were your child who'd been missing for a decade."

A moment later, Radhauser was on the phone to McBride. "Call Judge Wainwright. I need a warrant for a DNA sample from every boy who attended Tommy Bradshaw's memorial."

"Yes, sir."

"I want to get the samples today. I suspect all of them go to Sand Creek Elementary."

"I'm on it, boss. You want to tell me what this is all about?"

He told her.

"Holy crap," she said. "What are the chances?"

CHAPTER EIGHTEEN

Holly Patterson answered on the third ring.

"It's Detective Radhauser. Is Sean home with you?"

She laughed. "It's Monday, have you forgotten? He's at the university this morning." Sean was a clinical psychologist, a counselor at Medford High School, and part-time professor of psychology at Southern Oregon University.

"Is there any way you can call him and have him come home for a little while? I've got something I need to talk with you about. I'd like to have both of you there when I do."

"Is it Ryan?" She paused and blew out a series of short breaths. "Have you found his...Is he..." She stopped.

Radhauser could hear her swallow, almost hear her internal decision not to say the words, *body* or *dead*. "I have good reason to believe Ryan is alive."

She was silent for several seconds, only her breathing audible as if she couldn't quite believe what she'd just heard. "I'll call him. I'm sure he can come home. He doesn't have a class until this afternoon."

A half hour later, Radhauser rang the bell on the cottage-style bungalow he'd visited so often over the last decade.

Holly answered. "Detective Radhauser. Have you found Ryan? Please tell me he's still alive." Her voice held a combination of hope and fear.

"May I come inside?"

"Of course." She stepped aside so he could enter. "Please...Tell me you've found something."

He took off his cowboy hat. "I'd like to talk with both of you if

I can. Is Sean home yet?"

"Sean," she called. "Detective Radhauser is here."

Sean burst through a set of French doors Radhauser knew led into his study. He grabbed Holly's hand. "What is it? What have you found?"

"Okay if we sit down?"

"Of course," Holly said. "Where are my manners?"

She led them into a living room where a baby grand piano top still held a framed photo of their infant son. He set his cowboy hat beside the photo in order to remind himself to ask if he may take it with him when he left. The baby photo in the police file had been handled so much over the years, shown to so many people, that Ryan's baby features were no longer clear.

Once they were seated, the Pattersons on the sofa, Radhauser in a rocking chair across from them, he began. "You may have read about Blair Bradshaw's death in the paper?"

"So tragic," Sean said. "I understand she was an actress with the Shakespeare Theater. You're talking about the woman over on Sand Creek who just lost her son, right?"

"Yes. That's the one."

"The paper said the medical examiner was calling it a murder. Given what happened to her son, I thought it more likely a suicide." Holly's gaze darted to the infant photo of Ryan on the piano top.

"That thought entered my mind, too, but after going over the crime scene evidence and the medical examiner's report, we're positive it was murder."

She tilted her head, eyes narrowing. "It's a tragic story, but what's it got to do with us or Ryan's kidnapping?"

Under normal circumstances, he wouldn't divulge any details of his crime scene until the murder was solved, but these were the Pattersons, people he'd known for a decade. They deserved the truth. "When we investigated the crime scene, we found two hairs on the dead woman's skirt. The ME sent them away for DNA analysis, hoping it might lead us to a suspect."

Holly's hands were clutched together as if in prayer. "I still don't understand what that has to do with Ryan."

"Nothing except the fact that the DNA from one of the hairs was a match for Ryan's."

Sean flinched. "What…what…do you mean? Are you saying the Bradshaws' son, the boy who fell out of his treehouse, was really Ryan? Or are you saying you think Ryan had something to do with the woman's death?"

"Neither," Radhauser said. "Dr. Heron, the medical examiner, already eliminated the possibility Tommy Bradshaw was Ryan. And no, we don't think Ryan had anything to do with her death. I'm saying that one of the two hairs on the Blair Bradshaw's skirt was a match for someone in the system. Turns out that someone was Ryan."

Sean and Holly locked gazes. "Are you sure?" he asked. "How do you know after all this time?"

"Remember, I collected some of his clothing. A burp cloth with some of his spit-up on it. We had his DNA on file. We do that with all kidnapping victims."

Holly leapt to her feet. "You really do think it belongs to Ryan? You think he's still alive?"

"I'm positive. DNA doesn't lie. He was definitely alive and most likely at the memorial last Thursday night."

Sean stood, too. "Well, where is he? Let's go get him."

"At the moment, we don't know exactly where he is. But we're working on it. We think it's likely he goes to Sand Creek Elementary, is a fifth grader, and was a friend of Tommy Bradshaw. My new partner, Detective McBride, is at the school right now taking DNA samples from all the boys who attended the service. We'll get those samples over to the ME, and he'll put a rush on the results. I'm hoping to have Ryan back to you before the end of the week."

Holly's knees gave out.

Sean grabbed her before she fell and led her back to the sofa. They sat on the edges of the cushions. He didn't let go of her hand. "So, you think our son has been in Ashland all this time? Growing up right under our noses?"

"It looks that way," Radhauser said. "I'm so sorry."

"It's not your fault." Holly edged a little closer to Sean. "We've talked about how hard you've worked on our behalf so many times. Some other detectives would have probably labeled it a cold case and given up years ago."

"Do you think he's…I mean…do you think he's okay?" Sean's voice sounded like gnarled wood—grainy with too many knots. "Do you think he's been molested all this time? Kept in some kind of cage or rat-infested basement like those kids you hear about in the news?"

The air around them seemed to thicken and grow warmer.

Tears filled Sean's dark eyes, and his pulse was visible in his neck. But in every other way, he didn't appear to be crying. His breathing was calm and measured.

"Let's hope for the best," Radhauser said. "With an infant kidnapping, it could have been someone who desperately wanted a child to raise—maybe they'd lost one to leukemia or a miscarriage or something. Whoever took Ryan may have been good to him. Sand Creek Elementary is a top-notch school. Maybe he's been loved by his parents and had a happy and normal life."

"Parents?" Sean's nostrils flared. "Whoever kidnapped Ryan is a felon, not his parent."

"I'm sorry," Radhauser said. "I should have thought before I said that."

"No one could love him the way we do," Holly whispered, then hung her head and sobbed.

Sean tightened his grip on her hand. "What if they're hurting him? Doing things to him or selling him for sex? Shouldn't we go over to the school? We might recognize him if we got a look at all the fifth-grade boys who attended the memorial. We've got those age-projection photographs the FBI did. Remember Ryan had a birthmark right above his left nipple. It was shaped like a map of Africa."

Radhauser remembered.

Sean stood and paced across the room now like he was too excited to sit still. "We could ask the boys to take off their shirts.

If one of them has the birthmark, we'll know he's Ryan, and we won't have to wait, won't have to risk further abuse."

Had Radhauser made a mistake in telling the Pattersons before they had the boy in custody? Two strangers at the elementary school asking ten-year-old boys to take off their shirts was the last thing they needed. Taking DNA samples of the children would raise enough suspicion, even though he'd told McBride to leave out anything connected to the kidnapping and explain that they were eliminating suspects by getting the DNA of people present at the memorial.

"Please don't make me regret telling you this soon. I know how tempting it must be to go over to the school and demand to see every fifth-grade boy. I'd probably want to do the same thing if I were in your shoes. But let's go through the proper channels and let the authorities handle this. I knew I was taking a risk in telling you before we had a positive ID, but I also know how long you've waited and how hard it must have been to hold onto your hope. You were right. I thought you deserved to know."

"Thank you, Detective Radhauser." Sean offered his hand.

Radhauser shook it.

"You've made us happier than we've been since the day he was born. It's wonderful beyond anything we could have imagined. But it's also frightening to think about what..." He stopped himself from going on. "We'll do our best to wait until we hear from you."

Radhauser stood, then went over and picked up his Stetson. "That's great. I'll keep you informed at every step and get back with you as soon as I know anything. I promise. But in the meantime, I'd like to borrow this photo." He nodded toward the baby picture on the piano top. "I'll see to it you get it back."

Holly lifted the framed photo of the infant Ryan, kissed it, then handed it over to Radhauser.

He was on his way to the front door when the thought occurred to him. The police report included a description of Ryan's birthmark, but no photo. He stopped and turned to Holly. "This is going to sound like a strange request, but you wouldn't happen to have a photo of Ryan's birthmark, would you?"

She laughed. "Everything about that baby was so amazing to me. I took a close up in case it faded like birthmarks sometimes do. I thought we might show it to Ryan someday. Maybe even take him to Africa. I never dreamed I'd need it to identify my own son. But yes, I have a photo."

She returned a moment later with a partially filled baby book entitled, *Our Baby's First Year*. Holly flipped a few pages until she came to the close-up. They were right. The skin, just above the baby's left nipple, was a darker pigmentation and shaped like Africa.

Radhauser reached for the book. "May I borrow this, too? I promise to take very good care of it."

CHAPTER NINETEEN

While headed back to the Bradshaw house to execute his search, Radhauser got a call from McBride. "I'm over at the elementary school, and I have a problem. The school nurse refuses to allow me to swab the mouths of the boys who attended the memorial without parental consent."

"I thought Judge Wainwright granted the warrant?"

"He did. But the school nurse won't budge. I did everything but threaten her arrest."

"What's her problem?"

"It's probably me. As you've no doubt noticed, I'm not the most diplomatic person in the world."

Radhauser couldn't help but laugh. "Maybe if you took those rattlesnakes out of your ears, you'd have better luck making friends and getting people to do what you ask of them."

"When I called Wainwright, he said we should go ahead and get parental permission. That way, we can avoid any kind of shitstorm from parents who think their kids' rights have been violated."

"How many kids does it involve?"

"Ten attended the memorial, but only six of them were boys."

Murder cases were normally his top priority, but Holly and Sean Patterson had waited far too long already. If Heron was right, and Ryan had been living in Ashland all this time, Radhauser had failed the Pattersons in a big way. But murder cases grew cold in a hurry. He tried to weigh what was most important. Finding Blair's killer wouldn't bring her back. His search of the Bradshaw house could wait another day. The faster he got those DNA samples to Heron, the sooner Sean and Holly would have their son back.

152

Franklin Bradshaw's trial would likely last most of the week. Captain Murphy wouldn't be happy. The press was already pounding at his doors for an update on the status of the investigation. But Holly and Sean Patterson had already waited ten years.

Radhauser made a U-turn and headed toward Sand Creek Elementary. He'd deal with Murphy later.

McBride met him at the door with the warrant and the DNA kits. "This shouldn't have to take up both our time. What can I do to move things forward on the Bradshaw case while you're sweet-talking parents?"

"Interview Bradshaw's other partner, Donald Meyer. See what you can learn about Bradshaw's marriage and how his colleagues and staff viewed him, especially his secretary. They usually know the real story. He's got an alibi, but given it's from his girlfriend and the old lady next door, it's far from iron-clad."

"Consider it done, sir. I'm sorry about…well, my…my lack of diplomacy."

"Forget it, Mac. You were brilliant with Bradshaw earlier."

She smiled. "In case you don't know it, boss, I really appreciate your showing me the ropes. I hope to someday be half the detective you are."

He sighed a long and low sound. "If one of these six boys turns out to be Ryan Patterson, I wasn't much of a detective, now, was I?"

"Don't beat yourself up. It's not like you didn't give it all you had."

Radhauser watched McBride for a moment as she hurried into the parking lot, then he entered the double glass doors to Sand Creek Elementary and stepped up to the front desk. He introduced himself to the middle-aged woman who greeted him, showed his badge, and signed the visitor's register. He tipped his Stetson. "I'm here to see the school nurse."

"If you're carrying a firearm, we'll need to lock it in the safe," the woman said.

He took off his gun and holster and handed it to her, grateful for the new security put into effect in Ashland schools after the Columbine shootings.

She pointed to a hallway. "Down that corridor. Second door on the left. Her name is Linda Freeman."

He stood in the open doorway. Linda Freeman, RN, sat at a desk, working at a computer. Freeman was a petite, dark-haired woman of about forty and she wore a traditional white uniform and shoes with white stockings. She wore black-rimmed glasses over her brown eyes, and a stethoscope hung from her neck. The room was well organized and spotlessly clean. This was a woman who took pride in her work.

An extra chair nestled beside her desk. Two walls held built-in cabinets with locked doors, presumably for medical supplies. A small cot made up with crisp white sheets set along one wall—a pillow and blanket folded neatly on top. The room smelled like Pine Sol and rubbing alcohol.

"Nurse Freeman." He took off his Stetson and ran his hand through his hair. "I'm Detective Radhauser from the Ashland Police Department." He showed his badge. "May I speak with you for a moment?"

The veins pulsed in her forehead. "You may speak, but as I told Detective McBride, I don't intend to subject fifth-grade students to a police officer administering a DNA test without permission from their parents."

"I understand, ma'am, and I'm glad you take such good care of the children entrusted to your care. They're lucky to have you watching out for them."

Behind her glasses, her dark eyes widened. She seemed taken aback by his reply.

"Is it okay if I sit down?"

She gestured to the chair beside her desk.

He held his cowboy hat in his lap. "Technically, I have a warrant, so I don't need parental permission, but I understand your concern, and if it were my child, I'd appreciate a nurse who took every precaution to keep him safe." He was, as Gracie would say, *sucking up*, but he'd do what it took to get the job done.

She smiled then, and everything about her face softened.

"Suppose I tell you what's going on. And then, if you're in agreement, we'll call each parent and ask their permission. The test is non-invasive and involves a swab of the inside of the child's cheek. No discomfort and no danger."

"That sounds reasonable. Thank you for understanding my position."

Radhauser told Nurse Freeman about the kidnapped boy and the DNA they'd found at the crime scene.

"I understand," she said. "If the parents agree, I'll have the principal's office make an announcement for those boys to come in."

Radhauser called the parents of the boys in question, leaving Holden Houseman until last. He was respectful and polite as he told them who he was and that he was investigating the murder of Blair Bradshaw. He said multiple DNA samples were taken from the scene, and they now needed to eliminate the attendees who were there for the memorial. He praised Nurse Freeman for her diligence and when he finished his spiel, every parent he'd called so far, except Collier Zagorski's mother, agreed to the test.

"There is no pain involved for Collier," Radhauser said to Mrs. Zagorski. "And he won't be singled out. We'll call all six of the boys who attended the memorial to the nurse's station at the same time."

"I don't care. This means his DNA will be in the system and he might be accused of all kinds of things he didn't do. I need to talk to my husband."

"Would you please do that and call me back as soon as possible? I'm in the nurse's office now. This is important. I can see to it that Collier's DNA doesn't go into our database."

"Can I get that in writing?"

"You have my word."

"That's not good enough."

Radhauser wrote a note, signed it, and showed it to Nurse Freeman, then handed her the telephone.

She confirmed that Radhauser had written and signed the

waiver, said she'd hold it for them, then hung up.

"Do you know the Zagorski boy?" Radhauser asked.

"Of course," she said as if offended by the question. "I make a habit of knowing all the kids."

"Could you describe him for me?"

"Why?"

"Humor me, would you? I can always ask the principal to call him to the office for questioning or check the yearbook for his photo."

"You can't question him without his parents present," Nurse Freeman spoke with confidence, like an expert on the law.

Radhauser smiled to himself. "Actually, Nurse Freeman, that's a fallacy. Parents can demand to be present only if their child is a suspect in a felony."

She shot him a nasty look. "He's on the small side. Dark hair and dark eyes. I'd call him fine-featured. Maybe a little on the feminine side."

It definitely sounded like a child who could belong to Holly and Sean Patterson.

Mrs. Zagorski called back ten minutes later. "Okay," she said, more than a hint of reluctance in her voice. "My husband said to make damn sure Collier's DNA doesn't go into some kind of permanent record."

Five down. One more to go. Radhauser figured since Jung-Su took care of Holden after school, Jung-Su would have a direct line for Carl Houseman, and she did. He dreaded making the call, knew Mr. Houseman wouldn't be happy to hear from him.

When Houseman answered, Radhauser identified himself.

"What do you want now?"

He explained the situation.

"Haven't you put my son through enough? He already blames himself for Tommy's death, and he thinks Blair killed herself because of what happened to Tommy. That's a hell of a lot of guilt for one ten-year-old boy." Houseman told Radhauser about the broken spaceship he'd found in Holden's trashcan.

Radhauser was glad Holden had found a way to express his

rage over the deaths of two people he loved. "I understand, Mr. Houseman, but this is routine. We have permission to swab the five other boys who attended the memorial. It's not like we're singling Holden out. It might even make your son feel better to think he's helping us find who hurt Blair."

Houseman was quiet for a moment. "You'll present it to him that way?"

"Of course, I will, Mr. Houseman. I think you can tell, I really like Holden. You've done a fine job with that boy."

"He's been through a lot lately. I don't want to see him hurt or afraid again any time soon."

"I promise I won't let that happen. But I need you to give your verbal permission to Linda Freeman—she's the nurse and believe me, she has the back of the kids who attend her school."

He handed the receiver to Nurse Freeman.

When she gave Radhauser the thumbs up sign and a smile big enough to make her eyes dance, he knew Houseman had finally agreed to the test.

The process took much longer than he'd hoped, but three hours later, Radhauser left Sand Creek Elementary School with DNA samples for the six boys who attended Tommy Bradshaw's memorial.

From his car, Radhauser placed a call to Kurtis Lee Jackson at the FBI Portland Regional Office. Jackson had been an enormous help on a double murder case last year that involved civil rights violations. Radhauser had not only made himself a friend, but he'd also gotten an appreciation for how many more resources the FBI had at their fingertips. Maybe Jackson could speed up the DNA results.

The two men chatted for a few minutes. Jackson told Radhauser about his baby granddaughter and how she was walking and causing all kinds of delightful havoc. Radhauser, in turn, told stories about Lizzie and Jonathan.

"As much as I always love hearing from you," Jackson said. "I get the feeling there's a good reason for this call."

Radhauser told him what he needed.

"The closest lab to you that the FBI uses would be in Eugene. Can you get the samples up there today?"

Though it meant a six-hour round trip, Radhauser was willing to do it if it brought Ryan Patterson home to his parents more quickly. "I'll drive them up myself," Radhauser said. And then he asked Jackson for advice on how to best handle the transfer of the boy back to his biological parents.

Radhauser took a full page of notes. "Thanks, Jackson. As usual, I owe you one."

"No problem, buddy. You should have the results by tomorrow afternoon. Wednesday morning at the latest. I'll have the lab fax them directly to you."

CHAPTER TWENTY

When Radhauser arrived at the station on Tuesday morning members of the press had already gathered on the sidewalk like a murder of crows after roadkill. Local television station vans crammed their oversized vehicles into every available space on the Plaza where parking was already at a premium.

Radhauser was exhausted from last night's trip to Eugene and back. He'd wanted to get in and out unnoticed this morning, wanted to update Captain Murphy on what was happening with the Blair Bradshaw murder case and explain why he'd put it on hold yesterday in order to expedite the cold case kidnapping of Ryan Patterson. After that, he planned to drive over to the Bradshaw house and see what he could intuit about Blair from wandering through her home and examining her possessions. With any luck, she'd kept a diary.

Radhauser pulled into his reserved parking place, got out of his car, and headed toward his office at a fast clip.

A bald man in need of a shave, stepped up to him, waving a microphone in his face. He wore a pair of tattered blue jeans, a black T-shirt and a pair of high-top Converse sneakers with no socks. Whatever happened to the days when reporters wore dress shirts and ties?

"Aren't you Detective Winston Radhauser, the lead investigator in the Blair Bradshaw murder?"

"I am," he said. "And aren't you some leftover hippie from the sixties?" He grinned to let the reporter know he was messing with him.

The man laughed. "No, sir, just a struggling reporter, trying to get a story and pay the rent."

Something about his sense of humor and honest response made Radhauser stop. "What do you want to know?"

"Do you believe Blair Bradshaw was murdered because her husband let another murderer go free?"

"At this point, we're just beginning our investigation. But I can tell you this much. So far, we haven't found any connection to her husband's clients."

"Could she have committed suicide because of the tragic accident that killed her son just days before?"

"The medical examiner has eliminated that as a possibility."

"Do you currently have any suspects in custody?"

"We are interviewing persons of interest at this time, but we have no suspects in custody as yet. Now I really need to go."

"Thank you."

Just before he arrived at the station door, a Katie Couric lookalike jammed her microphone under Radhauser's nose. "Do you think Blair Bradshaw was murdered as revenge for her husband's unethical courtroom behavior? After all, he's known as the criminal defense attorney most likely to free the guilty." She had one of those honey-textured television voices that made butter soften.

It didn't work with Radhauser. "It is not in the best interest of our investigation to comment at this point. Captain Murphy will issue a statement later today." He ducked into the station, then closed the door.

Safely inside, he let out a long breath.

Hazel smiled her morning greeting, a telephone pressed between her ear and shoulder. She put whomever she was speaking with on hold and addressed Radhauser. "Did you survive the vulture attack?"

"Just barely. One of them got a bite out of me." He hurried straight to Murphy's office.

The captain sat behind his desk, his head in his hands as if the weight of the world was on his shoulders, and he could no longer hold it up.

Radhauser braced himself, then tapped on the door frame.

Murphy looked up, dark circles under his eyes. The man needed to find a girlfriend. He'd been miserable ever since his wife, Naomi, left him. "I hope you have something good."

Radhauser briefed the captain on everything he knew so far about the Bradshaw murder.

"But do you have a suspect? Are you close to putting this thing to bed?"

"No, sir. Not yet. We're working on checking alibis for the people of interest. It appears her husband has an alibi, but it's from a woman he's been sleeping with. The neighbor, an old lady, said she could swear Bradshaw's Jaguar was in his lover's driveway all night. But the old lady had to have slept part of the night, so I haven't cleared him as yet." He told Murphy about Jason Robertson and how the death of his sister ensured he'd become the sole owner of the family vineyard. "But I got a warrant for his phone records. They confirmed that he placed calls to the hospital in Medford at 11 pm. And then again at 12:15 a.m. So, I've pretty much eliminated him as a suspect. But I haven't given up on Blair's mother, a whack-job who lives out in Wildwood. She pointed a shotgun at me when I went to visit."

"I need to make a statement to the press this afternoon. They're lining up like scavengers out there," he said as if Radhauser didn't already know. "Can you get me something I can tell them?"

"We're trying, sir. I'm headed over to the Bradshaw house now. He's given me permission to spend time looking around. I'm hoping I can find something in her things that will lead me to a suspect."

"Do you have a warrant?"

"I have Bradshaw's permission."

"Get a warrant before you seize anything. We want all our is dotted and ts crossed in case we end up indicting that shark, Bradshaw."

"I will."

"What are you waiting for?"

"Something else has come up I should tell you about."

"What could be more important than the murder of the wife of that arrogant jackass?"

Radhauser filled Murphy in on the DNA they'd discovered at the scene and how it had come back as a match for Ryan Patterson. He told the captain about the samples he took from the six boys who'd attended the memorial for Tommy Bradshaw, and the fact he'd informed the Pattersons their son was still alive.

"Are you crazy?" Murphy said. "You should have waited until we had the Patterson boy in custody. One false move from those parents and that boy could disappear forever."

"I gave it a lot of thought, sir. I know them well. They've waited a long time. I thought they had a right to know."

Murphy stared at him for a moment, his eyes cold and flat. "Maybe you should have curtailed your thinking and consulted someone else. Like me."

"I'm sorry, sir. I did what I thought was right."

"I want you to turn the kidnapping case over to McBride. She's not emotionally involved."

"I can't do that, sir. I'm sorry, but this is my case. I've been working on it for a decade. The Pattersons trust me. And now we finally have a lead, I intend to see it through."

"You mean to tell me that missing boy has been living here in Ashland for the last decade? This is going to make the Ashland Police Department look like a bunch of incompetent fools."

"We don't know that for sure yet, sir. He may have just recently moved to Ashland. But we'll know more once we establish his identity."

Murphy dismissed Radhauser with a wave of his hand. "Get the hell out there and find me a suspect in the Bradshaw case. While you're at it, bring that boy home to his parents. Even if the Ashland police look like a bunch of idiots, the return of that boy will be the biggest and best news to hit Ashland in a decade."

* * *

Jung-Su greeted him at the front door with a big smile. "Detective Radhauser. Mr. Franklin say you look all you like. I not bother you."

Radhauser took off his Stetson and followed her into the entryway. It was tiled with slate and held a long table with a lamp and a small, and very expensive looking, bronze statue of an Arabian horse head. An ornate mirror, framed in gold leaf, hung above the table. The house smelled like cinnamon. "Something smells good."

"Snickerdoodles. I make for Holden for after school."

"Has his father told him about Mrs. Bradshaw's death?"

She nodded. "Holden very sad. That's why I make cookies. Snickerdoodles his favorite."

"Could you tell me where I'd find her bedroom?"

"On second floor," Jung-Su said. "It has double doors. Tommy's room is across hallway. You want me show you?"

"No. I prefer to look alone. It's less distracting."

"Okay. You need me, I be in kitchen."

"I'll stop in to see you before I leave."

She smiled. "I give you cookie."

Though he'd come to find out what he could about Blair Bradshaw, it was Tommy's door he opened first. He stood outside in the hallway and stared into a room that held two twin beds, a built-in desk in front of one of four windows, this one looking out on the pool. Bookshelves lined the walls on either side of the desk. A partially constructed Lego rocket ship, identical to the one he'd seen in Holden Houseman's living room, sat on the desk—tiny colorful parts in carefully separated piles all around it. Were the two boys having a contest to see who could finish it first? It wasn't difficult to imagine Tommy sitting at his desk, his head bent over his project, intent on building his ship.

It was at that precise moment Tommy Bradshaw rose out of the files of dead children to become a singular and irreplaceable little boy, just like his son Lucas had been. Radhauser studied the corkboard where Tommy had pinned a photo of himself with Holden Houseman. The two of them were wrestling, and though their bodies were twisted around each other, when the photo was snapped, both boys looked at the camera and smiled.

Tommy was a soccer fan and had cut photos from magazines of international soccer stars, names like Michael Owen and Hernan Crespo. Names Radhauser didn't recognize but must have meant something to Tommy because he'd pinned them on his corkboard. Radhauser glanced toward the walk-in closet where wooden rods held shirts, jackets, dress slacks and jeans. They hung on pale-blue plastic hangers, all facing the same way. Probably the work of Jung-Su. Tommy's T-shirts and sweaters were neatly folded on built-in shelves. His shoes were placed in a cabinet with an individual cubby hole for each pair. It was the closet of a rich boy whose mother valued organization.

A Cub Scout uniform hung on the upper rod with all the patches he'd earned sewn onto its sash. It also held all the empty spaces for the patches he'd never receive. There were clothes to play in and dress up for special occasions or go to church, clothes for soccer, baseball, and wrestling. Clothes for the changing seasons that Tommy would never experience again. And, of course, those small clothes suggested all the things this boy would never wear. A graduation cap and gown. A tuxedo at his senior prom and another at his wedding.

He'd never again play the shiny trumpet he'd placed on his bed, nor tap the keys on the computer that sat on top of his desk. Tommy Bradshaw would never whisper "I love you" to a wife or the child he might have someday fathered.

When he couldn't take another moment, couldn't allow himself one more thought about this lost boy, Radhauser silently left the room, closing the door behind him. He stood with his back against the wall and took several deep breaths. Once he'd regained his composure, he headed across the hallway and through the double doors.

The Bradshaws' master bedroom looked like something out of a magazine. It had a king-sized, four-poster, cherry-wood bed with matching end tables on both sides and a stone fireplace on the opposite wall set high enough to be seen when lying down. The bed was covered in a tapestry spread that matched walls painted a pale shade of gray. Assorted throw pillows in grays and blues were neatly arranged.

A sitting area with facing loveseats was situated at the far end of the suite with an entire wall of ceiling-to-floor windows that looked out on a breathtaking view of the Siskiyou Mountains. The adjoining bathroom was as big as Radhauser's entire bedroom with a huge sunken and jetted bathtub surrounded by stained glass windows, depicting a waterfall cascading down a mountainside into a turquoise pool that was circled with flowering pear and dogwood trees.

He guessed from the photograph of Tommy on the nightstand and the book of Rumi poems that the right side of the bed was Blair's. He pulled out the top drawer and examined the contents. A bag of cough drops. The half-filled bottle of valium Doctor Landenberg had prescribed on the day Tommy died. A stack of birthday and Mother's Day cards from her son. Had she been rereading them in bed while her husband was out with his young lover?

The drawer held an empty tablet with a pen attached. Was Blair Bradshaw the type of woman who thought of things in the middle of the night and needed to jot them down?

He picked up a gratitude journal in which she wrote five short entries every day. Things for which Blair Bradshaw was grateful. She was religious about it—even on the days after Tommy died. Radhauser read a few from the week of May 4th. *The sun falling on my bare shoulders. The smell of fresh-ground coffee brewing. A father who didn't forget me. A brother that I'd forgotten. The memorial Tommy's friends are raising in the woods behind our house. That my little boy didn't suffer long. The ten years, six months, and eleven days my son lived.*

Radhauser closed the book. He clamped his eyes shut for a moment, thinking about the woman who'd made those entries so soon after her son died. A part of him wanted to read more, but it felt too personal—as if he were eavesdropping on intimate thoughts that were none of his business.

But what if it contained something that could lead him to her murderer? He changed his mind and leafed back to late March and early April, to before she'd arranged to have the locks changed and the new security system installed. He scanned the entries but found nothing that implicated anyone—only her gratitude for the things most people took for granted.

He moved on to her dresser. It held the usual array of nightgowns, underwear, and T-shirts. Nothing unusual or out of the ordinary until his hand felt something solid as he rummaged through her sock drawer. He pulled a box of syringes from the inside of a black sock. The box appeared to be new and was labeled as containing a dozen syringes. He emptied them into his hand. Only one was missing.

Had Blair Bradshaw injected herself? Had she been trying to kill herself with heroin when the murderer appeared on the scene? Or was she merely trying to ease some of the pain of losing her son? Radhauser wasn't about to judge. If he'd had access to heroin after Laura and Lucas' funeral, he might have done the same thing.

He slipped one of the syringes into an evidence bag for comparison and tucked the remainder back into the sock and closed the drawer.

Her jewelry box was well-organized and held some beautiful pieces. Probably gifts her husband had given her over their years together.

Finding nothing of interest, he moved on to the closet. Like Tommy's, this one was custom-made and huge with built-in shelves and dressers. A bench in the center for pulling on socks and lacing shoes.

He started his search on Franklin's side and examined every suit for signs of blood. Picked up each athletic shoe and examined the bottom for blood or tread that resembled the print he'd found on the rock. He checked the size. Bradshaw wore a ten. Heron estimated the shoe that left the print was a size ten or eleven. The soles were all clean. His suits neatly pressed. His shirts hanging according to colors. White, blue, green. Ties hung from a rack— many of them grey or blue striped—the conservative wardrobe of a criminal defense attorney.

Blair's side was much the same. Compulsively neat. All the hangers pointing in the same direction. Her shoes were stored in see-through plastic containers, organized according to color.

Where would Blair Bradshaw hide something she didn't want

anyone to see? Probably not in her closet.

He looked up at the ceiling for a crawl space but found nothing. After checking with Jung-Su, Radhauser took a ladder from the garage, pushed up the panel in Tommy's closet and hoisted himself up into the empty space. It wasn't high enough to stand. He crouched and moved around the ten-by-ten feet space, using a flashlight to search, but found nothing. With a house this large, the Bradshaws probably didn't need their crawl space for storage.

On a hunch, he lifted a piece of plywood set over the rafters to provide a makeshift floor—and there it was. A small cardboard container, about the size of a shoebox, was taped shut and set between two joists. Someone had printed *childhood memories* in black marker on top.

Though he longed to slice it open and see what it contained, he decided to play it safe and get a warrant. Murphy would blow an aneurysm if there was something important to prosecuting the case inside and it was seized illegally.

Whatever was in that box could wait one more day.

CHAPTER TWENTY-ONE

After comparing the syringe he'd taken from Blair Bradshaw's sock drawer with the one in evidence and finding it a match, Radhauser spent the rest of the afternoon with McBride. They went over the interviews she'd conducted with Bradshaw's partner, his secretary, the artistic director of the Shakespeare Festival and several of its actors.

Meyer, Bradshaw's third partner, thought Franklin was arrogant but brought in more money than anyone else in the firm. He claimed Bradshaw got along with the other employees. Once McBride let Bradshaw's secretary know the police were aware of her boss' relationship with Sonya Clifford, she was cooperative and admitted she'd covered for Bradshaw a few times when his wife or son phoned.

Everyone McBride spoke with at the Shakespeare Company claimed Blair Bradshaw was well-liked, helpful to others, and humble about her own, pretty significant, accomplishments. No one could think of anyone who'd want to harm her. McBride went through her dressing room, examined the contents of the closet and drawers, but found absolutely nothing that might lead them to her killer.

She talked to the Human Resources director and requested a copy of Blair's employment application. It stated that she'd graduated from Gold Canyon High School in Portland in 1983 and Portland State University in 1987. "But here's the thing," McBride said. "Neither place has any record of her ever attending."

"Didn't Human Resources verify the information on her application?"

"Apparently not. A formal education is not a prerequisite for an acting career. Even as a teenager, Blair did a fair amount of little theater productions in the lead role. And once she tried out for Shakespeare Company, she was a superstar, and they didn't care about anything else."

"I need to find out where she was from 1980, when she left home at fifteen, until she began working with the Shakespeare Company in the summer of 1987."

Radhauser studied the murder board, added Sonya Clifford to the list of suspects with a note indicating she was pregnant with Franklin Bradshaw's child.

Around 6 p.m., Murphy, McBride and most of the other police officers and employees left the building to head home. McBride planned to visit Judge Wainwright first thing in the morning to see if he would issue a search warrant for the Bradshaw house.

Radhauser hung around a little longer, wanting to wait for the DNA results, even though he doubted they'd come in after 6 p.m.

He placed a call to the Pattersons and let them know the DNA samples from the ten-year-old boys who'd attended the memorial had been gathered, were at the lab in Eugene and with any luck they'd have the results soon.

"I don't suppose you'd give us their names." There was a new lilt in Sean's voice. "Or show us their school photos."

"You know I can't do that. But this will all be over soon. Maybe even before Friday." He knew he'd have the results by tomorrow, but wanted a little time to follow the plan Jackson had suggested. Radhauser figured as long as he kept them in the loop, the Pattersons were unlikely to show up at Sand Creek Elementary, or go out searching on their own.

It was 7:30 p.m. when Radhauser finally got home. He parked the car under the barn overhang and, as always, walked down the center aisle between the stalls, greeting each of their horses by name and feeding them their evening handful of sweet grain. The stallion, Ameer, rewarded him with a neck nuzzle. "Trying to make up for throwing me on my ass in front of my wife and kids, are you, boy?"

Ameer whinnied.

He scratched under the horse's chin. "Keep it up. It just might work."

* * *

Radhauser awakened at 5 a.m. on Wednesday, turned over and tried to go back to sleep, but the knowledge that the DNA results would arrive this morning prevented his eyes from staying shut. He felt a mixture of joy and fear. Joy that the Pattersons' nightmare was finally ending, but fear for what this revelation might do to the boy who'd believed for a decade that he was someone else.

After slipping out of bed, Radhauser tiptoed into the bathroom to shower and dress, then returned to the bedroom and leaned over to kiss Gracie on the cheek.

She opened one eye and groaned. "You smell good." She wrapped her arms around his neck. "Leaving already?"

"Today is the day the Pattersons get their son back. There was no way I could sleep another minute."

She kissed him on the cheek. "I'm so happy for you. And for them. But I can't help thinking about what that boy is going to feel."

He loosened her arms from his neck and pulled the covers over her shoulders. "Get some more sleep. The little monsters will be rising soon."

It was still dark when Radhauser arrived at the police station. To his relief, there were no reporters or television cameras lurking on the sidewalk. He unlocked the front door, waved to the night clerk, then hurried down the hallway to the fax machine.

And there they were. A cover sheet addressed to him and six pages, each containing the DNA results for one of the boys who'd attended Tommy's memorial. His chest tightened, and his right hand trembled as he reached for them. Without looking at the results, he carried the stack of papers into his office and closed the door.

When his chest lost a little of its tightness, he spread the papers across his desk and flipped on his lamp. One of them was stamped with the words, *Perfect Match*, in bright red ink. Before reading it, he made what he thought was an educated guess. Collier Zagorski. He picked up the page and read the name of the boy who'd been born Ryan Sean Patterson.

Radhauser's heart raced as if he'd been caught committing some sinful act. It had to be a mistake. That poor kid. How much more would he have to endure? Radhauser read the name again and was overwhelmed with tenderness. His throat thickened and the back of his eyes stung. For a moment, he thought he was going to tear up. Sentimental fool that he'd become.

The name was Holden Houseman. Tommy Bradshaw's best friend and the boy who'd been wrestling with Tommy when he fell to his death.

Stunned, Radhauser turned off the lamp and sat in the semi-darkness, rigid as a wax statue and watched the tree outside his window cast shifting shadows on the wall.

A half hour later, he was still holding the paper in his hands. The sun rose, shadows slowly disappeared, and his office filled with light.

It was time to set the plan Jackson had drawn out for him in motion.

But first, he had to spend some time with McBride, updating the case board and outlining the next steps in the Bradshaw murder investigation.

* * *

At 3 p.m. when school was about to let out, Radhauser met Carolyn Kelly, the social worker from Services to Children and Families, in the lobby of the Sand Creek Elementary School. Carolyn wore a tailored dark suit, sensible shoes, and a pinched expression. She was a slender woman with the posture of a wooden fence post. They introduced themselves, then explained the situation to the principal and asked if there was a private space where they could meet with Holden Houseman.

Once they were inside the room, which held a round table and four chairs along with a leather loveseat, Carolyn turned to him. "Judge Wainwright called me this morning. He's recused himself because he's Holly Patterson's brother. But he has appointed a guardian ad litem to represent the interests of the minor child. She'll visit both homes and interview the boy. I'm sure Judge Wainwright hopes we'll expedite this as soon as possible and get his nephew back where he belongs."

"There's nothing I'd rather see happen," Radhauser said, then thought about Carl Houseman and how much he obviously loved Holden. Nothing about this was going to be easy.

"I want you to stand aside on this. I've had a lot of experience with children in crisis situations."

"But I know this boy," Radhauser said. "He trusts me."

"We have a protocol in place for situations like this one."

Minutes later, Nurse Freeman led Holden into the private room where Radhauser and Carolyn waited. Holden wore a pair of dark blue slacks with a sharp crease and a clean white polo shirt with a blue alligator on the pocket. The school dress code required navy slacks and white shirts for the boys. Skirts or slacks for the girls. Holden's longish hair was neatly combed, bangs falling just above his eyebrows.

Again, Radhauser was struck by the boy's fragile beauty. Now he knew the truth, a resemblance to Holly's beautiful dark eyes, long, thick lashes, and fine features seemed obvious.

As soon as he spotted Radhauser, Holden tossed his backpack into a corner, hung his head, and stood very still, plowing the linoleum floor with the toe of his sneaker.

Radhauser touched his shoulder. "You don't need to be afraid. You're not in any trouble."

Holden blinked rapidly. "Then why are you here?"

Radhauser introduced Carolyn. "Ms. Kelly needs to talk to you about something important."

"Where's my dad?" He addressed his question to Radhauser.

"I suspect he's at work." It was Radhauser's plan to phone Carl Houseman as soon as they finished here and arrange to meet him at his house.

Carolyn pulled out a chair for Holden. "Why don't we sit?"

"Please." Holden shook his head and put his hands on his hips. "I don't want to sit. I want to talk to my dad."

"I'm sorry, but we can't do that right now. I'm going to take you to a nice place where someone will take care of you for a little while until we get this straightened out."

Holden's gaze darted between Carolyn and Radhauser. "Get what straightened out? You said it was an accident. You said it wasn't my fault Tommy died. You lied."

The drumbeat in Radhauser's chest quickened. He knelt in front of Holden. "Listen to me. Tommy's death wasn't your fault, and it has nothing to do with the reason you're here. I didn't lie. And you're not in any trouble."

He glared at Radhauser. "Then why can't I get on the bus and go home like I always do? Why do I have to go with her?" He shot an angry glance toward Carolyn, then back at Radhauser.

There was no place for the detective to hide. He held the boy's gaze for as long as he could but eventually dropped his own to the floor. This was going to be even more difficult than he'd thought. He shifted his gaze to Carolyn.

When she nodded, Radhauser assumed she meant for him to tell Holden what was happening.

"You told me the truth about Tommy, and I'm going to tell you the truth now. Remember when we swabbed the inside of your mouth and the mouths of the other boys who attended Tommy's memorial?"

Holden nodded. "You said it was to help find the person who hurt Miss Blair."

"It was. But DNA is a special test that..."

Carolyn touched his shoulder. "I'll take over now."

Radhauser stood and moved aside.

She crouched so she was eye level with Holden. "Every person in the world has unique DNA. No two people have the same. The police keep the DNA of children who have disappeared in their database. That way if they find a missing child and he no longer looks the same as he did when he disappeared, they use DNA. It helps prove they have the right child. Your DNA came back as a match for a boy who disappeared in 1991."

Holden's face was a mask of confusion. "But I was only just

173

born in 1991. I never disappeared. I've always lived on Sand Creek Road. Just ask my dad. He'll tell you."

Radhauser shot Carolyn a look he hoped would send her a message to slow down. This was a ten-year-old, very bewildered boy.

She ignored him. "There is no way you would remember. You were a little baby—just a few months old. Your name was Ryan Patterson. You lived with your mom, who was an operating room nurse, and your father, who was a clinical psychologist and guidance counselor at Medford High School. One day, when you were in your stroller at the Rogue Valley Mall with your babysitter, a person took you. The police looked everywhere, but you had disappeared. Your parents loved you very much. They still do. They are going to be so happy to see you."

"My mother is dead," he said, nostrils flaring. "Her name was Candace Houseman. She had cancer. She died when I was five. You have me mixed up with some other kid. I have a birth certificate and everything. Just call my dad. He'll show you." He paused and turned to Radhauser. "Tell her, Detective Radhauser. You know my dad. Tell her how wrong she is."

"I think we should go now." Carolyn took Holden's hand.

He jerked away and moved closer to Radhauser.

Carolyn's expression grew even more pinched. "Do you have any birthmarks, Holden?"

He stared at her for a moment before answering. "Yes. My dad says it looks like the continent of Africa. He told me we might go there someday. And I'd see lions and tigers and elephants and giraffes. If you go on a safari, you can see them up close." He talked fast as if to convince himself this trip would one day happen.

Radhauser sucked in a breath.

"Can you tell me where that mark is located on your body?" Carolyn asked.

He pointed to an area just above his left breast. "Right about here. Why? What does that have to do with anything?"

The last shred of doubt disappeared. This boy was Ryan Patterson.

Again, Radhauser crouched in front of Holden. Carolyn Kelly, with all her expertise in dealing with children, had overwhelmed and terrified the boy. "I'm going to talk to your dad and give him a chance to explain everything. But in the meantime, you need to go with Ms. Kelly."

"Your parents will pick you up after we get everything sorted," Carolyn said.

Holden threw his hands into the air. "How many times do I have to say it?" His voice was shrill. "I don't have parents. Only my dad. I want to see my dad."

"I know you're having a lot of feelings about this." Radhauser reached out and tried to touch him, but Holden wrenched away.

He stood at the window looking out at kids in single file in front of the school buses. Holden splayed his hands on the glass, his back to Radhauser and Carolyn.

Radhauser rushed closer and put both hands on the boy's shoulders. "I know you're upset, but we're going to sort it all out, I promise."

Holden turned to face them again. His moist palms left skeletal imprints on the glass. But even as Radhauser watched, they slowly evaporated and disappeared.

"I don't understand." Tears puddled in Holden's eyes and clung like fat diamonds to his eyelashes before one escaped and ran down his right cheek. He brushed it away. "Why can't I just get on the bus and go home to my house and my dad like I always do? Jung-Su watches me and makes me do my homework. My dad is a good dad. He would never take someone else's baby."

"I think he's a good man, too." Radhauser fastened his gaze on the boy's dark eyes. "And I won't stop until I get to the bottom of this."

"Get to the bottom of what? I know who I am. Carl Houseman is my dad. He's always been…" He trailed off and gave in to the tears, sobbing and wiping his eyes with his balled fists like a much younger child.

Radhauser couldn't help himself. He took the boy into his arms and held him until the crying subsided. He no longer gave a damn about Carolyn Kelly and her superior knowledge on how to handle children in crisis. He was going to do this his way. "Remember the talk we had a few nights ago about Tommy? I listened to you, didn't I?"

Holden bit down on his bottom lip and nodded.

"I need you to trust me again and to believe that I care about what happens to you, okay?"

The boy stared at him but said nothing.

Carolyn held the door open. "We need to go. Right now."

Holden stepped away from Radhauser, then picked up his backpack and slung it over his shoulder. He passed through the door slowly, head down, fists jammed into his pants pockets. But once in the hallway, he turned abruptly and ran back inside before throwing his arms around Radhauser's waist and hugging him tightly. "I don't want to go with her. I want to stay with you."

Instinctively, Radhauser cradled the boy's head against his body for a moment, wondering if he could take Holden home to their ranch. Gracie would be happy to watch over him. Being around Lizzie, Jonathan and the horses might be exactly what the kid needed now. Radhauser's questioning gaze met Carolyn's.

Having apparently read his thoughts, she gave him a rapid shake of her head. "I have procedures I must follow. It takes months to become a certified foster home."

Radhauser held Holden by the shoulders and looked him directly in the eyes again. "I'm going to come see you later today. I'll make sure you understand what's happening every step of the way, okay? Right now, I'm headed over to talk to your dad."

Holden nodded and tucked his chin into his chest. He was too polite to argue any more.

They all stepped outside.

After Holden climbed into her backseat and buckled his seatbelt, Carolyn closed the door, took Radhauser by the arm and led him away from the car so Holden wouldn't hear what she had to say. "I know you think I told him too much too soon, but lying to a child doesn't change anything. The sooner he accepts the situation he's facing, the better off everyone will be."

Radhauser said nothing. Holden did deserve the truth, but it could have been delivered with a little more sensitivity. "Let me know where you place him. His birth parents don't know the DNA results have come back and we've found Ryan. But as soon as they do, they'll want to see him."

"And you should grant them that wish," she replied. "Let them know they're lucky. It's rare to find a kid who's been loved and well cared for. The sad thing is, it might have been easier for his birth parents if he'd grown up with abuse, then he might see the Pattersons as his liberators. As it is, he'll most likely view them as the ones who stole him away from the dad he knew and loved."

Radhauser hung his head and thought about the joy and the pain involved with the solving of this decade-long kidnapping case. Out of nowhere, he remembered a quote Laura had once read to him from a book written by Kahlil Gibran, a nineteenth-century Lebanese poet. *Joy and sorrow are inseparable, together they came and where one sits alone with you at the board remember the other is asleep upon your bed.*

CHAPTER TWENTY-TWO

Radhauser called Carl Houseman at work and said he needed to see him as soon as possible.

"Can't this wait?" Houseman replied. "I'm about to go to an important meeting."

"No. It can't."

"What's this about, Detective?"

"It's about Holden. And it's really important."

"Is he okay? Is he hurt? Where is he?"

"Don't worry," Radhauser said. "He's safe. But there are a few things we need to straighten out about his birth."

"His birth? What the hell are you talking about?"

"Just meet me at your house in an hour. I'll explain everything."

An hour later, at about 4:30 p.m., Radhauser parked in the Houseman driveway and sat for a moment, dreading the encounter that awaited him. It had taken some doing to convince him, but the birthmark on Holden's chest had cinched it. He was now convinced Holden Houseman was Ryan Patterson and not the biological son of Carl and Candace. But there was no doubt in his mind Carl Houseman loved the boy. Radhauser was certain Holden loved the man he believed to be his father.

Radhauser could have arranged to have Houseman arrested and brought over to Ashland Holding, but he wanted—no, he needed—to hear the man's story before talking to Sean and Holly Patterson—before he let them see the son they'd waited ten years for Radhauser to find. He got out of his car, hurried up to the front door and rang the bell.

Houseman answered. He was dressed in a suit and tie, and a

pale blue oxford shirt. "Please, you have to tell me. Has something happened to my son?" He rubbed his hands on his pant legs, his brow furrowed.

"May I come inside?"

Houseman stepped aside so Radhauser could enter. He took off his Stetson. "Holden is safe and in good hands. Could we sit down and talk for a few minutes?"

Houseman led Radhauser into the living room where he took a seat on the rocker.

"You have to tell me where he is." Houseman sat on the edge of the sofa, tapping his foot against the carpet.

"At the moment, Services to Children and Families have placed him in a foster home in Jackson County."

Houseman's right hand flew up to his mouth for an instant. "A foster home? What the hell's going on here? Are you accusing me of abusing my son?" Houseman leapt to his feet. "I love that kid more than my own life. I've never even spanked him. Not once. What you're saying about Holden being in a foster home can't be true. I saw him get on the school bus this morning. Did they come and rip him from his classroom?"

"Sit down, Mr. Houseman. Holden is safe. I know you love him, and I want to give you a chance to tell your story before I bring you in to custody. But I'm here to arrest you for the May 4, 1991 kidnapping of three-month-old Ryan Sean Patterson."

Houseman's whole body grew rigid. "Arrest me? Kidnapping? What the hell are you talking about?"

"Please, Mr. Houseman, once you sit, I'll explain."

He sat. "I don't know anything about a Ryan Sean Patterson. You've got the wrong person. Holden is my son. I have his birth certificate and all his immunization and growth records." Again, he leapt to his feet, then hurried across the room to a roll-top desk near the entrance to the hallway, and pulled out a file drawer.

While Houseman leafed through his files, Radhauser looked around the room where he saw many items in support of Houseman's fathering and love for Holden. A baseball glove snuggled deep into the cushions of a burgundy side chair near the fireplace. On top of the television, a new photo sat, framed in wood. In it, Holden crouched in front of a backstop, in a red baseball uniform, a wide grin spread across his face. Three of *The Hardy Boys* books and two *5-Minute Mysteries* were stacked on the coffee table.

Less than a minute later, Houseman returned with a folder marked Holden's Records. He rummaged through the report cards and other papers, then pulled out a birth certificate and handed it to Radhauser.

He scanned the document. It looked absolutely legitimate. Listed the baby's birth on February 5, 1991, at 9:23 a.m. at Ashland Hospital. A baby boy born to Carl and Candace Houseman. Weight seven pounds, nine ounces, twenty-one inches long. A boy they'd named Holden Carl Houseman.

Radhauser frowned and turned back to Houseman. *What's going on here?* "I'm as confused by this as you are, Mr. Houseman. But there were two hairs on Blair Bradshaw's skirt the morning she was found murdered. We sent them to the lab for DNA analysis, hoping they might lead us to her killer. One of the hairs was not in our system. The other came back as a perfect match for Ryan Patterson. As you know, we tested the DNA of every male child who attended the memorial. I couldn't have been more shocked when that match turned out to be Holden."

Houseman unknotted his tie, jerked it from beneath his collar, and threw it onto the sofa, then began pacing again. "There has to be a mistake. You need to recheck the test results." He wrinkled his brow. "Maybe the lab screwed up. Or some DNA samples got switched. Mistakes happen," he said as if trying to reassure himself.

After hesitating for a moment, Radhauser stood and moved closer. What he was about to do didn't feel right, but DNA evidence couldn't lie. "Carl Houseman, you're under arrest for the kidnapping of Ryan Patterson on May 4, 1991. You have the right to remain silent. If you give up the right to remain silent, anything you say can and will be used against you in a court of law—"

"Wait a damn minute," Houseman said. "On May 4, 1991, I

was still in Kuwait, cleaning up after Operation Desert Storm. The fighting ended in February, but the country was a mess. Holden was born while I was away."

"Do you have your discharge papers? Or anything else that can prove you were there on that date?"

"Of course. I've got the papers and so would the US Marine Corp."

"I believe you." Radhauser returned to the rocking chair. This was going to take longer than he'd anticipated. "But I still need to verify."

Houseman let out a pent-up breath. "Fine." He spat out the word, then headed to the roll-top desk and came back with a folder that contained his discharge papers.

He handed it to Radhauser, then returned to his seat on the sofa. The documents were dated July, 1991. Another scenario began to develop in Radhauser's mind. "Where was your wife living during that time?"

"Here in Ashland. She was an only child, and we inherited this house after her mother died. About a year before Holden was born."

The person Radhauser had seen on the Rogue Valley Mall surveillance tape, pushing the baby carriage presumed to be Ryan's, was a female. "Was your wife pregnant when you left for Kuwait?"

"Not the first time. But when I was home on leave, we decided to try to get pregnant, and we succeeded. We planned the baby's birth for after my last tour, but they needed me for another six months. Candy and I talked about it. The money was good— better than anything I could make here. And, with the baby coming, we figured we'd need it. Holden was four months old when I saw him in person for the first time."

"Did your wife send photographs to Kuwait?"

"Of course."

"Do you still have them?"

"I don't know. Finding them might take a little time. But Candy kept a baby book." He stood, then headed over to the bottom shelf of one of the bookcases to retrieve it.

While Houseman stood in front of the rocker, Radhauser thumbed through the pages. The book held the usual birth information, a list of gifts received next to the name of the person who'd given them. A sterling silver baby cup and spoon, diaper service, assorted receiving blankets, and outfits. He turned to a page with a pocket and small envelope designed to hold a lock of hair.

Houseman jerked out the envelope and handed it to Radhauser. "Here. Take this. Get it tested. It will prove you're all wrong."

When Radhauser looked inside, the envelope was empty.

As if searching for the missing lock of hair, Houseman darted his gaze around the room. "It doesn't mean anything. Candy was soft and sentimental. Maybe she couldn't make herself cut his baby hair."

"Holden's birth certificate says he had blue eyes and blonde hair. Like you do, Mr. Houseman."

"Don't be ridiculous. You know as well as I do that a baby's eye color often changes from blue to brown. Baby hair sometimes falls out and comes in much darker. The opposite can be true, too. Besides, Candy's mother had dark hair and brown eyes."

Radhauser continued to turn the pages until he came to a photo of Holden taken at about three months. He pulled the small framed photo the Pattersons had given him from his pocket and compared the two. The babies certainly appeared to be the same child. He placed them side by side on the coffee table.

"Where did you get that photo of Holden?" Houseman clenched his jaw.

"It was the last photograph the Pattersons took of their son. They've had it on their piano for ten years, waiting for him to be found."

Houseman let out a long sigh. "Infants tend to look alike. This is insanity. I...I...can't believe this is happening."

"Does Holden have a birthmark?"

Houseman cocked his head and stared at Radhauser. "What does that have to do with anything?"

Radhauser took Ryan's baby book from his backpack and

turned to the page where Holly had posted the closeup of the birthmark that looked like Africa. "Does it look like this?"

Houseman grabbed the book from Radhauser's hands and held it close to his face. "Oh my God," he said, all the color draining from his cheeks. "It's true, isn't it?" He dropped the book onto the coffee table. "But if Holden isn't my son, what happened to the baby Candace and I had together?"

"That's a very good question, Mr. Houseman. Would you mind waiting a moment, while I call my partner?"

Radhauser slipped into the kitchen and placed a call to McBride. "I need you to check Vital Records. See if you can find a death certificate for a Holden Carl Houseman. He was born on February 5, 1991. I don't have a date of death, but I suspect it was within the next three months."

"I'm on it, boss. Anything else I can do for you?"

"Try to keep the press away from the kidnapping story until we get things a little more sorted out. I'm going to visit Ryan at the foster home in a little while and see how he's doing. The Pattersons don't know I have him yet."

"Too late. This is big news, and the press is all over it. Murphy said he'd be issuing a statement first thing in the morning. Someone must have leaked the DNA results."

"Great," Radhauser said. "Like Murphy knows anything about it. Tell the captain I'll update him early tomorrow. I suspect Vital Records won't have a death certificate for the Houseman baby, but we don't want to leave any loose ends."

A moment later, Radhauser returned to Houseman's living room.

"What am I supposed to do now?" Houseman said.

Radhauser tried to think of something he could do for this poor man who'd done nothing but love a boy he'd believed to be his son. "They've appointed a guardian ad litem to represent Holden's interests. They'll be coming to visit you, I suspect sometime today. I'm going to check on Holden later and see how he's doing. I'm sure he'd like to see you."

"What about the Pattersons?"

"I told them we might not have the DNA results until tomorrow or even later in the week. We have a little time." He decided not to mention the press.

Houseman broke down. His shoulders seemed to fold inward as he held his head in his hands and sobbed.

Radhauser looked the other way, gave him a moment to compose himself.

When Houseman gained control, he took out a handkerchief and blew his nose. "Of course, I want to see him. He must be terrified and wondering what the hell's going on. How much does he know?"

"He's aware his DNA came back as a match for a boy who went missing in 1991. He knows the Pattersons never gave up hope of finding their son alive. But most importantly to Holden, Carl, is that he knows you love him."

Houseman's face had grown ruddy, and the veins in his neck stuck out like cables. He clenched and unclenched his hands. "What am I supposed to tell him? That his mother stole him from a shopping mall when he was three months old? That he's not my son and never has been? That he has to pack up his things and go live in another house with some strangers who think his name is Ryan?"

"I suggest you tell him the truth in the kindest, most loving way possible. That boy trusts you and thinks of you as his father. I suspect a large part of him always will."

"But the Pattersons will never think of me that way."

"Probably not. Can you blame them? But they're wonderful people, and once they understand you had no part in the kidnapping, you may be surprised by their reaction. If it were me, I'd be grateful you took such good care of my boy."

Tears puddled in Houseman's eyes again. "Do you think they might let me see him? Maybe watch some of his baseball games? Or go to his soccer and wrestling matches?"

Radhauser shrugged. "I don't think they could stop you from attending his sporting events. I've known them for over a decade, and they're reasonable people. But it will take time to sort things out. We'll just have to wait and see."

"I know my son existed because Candy... she ...she sent a video from the hospital that was taken the day after he was born."

"It's only speculation at this point, but I think he might have died and your wife couldn't bear to tell you or even accept it herself. Maybe she couldn't face the enormity of that kind of loss, and something snapped. The kidnapping may have been a spontaneous act. Your wife may not have planned to take Ryan."

He told Houseman the circumstances surrounding the kidnapping, about the sixteen-year-old niece who'd taken the baby to the mall and left him asleep in his stroller while she hung out with her friends in the food court. "We'll never know what really happened, but maybe Candy saw him alone, maybe he started to cry, and she believed she was saving him. Grief can twist the mind into some pretty self-destructive behavior."

"But what do you suppose she did with our son's body? Wouldn't there be a death certificate? Some kind of medical examiner's report? Wouldn't people, like our next-door neighbors, and Candy's friends have known if our baby died?"

Radhauser had his suspicions and tomorrow he'd arrange for the Oregon State Police cadaver dogs to canvass the Houseman's backyard and the wooded area behind it. But the poor man had been through enough for one afternoon. "Not if she didn't notify the authorities or tell her friends and neighbors."

Houseman kept shaking his head. The look of confusion and fear on his face was heartbreaking.

"While you're waiting for the guardian, why don't you gather up some clothing, socks and underwear, pajamas, toothbrush and maybe a couple of *The Hardy Boys* books for Holden? I suspect he'll be more comfortable at the foster home with some of his own things. I'll swing by and pick you up later."

Houseman nodded. "But what am I supposed to say when he asks to come home?"

"The truth," Radhauser said.

"And what is the truth?"

"Start with the fact that you love him and always will."

CHAPTER TWENTY-THREE

Holden stood at the bedroom window in the foster home in Medford, staring out at the darkening yard, his back to the door. The foster parents, the Garfields, were older, maybe fifty, but seemed nice enough. They'd showed him around the house, gave him fried chicken, mashed potatoes, peas, and a glass of milk for dinner. With chocolate cake for dessert.

Afterward, they asked if he wanted to watch television or play a video game. When he said he wanted to be alone, they took him upstairs, handed him a clean towel and washcloth, along with a new toothbrush and one of those little tubes of toothpaste the dentist always gave him after his bi-annual visits.

The bedroom was clean and had two sets of bunk beds, with blue cord spreads, two double, maple dressers, and two desks with matching chairs. A room designed to house four boys if necessary. Mrs. Garfield told him he was expected to make his bed in the morning and keep the room tidy. No big deal. His dad expected the same thing.

According to Mrs. Garfield, Holden had the room to himself, at least for the time being. He didn't know if he was relieved to be alone or if he'd rather have another kid around to distract him. He did know he wanted his dad to come get him and take him home.

With the click of the bedroom door opening, Holden jerked around.

His dad stood in the doorway with Detective Radhauser.

A jolt of pure joy shot through Holden. Detective Radhauser had kept his promise and gotten everything straightened out. He held his breath and raced across the room toward his father. "Dad. Are you here to take me home?"

His dad tossed the duffel bag onto the floor and wrapped his arms around Holden. "It's okay, buddy. Everything's going to be okay."

When he finally unpeeled himself from his dad, he glanced over at Radhauser, who picked up the duffel bag and set it on top of one of the bottom bunks.

Holden kept his hand firmly planted on his dad's arm but addressed his words to Radhauser. "Did my dad show you my birth certificate? Did he prove I'm his son? Can I go home now? Is everything all straightened out?" He talked fast, and his voice sounded higher than usual, filled with hope.

"Why don't you sit down on the bed for a few minutes?" his dad said. "Detective Radhauser and I need to talk to you."

Holden shot Radhauser a look meant to say, *I don't want to talk to you. I want to go home.* The detective dangled his cowboy hat from his index finger like he was nervous or something. He wasn't the one being held against his will in some strange house when he had a perfectly good bedroom at home. What did Detective Radhauser have to be nervous about?

He liked Radhauser because of the way he'd listened and believed him when he told the truth about Tommy's accident, but he wasn't sure if he could trust him anymore. Not after what happened at school with that woman from Services to Children and Families. He gave voice to his thoughts. "I don't wanna talk to him now. I just wanna get out of here and go home. Can't we talk there, Dad?" His gaze shot back to his father, who looked sadder than Holden had ever seen him before.

"I'm afraid that isn't going to happen, son. At least not in the way you and I want it to."

Holden froze. A stream of panic rushed through him. "What do you mean it's not going to happen?"

His dad's face looked like it did after Holden's mother died—all white and twisted into a mask. "Please, son. Just sit down on the bed."

When Holden sat, his dad pulled the desk chair as close as he could to the bed.

187

Detective Radhauser took a seat across the room on the other bunk bed to give them some privacy.

"We've always been straight with each other, right?" his dad said.

Holden agreed.

"I've just learned some pretty shocking things about your mother..." He paused. "I mean about Candace. Detective Radhauser thinks that our baby boy died and Candace was very, very sad. Apparently, she saw you as a baby in a stroller at the mall, and she just pushed the stroller with you in it out of the mall, loaded you into the car, and brought you home to Sand Creek Road. When I returned from Kuwait, I believed you were our baby."

Everything around Holden slowed. He buried his face in his arms. He didn't know what was wrong with him. It was as if there were two Holdens—the boy who kept telling himself this was a nightmare, and he'd wake up soon in his own bed, and the other Holden who knew it was for real and hurt so bad he wanted to pound his fists into everyone who came near him.

His dad kept talking. "What she did was very wrong. And it's really sad news for me. In fact, it's devastating. But I'm trying to think about what happy news it is for Holly and Sean Patterson. They're your birth parents, Holden. It must have broken their hearts to lose you. Candace had no right to steal you away from them."

Holden leapt from the bottom bunk and pounded on his dad's chest. "No, that's not true. How can you say that? You're my dad. You've always been my dad. We go to the father-son picnic together at school every year. We go camping with the Boy Scouts. You always call me your son."

"I know how confusing this must be for you. It is for me, too. But I will always feel like your father. And you will always feel like my son. But we know the truth now. We can't pretend this terrible thing didn't happen. We can't go back to the way it was. Things will have to change."

"I don't want things to change. I want to play chess with you and drink hot chocolate and watch those dumb old movies you used to watch with Mom. I want you to yell at me when I don't clean my room or put my dirty clothes in the hamper. I want everything to be the way it usually is."

His dad wiped a tear from his cheek. "You have to remember it wasn't always this way. For five years, it was you and me and your mom. Do you remember how hard it was after she died? A lot of things changed because they had to." He reached out and lifted Holden's chin with his fingertip. "But we managed, didn't we, buddy? And we'll manage again."

Holden pushed his clenched fists against his temples. His whole body felt hot like he'd fallen asleep in the sun at Tommy's pool. "You go ahead and manage. I won't. Not ever." He tried to hold back the tears, but it was impossible.

"I know, son." His father took his handkerchief from his suit pocket and wiped Holden's cheeks. "But imagine how happy it makes Holly and Sean Patterson to know that their baby is still alive and that someone took good care of him."

"I don't care if they're happy. I don't even know them."

"They've waited ten years, and they want you back, Holden. By law, you belong to them. By law, your name is Ryan Sean Patterson."

"I don't want to belong to them. Who cares about the law? And I hate that dumb Ryan name." Holden stood and wrapped his arms around his father's neck, clinging as tight as he could. He didn't want to imagine living anywhere except in his house with the woods and creek behind it. The only home he'd ever known. "I'll tell them I want to be your son. And that I'll hate them forever if they make me leave you."

His dad hugged him, tears mingling now as they cascaded down both their faces before he turned to Radhauser. "Could you give us a few minutes alone?"

After Detective Radhauser left, his dad pulled him onto his lap like he was a little kid again. Ordinarily, he would have resisted, but not now. He tucked his face into his dad's chest. If he could, he'd climb inside his father's skin so no one could ever take him away.

"I want you to listen to me, son."

"I'm listening."

"Imagine you're all grown up and you've graduated from college and have a good job. You fall in love and get married. You and your wife are so happy, and after a few years, you decide to have a baby together. When that little baby boy arrives, you love him more than anything else in the world. More than you could ever imagine loving anything. You and your wife are happier than you've ever been. Then one day, a stranger comes along and steals your baby."

Holden knew it was a little kid thing to do, but he stuck his fingers in his ears. He didn't want to hear this made-up story.

His dad pulled them out. "You look everywhere, but you can't find him. You call the police, and they can't find him either. You pray, but God doesn't answer. Every year on his birthday, you make him a cake and sing happy birthday to him. You cry for him, you hope, and you pray with all your heart that by some miracle, you'll find your son alive and uninjured. You never give up. Then one day, you get the news that your baby has been found."

Holden lifted his head from his dad's chest. "But I'm not a baby. I'm ten years old. I don't know those people. And they don't know me."

"This is going to be the hardest thing either of us ever does, Holden. But you're a wonderful boy, and any man would be proud to be your father. You are kind, and you have empathy— that means you can feel what others feel—and I know you can imagine what this has been like for the Pattersons. You're going to meet them soon. I want you to make me proud the way you always have. Listen to them. Be kind. Try. Just promise me you'll try."

Holden couldn't make his legs stay still, and they trembled against his father's lap. "Try to do what?"

"To keep your heart open. If you do, maybe the Pattersons will come to see that your love is big enough to share with me. Someone from the court came to see me today. She was appointed to represent your best interests because you're a minor. She thinks that if you give them a chance, the Pattersons might allow us to spend time together. Maybe even go on another camping trip to Yellowstone, like we planned. Or—"

Holden pushed his hair out of his eyes. "But what if they don't? What if they never let me see you?"

"Detective Radhauser says the Pattersons are really nice people. If you do a good job of cooperating and if you tell them how you feel and ask politely to spend some time with me, I suspect they will."

Holden didn't want to cry anymore. He wanted to be the boy his father believed him to be, he wanted to make him proud, but... "What if they still don't? What if they blame you for what Mom did?"

"We'll have to cross that bridge when we come to it, son. But in the meantime, will you try?"

Holden nodded, afraid if he tried to speak, he'd burst into another round of tears. He tucked his head back into his father's chest and sat, very still, while his dad held him, rocking back and forth as if soothing a baby.

* * *

Radhauser stood in the hallway. It was all he could do not to cry with Holden and his dad. He reminded himself of how happy the Pattersons would be to have their son back. Of how long they'd waited for this day. The way they'd never given up their hope Ryan would be found alive.

It was easy to imagine the joy on Holly's face as she touched him for the first time in a decade. Would the Pattersons be able to recognize their own son? He definitely had their skin coloring. And Ryan looked like his mother, his face held her fragile beauty and her dark hair and eyes.

As happy as he was for the Pattersons, and for being able to close this case at last, Radhauser had ambivalent feelings. Holden was Sean and Holly's son by birth, but in his every memory he belonged to Carl and Candace Houseman. Should Holden stay with the only father he'd ever known? Radhauser tried to imagine how he'd feel if this were Jonathan. Would he be able to put his own feelings aside and think of what was best for his son?

But what was best for Holden? The boy had told Radhauser how much he wanted a mother and thought he'd found one in Blair Bradshaw. Holly Patterson would be a great mom. Holden would have homemade cupcakes at school on his birthday, someone to tuck him into bed at night, to be the team mother on his Little League team. She'd make a banner and bring sliced oranges for halftime. He'd finally be, as he'd longed to, like the other boys in his class.

Houseman opened the bedroom door and slipped into the hallway, closing it carefully behind him. "Poor kid is exhausted. He fell asleep on my lap," he whispered. "But before he did, he told me he wants to get it over with tonight. He wants to meet the Pattersons. He asked me to be with him when he did. I told him that wasn't possible. Holden asked if you'd be willing to stay with him."

Radhauser nodded. It was the least he could do.

CHAPTER TWENTY-FOUR

Detective Radhauser knew he needed to find a way to focus his attention back on the Bradshaw murder case. To check with McBride about the death certificate for Holden Houseman and the warrant for the Bradshaws' house. He had to collect the box from the crawl space above Tommy's closet and see if it held any clues that might lead him to her killer. If he didn't find a viable suspect soon, Murphy would either have a stroke or Radhauser's badge.

As soon as he dropped Houseman off at his home, Radhauser phoned McBride from the driveway. She had the warrant. "Leave it on my desk," he said. "I'll pick it up first thing in the morning."

"Vital Records has no death certificate for Holden Houseman."

"I figured as much," Radhauser said.

"How's it going with the Pattersons?"

"I'm about to take them to see their son."

"Oh, my God. I imagine it's the best feeling in the world for you to finally get that case closed. It's haunted you for a decade."

He closed his eyes for a moment. What he felt was about as far from the best as he could imagine. "I wish it were that simple. Carl Houseman was in Kuwait when Ryan was kidnapped, and he had no idea Holden was not his biological son. I suspect his birth son died, and his wife buried him without letting the authorities know." He told her Holden was unhappy and begged to go home with Houseman. "As much as I wish it were different, I don't think this long-awaited reunion is going to be a happy one."

"Sorry, boss. Is there anything I can do to help?"

"Try to locate some of Blair Bradshaw's high school classmates.

She would have been known as Meadow Finney or Meadowlark Finney. She was born in 1965, so I suspect she was in Wildwood High School somewhere between 1979 and 1983."

"I'll get on that. Anything else?"

"Call the state police and see if they can bring cadaver dogs to canvass the area behind the Houseman property on Sand Creek tomorrow morning. Check with Heron about getting some forensic guys out there, too, in case the dogs find what I suspect they're going to."

"You think she buried her kid in her backyard?"

"If she didn't call the authorities, she obviously didn't want anyone to know he died. And I doubt she would have buried him somewhere she couldn't visit easily. You got a better idea?"

"No, sir. I'm sure you're right."

After completing his instructions to McBride, he phoned the Pattersons. It was 6:30 p.m. "I know it's on the late side, and you're probably having dinner, but I wonder if I might stop by. I have some news about Ryan."

"Are you kidding? With that kind of news, you'd be welcome at midnight," Sean said. "We'll be waiting for you."

When he arrived, Holly made him a cup of tea, and they sat in the living room like they had on so many other occasions over the last decade.

The Pattersons were literally sitting on the edge of their seats.

"The DNA came back. We've found Ryan."

"Where is he?" Holly asked, her eyes wide.

Before he could stop her, Holly hurried to the window and looked out at Radhauser's car.

"He's not with me. Until we get this all squared away, Ryan is in a foster home in Medford."

Sean leaped to his feet. "Get what squared away? He's our son. You've got the DNA to prove it. What's to get squared away? Haven't we waited long enough?"

Holly's face went soft. "Oh, my God. Is he okay? Did anyone hurt…I mean…was he?" She paused, unable to finish any of her questions.

"Ryan is uninjured. He was raised by Carl and Candace Houseman." Radhauser told them Candace was a stay-at-home mom who died when Ryan was five. Carl was in the US Marine Corp and did two tours in Kuwait and was now an executive with Aviator Helicopter Service in Medford. That they'd lived in the same house, out on Sand Creek Road, for the last eleven years.

Sean sat.

"After his wife died," Radhauser continued, "Carl raised the boy on his own. Up until today, Ryan, who is called Holden, believed Carl was his father."

"They sound like regular, decent people," Holly said. "What made them steal our baby?"

Radhauser explained the circumstances of the abduction, the fact that Carl Houseman was in Kuwait at the time of the birth and the kidnapping and had no knowledge that Holden was not his biological son. He told them he suspected the Housemans' birth son died, that Candace had some kind of breakdown that may have led to the kidnapping. That when she stole Ryan, she did so with the intent to rear him as her own. "Maybe she even convinced herself that her son didn't die."

He let them know that McBride was calling the Oregon State Police to arrange for cadaver dogs to search the area behind the Housemans' home on Sand Creek Road the following day. "I suspect we'll find the remains of the real Holden Houseman."

Holly wiped at her eyes. "How sad for Carl Houseman. He must be devastated."

Sean didn't appear so sympathetic. "And what do you think we've been for the last decade if not devastated?"

Shame was a shot that rang in Radhauser's ears. "No one is disputing that fact. And I'm sorry I didn't find him. But I have to warn you this isn't going to be easy. The social worker explained the situation to him, but Holden wants to stay with Carl. The boy was so upset about going to the foster home that I took Carl to see him earlier."

"You did what?" Sean snapped.

Holly lifted her hand, palm out. "Please, Sean. Let him tell us what's happening with our son."

"Houseman did a great job of explaining the circumstances, of telling the boy how happy you were and pleading with him to give you a chance. Holden begged Houseman to take him home. You can't really blame him—he's never known anything else. But I have to hand it to Carl, he handled the situation as well as anyone could have."

Radhauser paused and surveyed their faces. "We have to give the boy a little time to adjust." He told them about the recent trauma Holden had experienced with the death of his best friend, Tommy, and then the murder of Blair Bradshaw, who'd stepped into the mother role for Holden after Candace died.

Holly crossed her arms over her chest but said nothing.

Sean's expression softened. "Poor kid. What can you tell us about him? What's he like? Is he an outgoing boy, or is he shy?"

"I can tell you this much for sure, your son has been well loved. He gets good grades at Sand Creek Elementary, plays soccer and baseball. He's on the small side but wants to wrestle on the Mountain View High School team when he's older. He's good at chess. He likes to read *The Hardy Boys* and *5-Minute Mysteries*. He's a beautiful and very well-mannered boy. He's got your dark hair, Sean. And Holly's big brown eyes. In spite of the recent traumas with the Bradshaws, he appears to be a well-adjusted, ten-year-old boy."

Holly closed her eyes. "Thank God for that."

"God may have played his part, but I think it's Carl Houseman you'll need to thank," Radhauser said. "From everything I've seen, he's been an exceptional single parent. Are you ready to see Ryan?"

Sean was the first to stand and head toward the door. "Should we take something for him? Maybe that soccer ball we bought him for his last birthday?"

Radhauser thought about that for a moment. It wouldn't be good if Holden thought the Pattersons were trying to buy his love. "I think this time it would be better to come empty-handed and just meet him."

Holly pressed her lips together and touched her hand to her chest, over her heart. "What a horrible, sad thing. Being introduced to your own son when he's ten years old."

"At least he's alive and uninjured," Sean said. "We changed the sheets on his bed and have everything all ready. We'll be bringing him home, right?"

"I suspect the court will want to give him a little time to adjust," Radhauser said. "Ultimately, it's the judge's decision. Judge Wainwright has recused himself and another judge, Hawkins, has the case. A guardian ad litem to represent the boy's interests."

Holly gave him a shy smile and told him what he already knew. "You'll find out soon enough. Arthur Wainwright is my brother."

"I know," Radhauser said. "And I admire him for recusing himself. I'm hoping Judge Hawkins will be fair to both the boy and to Carl Houseman."

Sean stiffened. "We did nothing wrong. What's fair is for us to get our son back."

Holly spoke up with the voice of reason. "We have to remember, sweetheart, Carl Houseman did nothing wrong either. From everything we've heard, he's taken good care of Ryan."

The Pattersons wanted to ride together so Radhauser opened the back door and waited while they climbed into his car and sat so close you'd think they were high school kids going steady.

"I'm excited and scared half to death all at the same time," Holly said. "And I'm trying to imagine how it must feel for Ryan."

Sean took her hand. "It's going to take time and patience, sweetheart. Something like this shakes the very foundation of who a person is and who he believed his parents to be. Imagine being ten years old and discovering everything about your life has been a lie, and you've had a family out there grieving and looking for you."

"What if he hates us?" Holly whispered.

Radhauser saw Sean tightened his grip on her hand.

"Don't expect too much, too fast," Radhauser warned, then closed the back door, got into the driver's seat and drove toward the Garfield house in Medford.

* * *

When Holden heard the sound of multiple footsteps on the

197

wooden stairs and then the hallway outside the bedroom door, he stopped doing his homework and stood, frozen in place, his arms hanging thick and useless at his sides. Was he about to meet his birth parents?

The door opened.

Detective Radhauser and a man and woman he knew must be the Pattersons stepped into the room.

Holly Patterson, the woman who was supposedly his mother, was small and pretty with dark eyes. Her hair was dark brown and fell to her shoulders. She looked a little bit like Audrey Hepburn in the old movie, *Breakfast at Tiffany's*, he'd watched a few weeks ago with his dad.

She moved closer, squatted in front of him and held his face in her hands for a moment, just staring at him. "You're so beautiful." She ran her fingertips down the side of his face from his hairline to his chin. Her eyes got all watery.

It felt creepy, and Holden wanted to shove her hands away but remembered what his dad had said about being polite and kind. "I'm Holden Carl Houseman," he said, using his best manners. "I'm very happy to meet you."

Holly took a step back and forced a smile. "I'm Holly Anne Patterson. I gave birth to you on January 15, 1991. And your dad and I named you Ryan Sean Patterson. I'm very happy to meet you, too. I know this must all be very hard for you to understand. How are you doing?"

"I'm okay, I guess." Holden glanced at Radhauser. He wanted to tell the Pattersons his name wasn't Ryan, and he celebrated his birthday on February 5th but held back. "Where's my dad?"

"I'm right here." Sean smiled, moving closer to Holden.

"I didn't mean…" He stopped himself. He reached out his right hand, determined to make Carl, his real dad, proud. "How do you do, sir?"

The smile on Sean's face wilted. He shook the boy's outstretched hand. "Well, aren't you a perfect little gentleman?"

When Holly tried to hug him, Holden couldn't help himself, he stiffened and backed away, reaching for Radhauser.

Radhauser dropped his hand on Holden's shoulder, pulled him in a little closer, and then glanced at Holly. "I'm sorry."

"Don't be," she said. "This isn't easy, but it's still the second-best day of our lives."

Holly moved aside, and Sean crouched in front of Holden. "The best day was the day you were born. I know this is very confusing for you. It's going to take some time for us to work through things, and get to know each other again. But I hope you'll give your mother…I hope you'll give Holly and me a chance to show you how much we love you. What good parents we'll be if you give us the opportunity."

Holden cringed and nudged a little closer to Radhauser.

Sean stood.

"I'm really sorry someone stole your baby, Mr. and Mrs. Patterson. From what everyone is telling me, it was my mom. But I didn't do anything wrong. I don't know you, and I just want to be with my dad." Holden's voice cracked. "Please, Mr. Patterson," he finally gulped out. "I want to live with my dad like I always have."

Again, Sean crouched in front of Holden. "You seem like a very nice boy. And I think your dad, I think Carl, did a good job raising you. But you're our son and we can't…we won't lose you to anyone, not ever again."

Holden kept backing up until he hit the bunk bed. He sat on the edge of the mattress and hung his head. He sucked as much air into his chest as it would hold, told himself he had to be nice to these people or he'd never get to see his dad again.

Radhauser gestured toward the door. "How about you give me a few moments alone with him? Would you mind?"

Holly sighed, took Sean's hand, and the two of them stepped out into the hallway, and closed the door behind them.

Radhauser sat on the bed next to Holden. "You can stay here for a few days if you want to give yourself a little time to adjust. Or you can go home with the Pattersons tonight—just to try it out and see how it feels."

"I want to go home to my own house. And sleep in my room."

"I'm sorry…I really am…but that probably won't happen. The law usually rules in favor of the birth parents."

"But that's not fair."

"I know," Radhauser said, dropping his arm over Holden's shoulder again. "Tonight, you have two choices. This is the way I see it. The Garfields are strangers to you. And the Pattersons are strangers. But the Pattersons are your parents, and they love you. They have a bedroom all ready, and they've waited a long time for you to be returned to them. I suspect the Garfields will take good care of you, feed you, and make sure you get to school and do your homework, but they won't love you the way the Pattersons do. I know what I'd choose if I were you. But it isn't my choice. It's yours."

"Don't you see? If the Pattersons love me, it makes it harder to ever go home again. I promised my dad I'd be kind and try to understand what they feel. I want to keep that promise. So, I'd like to stay here with the Garfields until I can go home and live with my real dad."

This was more than Radhauser had bargained for. He wanted Holden to give the Pattersons a chance, but he also understood how much the boy wanted things to remain the same. "In terms of the law, Sean Patterson is your real dad. The law probably won't give custody to Carl Houseman."

Holden blinked and pressed his elbows against his sides. "Would the law make me go live with them?"

"Probably not tonight."

Radhauser hated to leave that bedroom and face the Pattersons without Ryan beside him. Such a no-win situation for the kid and Radhauser felt sorry for him as well. What Ryan wanted, more than anything, was to go home to Carl Houseman and resume his life, as Holden, the way he'd always known it. And who could blame him?

It was a bit of a dirty trick, but Radhauser decided to give it a try. What difference did it make if the boy spent the night with the Garfields or with Sean and Holly? Either way, it wouldn't be what he wanted.

"One more thing before I leave," Radhauser said. "If you stay with the Garfields, you'll have to be enrolled in the Medford school district."

Ryan cocked his head and glared at Radhauser. "You mean I can't go to my school?"

"I'm afraid not."

"But I want to be with my friends. How about my soccer and baseball teams?"

"You might be able to remain on your teams if the Garfields are willing to drive you into Ashland to all your practices and games."

His dark eyes widened. "And if I go home with the Pattersons, does that mean I can still go to Sand Creek Elementary?"

"You'll have to ask them, but I'll bet they'd make that happen for you, no matter what it took. You'd get to stay on the same baseball and soccer teams."

Without another word, Ryan picked up the books on the desk, tucked them into his backpack, and slung it over his shoulder.

Radhauser grabbed the duffel bag Carl had packed, and together he and Ryan stepped out into the hallway to join the Pattersons.

CHAPTER TWENTY-FIVE

Thursday morning was bright and warm, the maples in full lime-colored leaf. The sky spread out in that deep blue of late Oregon spring, with two or three small clouds scudding across it. Crows called from the oak trees in the woods behind the manicured portion of the Housemans' backyard. If they weren't about to search for the remains of a three-month-old baby, the day would be picture perfect.

Radhauser stood beside Doctor Heron, just outside the search area police had roped off. They watched as the Oregon State Police car circled the driveway, headed around the back of the dwelling and came to a stop. Two handlers with beautiful German Shepherds on leashes got out. One of the dogs was tan and black, the other solid black. Their thick coats gleamed in the sunlight. These were cadaver dogs—trained to detect the scent of human decomposition rising from the soil.

The way these dogs could uncover bodies buried for decades always amazed Radhauser. But this morning, he both hoped his hunch was correct and prayed it wasn't for the sake of Carl Houseman, who had just appeared at his kitchen window. He looked pale and desperate—obviously unable to leave for work and unable to be fully present for the search. Radhauser couldn't blame the man. Faced with Houseman's circumstances, Radhauser might have remained inside as well.

A two-man forensic team in white coveralls waited on the sidelines, shovels, and rakes in hand.

Radhauser hurried over to the handlers, introduced himself, and gave them a brief account of what he was looking for and

202

what he thought were the circumstances surrounding the baby's death and burial. "I suspect the child was not embalmed. His mother probably dug the grave, so it's likely not very deep."

Thomas, the shorter of the two handlers, smiled. "It doesn't matter how deep she dug. These guys can easily smell things buried thirty feet below the surface."

The taller one, a man named Louie, introduced the dogs. "This is Seeker." The tan and black animal sat and lifted his paw, tail wagging.

Radhauser couldn't help but smile as he took the paw and shook it.

The other, Dante, went through the same introductory ritual.

In awe of these astonishing creatures, Radhauser watched them for a moment as they sat, still and quiet, on the ground beside their handlers. Lizzie had been begging him for a dog. Maybe it was time he talked with Gracie and brought a German Shepherd puppy home.

After receiving Radhauser's briefing, the handlers let the dogs loose. Both animals stood still, sniffing the air around them. And then ran in circles for a few moments, pushing their noses into the areas around the bases of trees and landscape rocks.

Their handlers followed, but kept some distance, giving them their needed space. Eventually, Dante stopped in a lush garden of spring flowers—orange and yellow marigolds, purple cone flowers, wave petunias, shasta daisies and a ground cover of tiny yellow flowers Radhauser couldn't identify. A small statue of a smiling Buddha sat in the center of the flowerbed.

Dante sniffed the ground, circled the Buddha and sniffed again. Within a minute, Seeker joined in. Almost in unison, the dogs sat, then let out a crisp, single bark.

The white-clad forensic guys ran over with their shovels and rakes, the dog handlers right behind them.

The handlers re-attached the leashes to their harnesses, moved away from the flowerbed and waited, their dogs sitting quietly beside them. One of the handlers pulled two treats from his jacket pocket and rewarded them for a job well done.

Moments ticked by like a breath inhaled and not let out. The only sound that could be heard was the shovel as it plunged through the ground, releasing its moist, earthen smell. Silence, followed by the scraping sound of the rake as it sifted.

And then, like a clap of thunder, the shovel hit something solid. A strike of metal hitting metal.

One of the forensic guys held up his dirt-caked fist and shouted, "We've found something. Over here."

It was only a matter of minutes before the men raised a metal trunk, about thirty inches long and fifteen inches wide, from the hole they'd dug in the ground. Though some of the paint had worn off, the trunk had once been blue and painted with stuffed bunnies, lambs and teddy bears romping in a field of wildflowers beneath a rainbow-filled sky.

Radhauser closed his eyes. How had this baby died? It was hard for him to believe, given the way Holden thought about his parents, that Candace had ever deliberately hurt the baby. Though they might never be sure, in all likelihood, the child had died of natural causes. He tried to imagine what it had been like for Candace Houseman to face the death of their son alone. Had she shopped for a container to house their son in his final resting place? Or could it have been a toy chest she'd purchased for her living child? How does anyone say goodbye to their three-month-old baby? She'd probably shared the sad news of Holden's death with no one. In spite of what she'd later done, Radhauser felt sympathy for Candace.

Heron grabbed his shoulder and shook him out of his reverie. "What's the matter with you? Have you gone to sleep? Come on, our work has just begun."

They hurried over to the flowerbed where Heron knelt and used a brush to carefully clean dirt and debris from the trunk, then slowly opened the lid.

A tiny skeleton lay on top of a very stained, but still blue, flannel blanket.

The air was tinged with the faint smell of decomposition, and it felt heavy and hard to breathe. Radhauser closed his eyes for an instant, opened them again, and swallowed hard.

Once he'd confirmed it was human remains, Heron closed the lid, then carried the trunk to his van as carefully as if he were carrying a precious antique. "I'll take him over to the lab and see what I can discover. Get me a DNA sample from Carl Houseman, and I'll send both off for comparison. But unless there are broken or crushed bones, I probably won't be able to give you a definitive cause of death. I should have something by this afternoon."

Radhauser waited until everyone had left and the crows called from the oak trees again before he marched up to the back door and knocked.

When he found it unlocked, he opened it and stepped inside. "Mr. Houseman. It's Detective Radhauser." No matter how much it hurt, Houseman needed to know what they'd found—though Radhauser suspected the man had seen the small trunk being lifted from the ground and knew exactly what it held.

Houseman sat at the kitchen table, his head in his hands. Half-moons of perspiration stained the armpits of his dress shirt. His blond hair spilled out between his fingers, and his elbows rested on the tabletop. There was a half-filled coffee cup beside his right elbow and an empty bourbon bottle and small glass in front of him, along with the folder housing Holden's records. He made no effort to respond.

Radhauser cleared his throat. "Mr. Houseman."

Carl Houseman looked up slowly, his eyes red and watery. He wore the same clothes he'd worn when they visited Holden at the Garfields' last night. The front of his blue shirt was wrinkled. Houseman stared at Radhauser like he was trying to place him from somewhere in the distant past. Someone he once knew but could no longer bring into focus. "I sent that box home from Ku...Kuwait. Candy claimed it ne...ne...never got here." He slurred his words.

The man was drunk. And it appeared he'd been up all night.

"I need to take DNA for comparison with the remains we found." Radhauser retrieved a kit from his backpack and swabbed the inside of Houseman's cheek, then sealed the container. He helped the drunk man to his feet, then grabbed his elbow as he staggered toward the hallway. "Let's get you into bed." Radhauser wasn't about to judge. He'd had his own love affair with scotch after losing his first wife and son.

In truth, he felt a lot of sympathy for Houseman. If ever a man had a good reason to get drunk, it was this one. Radhauser walked him down the hallway. "I'll call your office and tell them you won't be in today."

Houseman stopped in front of Holden's bedroom and stared into the pale morning light seeping through the windows as if memorizing what was inside. A place filled with *The Hardy Boys* books, Legos and the unmistakable pine sap and sweaty sneakers smell of the boy who no longer inhabited it. Without a word, he lowered his head and closed the door.

In the master bedroom, Houseman collapsed onto the bed.

Radhauser straightened the man's legs, slipped off his shoes and covered him with a patchwork quilt he'd found folded on the cedar chest at the foot of the bed.

"My wife buried our son in the back yard." He shut his eyes and didn't open them again.

Radhauser watched the steady rise and fall of Houseman's chest for a moment, then lumbered into the kitchen, his legs as heavy as boulders, and called Aviator Helicopter Service.

* * *

Just as he'd hoped, Franklin Bradshaw had already left for the courthouse when Radhauser knocked on the front door, search warrant in hand. He'd drop off Houseman's DNA after he retrieved the box from the crawl space in Tommy Bradshaw's closet.

Jung-Su smiled and seemed relieved to see him. "Detective Radhauser. I see police cars and dogs at Housemans'. What is happen? Holden, he is okay? He no come after school yesterday."

When he picked up the search warrant this morning at the station, he'd found a note from McBride. The press was already calling about the Patterson kidnapping case. It never ceased to amaze him how quickly reporters got a hold of the stories he most wanted to protect. There would surely be something on the news and in the local papers by tonight.

"May I come inside?"

"Of course." She stepped aside to let him pass.

He showed her the warrant. "I've come for a box of Blair's memorabilia I discovered in the crawl space above Tommy's closet. I'm hoping there might be something in her past that could lead me to her killer."

She cocked her head and gave him a confused look. "Miss Blair. She hide box up there?"

"I think she did."

"Maybe she no want you to see inside."

"That may have been true when she was alive. But I think she'd want me to do everything in my power to bring her killer to justice."

Jung-Su nodded. "Yes, you are right. But I worried. I see police cars in Houseman driveway. Holden, he is okay, no?"

Radhauser felt a headache coming on and feared it might be caffeine withdrawal since he'd left his ranch early without his morning coffee. "You wouldn't happen to have a cup of coffee, would you?"

She smiled and led him into the kitchen. After pouring his coffee, she sat with him at the table, and he told her what he knew would be on the news that evening.

"Oh, poor Holden. He love Carl very much."

"I know," Radhauser said. "It's going to be a very difficult transition for both of them." And then it occurred to him that Jung-Su might have known Candace Houseman. "Did you know Carl's wife?"

"Not so well. She quiet and stay to herself. One day in summer, I see her walking baby in stroller when I walk Tommy. We talk. I invite her and Holden come over for what you call it. Play date."

"Did she seem off? Like someone who would steal another woman's baby?"

"She very protective of Holden. Love him very much, and no want him out of her sight. I offer babysit, but she no ask me. But I no think she steal baby." Jung-Su shook her head like she couldn't imagine anyone doing something so horrendous.

After finishing his coffee, Radhauser excused himself, took the ladder off its hook in the garage and carried it up to Tommy's room to retrieve the box.

Once he'd closed up the crawl space, he carried the box into the sitting area in the Bradshaws' bedroom, took out his penknife and sliced through the tape, then placed the box on the table in front of the loveseat. It held the kind of things a high school girl might paste into a scrapbook. A red, varsity school letter for being the star of the drama club at Wildwood High School, home of the Cougars, was nestled toward the bottom of the box. Playbills from a half-dozen or so junior high, one high school, and three little theater productions.

One by one, he opened them and checked the cast. Meadow Finney in the role of Scout Finch in *To Kill A Mockingbird*. Meadow Finney cast as Blanche in *A Street Car Named Desire*, in the role of Juliet in *Romeo and Juliet*.

Meadow Finney would have graduated about eighteen years ago. He wondered if anyone still working at the high school might remember her.

Radhauser carefully sorted through the box, stacking the playbills and report cards. Photographs of a kitten and some class photos from Wildwood Elementary and Junior High Schools. So, Meadow Finney was a sentimental girl—the kind who grew into a woman who protected and preserved something of a past others might have wanted to forget. He thought again about what Franklin Bradshaw had said about his wife. Blair loved her secrets.

He picked up a tattered and well-read book of W.H. Auden's poetry and skimmed through the poems. Many of the pages were turned down and someone, probably Meadow, had underlined words and passages, made notes in the margins. Hoping to find a name or inscription, he turned to the front pages.

For Meadow. May you find hope and inspiration in these words.

It was dated February 2, 1980 and signed *Mr. Townsend.*

Was he one of her teachers? A neighbor who'd taken an interest? He gathered up everything and put it back in the box, wrote out an inventory of what he'd taken and left a copy on the dining room table for Bradshaw.

None of the contents in the box seemed all that significant. Just memorabilia kept by a teenaged girl. Had he reached the end of the road where not one of his leads had led to her murderer? The place a detective arrived when he no longer believed that something might intervene on his behalf—some piece of luck or a blaze of intuition that would keep this case from becoming yet another unsolved murder investigation? Radhauser couldn't let that happen. Blair Bradshaw deserved justice. And somehow, he'd find a way.

As he drove toward the police station, he thought about the final name in Tommy Bradshaw's memorial book. Auden F. Bradshaw. Was it the signature of the murderer? But if so, why couldn't they find him through motor vehicle records? Or might Blair have written that name in the book before she was murdered? But why would she have disguised her handwriting?

The F could stand for Finney, her maiden name. The poet, Auden, had obviously meant something to the young Meadow. Was it the name she'd wanted for Tommy? Or was it a mere coincidence?

Maybe.

But Winston Radhauser wasn't the kind of detective who believed in coincidences.

CHAPTER TWENTY-SIX

For Holden Houseman, the minutes bled into each other and then into hours, eventually becoming a whole night. He watched the unfamiliar trees outside the bedroom window cast strange shadows on the walls. When the sun finally began to rise, it took him a moment to remember where he was and everything that had happened. The bed was warm and comfortable with sheets that smelled like sunshine. Beams of morning light streamed through the window, painted the white walls a quiet yellow, and landed in soft squares on the hardwood floor. But he felt empty. And afraid of everything that wasn't familiar. He wanted to go home to Carl Houseman and the only life he remembered.

He sat on the edge of the mattress for a moment, imagining his dad in their kitchen, pouring orange juice into glasses and setting cereal boxes, cornflakes for himself, Rice Crispies for Holden, and a carton of 2% milk on the kitchen table. When his bottom lip started to tremble, he touched it with the back of his hand to make it go still. Except for the fact he was wearing his own pajamas, everything around him was unfamiliar and strange.

As the smell of bacon wafted into the room, he stood and headed for the attached bathroom where he brushed his teeth, combed his hair and put on a pair of blue slacks and a white polo shirt—the basic school uniform for Sand Creek Elementary. It was one of two outfits he'd found in the duffel bag his dad had brought to the foster home last night. He held the bag to his nose for a moment. The handle smelled like the cedar-scented aftershave his dad always wore. Holden felt his dad's absence deep in his belly.

After making his bed, he packed his backpack for school with his textbooks and homework assignments, then sat on the desk chair, wondering what to do next. Should he appear in the kitchen, smile, and ask Holly, "What's for breakfast, Mom?" She'd love that, but he couldn't make himself do it. He wondered what his dad was doing now. Had he already left for work? Or was he having his second cup of coffee at their kitchen table? Did he think about his son? Would he be able to find a way to bring Holden back home?

A phone rang, but no one picked it up. Holden counted the rings. Ten and then the phone grew quiet. In the stillness left behind, the last ring hung, vibrating, in the air around him. He shuddered.

Less than a minute later, someone tapped on the bedroom door. "Breakfast is almost ready." Holly opened the door and gave him a heartbreaking smile. She had on a pale blue robe with a nightgown underneath and a pair of Oregon Ducks slippers.

He almost smiled, being a Ducks fan himself.

"Look at you. All ready for school. I hope you're hungry."

They were interrupted by the sound of voices. Holly hurried over to the window that looked out on the front yard, Holden a few steps behind her.

Vans from the local television and radio stations were parked along the curb. A clump of reporters, microphones in their hands, stood on the sidewalk leading up to the house.

Across the street, neighbors lingered on their porches in their robes, slippers, and pajamas—all their faces turned toward the Patterson house.

"It's the television and newspaper reporters," Holly said. "They've been calling here all morning."

So that's why no one answered the phone. "What do they want?"

She shook her head sadly. "They want our story. When you disappeared ten years ago, it was big news in Ashland. The newspaper and television reporters hounded us for months. And then for a couple years afterward every May 4th they'd show up in our driveway. That's the day you went missing."

"Do you think I could go home and see my…I mean go back to Sand Creek Road after school today?"

She tugged on a piece of her hair. "This is your home now, Ryan."

He swallowed. "I'm sorry. But my name is Holden."

Holly's gaze fixed on him like two headlight beams. She opened her mouth. Her chin and bottom lip quivered. "Okay," she finally said. "I know having a new name isn't easy, and I have an idea. I'm going to talk to your father…to Sean… about getting your name legally changed to Holden. It's a lovely name. It suits you. How does Holden Ryan Patterson sound?"

Holden felt the tears rising. He didn't expect her to be so kind. But his name was Holden Carl Houseman. It had been his name for the last ten years. Why did he have to change it now?

He considered what his dad said about being nice and cooperative with the Pattersons and that maybe if he did that, they'd allow him and his dad to spend time together. Keeping the name Holden was a small victory. "Thank you. All my friends at school and the teachers call me Holden."

An hour later, after a breakfast where Sean and Holly asked him a million questions, Sean went outside to talk to the reporters before going to work, and Holly dressed to take Holden to school.

They locked the car doors while still in the garage and backed out slowly through the wall of reporters who huddled, waiting for a glimpse of him. One man, wearing a backward baseball cap, stuck his camera up to the passenger window and snapped photographs in rapid succession. Holden clamped his eyes shut and put his hands over his face. "Why won't they leave us alone?"

"Your dad…Sean…is talking to them. He'll explain what's going on. Hopefully, that will satisfy them, and they'll find someone else to harass."

Holly dropped him off in the parking lot in front of his school. "I'll be right here to pick you up at 3:15, okay?"

He nodded, but Holden had no intention of going home with Holly or Sean Patterson—not ever again.

* * *

Amos Townsend, an English literature teacher at Wildwood High School, was a small man with very fine features, a soft voice and one of those tiny but open faces that induce trust. He was no more than five-feet, five inches tall and extremely thin. Wire-rimmed glasses covered his wide-set blue eyes, and his hair was more gray than brown, with a circular bald spot in the back. He wore belted khaki dockers and a pale blue shirt tucked in and open at the collar. Radhauser guessed him to be about sixty years old—nearing retirement after teaching at Wildwood for thirty-five years.

The assistant principal agreed to take his class while Townsend talked to Radhauser. They sat across a round table in the teacher's lounge—the place where many of the faculty members ate lunch. The room smelled like chocolate, orange peels, and too-ripe bananas.

After taking off his Stetson, Radhauser set it crown side down on the tabletop.

Townsend crossed his legs and removed his glasses before wiping them clean with a tissue he'd taken from the box on the table. "What can I do for you, Detective?" He put his glasses back on. There was a gentle kindness in his smile.

Radhauser pulled the W.H. Auden book from his backpack and set it on the table.

"Oh," Townsend said. "Nothing makes my heart sing like a well-worn poetry book. So, you're an Auden fan. That makes two of us. He's one of the all-time greats."

"I can't truthfully say I've read him, but this book was obviously very important to one of your former students." Radhauser opened the book to the inscription.

Townsend stared at his own words for a moment. His face paled as if he were staring at a ghost. "Meadow Finney. I haven't thought about her for years. She isn't in any trouble, is she?"

"Do you make a habit of buying gifts for your students?"

The kindness in his smile disappeared. "Only the pretty female ones. I know where you're going with this, Detective, and you're way off base," he said righteous indignation in his voice.

"I didn't mean any offense."

Townsend brought the fingers of his two hands together and stared at them. "I've never had an inappropriate relationship with a student. And I resent your implication. Meadow Finney was a special kid. I've often wondered what became of her." He shook his head. "So much promise in that girl."

"Meadow grew up, changed her name to Blair, married an attorney, and became a noted Shakespearean actress in Ashland."

His face lit up like a man who'd just won the lottery. "Quite a transformation. But, good for her. I always knew she had it in her." He paused and stared at his hands for a moment. "Blair Bradshaw. I heard about her on the news. I've seen her act in Ashland many times, but had no idea she was the grown-up Meadow Finney."

"I'm afraid I have some bad news," Radhauser told Townsend about Blair being found lying among the flowers in her son's memorial.

The loss seemed to drain something out of Townsend, and his voice grew flat. "I read about her death in the paper, but had no idea…Poor Meadow. She always wanted to be an actress. At least it sounds like she had some happiness in her life."

"When was the last time you saw her?"

"Aside from the Shakespeare Theater when I didn't know it was Meadow I was watching, I'd say ninth grade. One day she just stopped coming to school."

"Do you have any idea why she quit?"

"We get a lot of dropouts here. Drugs and teen pregnancies are pretty common. Wildwood and its surroundings have a large counter-culture population, many of whom don't believe in formal education. But Meadow was different. I really thought she'd get a scholarship to college."

"Did you call the police? Did you look for her?"

"Like I said, dropping out of high school is a common occurrence here. But this was Meadow. I was, quite frankly, shocked."

"But did you look for her?"

He crossed his arms over his chest and stared at Radhauser.

"Are you going to accuse me of caring too much if I tell you I drove out to her house, but her mother said she had no idea where she'd gone? Actually, she told me as far as she was concerned, it was good riddance. She had some dirty-looking, tattooed guy with a Harley living with her. He told me to mind my own business, get the hell out, and not to come back."

"Do you know if Meadow had a boyfriend back then?"

"I never saw her with a boy. So, if she did, I'm pretty sure he didn't go to school here."

Radhauser thought about the things that could make a fifteen-year-old girl want to leave home and disappear. "Do you think it's possible she could have been pregnant?"

He glared at Radhauser. "Not by me, if that's what you're getting at."

Radhauser scrubbed his hand over his face. "Your involvement with Meadow in any inappropriate way was the furthest thing from my mind. Look, somehow, we got off on the wrong foot. I'm merely trying to find out who killed your former student and why."

"Maybe I'm overly sensitive. I've been teaching at this school all my adult life, and no one has ever accused me of behaving inappropriately with one of my female students before."

"I'm sorry if my questions felt like an accusation. I didn't intend it that way," Radhauser said.

"It's possible she dropped out because she was pregnant, I guess. But I never saw any signs of it." Townsend's voice had deepened, his gaze soft now.

"Do you often give students books?"

"No. And I'm sure it would be frowned upon by some of my colleagues, but Meadow was a special case. She was smart and interested. The class had read Auden's poem, *The Age of Anxiety*, and she understood it on a level that was amazing for a kid her age and from her background. Poetry has the power to change young lives. God knows hers needed changing. I don't know if you've talked to her mother, but—"

"I have," Radhauser said. "She met me at my car with a shotgun in one hand and a dead possum in the other."

Townsend laughed, and a little bit of the tension between them eased.

"How about a best friend? Someone who might have taken her in or at least knows where she went."

"Nora Crestwell."

"Did Nora graduate?"

"She did. And went on to the University of Oregon in Eugene. From what I understand, she taught for a few years at the elementary school here before she became a stay-at-home mom."

"Do you have any idea where I can find her?"

"Check with the alumni director. I believe she came to the class reunion a couple years ago. Now, if you don't have anything else to ask, insinuate, or accuse me of, I'd like to get back to my class." Townsend smiled as if to let Radhauser know he was kidding, then stood.

"Again, Mr. Townsend, I didn't mean any offense. I'm just doing my job."

Townsend nodded. "If anyone knows where Meadow went, it would be Nora. Those two were inseparable back then."

"I really do appreciate your help, Mr. Townsend."

After hurrying down the hallway to the main office, Radhauser asked if he could talk with the alumni director. Mr. Haldeman was two doors down on the right. Radhauser tapped on the door frame. "Come on in," Haldeman said.

He questioned Haldeman about Meadow and her best friend, Nora Crestwell. A moment later, the detective left with a name and address.

The former student was now Nora Mason, and she lived in Wildwood, just a few blocks from the school.

CHAPTER TWENTY-SEVEN

The Mason house was a recently painted and well-kept, double-wide trailer set on a wooded piece of land with no neighbors in sight on either side.

Radhauser's tires crunched their way up the gravel drive. He parked, then hurried up a walkway made from sixteen-inch square paving stones to a wooden deck. The air smelled like pine sap and cedar chips from the recently mulched beds and flower boxes of hot pink and white wave petunias and cone flowers attached to the deck railing.

When he arrived on the deck, a dark-haired woman was already standing in the doorway. If she was Nora, life hadn't been as kind to her as it had been to Blair Bradshaw. This woman looked much older than thirty-five. She wore a pair of sweatpants and a vintage, tie-dyed T-shirt with a picture of Jerry Garcia and the words *Grateful Dead* on the front. Her feet were bare.

"Are you Nora Mason, formerly Nora Crestwell?"

"I am." She stared at him for a long moment. "And who might you be?"

Radhauser tipped his Stetson and introduced himself, then showed Nora his badge.

She shot him a suspicious look.

"Don't worry," he said. "You're not in any trouble. I'm sorry to say your old friend, Meadow Finney, was murdered last week. Every one of my leads has turned into nothing. I'm hoping you might help me piece together some things about her early life. With any luck, it might lead me to a viable suspect."

She moved aside so he could enter. "I don't know how much

help I can be, Detective Radhauser. I haven't seen Meadow in years. But we were good friends back in the day."

He took off his cowboy hat as she led him into the living room. The trailer was clean and very neat. A basket of toys, looking as if they belonged to a preschool-aged child, was set in the corner, along with a Fisher Price garage and barnyard. A couple of toys Radhauser knew well.

She motioned toward two chairs set in front of the window with a table between them.

Radhauser took one, then placed his cowboy hat in his lap.

Nora sat in the other.

"I talked to Mr. Townsend over at the high school. He suggested you might be able to help me."

She squealed. "Oh my God, Mr. Townsend. Is he still teaching at Wildwood High?"

"Thirty-five years."

"He was a great teacher. My favorite, and Meadow's too. He was the kind of teacher I wanted to be. The kind who changed lives, if you know what I mean. I guess you could say he's the reason I became a teacher. And he encouraged both Meadow and me to get an education. I probably would never have gone to college, or taught, if it weren't for him. But Meadow didn't have much support at home, that's for sure."

The entire trailer was filled with the rich, brown-sugary smell of something in the oven—a pie or maybe some kind of cake. "Whatever you're baking smells delicious."

"Pineapple upside down cake. It's my husband's favorite. I have to bake while the monsters are taking their naps." She lifted her hands, palm sides up, in a helpless gesture. "Twin, three-year-old boys."

"I have a six-year-old girl and a seventeen-month-old boy." Sensing she was nervous, he tried to put her at ease. "So, I know you've got your hands full."

"That's putting it mildly."

"When was the last time you spoke with Meadow?"

"Ninth grade. We were fifteen and thought we'd be best friends forever. One day, she just didn't show up at school. When I went over to her house, her mother told me she was gone, and she wasn't coming back. I asked where she went, but Sunny was never much for explanations. I saw Meadow again, a couple years ago, when I took my mother to the Shakespeare Theater for her birthday. Imagine how shocked I was to see her. But she was no longer Meadow. She was someone different, who called herself Blair Bradshaw. I did some research afterward and found out she was married to some hot-shot lawyer. I guess Meadow did okay for herself after all."

"Did you talk to her after the play?"

"No. It was late, and my mother was tired and wanted to go home. And…I don't know…it felt really weird to know she'd been around all those years and never got in touch."

"Can you think of anyone who might want to hurt her? Any enemies? Someone who might have carried a grudge?"

"She hated her mother's loser boyfriend. Some biker dude named Spider. But, far as I know, he's not been around for years."

"Do you have any idea why she hated him?"

"I don't like to talk behind someone's back even if they're not my friend anymore."

"Your former friend is dead. You must have loved her once. Don't you want me to get justice for her?"

She bit her bottom lip. "Meadow didn't want anyone to know. She made me promise I'd never tell a single soul. Not ever."

"I don't think anything you say to me would bother her now, Nora."

"It's pretty personal. It wasn't her fault. But she was embarrassed and ashamed."

"Like I said, I don't think Meadow would be worried about that now."

A flush rose on her neck and cheeks. "A promise is a promise."

"It was a brutal murder, and I just want to bring whoever did it to justice." He told her about the femoral arteries and how she'd been placed in front of the memorial her son's classmates had made for him. "There were other things about the murder that seemed very personal. Like revenge. Please. If you know anything…"

She stared at him for what seemed like a long time. "Poor Meadow. I read about what happened to her son. I don't think I could go on living if anything happened to one of my boys."

He told Nora that Meadow's husband had thought it was a suicide. "But the medical examiner believed otherwise. And we found no weapon near her body."

"Okay. Maybe you're right. Maybe Meadow would want you to know the truth. Spider was sneaking into her bedroom at night after Sunny was asleep. Making her do things to him."

"Do you think that's why she left?"

"I'm not sure. I only know that she planned to tell her mother the night before. But then she disappeared, and I never knew if she did tell Sunny. Or how her mother reacted." She fiddled with the edge of her T-shirt and didn't make eye contact. Was she telling the truth?

"Did Meadow have a boyfriend? Anyone she might have run away with?"

She looked at him when she answered. "No. She didn't get involved with any boys. Meadow was the most determined person I've ever known. She had goals—a big plan for her life. She wasn't going to let anything get in the way. She wanted to get out of Wildwood. Had hopes of going to acting school in New York or Hollywood. Mr. Townsend thought she could get a scholarship. She was that talented. Truthfully, I wasn't all that surprised when I discovered she'd changed her name and had a job with the Shakespeare Theater."

"Why didn't you ever try to find her?"

She shook her head. "You know how it is when you go through something kind of terrible together. When it's over, it's like you want to pretend it never happened and that person who went through it with you is just a reminder of something you'd rather forget. Meadow knew where I was. When she didn't contact me again, I figured she'd headed for New York or Hollywood and didn't want to be found."

"What did you go through together that was so awful?"

"You know, just that stuff with Spider and her mother not believing…" She clamped her mouth shut, realizing she'd just contradicted herself.

Radhauser was convinced she was hiding something.

A moment later, she stood and showed him to the door. "I've got to get that cake out of the oven before the twins wake up. I hope you find whoever killed her, Detective Radhauser. She was a good person and didn't deserve to die like that."

He gave her his card. "Call me if you remember anything else. Memory can be like a floodgate, once you open it. Sometimes it's hard to close. I think you know more than you're saying. I hope you'll decide to tell me the whole truth. Your friend deserves justice."

After Radhauser stepped onto the deck, Nora Mason slammed the door.

* * *

Holden hunkered inside the school lobby, near the front door, watching the reporters with their cameras and microphones gather in the parking lot. Sand Creek Elementary School was a sprawling, modern structure, made from brick, stone and lots of glass. It sat on a hill and had a lush, green lawn that stretched down the hillside to the parking lot. A wide concrete walkway, trimmed on both sides with bricks, led to the front entrance which was landscaped with evergreen and flowering bushes. With the backdrop of the Siskiyou Mountains behind it, his school was as beautiful as a postcard picture.

The reporters must be waiting for Holly, hoping for a chance to question her or maybe even him. He didn't want to talk to them. What could he say? Except for Tommy dying, none of this was his fault. Was God punishing him because of what happened to his best friend? More than anything, Holden wanted to board his old bus, go home and wait for his dad. He wanted a regular night where Jung-Su fixed him a snack, and he did his homework before dinner. Maybe a game of chess with his dad and a cup of hot chocolate before bed.

He dawdled at the front door, letting the surge of bodies swarm around him, making him invisible. When he spotted Holly's car, parked near the bottom of the walkway, and the reporters hovered around it, he raced across the wide yard toward the area where the school buses parked. He tried to hide himself behind Larson Pugh and John Goldman, a couple of hefty sixth graders already in the line to get on the bus. Holden took the steps two at a time and hurried into a seat behind the driver without anyone noticing.

As he dropped his backpack into the seat beside him, hoping to avoid anyone sitting there, he couldn't help but think about Tommy. How the two of them had always sat in the back and stretched their mouths and eyes into grotesque masks at the drivers in cars behind the bus—trying to make them laugh. Tommy was friendlier than Holden and said hello and slapped hands with everyone as they made their way to the back seats.

Now, Holden sat alone and didn't talk to anyone. As the bus pulled out of the parking lot, he watched Holly get out of her car, push her way past the reporters, and head up the walkway toward the entrance. He ducked down into the seat so she wouldn't spot him.

He was going home to his house on Sand Creek Road.

Home. It was a word that glowed inside him like a secret gem.

He got off at his usual spot, but instead of going to Tommy's house, he headed to his own to wait for his dad. It was 3:30. Two more hours and his dad would be home. Maybe they'd order a pizza and eat it in front of the television, watching one of the old movies his dad and mom once watched together. Tonight, he'd sleep in his own bed. They'd read the next chapter of *Tom Sawyer.*

When he walked around to the back of his house, his mother's special flowerbed had been dug up. Many of the flowers he and his dad had planted were uprooted and dying in the sun. The smiling Buddha laid on its side with mounds of dark earth beside him. Holden hurried into the garden and tried to straighten the Buddha. Loose dirt seeped into his shoes. He strained to lift the statue, but he wasn't strong enough and finally gave up. What had happened here?

Just like they did every spring, Holden and his dad spent a whole weekend planting all the flowers his mother loved. Something was very wrong. Why would anyone destroy his mom's garden?

He used his key to open the back door. The kitchen was dark and quiet, and it smelled funny—kind of bitter and sour like maybe his dad forgot to empty the garbage can. The phone rang. Holden jumped. It was probably Holly looking for him. He didn't answer. He counted the rings. Twelve before it finally stopped and the kitchen grew quiet again.

An empty bottle of Jack Daniel's bourbon sat on the table, alongside a glass with a ring of something brown at the bottom and a coffee cup. Had his dad been drinking? He hardly ever drank. Something wasn't right. The house was quiet, but it was a different kind of quiet. The kind that has a ticking heartbeat. He tiptoed down the hallway. Holden's bedroom door was shut. Had his dad closed it because it was too hard for him to look inside?

Holden kept walking until he reached his dad's bedroom, then stood in the doorway. The curtains were drawn, and the room was darker than usual at this time of day. His dad lay on top of the bedspread, covered in the patchwork quilt Holden's mother had made—the one he always wanted when he was sick. It was one of the few memories he had of his mother. Whenever he caught a cold or the flu and had to stay home in bed, his mom had covered him with it and told him a quilt was a blanket of love. Holden believed she was right, and that quilt would make him get better faster.

His dad's bedroom smelled funny like he might have thrown up. And his shoes were placed side by side on the floor next to the bed. The phone on his bedside table was unplugged, the wire dangling over the lampshade. What was going on?

Holden stood watching his father for a long time until his back ached a little, and his legs began to throb. Finally, he tiptoed over to the bed. "Dad," he whispered. "Are you okay?"

It took a second, but his father opened one eye and then the other. He smiled, reached up slowly, and patted Holden's cheek.

And then something flashed in his dad's eyes, and he struggled to sit up. He still wore the suit and pale blue shirt he'd worn when he brought the duffel bag to the foster home last night.

When his dad dropped back against the pillow, Holden, with tears heating the space behind his eyes, put his hand on his father's forehead. "Are you sick, Dad?"

His father's face was all blotchy and stubbled with prickly hairs. He hadn't shaved that morning. His dad always shaved before going to work. And he always smelled good, like cedar trees. "What are you doing here? You're supposed to be at the Pattersons'."

"I took the school bus. I wanted to come home."

There were red lines of worry in his father's blue eyes. "But the Pattersons' house is your home now."

"No, it isn't. I want to stay with you. This is my home. It's always gonna be my home." Holden watched his father's face, trying to see if the words he'd said could change anything—if they could recast events that had already taken place. If they could erase the awful things that happened during the last two days and bring Holden home again.

"Oh, son." He threw his legs over the side of the bed. "I need to take a shower. Then I'm going to take you back to the Pattersons'."

"No. I'm not going back. I hate it there. I never want to go back."

"Come on, son. You promised you'd try. You haven't given it a fair chance."

"I stayed there all night last night."

"That's not much of a chance. It takes time to get to know people. But we can talk about that after I shower. Right now, let's get you a snack." He placed a hand on Holden's cheek.

Holden leaned into it. And it felt like his dad was trying to tell him something without saying any words. Something about what connected them to each other—something Holden wanted to hear. "I love you, Dad."

His dad winced as if something was hurting him. "You must be starving." His father lumbered down the hallway, his footsteps so much heavier than they used to be. In the kitchen, he tossed the empty bourbon bottle into the recycling bin, wiped off the table, then poured Holden a glass of milk. "We've still got some chocolate chip cookies from the bakery. How does that sound?"

"Cookies would be great." He told his dad about the destroyed flower garden. "Somebody knocked over the laughing Buddha."

"I know." He set a plate of cookies in front of Holden. "The police brought special dogs out this morning to search for human remains."

Holden gulped and stared at the kitchen floor. "Human remains? You mean like a dead person in Mom's garden?"

His dad knelt in front of him. "This is going to be kind of hard to hear, buddy. But you and I—we tell each other the truth, right?"

Holden nodded, scared all the way to his toes.

"The police dogs found the skeleton of a little baby in a trunk in your mother's…in Candy's…garden. I didn't know what she'd done, but now I understand why that flowerbed was always so important to her. Remember how upset she got when there were any weeds in it?"

Holden remembered. "One time, she cried because of the crabgrass."

"The police think she buried our baby boy after he died. She never told anyone. She never got any help. They think that's why she kidnapped you. She couldn't…" He stopped and started again. "But don't you worry. I'm going to replant the garden and make it good as new again."

Holden felt a pang of sadness with the words *our baby boy*. He was their baby, not some old bones in a trunk. "I can help you. After your shower, we can go to the plant store and buy more flowers. We can get it all fixed up before dark if we hurry."

"We'll see." He didn't meet Holden's gaze. "Why don't you finish your snack, then start your homework while I get cleaned up." Without another word, he headed down the hallway to shower.

Holden choked down the cookies, drank his milk, rinsed out the glass and put it in the dishwasher, then wiped the cookie crumbs from the tabletop. He wanted to do everything right.

Wanted to make his dad proud.

Wanted to stay here in this house on Sand Creek Road forever.

CHAPTER TWENTY-EIGHT

Radhauser was on his way to pay a second visit to Sunflower Finney when his cell phone rang. It was Holly Patterson.

"Ryan's disappeared again. I went to pick him up from school, and he was gone. I think Carl Houseman may have taken him. I called their house. The phone rang and rang, but no one answered. What if they boarded a plane and he took him out of the country? To Mexico or something? Please, Detective Radhauser, you have to help me. We can't lose our son again."

"Did you check with his teacher? Was he in class today?"

"Yes."

The last time Radhauser had seen Houseman, he was in no shape to take himself out of the house, let alone a boy out of the country. "Calm down, Holly. I'm on my way."

Dark was descending when he arrived at the Patterson house. The trees were shrouded in night, thin clouds kissed at the edges of the nearly full moon, the songs of crickets and tree frogs rang out in the distance.

Holly and Sean met him at the door. "Do you have any news?"

"I was on my way to Wildwood when you called. But I alerted the airport and the bus station to be on the lookout for him. I'm sure I'd have heard something by now if they tried to board a plane or bus. Let's sit down, and you can tell me exactly what happened."

The doorbell rang.

All three of them leaped up and went to the door to answer.

Holden and Carl Houseman stood in the warm golden glow of the porch light. Houseman had his hand on Holden's head, gently nudging him forward.

The boy turned toward Houseman, who nodded and urged him to step inside.

Radhauser opened the door. He could smell milk and chocolate on Holden's breath.

Houseman appeared drawn and exhausted, but at least he was cleaned up and sober now. "I'm so sorry, Mr. and Mrs. Patterson. But Holden took the bus back to our house." His glance shifted to Radhauser. "I was feeling a bit under the weather today and stayed home from work. I ignored the phone. I'm sorry. I brought him back as soon as I could get out of bed, shower, and shave."

"Thank you," Holly said, then crouched so she was eye level with Holden. "I know this is hard and confusing for you. But you can't run away and scare us like this again. I want you to go to your room and do your homework while we talk to Carl."

"I already did my homework at my house while Dad was in the shower. Don't you get it?" A single tear slipped from his right eye and slid down his cheek. He made no effort to wipe it away. "I don't want to live here. That room is nice, but it isn't my room. It doesn't have any of my stuff in it." He turned to Carl. "Dad, tell them. You want me to come home, don't you?"

Houseman looked like he was about to cry. His misery and discomfort so real it seemed like there was another person in the room. He looked at Sean, then Holly, then Radhauser. Finally, his gaze landed on the boy. "Of course I do, Holden. I love you more than I've ever loved anything or anyone, and you are my son in all the ways that really matter." His gaze shifted back to Holly and Sean. "I'm sorry. It's the way I feel. And the way I'll always feel." He stared directly into Holden's eyes. "But you're not my biological son. You belong to Holly and Sean."

"I don't! I belong to you."

Sean took Holly's place, crouching in front of Holden. "You can't really expect us to give you to the husband of the woman who kidnapped you. Do you have any idea what she did to our lives? What your mother...what Holly and I have been through during the last ten years?"

"Yeah. I'm not stupid, and I can figure out it was awful for you. My mom did a bad thing. But me and my dad didn't do anything to you." He turned, then ran down the hallway. The door slammed.

Holly ran after him.

Sean spoke first. "Why don't we all sit down?"

They settled in the living room, Houseman on the rocking chair across from Radhauser and Sean.

"I can't help but wonder if by finding Ryan, we may be somehow destroying him," Sean said. "But, sweet Jesus, how can we let him go?"

"May I offer a suggestion?" Radhauser said.

"At this point, I'll listen to anything." Sean gave him a sad smile.

Holly returned and sat on the sofa between Radhauser and her husband.

"Is he okay?" Sean asked.

"The poor little guy," she said. "He's face down on the bed, sobbing his heart out."

Houseman sucked in a long breath. "I'm so sorry."

"We don't blame you, Carl. It's obvious how much you care about him. What an excellent job you've done with him. He's beautiful, well-mannered, and a very sweet boy." Holly choked up and took a moment to regain control. "I used to imagine what his life might be like and, believe me, I never saw him happy and well cared for. Never imagined him loved." Tears streamed down her face.

"It seems that everyone in this room wants to do right by Holden," Radhauser said. "Maybe you could come up with some kind of joint custody arrangement."

Sean gulped. "We've only had our son back for a little over a day, and you want us to give him up again?"

Houseman stood. "I think I should leave now and let you talk more freely. I'm really sorry this happened, and I hope you know I had nothing to do with it. I love that boy, but I also know Candy, my wife, did a terrible thing to both of you. I think of Holden as my son and, of course, I want to be a part of his life. But I'll agree to do whatever you decide."

Sean and Holly started to stand and see him to the door.

He waved them back with a weary hand motion. "I can see myself out." He left without another word.

"The social worker warned us about this," Sean said. "It's going to take a long time, and it isn't going to be easy. He's got identity confusion and all that goes along with it."

Holly blew her nose and turned to her husband. "He's so unhappy. And I don't think time is going to change that. Houseman has ten years on his side. Holden will be twenty-years-old by the time we catch up. Maybe we should consider some joint custody arrangement, at least for now. Lots of divorced couples make it work. We live in the same town as Carl. Will you at least think about that?"

Sean stared at his feet, then up at Holly. "I have. And it's different for you. You don't have to compete with Candace Houseman. You're the only mother in the picture. It's different for me. I want to be my son's dad. Don't you get it?"

Holly touched his arm. "Remember how we wouldn't let ourselves say it out loud, but we both thought about what might be happening to Holden? He could have been molested. Abused. Kept in a cage in someone's basement. But he was loved. After Candace died, Carl took care of our son. Good care. Don't you think he deserves something in return?"

Sean lowered his head as if ashamed. A moment later, he spoke. "Okay. As long as it's informal and we're not bound by any legal restrictions. And he spends most of his time with us. Who knows, maybe Carl Houseman will remarry and start another family someday."

Radhauser certainly hoped so, for Houseman's sake. He knew it was possible. It had happened for him with Gracie and their kids. He stood to leave. "I know you'll do whatever is best for him. Call me if there is anything I can do to help. I mean that. Anything."

Holly looked frightened but determined. "I'm going to talk to Ryan...I mean Holden. Maybe if we let him come up with a compromise, he'll be more likely to accept being here."

* * *

Holden lay face down on the bed, his right hand under his head. He tried to take deep breaths, the way his dad had taught him, to slow down the hard thump of his heart, but it wasn't working.

The bedroom door opened.

He turned his head toward the sound.

Holly stepped over to the bed and sat on the edge of the mattress. She put her hand on his back and ran it slowly from side to side. For a long time, she didn't say anything, just rubbed his back.

Holden was glad. He wasn't in the mood to talk, and even if he was, he didn't know what to say or how to make things right. He had no idea what the right thing even was. All he really knew was that he loved Carl Houseman and wanted their life together back.

Finally, he turned over. His right hand had gone to sleep under the weight of his head, and he held it in his left hand. It was lifeless and a little too white. He thought about Tommy's white skin with the slightly blue tint. He looked at Holly.

Tears cascaded down her cheeks. She looked like a little kid as she wiped them away with her palms and turned her face toward the door.

He sucked his bottom lip behind his front teeth. "I'm sorry. I don't mean to make you sad."

"Have you had any supper?" Her face was still turned to the door.

"My dad fixed me some milk and cookies."

She turned back to face him again. Her dark eyes were no longer lit from the inside. "How about I make you a grilled cheese sandwich and some tomato soup? My mom used to make that for my lunch whenever I stayed home from school because I was sick. I know you're feeling sad and confused, too. Your dad…Sean and I don't want to hurt you either, but we know that you are hurting. We all are. The reality is that we're all victims here. The person at fault isn't around anymore."

She was right. His mom, or the person he thought was his mom, was dead. "Do you hate her…do you hate my mom?"

Holly winced.

Holden realized he'd made a mistake. "I mean do you hate Candy for taking me from the mall that day?"

"No," she said so fast he actually believed her. "I feel sorry for Candy. Losing your child can mess with your head."

"Do you think she was crazy?"

Holly reached out and took his hand.

He let her.

"I don't know," she said. "But that's in the past, and there's nothing we can do about it now. Let's talk about you. What would make you happy?"

He thought about that for a moment. Thought about the way he'd laughingly taken Tommy down on the treehouse platform, the way they wrestled, then rolled in opposite directions. "It would make me happy if none of this ever happened. And I could just go back to being Holden Houseman, living over on Sand Creek Road. It would make me happy if Tommy Bradshaw was still alive and my best friend."

"Okay," she said, sadness in her eyes. "That's a start. It would make me happy if my niece never took you to the mall that day, didn't leave you alone in the food court. That she and my brother didn't have to carry all the guilt around. It would make me happy if Candy's baby didn't die, and she had no reason to take you away from us. But we both know all of that has happened. Tommy died. The woman you thought was your mom died. Sean and I found out our son was still alive. We found out he was you. We can't undo any of that now, can we?"

He looked up at her and shook his head.

"So, given that situation, what do you think would be a fair compromise? Do you know what it means to compromise?"

"Sure. It was one of my vocabulary words last month. I always get a hundred. My dad and me make flash cards, and he tests me before the quiz. Compromise means that people disagree, but each of them decides to give in a little to the other person, and they meet someplace in the middle. And everyone is at least a little bit happy."

She smiled then, and the light returned to her dark eyes. "That's exactly right. So, let's think about some kind of compromise. Something that allows you to see and spend time with your… with Carl…but still allows Sean and me to have our son back in our lives."

He sat up. "Do you mean it? You would really let me see my dad…I mean, see Carl."

"Yes, I mean it. When you love someone as much as I love you, you want to do what is best for them, not yourself."

Holden felt that warm feeling behind his eyes that meant tears were coming. He didn't expect her to be so nice to him. Like a real mother.

She kept her gaze on his face. "Do you have any ideas on how we might accomplish this compromise?"

"You're going to let me decide?"

She smiled, then let go of his hand and stood.

This woman, Holly, his mother, was really pretty when she smiled. It was hard not to notice that something shined in her eyes when she looked at him, as plain and simple as love.

"You strike me as a very smart boy who is kind and fair. I'm going to trust you to come up with a solution that works for all of us. You give it some thought, Holden. Sean and I will think about it, too. We'll be out in the kitchen when you're ready to talk."

So happy he could barely speak, he scrambled to his feet and stood on the mattress to wrap his arms around her neck. He hugged her hard. She smelled like flowers, a little bit like Blair Bradshaw had always smelled.

Holly held him so tight that Holden could feel it, that need to never let go.

CHAPTER TWENTY-NINE

After leaving Holly and Sean's house Thursday evening, Radhauser stopped by his office to complete a little paperwork and phone Heron. "What have you got on the Houseman baby?"

"It's not good news," Heron said. "The infant had three rib fractures. That's a strong sign of abuse in babies because their thoracic region is extremely flexible."

Radhauser leaned back in his chair and closed his eyes. What more could this day hold? "What exactly are you saying?"

"That the Houseman child might have been murdered."

"Might?"

"It's impossible to say for sure since the body has decomposed and I don't have anything except the bones to work with."

"Could the ribs have been fractured by a layperson doing CPR without any training on infants?"

"Conceivable, but unlikely."

"Could that be consistent with Sudden Infant Death Syndrome? Might a distraught mother, in a state of panic, break his ribs trying to do CPR on her dead baby?"

"Maybe. But Candace Houseman isn't around to question or hold responsible if her answers don't pan out. I'm calling it death from unknown causes. And that's what I'll put on the death certificate. You can tell Carl Houseman whatever you want."

Radhauser hung up. He tried to imagine the cost to Carl Houseman of knowing three of his son's ribs were broken— of being presented a version of his dead wife he'd be better off without.

Exhausted, Radhauser's whole body was one pulsing ache, but

he documented his interviews with Townsend and Nora Mason. After completing the final paperwork on the Ryan Patterson kidnapping case, he stamped the file *closed* and dropped it onto Hazel's desk, ready to call it a night.

It was after 8 p.m. when Radhauser pulled into his driveway. He made his usual visit to the barn, then hurried down the gravel lane to his house. Gracie had already bathed the kids and put them to bed and was having a cup of tea at the kitchen table. He set the box he'd taken from the crawl space on the counter and kissed her on the cheek. After dropping his backpack on the floor, he pulled out the chair across from her and sat.

She looked up at him and smiled. "Guess what your son said today?"

"Was it a cuss word or the answer to one of Lizzie's knock-knock jokes?"

She gave him one of her dimpled smiles, like the one that made his heart skip a beat the first time he ever saw her. "Neither. He said 'cowboy,' then he added another word, 'Daddy.'"

A feeling of warmth radiated through his body, and he felt like the luckiest man in the world to be given another chance—another son. "That's my boy."

Gracie studied him for a moment. "You look whipped. I've got leftover meatloaf and mashed potatoes if you're hungry."

"I'm too tired to even eat."

"Rough day?"

He nodded.

"You want to talk about it?"

He told her about the baby skeleton they'd found buried in the Houseman's backyard under the laughing Buddha. The way he'd found Carl Houseman drunk at his kitchen table. His learning from Heron the dead baby had three broken ribs and may have been murdered. He told her about his trip to Blair's old high school and his meeting with her English teacher, Mr. Townsend. The way that meeting led to her best friend, Nora, who said the mother's live-in boyfriend was sneaking into Meadow's room at night and she believed that was the reason Meadow left Wildwood and never returned.

Gracie listened but said nothing.

"I was about to pay a second visit to Sunflower Finney when the phone rang, and it was Holly saying that Holden had run away." He told her he'd abandoned his plan and returned to Ashland. How Holden had taken the school bus to his old house and finally, the way Carl Houseman brought Holden back to the Pattersons.

"That poor kid," she said. "Not to mention what this is like for Carl Houseman. It's always easy to say what you'd do when you hear about a birth mother wanting her child back years after giving it up for adoption, but it's a little more difficult when you're the birth mother of a child that was stolen. I have no idea what I'd do if it were Lizzie or Jonathan."

"I'd like to think we'd do what was best for our child," Radhauser said.

"And what would that be in this case?"

"I wish I knew. The poor kid wanted a mother so badly that he used to pretend the next-door neighbor was his mom." Radhauser just shook his head. It was way too complicated to figure out tonight. "Sean and Holly love that boy. And they've kept living and hoping for a decade. But Houseman adores Holden, and he's been a damn good father. I just have to believe the four of them will figure something out."

"Have you eaten at all today?"

"I grabbed a muffin at the station before I met the state police and the cadaver dogs at the Houseman property. After that, I pretty much lost my appetite. I did have a cup of coffee with the Bradshaws' housekeeper."

"You have to eat something. You're going to make yourself sick." She stood, dished up a plate of meatloaf, mashed potatoes, and green beans, then heated it in the microwave.

When she placed it in front of him with a cold Sam Adams Boston Lager, he ate.

"Is there anything I can help you with?" She pulled out the chair and sat across from him again.

"You know I don't like to bring my work home."

She reached across the table and touched his hand. "It's pretty hard to avoid when you've had a day like this one. It's written all over your face."

He cocked his head and studied her. "Are you sure you wouldn't rather talk about the kids?"

"Absolutely. I hang out with a six-year-old and seventeen-month-old all day long. I'm ready for some more challenging conversations."

He told her about the box he'd taken from the Bradshaws' crawl space and how it contained the only clues he'd found to Meadow Finney's childhood. "She disappeared when she was fifteen and didn't resurface until she was in her twenties and started working as an actress with the Shakespeare Company. You might be able to make more sense of its contents than I've been able to. As soon as I finish eating, I'll show you."

Ten minutes later, after Gracie cleared the table, Radhauser emptied the contents of the box and spread them across its surface. His wife was both smart and intuitive and might think of something Radhauser hadn't.

She pulled out a chair and sat, then picked up each item and studied it for a moment. The school letter Meadow had received in ninth grade for being the star of the drama club, each playbill where she had a starring role. "Looks like she was very talented, even as a young girl. Not to mention focused on what she wanted."

Radhauser told Gracie that after Meadow changed her name to Blair, she'd gone on to starring roles in many of the Ashland Shakespeare Theater productions. "According to the artistic director, she was popular and well-liked by the other company members—surprising since she got almost every part she tried out for."

Gracie opened Meadow's report cards. "Nine years of straight As and glowing comments from her teachers. What do you know about her life after she left Wildwood? Did she manage to finish high school? Go to college? Study theater arts or drama? She was just a kid. Where did she live? Have you checked with Services to Children and Families? Maybe she was in a foster home. Or some kind of youth shelter. How about relatives?"

Radhauser shrugged. "You're worse than Murphy. I wish I knew the answers to those questions. I do know she lied on her application for the theater. Claimed she'd graduated from high school and college in Portland, but the schools she listed had no record of her attending. It's like she dropped off the face of the earth for a while, then reappeared as Blair Bradshaw. Her mother was no help. She didn't even bother to look for Meadow after she disappeared."

She shot him her look, the one that said he needed to delegate more. "You've got a partner again. Let McBride do some of the leg work."

"Believe me, McBride has been working her ass off. You should have seen her interviewing Bradshaw. Backed him into a corner and wouldn't let up. She did those rattlesnake earrings justice."

"Did Blair's husband reveal anything about that period of time in her life? You told me she was about to divorce him, but that doesn't mean they didn't talk early in their relationship. You remember how many hours we spent talking about our childhoods, my growing up here in Southern Oregon and the way you loved visiting your Uncle Roger's ranch in Phoenix."

"I didn't exactly get off to a good start with Bradshaw. In the first three interviews, he was my prime suspect, and I pissed him off more than a little bit."

Gracie smiled, then leaned toward him and planted a kiss on his cheek. "Put on your charming hat and talk to him again tomorrow." She sat, picked up the book of W.H. Auden poems, and read the inscription.

"I managed to piss Mr. Townsend off too. He thought I was accusing him of having a sexual relationship with Meadow."

"Damn, boy. You're batting a thousand. Whatever happened to Mr. Diplomatic Nice Guy?"

"He got handed a murder case where every one of his suspects has led nowhere." Radhauser knew this meant he needed to go back to the beginning and reexamine everything he'd already done. Every instinct told him he needed to bring Blair Bradshaw back from the grave and learn what he could about her life.

Gracie sat and leafed through the poetry book, paying attention to everything that had been underlined, reading every comment in the margins. "Look at this," she said, pointing to a poem called *Anthem For Saint Cecilia's Day*. "Why would she circle those two lines in red and put hearts beside them? They must have meant something to her."

Radhauser took the book and read the two lines circled in red.
O weep, child weep, o weep away the stain...
Weep for the lives your wishes never led.

Never much for poetry, he turned to Gracie and shrugged. "What does that mean to you?"

"It could mean a couple things. It could be Meadow identified with those lines—wanting to wipe away the stain of her life in Wildwood or what Spider may have been doing to her. Or it might have also represented her desire to be an actress, to escape and live those wishes, rather than weep for them."

"You're pretty smart, you know that?"

"I married you, didn't I?"

He grinned. "Smartest thing you ever did. Now let me ask you something else. From the point of view of a woman, who was a fifteen-year-old about the same time Meadow was, what would make a girl with straight As and a burning need to be an actress drop out of school and disappear?"

"Pregnancy," Gracie said, without giving it much thought. "Or some kind of abuse in the home she wanted to escape."

"Did Meadow ever tell her mother what Spider was doing to her?"

"Nora claimed she didn't know. But I got the distinct sense she was lying."

"Then you need to be more charming. Talk to her again."

"I plan to do that, boss."

"What's her mother like?"

He told her. "She pretended to hate her daughter, but when I told her Meadow was dead, I detected some sadness cross her face. She told me she called after she heard about Tommy dying—

thought they might have something in common since Sunny had lost a son, too."

"And?"

"Blair didn't want anything to do with her."

"That's a lot of hate," Gracie said. "You need to find out what happened between them. And where Meadow went and what she did between Wildwood and becoming Mrs. Franklin Bradshaw. Filling in those blanks could be the key to your case."

"You should be a detective. Now hand me that box."

When she picked it up and handed it to him, something fell out and landed face down on the tabletop. It looked like a Polaroid photograph that had slipped between the cardboard flaps on the bottom of the box. Gracie stood and flipped it over.

The newborn in the faded colored photograph had what appeared to be a cleft palate and lip. He wore a blue knitted cap, the kind hospitals often put on newborns to keep their heads warm and to indicate the baby's sex. The tiny face was grotesque—like the photos you sometimes see of children in poverty-stricken areas of Mexico begging for dimes and selling sticks of gum on street corners. The kind charitable organizations like Save the Children used to solicit donations.

Why would Blair/Meadow have saved that photo? Was it a high school project she'd taken on? Had she seen this baby's photo, felt sympathy, and donated money? Was it a child she had once sponsored?

Another possibility occurred to him. From everything he'd learned so far about Blair's mother, she was a drug addict who might have given birth to a deformed child. But this baby was not Jason. When Radhauser visited the vineyard, Jason's face was handsome and clean-shaven. Radhauser would have noticed the scars—even if the deformity had been surgically repaired. Could this photo be of another little brother?

And, of course, there was another possible scenario. Had Spider's nightly visits to Meadow's room led to a pregnancy?

One thing was certain, he needed to talk to both Sunflower Finney and Nora Mason again. Maybe one of them could shed some light on the photograph and why Blair had saved it.

He turned it over to see if there was a date or any indication as to where it was taken. But the back was blank. He slipped the photo into an evidence bag, tucked it into his backpack, then carefully replaced all the items in the box.

He made a list of things he still needed to investigate.

Tomorrow, he'd return the box to Bradshaw and talk to him about Blair's past. Would Franklin recognize the photograph? Would he even know if his wife had given birth before they met? And what about the syringes? Did Franklin Bradshaw suspect his wife of being a drug user?

In all probability, this photo had nothing to do with Blair's death, but there was something compelling about the fact that she'd saved it for twenty years.

And he wouldn't rest until he knew why.

* * *

Holden stood in the doorway into the kitchen and watched the two strangers who were his birth parents. They spoke in whispers and sat across from each other at their kitchen table with only a candle lighting the space between them.

"We have to think about him now," Holly whispered, her face softly lit by the candlelight. "About what's best for Ryan in the long run."

"The social worker said this wasn't going to be easy. But he's our son, not Houseman's."

"We know that. We've known it every day since he went missing. But he just found out. Think about what it feels like for our little boy."

Holden felt like he was doing something bad by listening to their private conversation about him. He used his best manners to announce his presence. "Please excuse me for interrupting."

They both swung around and stared at him.

Nervous, he shifted from one foot to the other and hung his head.

"Would you like to join us?" Holly got up and turned on the overhead light. "We're having a glass of wine. How about some grape juice?"

She poured his juice into a wine glass and pulled out a chair for him.

He sat and took a sip of the juice, then carefully set the glass back on the table. This was the first time he'd ever drunk from a stemmed glass. "I been doing what you said. Thinking about a compromise."

Sean cleared his throat and started to speak.

Holly shot him a glance that made him silent. "I asked him to think about some custody arrangement that might work for all of us."

"Are you crazy?" Sean said. "He's a little boy. What does he know about what's best for all of us?"

When Holden picked up his glass, his hand trembled.

"It's okay, honey. We want to hear what you have to say, don't we, Sean?"

Sean said nothing.

Underneath the table, Holly took Holden's hand and squeezed hard.

So this was what it felt like to have a mother's encouragement. Her touch gave him courage. "I don't know you…I mean… I…I guess the DNA showed that you're my parents. Detective Radhauser says DNA doesn't lie. But for ten whole years, I didn't know that. I thought Carl and Candy Houseman were my mom and dad. Now, I know that wasn't the truth…and…" His eyes filled with tears.

Holly squeezed his hand again. "It's okay, honey. We want to know how you feel, don't we, Sean?"

Once again, Sean didn't speak.

Holden swallowed hard and gave himself a moment to stop the tears from falling. "My compromise is this. How about I stay here during the school week? And spend the weekends with my real dad."

Sean stood so fast he sent his chair tumbling backward. "I am your real dad, son. And that's not going to work for me."

Holden jumped at the sound of the chair landing, then scooted his chair a little closer to Holly. "I'm sorry. It's just that…" His bottom lip trembled.

Holly placed her reassuring hand on his leg.

"Sit down," she said to Sean, a new firmness in her voice. "Holden spent time coming up with a compromise, and it deserves our consideration."

Sean straightened his chair and sat. When he looked at Holden, his gaze softened. "I'm sorry, son. I overreacted. This is just so hard for all of us. Please, forgive me. I didn't mean to lose my temper. We've waited so long for you to be returned to us."

Holden curled his toes in his sneakers. "It's okay. I've been pretty mad about everything that's happened, too."

"That was very smart of you to develop a compromise." Even Sean's voice was softer now. "Maybe we can fine tune it a little bit, so it works for all of us. Would that be okay?"

Holden's body loosened. "Yes. That's how people compromise."

Sean smiled and continued. "How would you feel about spending every other weekend with Carl? I'd like a chance to get to know you better. Since I work during the week, the weekends you're with us would be our best time together."

Holden was so happy he didn't trust himself to speak. He took a couple deep breaths until the air went in and out of his chest without catching. "If something special came up, like a Boy Scout camping trip, could I go with my...with Carl? He's my Scout leader."

"Absolutely," Sean said. "And maybe he could use a parent helper. I was an Eagle Scout when I was a boy."

Holden grinned, then clapped, filled with more joy than he'd felt since before Tommy died. "That's a great compromise. Can I call my...can I call Carl and tell him?"

"Of course." Holly handed him the phone, then mouthed the words *thank you* to Sean, took him by the hand and led him out of the kitchen.

CHAPTER THIRTY

It's been a while since anyone heard a word from you. You've been minding your own business, showing up for work and doing your job to the best of your ability. And, of course, you've been thinking about what you did to Blair Bradshaw—even trying to justify your actions. You've read a lot of articles about murderers and, given the right set of circumstances, some experts believe everyone is capable of murder. All people need is a motive that makes sense to them, the need to end a threat to their well-being or that of someone they love. Or, in your case, the need to avenge some terrible wrong.

You've also been following the story of that kid who was stolen from the Rogue Valley Mall in 1991. If you hadn't killed Blair Bradshaw, that boy, Holden Houseman, would never have known he was kidnapped. Sean and Holly Patterson would have spent the rest of their lives living a nightmare—traumatized and worried about their son. Was he dead? Was he alive? Was he starving and locked in a cage in someone's dark basement? What heinous acts had been done to him? And you, of all people, know a lot about heinous acts done to kids.

Even under the best of circumstances, Holden would have grown up somewhere he didn't belong. Most likely, he would never have been returned to his rightful parents. Or know his real name was Ryan Sean Patterson.

Every kid should know who his or her birth parents are. It's crucial to understand where you came from in order to know where you're going. It doesn't take a philosopher or a criminologist to figure that out.

This kidnapped kid is big news, and everyone in Ashland is talking about it. How that boy has been living here, right under his real

244

parents' noses, for his whole life. Not to mention right under Detective Radhauser's nose as well. Pretty amazing, don't you think?

A part of you wants to brag about what you've done, but, of course, that wouldn't be smart. But you're starting to think of yourself as a local hero for bringing Ryan Patterson home.

Captain Murphy held a press conference about Blair's murder. He claimed they were interviewing several suspects and persons of interest in the case. That they were getting close to making an arrest. What a crock of crap that is. They don't have a clue about you. Maybe Detective Radhauser isn't as clever as you'd once believed him to be.

Since the night you severed her femoral arteries, you've discovered that vengeance is like cold coffee. It didn't warm the emptiness inside you or bring you any peace about what she did to you. The warm feeling you had when the blood gushed from her body disappeared way too soon.

And you're afraid that the day will come when you want that feeling back.

* * *

Bradshaw agreed to meet Radhauser at 7 a.m. on Friday before day five of the famed attorney's trial began. An entire week had passed since Blair's body was discovered. Radhauser had hit one dead end after another. What was he missing?

He and Bradshaw talked over coffee and blueberry muffins at the table in the Bradshaws' kitchen. Like a concerned neighbor, he asked about Holden Houseman, and Radhauser told him they were working on some sort of joint custody arrangement so that Carl might continue to see the boy.

"Houseman and I didn't have a lot in common, but he was a good father to Holden. And he stepped up to the plate a few times for Tommy, too."

The radio was set to a classical station and some violin concerto Radhauser didn't recognize played softly in the background. It made him think of Heron.

After handing the box to Bradshaw, Radhauser told him there was nothing missing except for one photograph, but that he would return it once the case was closed.

"Whatever you need," Bradshaw said, the epitome of cooperation now. But Radhauser found it slightly odd he didn't want to know what photograph Radhauser had kept and why.

"What can you tell me about Meadow Finney?"

Bradshaw scratched his cheek. "Absolutely nothing. I know Blair's maiden name was Finney so it might be one of her relatives. But I've never met anyone named Meadow."

"Meadowlark Finney was your wife's birth name. She changed it to Blair sometime after she turned fifteen and left Wildwood."

Bradshaw stiffened. "You've got to be kidding me."

"It's true. I spoke with her mother and her father in hospice."

Bradshaw shook his head. "Except for the last name, Finney, that's news to me. But, as I told you before, Detective Radhauser, Blair loved her secrets."

"Would you mind telling me how the two of you met?"

He gave Radhauser a questioning look. "I don't know what that has to do with her murder investigation."

"On the surface, nothing. But in all my murder investigations, I try hard to get a feel for the victim. And, let me tell you, it's not been easy with your wife. Just when I think I have at least something about her figured out, I'm hit with a new surprise."

Bradshaw laughed. "Welcome to my life. That's because Blair could shift character roles as fast as some people can change their shoes. I was never quite sure who'd be there when I got home from work—was I talking to my wife or some character she'd invented?"

"So how did you meet?"

"One summer evening, back in 1988, I took another woman to see *Romeo and Juliet* at the Elizabethan Theater. Blair played Juliet, and I was smitten from the moment I saw her. I came back the next night without a date. Following the play, I hung around and talked to her at the Actors' Meet and Greet event." He smiled. Clearly, the memory was a good one. "I saw her play Juliet so many times that summer I could repeat the lines verbatim. We married before the year ended." There was a tenderness in Bradshaw's eyes Radhauser hadn't seen before. Maybe there was a time when he genuinely loved his wife. Or maybe he still loved her in spite of his pregnant girlfriend.

"What was she like then?"

"Beautiful. Charming. But complicated. She was twenty-three years old, and her acting ability was already phenomenal. She could be anyone she wanted to be. She was that good. At first, I liked that about her, but after a while, nothing felt real. When I look back on it now, I think the only true thing in her life was our son…was Tommy." His voice broke.

Radhauser gave him a moment to compose himself. "Did she ever tell you anything about her teenage years?"

"Just that her parents were hippies, flower children, who moved up from San Francisco when she was a toddler and bought some land out in Wildwood. They divorced when she was about five. She hated her mother and escaped as soon as she could. Blair told me she headed up to Portland after she left Wildwood, stayed with a friend while she finished high school, then got a scholarship to Portland University. When she graduated, she tried out for a Shakespeare play in Ashland and the rest, as they say, is history."

"Would it surprise you to learn that neither the high school she claimed to have attended nor Portland University has any record of a Meadow or Blair Finney attending or graduating? My partner checked with Human Resources at the Shakespeare Festival. Apparently, Blair lied on her employment application."

He jerked at the knot in his tie as if it were choking him. "I've come to the point where nothing would surprise me about Blair."

Radhauser flinched at the coldness in his voice, then pulled the evidence bag with the Polaroid from his backpack and handed it to Bradshaw.

At first glance, he gasped, then studied the photo for a moment, a look of genuine pain on his face. "Poor little bastard. Who is it? And what's it got to do with Blair?"

"I was hoping you could tell me."

Bradshaw handed the photo back. "I've never seen that before in my life. I never owned a Polaroid camera. Believe me, I have absolutely no idea who that baby is."

"The photograph was in that cardboard box I found hidden under the plywood floor in the crawl space above your son's closet.

We think it's conceivable your wife gave birth to this boy in 1980."

"Impossible," he said. "She would have been fifteen years old." He tapped his fingertips against the edge of the table and stared out the window for a moment. "I used to ask Blair about her childhood when we first got married. I saw the box and was curious and wanted to know what was inside. She said it was a bunch of old junk she wasn't ready to part with, but that someday she planned to burn the entire box in a bonfire and forget that time ever existed. I hadn't seen the box for years, and I assumed she'd done that."

"Why do you think it's impossible your wife gave birth when she was fifteen?"

He blinked as if a flashbulb had gone off in front of him. "No good reason. And I'm probably wrong. Anything is possible with Blair. Come to think of it, she did have some stretch marks on her abdomen, but she told me she'd been obese as an adolescent and the marks appeared after she lost a lot of weight. I never thought anything more about it."

Radhauser told Bradshaw about the box of syringes he'd found hidden in Blair's sock drawer and how the missing syringe was a match for the one they'd found in the creek. "Was she diabetic, or can you think of some legitimate reason she'd have a box of syringes?"

"No." Bradshaw twisted his neck back and forth. "And if there was a legitimate reason, why would she hide them?"

He was right, Radhauser thought. Maybe Blair bought them after Tommy died. Maybe she intended to kill herself with a heroin overdose. Someone else beat her to it.

"Can you think of anyone, anyone at all, who might be able to fill in some of these blanks for me?"

"I wish I could help you, but I was married to her for twelve years, and I have no idea who she really was."

Radhauser told him how Sunny had met him with a shotgun in one hand and a dead possum in the other. "She claimed she hadn't seen Meadow since she left home at fifteen. But she did phone your house after she heard about Tommy's death."

For a moment, Bradshaw stared at his empty plate. "So that's why Blair was so insistent on that security system."

"I don't think so," Radhauser said. "It was installed almost a month before Tommy's accident. Did Blair have any girlfriends? Someone she might have confided in about her past?"

"She was friendly to everyone but had no real friends as far as I know. She never went out for a drink, a movie, or dinner with a girlfriend. Maybe that's why I find Sonya so appealing. She's a simple woman—what you see is what you get."

Maybe you feel that way now, Radhauser thought, but Sonya was pregnant, about to become a mother when she was barely more than a child herself. Bradshaw may not know it yet, but everything about Sonya Clifford was about to get more complex.

"I need to get going." Bradshaw checked his watch. "Please let me know if you need anything else from me." He stood, then turned and left the room, leaving nothing behind but the smell of his expensive aftershave.

Radhauser showed himself out. He understood that for many people, their truest self was often the person they allowed no one else to see. Who did Blair Bradshaw see when she was all alone and looked in the mirror?

For the rest of the world, including her husband, she'd obviously edited and recast herself into whatever role fit the situation. She evaded and concealed. Somehow Radhauser knew in order to find her killer, he needed to find the fifteen-year-old Meadow Finney. Maybe then he'd discover the woman behind the mask.

CHAPTER THIRTY-ONE

When Radhauser arrived back at the police station, Murphy had taken off his tie, loosened his shirt collar, and was pacing across his office. It wasn't a good sign. "I don't care what it takes. Bring me a viable suspect. This is a high-profile case. The mayor is breathing down my neck."

Radhauser took a step back and crossed his arms over his chest. "Seems the mayor cares more about Blair's murder than her husband does."

Murphy gave a slow and disbelieving shake of his head. "What's wrong with that prick, Bradshaw, anyway?"

"He's in the middle of a murder trial. And I suspect he knows his girlfriend is pregnant by now. He probably thinks he's got bigger things to worry about."

"Sounds to me like he should be your prime suspect. Why isn't he in custody?"

"Because he's got an alibi."

Murphy curled his shoulders and limbered up his neck as if he were a linebacker getting ready for an important tackle. He wagged his index finger and raised his voice. "His pregnant girlfriend says he was with her all night, right? Come on, Radhauser, you're a better investigator than that."

Murphy, like McBride, had a cheating spouse that led to a divorce, and both of them were a little sensitive on the subject of infidelity. "McBride went after him like the rattlesnake you know she can be. Besides, the girlfriend's neighbor corroborates his alibi. The truth is, sir, I don't think Bradshaw did it."

Color rose in Murphy's cheeks. He'd been having problems

with his blood pressure ever since his wife, Naomi, left him. "Since when does anyone care what you think? Go with the evidence."

Radhauser took a deep breath and held it for a moment, trying to keep from saying something he might regret. After he let out his breath, he decided to say it anyhow. "Did someone take a leak in your cereal this morning? You know as well as I do that a lot of police work takes place in the detective's head and gut. I'm working this case, night and day. Even from home."

"No, you're not." Murphy shook his head. His gaze hardened. "You've been spending most of your time on the old kidnapping case. The kid was found right under our noses by a fluke and not because of good police work. It makes us look incompetent."

So that was it. Murphy was still stinging because of the newspaper article that slammed the Ashland Police Department for not finding Ryan Patterson sooner.

"He's back with his parents," Murphy's voice was lower now. "Count your lucky stars and move on. The adjustment problems the Pattersons and Carl Houseman are having aren't the problem of the Ashland Police Department. So, start concentrating on the Bradshaw case. Do you hear me?"

"I hear you, sir. And I'm on it with one hundred percent of my attention now. I have a new lead I'm following up on today."

"Good."

Radhauser remained silent, not sure Murphy was finished.

"So, what the hell are you waiting for?"

Though he had plenty to say in his defense, Radhauser turned and left without another word. He'd worked with Murphy long enough to know when it was best to keep silent. Radhauser knew himself. He'd do everything in his power to find whoever killed Blair Bradshaw no matter what it took to do it. He headed to his office and sat for a moment, drinking a cup of coffee and licking his wounds, then asked McBride to join him. "Murphy's pissed and up on his high horse."

She gave him a sad smile. "Tell me about it. Naomi's attorney sent over the divorce papers to sign this morning."

"I asked him who pissed in his cornflakes," Radhauser said.

"Now I know it was Naomi."

"What's going on with the Bradshaw case?"

He made a copy of the infant Polaroid photo and gave it to McBride, then filled her in on everything he knew so far. "I want you to see if you can find out who this kid is. I don't have much more than a strong hunch at this point, but I suspect Meadow Finney gave birth to him when she was fifteen—some time in 1980."

Radhauser asked McBride to phone Services to Children and Families in Jackson and Josephine counties—look into the foster care system and see if they had any records on Meadow Finney or Blair Finney. "Check area hospitals, group homes, and homeless shelters. That fifteen-year-old had to be living somewhere after she left Wildwood. And, if I'm right, someone has to remember a kid born with a cleft palate and lip."

After they finished, Radhauser headed out to his car but was accosted by an overzealous reporter who spoke into a microphone. "Peter Taylor, Channel 5 News. I'm outside the Ashland Police Department speaking with Detective Radhauser, lead investigator in the ten-year-old Ryan Patterson kidnapping case. What's the latest on the case? Has the boy been returned to the Pattersons?" He stuck the microphone in front of Radhauser's face.

Radhauser put his hand on the head of the microphone and gave Peter a look meant to say, *I have better things to do.* "Don't you watch your own local news?" He lifted his hand and spoke into the microphone. "Ryan Patterson went home last night."

"Will charges be brought against Carl Houseman?"

After Radhauser told him Houseman was in Kuwait and unaware of what his wife had done, the reporter asked one more question. "How is Ryan Patterson adjusting to his new identity?"

"Everyone involved cares deeply about him and is doing everything in their power to make his transition as smooth as possible. Now, if you'll excuse me, I have a murder case to investigate."

Once again, Radhauser headed toward Wildwood to talk to Nora Mason and Sunny Finney—confront them with the infant photo and see if it jogged either of their memories. Because he wanted to time his visit to Nora so the twins would be napping and she'd be free to talk, he headed to Sunny's place first.

After bouncing up her rutted driveway, trying to avoid potholes still filled with rainwater, he parked his car at the top of the hill. He hooked his backpack over his shoulder and headed up the gravel drive to the sagging wooden structure, climbed the cinderblock step, and tapped on the door. An old-time washing machine with a hand wringer sat on the far end of the porch, and a drooping clothesline stretched between two oak trees in the side yard.

Something stirred inside the shack, then the door opened, and Sunny stood backlit in the doorway, her body in black silhouette. She made no effort to invite him inside. When she stepped out onto the porch, Sunny smelled like lye soap, a little better than the last time he'd visited.

"I ain't got nothin' else to say to you." Her voice wasn't any less raspy. She wore a shapeless dress that fell over her bony shoulders like a tent, yellow with big blue flowers whose colors had faded from too many trips through the wringer. Her shoes were worn hiking boots with broken laces she'd tied back together with knots.

Radhauser touched the brim of his Stetson. "I'm sorry to bother you again, Miss Sunny, but I have some more questions for you, and if you aren't willing to answer them here, I'll have to place you under arrest and bring you into the Ashland police station."

She forced a laugh. "What for? I ain't done nothin'."

"For failure to cooperate in a murder investigation."

"Failure to cooperate? Are you crazy? I could of shot that pretty, gray Stetson right off your head if I had a mind to. But I didn't. I talked to you last time you was here, and I cooperated. What more do you want?"

"As a case develops, more questions arise. We often revisit people of interest more than once."

"So I'm one of them people of interest, am I? Well, I sure as hell ain't interested in the likes of you." She flopped into one of the rocking chairs, then watched as Radhauser pulled over the other one and sat.

"It's about Meadow. I'm trying to account for her whereabouts from the time she left here in 1980 until she joined the Shakespeare Festival in 1987. That's seven years when nobody seems to know where she was or what happened to her."

"I done told you that lyin' bitch up and left for no good reason. Dropped out of school even though she was doin' real good. One of her teachers even come lookin' for her."

"Mr. Townsend, her English teacher."

"Yeah, that's right. How did you know?"

"I spoke with him. He was fond of Meadow and thought she was smart enough to win a scholarship to college. Now, tell me again. When was the last time you saw your daughter?"

"That ain't changed from the last time I told you. It was the day she up and left. I think it was sometime in April 1980. I remember that forsythia bush out back had stopped its bloomin'."

"Do you have any idea why she left?"

She grabbed a pack of cigarettes from the pocket of her dress, thumbed one out of the box. After lighting it, she licked her index finger then extinguished the match between it and her thumb. "None whatsoever." She took a quick drag on the cigarette.

"I talked to her best friend, Nora. Her last name was Crestwell back when the girls were in high school."

"Don't you think I know that? Her mother, Maybelle, she died last year, but she used to be a friend of mine."

"Nora said Meadow told her your boyfriend at the time, someone called Spider, was sneaking into her bedroom at night after you went to sleep, making her do things she didn't want to do. Apparently, Meadow planned to tell you what Spider was doing to her that same night she disappeared."

Sunny winced. "All right. All right. Why you askin' me if you already know anyhow? That's why she left. I said it was a bald-faced lie. Spider was my man, and he told me himself he liked his women with a little flesh and seasoning. Not some skinny-ass, milk-faced teenager."

"Did you try to find her?"

She hung her head. "I called Meadow a lyin' bitch and said that she could just get the hell out of here and live somewhere else if she was gonna go around spreadin' rumors about Spider."

Though he didn't have confirmation yet, his hunch was strong, and he decided to take a chance. "Did she tell you she was pregnant?"

"Yeah. She told me. But at the time, I didn't believe a word of it. I never even seen her with a boy. I was startin' to think she might be a lesbian. That was okay with me. All she was interested in was goin' to acting school and getting rich and famous. I thought she was tellin' me Spider was sneaking into her room to get even with me or Spider for somethin' she thought we done or didn't do. You know how kids are."

Radhauser shook his head, slow and disbelieving—his sympathy for the young Meadow growing by the minute. "You said *at the time*. Did you come to believe her later?"

Her shoulders drooped, and for a moment she stared, vacantly, out into the yard where a set of yellowed sheets and three, blue-striped towels hung on the clothesline. "Matter of fact, I did."

"What happened to change your mind?"

"There was two things." She took another puff on her cigarette, then let the ash drop onto the porch floor. "One was the fact that Spider proved himself a big, fat liar a few years later when he got arrested for statutory rape. Guess he was fond of skinny-ass jailbait, after all. He got what he had comin' to him and, far as I know, he's still in the Jackson County Jail. Servin' a twenty-year sentence for aggravated rape. He hurt the girl pretty bad." A ribbon of smoke drifted from her mouth.

In his mind, Radhauser checked Spider off his list of suspects. He asked the question again, hoping she might answer it this time. "Did you try to find Meadow after you learned the truth?"

A spark of regret fired in her eyes. "In case you ain't noticed, I'm a proud and stubborn old bitch, and I ain't much good at admittin' I'm wrong or sayin' I'm sorry. So, I just went right on tellin' myself I was better off without that stuck-up girl."

"And what was the other thing that made you believe Meadow was telling the truth?"

"I met him," she said, then dropped the butt of her cigarette onto the floor and thumped another from the pack.

"I don't understand. You already knew Spider."

She wrinkled her nose and spit on the porch floor. "I ain't talkin' about him. Believe me, I was done with that disgusting pervert."

Radhauser tapped his cowboy boot against the porch floor, his impatience mounting. "You met who, then?"

"The baby boy Meadow had. He favored Spider but was even more handsome."

After sucking in a breath to calm himself, Radhauser grabbed his backpack from the porch floor and pulled out the evidence bag with the infant's photo inside. He handed it to Sunny. "Is this the baby you met?"

She laughed. "The grandson I met must be about twenty or twenty-one now. If he was born lookin' like this, he must have had some major plastic surgery done."

"When did you meet him?"

"Must a been a month or two ago."

"Was there some reason you didn't tell me that the last time I was here?"

"I don't have any recollection of you askin'. And you didn't threaten to drag me into the Ashland police station for questioning either."

She was right. During his last visit, he hadn't yet spoken to Nora, didn't know, or even suspect, Meadow was abused by her mother's boyfriend. "You seem like a pretty suspicious character to me, Sunny. What made you believe this so-called grandson was telling the truth?"

"He said he thought I was his grandmother and that he believed his mother was Meadow Finney."

"Did he give you his name?"

"My memory ain't as good as it used to be. I smoked my share of weed back in the day." She paused and gave him her gap-toothed grin. "Still do, if the truth be known. But I think he said it was Carlson or Carter. One of them C names. He looked like a nice young man, clean cut and pretty darn handsome. Dark like

Spider. But with Meadow's blue eyes. If he had any scars under his nose or anywhere else on his face, I didn't notice them. But he did have a mustache."

Radhauser knew that adult males who'd had plastic surgery for cleft lip often wore a mustache to hide the scars. "No last name."

"Not that I recall."

"What did he want?"

"He wanted to know stuff about his family history. He wanted to know who his father was."

"Did you tell him?"

She shot Radhauser a look that could have boiled cabbage. "That his father was a good for nothing pedophile who raped his teenaged mother right under the nose of the woman he claimed to love?" Her tone had sharpened. "I might be leftover hippy trailer trash, but I don't stoop that low."

"Did he ask about Meadow?"

"Of course he did. It was the whole purpose of his visit. He wanted to find his mom like most of them people who are thrown away or adopted want to do."

"Did you tell him where she was?"

"I told him what I knew. She'd changed her name to Blair. Married some hot-shot attorney and that she was an actress with the Shakespeare Theater in Ashland."

"You recognized that baby rattle, didn't you? I could see it on your face."

A vague nostalgia touched her eyes. "All right, I'll tell you the truth. That baby rattle belonged to my momma. My grandmother, a vaudeville actress in New York, had given it to momma when she was born. I gave it to Meadow when she was a baby, and she wouldn't part with it. You'd of thought it was pure gold. She took it to school for show and tell. Polished it up, even though that silver polish made her hands blister. Meadow didn't take much when she left here, just a duffle bag with some clothes and that damn poetry book she carried around everywhere she went. But I'm sure she took that rattle." As Sunny spoke, her face swam in and out between undulating waves of smoke. "I don't know where you found the rattle, but if you found it on her body, maybe she wanted to take it with her."

"But your daughter didn't kill herself, Sunny. She was murdered."

Finally, he was getting somewhere. And at least a few things were starting to make sense. "I've got a couple more questions, and then I'll get out of your hair. Do you have any idea where Meadow gave birth?"

"Carlson or Carter, or whatever the hell his name was, told me his birth certificate listed him as a home birth. It said both his parents was unknown. If you ask me, that's downright pitiful."

Radhauser pushed back against the rocker. A cool breeze off the river lifted his hair. "Without a last name for either of his parents, what led him to you?"

Sunny blew a column of smoke into the air above her. "I guess I should of asked him how he found me. But I didn't."

"So, you're telling me you have no idea where Meadow was living or where she gave birth?"

"None. But if anyone knows it would be Nora Crestwell. Those two were thick as thieves back then. And Nora's mother was a midwife in Wildwood for years. She delivered my Raven. Nora used to help her."

Sunny heaved herself up and out of the chair. "If you ain't got no more business with me, Detective Radhauser, I've got chores needin' to be done."

He stood and handed her his card. "If you should remember anything more about the young man who came to see you, especially a name, please call me. I don't care what time. My home phone number is on there, too." He reached out his hand.

Sunny shook it. Her hand was dry, palm calloused.

"Thanks for your cooperation."

She gave him her toothless and mischievous grin. "It ain't like you gave me much choice in the matter. But if you find my grandson, tell him I wouldn't mind seeing him again." As she spoke, Radhauser could almost see it tighten up inside her, the hard knot of her aloneness.

He walked out to his car, paused to look back. When he saw her watching from her doorway, he waved.

She returned the gesture with a slight movement of her tobacco-stained fingertips.

No doubt about it, Sunny Finney, for all her bravado, was a lonely old woman.

CHAPTER THIRTY-TWO

It only took him about ten minutes to drive to Nora Mason's double wide on the wooded hillside. He checked his watch. 12:45 p.m. If she was anything like Gracie, she'd put the twins down for their nap after lunch. He draped one of his backpack straps over his right shoulder and headed up the paving stones to the front deck.

Not taking any chances on waking her kids, he avoided the doorbell and tapped lightly on the front door. Just like the last time he was there, the air around him smelled like pine sap and cedar shavings. He sucked in a deep breath. Nothing like the clean smell of an Oregon forest.

A moment later, Nora opened the door. Today, she wore a pair of denim leggings with an oversized man's light blue, chambray shirt. Her dark hair was pulled into a ponytail, and she was, again, barefoot. Her face reflected her surprise. "Detective Radhauser. What are you doing here?"

He touched the rim of his cowboy hat. "I have some more questions I need to ask about your friend, Meadow Finney."

She dropped her shoulders and let out an exaggerated sigh. "I've already told you everything I know. I haven't seen Meadow since she was fifteen." She closed her eyes as if there was no other gesture that could possibly convey her frustration.

"I have some new evidence I'd like to show you. May I please come in for a few minutes?"

"No," she said. "I just got the twins down for their nap. These are the only two hours I have when I can get anything done."

Radhauser stared at her, one eyebrow raised. "Here's the thing,

Mrs. Mason. Given your relationship with Meadow and my suspicions about what you do know, I could easily get a warrant and take you into the Ashland police station for questioning. I suspect that would wreck a lot more of that time you have for yourself."

"On what grounds?"

"Failure to cooperate in a murder investigation, for starters."

She tossed her hands, palm-side up in front of her. "You win. But I don't know what else I can tell you."

"We can start with the truth."

"So you're calling me a liar now."

"Not so much lies. More like selective memory and avoidance."

She shrugged and stepped aside so he could enter, then led him into the living room where they sat in the same two chairs in front of the window.

Radhauser set his Stetson on the table and dropped his backpack to the floor beside him.

"I hope you can make this quick," she said.

"A lot will depend on you. First, I'd like to show you a couple things."

He unzipped his pack and removed the evidence bag containing the infant photo and handed it to Nora.

As she studied the photo, he watched her eyes closely, knowing eyes that shifted nervously usually indicated either guilt or that the subject was withholding something.

Nora couldn't hide her recognition. "Oh my God. Where did you get this?"

"It was found in a sealed cardboard box, hidden beneath the floor of a crawl space in Meadow's house. The box also held nine years' worth of report cards, the school letter she'd earned from drama club and a few other sentimental things."

When Nora looked at Radhauser again, her eyes were flooded with tears.

"I already know this is the child Meadow delivered in 1980," he said. "But I'm trying to find out where she gave birth and who helped her. Sunny said if anyone knew, it would be you."

A tear escaped Nora's right eye and raced down her cheek. She wiped it away with her clenched fist. "I promised Meadow I'd take her secret to my grave."

"When she extracted that promise from you, Nora, Meadow couldn't know she'd be murdered two decades later, and your secret could be the key to solving the case and bringing her murderer to justice."

Nora closed her eyes for a long moment. When she finally opened them again, a new determination lit her face. She handed him back the photo. "My mother was a midwife for years. In her spare time, she knitted pink and blue baby caps for the infants she delivered. Every time she was called to make a delivery, she brought one of each color with her."

"Is Meadow's baby wearing one of those caps?"

Her gaze drifted toward her bare feet, one of which was bouncing like she couldn't keep still.

She reminded Radhauser of an electrical line that had snapped during a windstorm. He could almost believe if anyone touched her arm, sparks would shoot out.

"Yes, that's one of my mother's caps."

"Meadow called you when she went into labor, didn't she?"

Her shoulders stiffened, and her eyes clouded with suspicion. She looked at Radhauser like he was holding an explosive device, but answered him anyway. "Meadow was so scared. Her water broke early, and she had no idea what to do, where to go, what to expect."

"Where was she living?"

"On the streets, mostly. Or in a vacant warehouse near Medford with some other homeless kids. It was a terrible place. Dirty and rat-infested. No place to have a baby. There was a shelter within walking distance where she sometimes stayed or got food. I think it was called Mission of Hearts Youth Center. I suggested she go there. But she said they were full and had locked the doors for the night."

"Tell me what happened after she called you."

Nora leaned forward in her chair and put her hands between

her knees. "Meadow wanted me to find a way to get into town so I could help her. She didn't want me to tell my mother. You see, Mom and Sunny were friends, and Meadow didn't want Sunny to find her." Again, she paused and looked over at Radhauser as if she needed his permission to continue.

He nodded for her to go on.

"I used to help my mom out with deliveries, but I'd never even come close to doing one on my own. I told Meadow I didn't know what to do without Mom. She said if I couldn't come alone, not to come at all." Nora's hands fluttered like little pink birds between her knees.

"Did you tell your mother?"

"I kept thinking about Meadow all alone and scared, so yes, I told my mother. And she didn't ask any questions. Mom was really good like that. Never judgmental. She kept her gear loaded in the trunk of her car and went wherever she was needed."

"So, you drove into Medford? Tell me everything you remember about that night."

"It was late. I was still home from school for summer vacation, and it was a really hot August, too hot to sleep. Mom and I were on the porch when the phone rang about 11 p.m. I ran inside to answer." Her eyes lost their focus as she went deeper into the memory.

"The drive from Wildwood was very dark, with only a few lights burning in some of the houses on either side of the road. Meadow met us on a street corner somewhere in Medford where there was a bench for a bus stop. She was clutching her backpack in her lap, bent over in pain, and doing her best not to scream and draw attention to herself. She looked awful like she hadn't bathed or washed her hair in weeks."

Radhauser imagined the fifteen-year-old curled up on the bench, cradling her unborn child and trying to be brave. He thought about Lizzie and prayed she'd never experience anything close to what Meadow had.

"I hadn't seen Meadow since she left." She paused. "It's the truth, I swear to God. It must have been about four months. Even though the night had cooled off a little, she was sweating and had an almost crazed look in her eyes. It was probably from the pain. Before Mom even came to a complete stop, I jumped out of the car. I knew Meadow wouldn't accept my mother's help without some sign from me. I didn't have to think about it, not even for a second. I just opened my arms, and she slipped into them. I told her it was okay. That Mom and I would take her secret to our graves."

"You were a very good friend to her," Radhauser said. "She was lucky to have you."

Nora started to cry in earnest then. "But I'm breaking my promise."

Radhauser waited for a moment while Nora blew her nose. "Neither you nor Meadow ever expected murder."

"Mom planned to bring her back to our house for the delivery, but there wasn't time."

"So what did you do?"

"There was no safe place for us to go, so Mom rented a room at a motel that had air conditioning. We ran a bath for Meadow and got her in, thinking she might be more comfortable and Mom wanted to get her clean before the baby came. We washed her hair. Afterward, we wrapped her in towels and put her on the bed. We delivered the baby there."

"Then what happened?"

"I knew right away there was something wrong with him. I wanted to scream, but my mom shot me a look I understood meant I should be quiet. We'd delivered a deformed baby once before, but I'd never seen anything like this. I understood, even at the time, that Mom didn't want to upset Meadow. My mother cut the umbilical cord. While she delivered the placenta, I cleaned the baby up, dressed him in a diaper and little undershirt my mom brought with her and put on the blue knitted cap. I snapped that Polaroid, just like I always did when I helped Mom with a delivery."

"I need to know what you did with the baby."

"He was crying. We tried to get him to latch on and nurse, but every time he tried to suck, the milk, or I guess it was colostrum, came out his nose, and he started sneezing and coughing like he was choking or something. Meadow freaked."

"Then what?"

"My mom tried some things, like changing the position of the baby, making him more upright. And she held his chin up."

"Did that work?"

"A little better. He went to sleep. My mom took one of the pillows from the bed and tucked it into the laundry basket she used for her supplies and laid the baby on top."

"I need to know what you did with the baby."

"Am I in trouble?"

"Absolutely not."

"My mom talked to Meadow. She explained that babies born with a cleft palate often can't get enough suction to draw milk from a breast or even a regular baby bottle.

She told her the baby was going to need surgery and maybe some special nipples to help him get more nourishment until he was old enough to withstand the operation. She asked Meadow if she planned to keep him."

"And what did Meadow say?"

"She was crying really hard, hiccupping and sobbing like a little kid. Eventually, when she was able to talk, she said it was hard for her to look at him because of the rape. She looked up at my mom with those big blue eyes of hers and asked, 'what if I can't ever love him?' She said she was too young, and she didn't have a place to live yet or any money for his food or clothes. My mom told her she knew a priest who could help. That she'd taken other babies to him from mothers too young to care for them. She assured Meadow that this priest would make sure he got the baby to the hospital where he would get the special care he needed. That the priest always kept the mother's name confidential, and no one would ever have to know. There were places out there where her baby could stay until they found a good home for him."

"Did Meadow agree?"

She gave him a sad smile that didn't reach her eyes. "She did.

So we checked out of the hotel and drove to this church."

"Do you remember the name?" Radhauser was furiously taking notes.

"I don't. Meadow and I waited in the car. But before my mom left with the baby, Meadow tucked her rattle and a little envelope in the basket with him. I don't have any idea what was inside."

"Did you see this priest?"

"No. Like I said, we waited in the car. About ten minutes later, my mom came back, and we drove home. Meadow asked me if she could keep the Polaroid and I gave it to her. She stayed with us for about a week, and then she disappeared, and I never heard from her again."

"But you saw her at a play in Ashland, right?"

"Years later. That's how I knew she'd changed her name. And that she'd made something of her life. It's crazy, isn't it? How many people have dreams that never come true? But somehow, against all the odds, Meadow accomplished hers."

"Did your mother keep any records of the babies she birthed?"

"Yes, but everything was lost, including my mother, when her house burned down two years ago."

"I'm sorry," Radhauser said. "I can tell by the way you talk about her that you loved and respected your mother. Did she even get to meet her grandsons?"

Nora smiled then. "She loved them to pieces for the one year she had with them."

"Thank you for telling me the truth, Nora. It was very brave of you, and knowing these things will help me solve the case."

"How? It was so long ago. More than twenty years. What does that night have to do with Meadow's, I mean Blair's, murder?"

"I'm trying to find this son and see if he has any connection to the case."

"What makes you think he does?"

Radhauser pulled the other evidence bag from his backpack and handed her the rattle. "Because of this. It was with Blair's body. Do you recognize it as the one Blair tucked into the baby's basket?" He could already tell by the troubled look on her face that she did.

"It belonged to Meadow. She always said it was her good luck charm. Whenever she was about to give a performance or take a test, she rubbed it three times, then held it in the palm of her hand and said a little prayer."

"Is it the same rattle she tucked into the baby's basket?"

She grabbed his arm. "Oh, my God. You think her son was the one who killed her, don't you?"

His spine zipped straight. At this point, he didn't have any other viable suspects. He got that feeling that always washed over him when he was zeroing in on a suspect. "He's certainly a person of interest at this point. But do me one more favor. Don't talk about this to anyone, not even your husband, until I've found Meadow's son. Do I have your word?"

"You do." She gave him a big smile, one that lit her eyes this time. "And you already know I'm pretty damn good at keeping my promises. I'm sorry, Detective Radhauser. I should have told you everything from the beginning."

He stood and put out his hand. "I'm sure they'd have to pull out your toenails before you'd cave."

She laughed and shook his hand.

"You still have my card."

"I do."

"Please let me know if you remember anything about the church or the name of the priest who took the baby."

CHAPTER THIRTY-THREE

On the trip back to Ashland, Radhauser found himself thinking about fifteen-year-old Meadow Finney, what she must have gone through on that hot August night in 1980. Not only the pain of childbirth but the anguish and mixed feelings of bringing the child of her rapist into the world. Then, despite the circumstances of his conception, having enough compassion for the child to give him the good luck charm she'd carried her entire life. He wondered what message was in the envelope she'd left for her son.

What courage it must have taken, after all she'd been through, for Meadow to rise above her circumstances and follow her dream of being an actress. His admiration for the woman grew by the minute. And with it, his need to bring her murderer to justice.

With any luck, McBride had uncovered something that might lead them to the priest.

It was 4 p.m. by the time he finished briefing Murphy. Radhauser found McBride at her desk, the telephone propped against her ear, a pen poised in her hand and a yellow legal pad in front of her. "I'm on hold," she said. "Have a seat, I'll be right with you."

He dropped into the chair beside her desk and stretched out his long, jeans-clad legs.

"That's great," she suddenly said, scribbling something on the pad in front of her. When she finished writing, she thanked the person on the other end of the line for their help and hung up. She massaged her right arm at the bicep. "Feels like I've been on the phone for hours." She glanced at her watch. "Could it be because I have been?"

"What did you find out?"

"I checked with Services to Children and Families in both Jackson and Josephine Counties. Jackson had no records of a Meadow Finney or Blair Finney being in the system between 1980 and 1983 when she would have turned eighteen. I'm waiting to hear back from Josephine."

"How could a fifteen-year-old pregnant kid just disappear?"

"Apparently, she somehow made it on the streets. I spoke with a youth shelter in Medford." She paused and checked her notes. "Something called Mission Hearts."

That was close enough to the one Nora mentioned to be authentic.

"Apparently they keep their sign-in sheets. I had them check from the summer of 1980 forward. Meadow Finney was on the roster pretty frequently during the summer through the winter of 1980."

"How about the baby with the cleft lip and palate? Did you learn anything about him?"

"I called St Mary's Hospital in Medford, Ashland Hospital, and Josephine County Hospital in Grants Pass. Saint Mary's was a hit. One of the nurses in the neonatal unit is still working there. Kate Rickert was on duty the night of August 20, 1980, when a priest brought in a baby with both a hair lip and cleft palate."

"Good work, McBride." He told her what he'd learned from Meadow's childhood friend. "I want to talk to Nurse Rickert."

"I figured you would, sir. She's on duty tonight until 6 p.m."

"Do you want to go with me?"

"I'm waiting for a call back from Josephine County. And a couple youth group homes."

"Will you still be here when I get back?"

"I'm not going anywhere," she said.

* * *

At Saint Mary's Hospital, Radhauser entered the lobby and stepped up to the information booth. He swallowed the usual nausea he felt whenever he entered a hospital, introduced himself, and showed his badge to the elderly volunteer behind the desk.

"I'm looking for one of your nurses, Kate Rickert. She works in pediatrics and neonatal."

The volunteer entered the name into her computer, then directed him to the third floor.

Ordinarily, he'd take the stairs, but it had been a long day, he hadn't had any lunch or dinner, and his head was pounding. Radhauser boarded the elevator. When he got off on the third floor, he hurried over to the nurses' station, introduced himself to the young, dark-haired nurse with a nametag that read *Tammy Rawlings, RN* and showed his badge. "I'm here to see Kate Rickert. I called ahead. She's expecting me."

"Kate is with a patient right now, but there's a small waiting room at the end of the hall. I'll send her over as soon as she's free."

Radhauser headed down the hallway past the food carts with their dinner smells of meatloaf, chicken, and broccoli mingling with something chocolate. A young nurse smiled as she hurried by him, pushing a newborn in his plastic bassinet. Like Meadow's baby, he wore a blue knitted cap and was wrapped in a blue receiving blanket.

The waiting room was empty. It held a brown and blue striped loveseat and six side chairs, their seat cushions covered in the same striped fabric, their backs pushed against the opposite wall. Radhauser sat in a chair in front of the window, took off his Stetson, and waited. His pulse pounded in his temples. He searched his backpack for some aspirin and swallowed three tablets. It wasn't easy to get them down without water, but he managed, then absently thumbed through an old copy of *Sports Illustrated*.

Less than five minutes later, the door opened, and a woman he assumed was Nurse Rickert, marched into the room.

Radhauser stood.

Kate was a woman in her fifties, tall and stocky, at least five feet nine, and well put together. Like most of the nurses he'd seen on the floor, she wore a pair of crisp, white slacks with a blue smock covered in pink and blue teddy bears. Her hair was salt and pepper, heavy on the salt, and very short in the back. The sides were longer around her face, and it gave her a softer look. "Sorry to keep you waiting, Detective Radhauser." She introduced herself and offered her right hand.

Radhauser shook it.

"Please, call me Kate." Her handshake was as firm as any man's. An imposing woman, she got right to the point. "I've been expecting you, Detective Radhauser. What can I do for you?"

Radhauser liked her no-nonsense approach. "Okay if we sit down and talk for a moment?"

She took the loveseat.

He pulled one of the side chairs closer, so he was facing her, their knees not more than a foot apart.

"I'm investigating a homicide, trying to find the victim's son—a child I have reason to believe was dropped off at Saint Mary's by a priest in August of 1980, right after his birth."

"I spoke with your partner on the phone briefly. I told her I was on duty that night and remember the incident."

Radhauser took the evidence bag containing the photograph and handed it to Kate. "Is this the child?"

"It's been a long time. But you don't see a lot of infants born with both a cleft lip and cleft palate in this country. I'll never forget this poor little fellow."

"Do you remember the priest who brought him in?"

"I do. But I don't want to get him in any trouble. To tell you the truth, I believe this particular priest was a hero and did the world a great service. This was long before any safe haven laws had been passed. I suspect this priest saved a lot of babies' lives."

"He won't be in any trouble," Radhauser said. "I agree with you, Kate. Dropping an unwanted newborn in a safe place beats some of the other, far less desirable alternatives, that's for sure."

"Do I have your word?"

"You do," Radhauser said and meant it.

"His name is Father Joseph. He was the priest at a small Catholic church in Medford called Saint Pancras. I'd guess he was in his fifties back then, so he may have retired or even died by now."

Radhauser made a note of the name.

"I grew up Catholic," Kate said. "And Saint Pancras is the Patron Saint of Children. It always seemed right somehow that a desperate mother might drop off her baby there."

"When was the last time you saw Father Joseph?"

"It's been years. I don't expect we'll see him anymore now that we have safe haven laws in place."

"Do you know what happened to the baby?"

She got a strange look on her face, then answered his specific question. "Only that we examined the infant thoroughly. He was alert, clean, and well cared for. His umbilicus was neatly cut and tied off. We got some special nipples that would help him swallow more nourishment, and then we released him into the foster care system."

"Did you notify the police?"

"Am I in trouble?"

"No. I'm just wondering."

"We had an unspoken arrangement with Father Joseph to keep these drop-offs confidential. It wouldn't have done any good. We had no identifying information about the parents of any of the infants he left with us."

"Did it happen frequently?"

"Maybe fifteen or so times in the last twenty years."

"Is it possible this child came to see you recently as an adult?"

She stared at him for a long moment like she was assessing his motives. "It is."

He smiled to let her know neither she nor the priest were in jeopardy. "Care to tell me about it?"

"The young man came here, asking questions about two months ago. One of the nurses called me because she knew I've been here for a long time. And I did speak to him."

"Did you confirm that he was left here shortly after his birth?"

"I did. Adoption records had been opened, and I thought he had a right to know."

"What can you tell me about him?"

"He seemed like a very nice young man—tall, clean-cut and

handsome with dark hair and bright blue eyes. He was soft-spoken and very polite. It was obvious he'd had surgery for the cleft lip and palate. His scarring was mostly covered by his mustache."

"How did you know he was the baby from 1980?"

"He had his medical record. The first entry was the examination we gave him here at Saint Mary's. The handwriting was my own. And there was something else."

"Was it a sterling silver rattle? An old one?"

She gave him an odd look like he possessed some kind of magical powers. "I remembered it from that night when he was brought in. It was heartbreaking. Father Joseph had told me his mother was fifteen, and the baby was a product of rape. I found it so touching that she'd leave a rattle and a note for him. I asked the social worker who picked him up to be sure and keep it with him. But I never dreamed it would survive for more than twenty years."

"Did you read the note?"

"Not then. But he brought it with him."

"Would you mind telling me what it said?"

"It was a quote from the poet W.H. Auden. Something about wishes—or weeping for wishes your lives never led. He thought it was an indication of her regret in not being able to keep him."

At last, he was on the right track. But why would that soft-spoken young man want to kill the mother he'd tried so hard to find? "Do you happen to remember his name?"

"I should remember it. I know it started with a C. Carl or Colton. Something like that. Father Joseph filled out all the paperwork for a foundling birth certificate. It's something the state requires within five days of accepting custody. Father Joseph always named the infants. He couldn't bear to write Baby Doe on the paperwork. Who knows if the name he gave that baby actually followed the child? If he was adopted, the child was no doubt given the name of his adoptive parents. What a pity his mother was killed before they had a chance to reconnect. I think she would have been proud of the young man he became."

There must have been something on Radhauser's face that gave his thoughts away. "You can't think he had anything to do with her murder," she said. "He seemed like such a kind young man."

Radhauser didn't respond. After a moment, he thanked her for her time.

She stood and turned to go, then changed her mind. "If you find Father Joseph, tell him Kate from Saint Mary's said hello."

"I'll do that," Radhauser said. He hoped this young man hadn't murdered Blair, too. But what else would explain the rattle glued over her heart?

It was after 6 p.m. when he left the hospital.

Another day had passed without Radhauser finding the killer. But he was getting closer, he could feel it down to the center of his bones.

CHAPTER THIRTY-FOUR

St. Pancras Catholic Church sat on the corner of 10th and Hamilton streets in Medford. It was a small, brick and clapboard structure with a bell tower and one long wing off to the right that probably served as living quarters and offices, maybe held some classrooms as well. Radhauser parked in the asphalt lot. He was uncertain if he should enter by the front door, or try the side door that led into the wing instead.

He opted for the side door.

A nun answered. She wore the traditional black robe and scapular with a headscarf and wimple. None of her hair was showing and if Radhauser had to guess he'd say she was young, barely more than a girl.

"If you're here for confessions, go ahead and enter through the main doors into the sanctuary."

"I'm not here for confession." He introduced himself and showed his badge. "I'm looking for Father Joseph. I have some questions I need to ask him."

Her pale blue eyes widened. "Oh my," she said, obviously flustered. "Father Joseph is no longer with Saint Pancras. But from what everyone says, he's a wonderful man. I'm sure he hasn't done anything wrong. We've had a new priest, Father Michael, for over a year now."

"May I speak with Father Michael?"

"He's taking his confessions this evening so you'll have to wait your turn. Follow me."

She led him around the front of the church and up five steps, then pushed open the carved doors into the sanctuary. They moved

275

silently through the thick, sweet perfume of ancient devotionals, of candle wax and cedar incense—the smell of death and baptism. Flickering on either side of the altar, five rows of votive candles in red glass containers the size of shot glasses had been lit for the dead.

The nun ushered him to one of the front pews. "Just wait here. We work on the honor system. Father Michael will hear you out when it's your turn."

Radhauser drew in a breath and waited until his eyes had adjusted to the dimness. He was surrounded by stained glass windows depicting the life of Jesus. The late day sun streamed through the windows on the west side and painted sections of the polished wooden pews and industrial carpet with rainbow colors.

There was one older woman ahead of him. She sat, head bowed, her gray curls covered in a black lace scarf.

When a man stepped out of the old and elaborately-carved confessional, not much larger than a phone booth, the woman entered. Radhauser moved forward two pews. He now sat adjacent to the structure and waited.

Five minutes later, the woman exited.

He stepped inside.

Through the darkened screen that separated them, he got a glimpse of the young priest.

Radhauser sat on the wooden bench, introduced himself, and stated his business.

"I'm sorry, Detective. But the confessional is a sacred place. Please wait outside. I'll be with you in a few minutes."

Radhauser flushed. He stood, quickly opened the door and returned to his seat in one of the front pews.

A teenaged boy entered the confessional.

About a half hour later, the priest, who appeared to be about thirty years old, joined Radhauser. He was dressed in his black cassock with a purple satin shawl draped around his neck. His skin was very tanned, and his chin sported a black goatee. He wore his dark hair long and shaggy in the style of a man who drove a convertible and patronized Bob Marley concerts.

"I'm terribly sorry, Father. I hope you can forgive my ignorance. I'm not Catholic, and I had no idea what I was supposed to do. The nun who answered the side door must have misunderstood and thought I'd come to confess my sins."

Father Michael's amused smile indented two dimples on either side of his mouth. His dark eyes laughed and put Radhauser instantly at ease. "Surely you have some sins you're in need of confessing, Detective."

"Probably," Radhauser said. "But right now, I'd like to talk to you about your predecessor, Father Joseph."

"A wonderful man and mentor to me. Are you a friend of his?"

"We've never met," Radhauser said. "But I do admire the work he did with unwanted infants."

Father Michael's face went blank for a moment. Maybe his predecessor hadn't mentioned this work to his protégée, or maybe Father Michael was trying to protect the old priest.

Radhauser decided to be careful as he explained his mission. He told Father Michael about Blair's murder. About the child she'd delivered in August 1980. He pretended Father Joseph had counseled her. "I'm looking for the child. He'd be a grown man now. I was hoping Father Joseph might be able to help me find him."

"That could very well be the young man who paid me a visit a little while back."

"How long ago?"

"Five or six weeks. A young man came by. He said he was looking for his birth mother. He was both respectful and polite. Told me that he believed his birth mother had dropped him off at Saint Pancras as an infant—shortly after she gave birth. He said it was August 1980. Is Father Joseph in trouble? Will he be prosecuted for hiding the identity of those mothers from the police?"

"No. That's the furthest thing from my intent."

Father Michael smiled and looked up for an instant as if thanking the heavens for this joyous news. "To me, Father Joseph was a hero, saving all those babies who might have otherwise ended up in dumpsters or worse. Now we've got safe haven laws, but before that, Father Joseph was a beacon of hope."

"I agree with you," Radhauser said. "And I want to talk to Father Joseph to see if he has any idea where I might find this young man. Do you know where Father Joseph lives now? Is he still in Oregon?"

"Father Joseph has retired and lives in a monastery in a little town called Murphy—about seven miles outside of Grants Pass on Route 238. It's a beautiful, secluded place on the Applegate River. I may go there myself when the time comes." He jotted down the address, and phone number then checked his watch. "It's a place that enforces silence after 7 p.m. so you best wait until morning to pay him a visit."

"Before I go, I'd like to ask one more question. Did this young man give you his name?"

"Carter. I remember because I don't think I've ever known anyone with that first name before. But he said he believed Auden was the name his birth mother would have given him had she kept him. When I asked about a last name, he said he'd had so many different foster families that he'd decided to go by only his first name."

Once Radhauser returned to his vehicle, he leaned forward, sank his face into his hands and thought again of the long week's efforts to discover both the killer and his motivation. All the interrogations that had led him nowhere.

He was finally onto something.

That last signature in the memorial book for Tommy Bradshaw. Auden F. Bradshaw. Blair's son believed that would have been his name had she kept him. He would have started life as Auden Finney. When his mother married Franklin Bradshaw, the boy would have been eight years old. If Bradshaw had adopted him, which would have been likely, the kid's name would be Auden Bradshaw.

Auden F. Bradshaw. Had he signed that name in an attempt to reclaim what he believed should be his?

It was all beginning to make some kind of strange sense.

* * *

Early the following morning, Radhauser drove along the asphalt ribbon of road that wound through the Applegate Valley. A thick forest of Douglas fir, red cedar, and big leaf maple engulfed both sides of the highway, surrendering to the occasional farm, vineyard, private home or ranch. The places on the left side of the road backed up to the Applegate River, and their low, rolling banks were lush green during the spring when rain was plentiful.

When he located the monastery, he turned into the driveway, parked and stepped up to the door of a log building. It was surrounded by a semi-circle of a half dozen individual cabins, nestled into the manicured woods, all of them facing the river. If Radhauser had the opportunity to retire to a place like this, he'd do it in a heartbeat.

He knocked.

A middle-aged nun answered.

"I'm Detective Radhauser from the Ashland Police Department. I called ahead to talk with Father Joseph."

She smiled. "Yes, of course. I'm the one you spoke with. Father is expecting you."

The inside of the log house was bright with vaulted ceilings and a wall of windows looking out on the river. The top row of windows was set in multicolored stained glass panels that painted the interior log walls with color. A massive rock fireplace rose at least twenty feet from the hardwood floor to the cedar planked ceiling. The air smelled like breakfast—coffee, bacon, and sausage. A hint of maple syrup.

Radhauser's stomach growled. When was the last time he'd eaten breakfast? "This place is beautiful."

"It is lovely, isn't it? Father Joseph likes to have his morning coffee outside when the weather permits. Follow me." She led him through the big room to the back door and opened it for him, then indicated two bright yellow Adirondack chairs on the grassy banks of the river.

Radhauser hurried across a lawn, as thick and manicured as a golf course, toward a wooded area around the small cabins where he assumed the retired priests lived. He breathed in the thick odor of moss from the river and the perfumed scent from the fields of wildflowers on the adjourning farm. The trees were completely leafed out now and hung like a lime-green canopy over the Adirondack chairs. Steelhead darted in and out of the clear water that flowed down the mountainside and bubbled over the rocks below them. The water lapping on the shore was as comforting as a lullaby.

No wonder the old priest liked to sit here, have his coffee, and watch the day awaken around him.

The former priest of Saint Pancras Catholic Church was in his mid to late seventies. Even though he'd retired, he still wore the black slacks, shirt, and collar of an active priest. He sat, eyes closed, face lifted to the morning sun, his hands folded over the Bible he held in his lap.

Radhauser studied him for a moment. The man's face was smooth and unlined—his skin flawless and almost translucent. He wore his thick, gray hair long on top and neatly parted on the right side. His expression held a tranquility, a peace Radhauser had rarely seen. Perhaps it was something that came from a long life of service.

After lowering himself into the other chair, Radhauser stretched out his jean-clad legs and stared out at the river.

"What can I do for you, Detective Radhauser?"

Having thought the priest was asleep, Radhauser startled, then turned to face Father Joseph. "I hate to interrupt your meditative time, Father. But I'm in the middle of a murder investigation, and your name came up."

Father Joseph raised his thick gray eyebrows and smiled. His eyes were a deep and very clear blue that seemed to be lit from within. He chuckled. "Is that so? A murder investigation? I must be a far more interesting character than I thought."

Radhauser laughed. "You're not a suspect if that's what you're thinking. But I understand you operated a type of safe haven for unwanted babies before we had laws to provide for them."

The priest's smooth fingers tightened around his Bible. "I

280

performed that service whenever I was called upon. Young women who were unable to take care of their infants didn't have a lot of choices back then. I suppose some might think what I did was a crime. Are you here to arrest me?"

"On the contrary," Radhauser said. "If it were up to me, I'd give you a medal for all the young lives you probably saved—both the infants and the mothers."

Father Joseph leaned back in his chair and spoke slowly, his voice soft and low. "God led me to Saint Pancras Catholic Church in Medford, where I served as their priest for more than four decades. Did you know that Saint Pancras was the patron saint of children?"

"I only learned that yesterday."

"When I got the assignment, it seemed destined for me to do what I did. To do what I could to prevent people like you from having to dig dead babies out of landfills, sewers or drug-filled flophouses. No one was happier than I when the safe haven laws were put into effect, and I could retire from the sad business of unwanted babies. But what's that got to do with your murder case?"

"I'm beginning to think it has everything to do with it." Radhauser was as certain as he'd ever been that if he found the son Meadow Finney gave birth to, and Maybelle Crestwell handed over to Father Joseph, he'd find the key to his case.

Father Joseph scooted forward in his chair. "Please. Enlighten me."

Radhauser told the priest what he knew about Meadow Finney, her period of homelessness when she gave birth to a son with a cleft lip and palate. "I also spoke with the daughter of the midwife who delivered him. Nora Mason still lives in Wildwood and told me her mother brought the newborn to Saint Pancras. Do you remember receiving that baby? It would have been sometime in August 1980?"

"That baby boy would be hard for anyone to forget—even an aged priest with a touch of dementia," Father Joseph said. "Maybelle Crestwell was no stranger to me. She'd brought other newborns to

Saint Pancras, but never one that looked like that poor little angel."

"Nora told me Maybelle was killed in a fire about a year ago. All her records were lost in the same blaze."

"I'm sorry to hear that. She was a good woman, and I suspect she'll receive her heavenly rewards." Father Joseph smiled sadly. "I had the utmost respect for the work she did."

"I know you took the baby to Saint Mary's. I've already spoken to one of the nurses there. Kate Rickert. She told me to say hello to you."

"Ah, yes. Right there is another of God's angels."

"What I need to know from you is what you told that young man when he came looking for his birth mother?"

The priest gave him a bemused smile. "And how would you know he came to me?"

"He came to Saint Mary's and talked with Kate. She told me she suggested you might have kept a record of the babies who were entrusted to you."

"Kate is right. I did."

"And did you give this young man Meadow Finney's name?"

"He was quite charming and convincing, too. He said he'd wanted to find her his entire life. He had the baby rattle and note she'd left in the basket with him when he was dropped off at Saint Pancras. He told me he wanted to thank her for having the courage to give birth at fifteen and not have an abortion. That he wanted to set her mind at ease that he'd done all right in life. He'd hoped the two of them might have some kind of relationship."

"But did you give him Meadow's name?"

"I did. I kept a log of names and addresses, if they were available, in case a mother changed her mind. After Oregon passed new laws a couple years ago to give adoptees access to their original birth records, I thought this boy had the right to know the name of his birth mother. That poor kid was never adopted. He actually grew up in the foster care system with several different sets of parents. But unlike so many kids, he managed to graduate from high school and make a life for himself. If I did something wrong in the eyes of the police, I don't think it was wrong in the eyes of the Lord."

"I don't disagree with you," Radhauser said. "I think kids have a right to know where they came from. Do you happen to know the boy's name?"

Father Joseph smiled. "I should. I'm the one who named him. The state required paperwork to be filed within five days of taking custody of an infant. I couldn't bear to call him Baby John Doe. He already had so many strikes against him with the deformities. I carefully chose a name I thought would fit him—maybe even encourage him to make something out of his life."

"May I ask what that name was?"

Again, Father Joseph gave Radhauser a smooth-faced grin. "Patience, son. I was about to tell you. I gave him the name, Carter Heartson. And I filled out his paperwork. Carter because Jimmy Carter was president in 1980 and he was a good and honest man—a Christian man and I respected him. I chose Heartson, not that I'd ever heard the name before, but because of the rattle and the note that young girl left with him. It made me believe that she cared. That he was the son of her heart."

From somewhere in the recesses of his mind, Radhauser heard a wheel turn, a gear unlock, felt something fall like a coin into a slot machine.

The awful truth cut through his mind.

Blair Bradshaw had rejected her son.

A chill ran all the way up Radhauser's back and settled in his neck. Had Carter glued the rattle over his mother's heart because she'd failed to live up to the promise in his name?

That thought led him to the clump of hair that had been cut from the back of Blair Bradshaw's head. Mothers often kept a lock of their baby's hair. Did Carter perform a different sort of ritual? Some bizarre form of a birthing in reverse?

He thanked Father Joseph and hurried back to his car.

Was her long-lost son the visitor who prompted Blair Bradshaw to install that elaborate security system?

One way or another, it was time for Radhauser to find Carter Heartson and pay him a visit.

CHAPTER THIRTY-FIVE

Radhauser drove back to the station, mulling over the new evidence he'd gathered from Kate Rickert and Father Joseph. He had that tight feeling in his chest, a combination of excitement and relief, knowing he was zeroing in on a suspect.

Even though it was a Saturday morning, he found McBride, Officer Corbin, and Chief Murphy studying the crime board in the conference room.

Murphy glanced up when Radhauser entered. "I think you should bring Bradshaw and his lover, Sonya Clifford, back in for questioning. Put them in separate interview rooms. Pit them against each other. Drill them until one of them breaks."

When Radhauser said nothing, Murphy added, "McBride agrees."

She gave her partner a look that said she didn't.

"I'm not bringing them back in," Radhauser said. "Because they're innocent of everything except adultery, and last time I looked, cheating on your spouse wasn't against the law."

"Maybe it should be," Murphy said, obviously thinking about his soon-to-be ex-wife.

Radhauser gave them a quick briefing, putting into words the theory he'd been developing about the son fifteen-year-old Meadow Finney had given up.

"And what makes you so sure?"

"The evidence. The rattle that was once Meadow Finney's good luck charm. The testimony from her best friend, Nora Mason, stating Meadow placed it in the basket that held the baby before he was dropped off at Saint Pancras. The souvenir clump of hair

284

the killer cut from the back of her head. Even the name he signed in the memorial guest book. It all makes sense to me now."

He explained what he meant. "Think of it like a birthing in reverse. Even his name, Carter Heartson played into his scenario. Carter went through his life, believing his mother loved him, gave him up because she had to. That he was, indeed, the son of her heart. That's the reason he glued the rattle over her left breast—a way to remind her of the promise she'd made. I suspect he visited her and she rejected him, even went so far as to install a security system to keep him away."

"I'll check for a sheet and DMV records. See if we can get a hit on a Carter Heartson," McBride said, then hurried from the room.

Less than five minutes later, McBride returned with a photo. She tacked it onto the board. "He lives in an apartment in Ashland and works for *Custom Decorators* in Medford as a painter and wallpaper hanger."

Carter probably kept his tools in his vehicle. If they could find them, they'd have their murder weapon. With any luck, Blair Bradshaw's DNA would be on Carter's cutting tool.

In the photograph, Carter Heartson was a good-looking young man with thick, dark hair, piercing blue eyes, and a mustache. He bore no resemblance to the baby photo Radhauser had been carrying around.

"What are you waiting for?" Murphy said. "Get yourselves search and arrest warrants and go pick the bastard up."

* * *

It was nearly 4 p.m. by the time Radhauser had the warrants. He wanted to do this right, wanted to wrap up the case and hand it over to the DA with all the loose ends tied up, all the evidence obtained legally. Corbin and McBride took the search warrant for Heartson's vehicle and followed Radhauser in Corbin's cruiser.

Carter Heartson lived in a modest apartment complex near the corner of Iowa and Avery streets. A white paneled van was parked in the lot with the words Custom Decorators painted in blue letters on the sides.

Radhauser parked, got out of his vehicle, then stepped over to Corbin's car and gave them directions to search the van for a cutting utensil and anything else that might be connected to the case. He instructed them to use luminol to check for blood on the seats and carpet.

In the meantime, Radhauser searched for Building C, Apartment 4. He found it easily, climbed the two sets of stairs, and knocked on the door.

Silence followed.

He knocked harder, leaned in a little closer, and heard the creak of footsteps headed toward the door. The creaking sound stopped.

Radhauser knocked again.

A handsome young man, with dark hair, neatly parted and combed to one side, bright blue eyes and a black mustache drew the chain from its cradle and opened the door. He was dressed in dark brown slacks with a pale blue, button-down oxford shirt, tucked in at the waist and a pair of polished loafers. He could have easily passed for a preppy Harvard student.

"I'm looking for Carter Heartson." Radhauser introduced himself and showed his badge. If Carter was the killer, he now knew his game was up.

"That would be me," the man said.

Radhauser waited for Carter to inquire about the nature of the visit, but he said nothing and made no effort to step aside so the detective could enter.

"May I come inside?"

"I'm kind of busy right now. Any possibility you could come back later?"

Right, I'll leave and give you time to pack up and disappear. "I'm afraid that won't be possible." He kept his hand casually by his right hip where his Glock waited in its holster.

Carter stepped to one side so Radhauser could enter.

The living room smelled like lemon furniture polish and was in the shape of an L. It was spacious and modestly furnished with a scuffed leather sectional sofa and two end tables. The carpet held wheel and brush marks like it had been recently vacuumed. A round maple table with four chairs pushed beneath it occupied the shorter section of the L. Everything in the room was neat.

The books in the two bookshelves adjacent to the sofa were lined up perfectly as if a ruler had been used to justify each binding. The magazines on the coffee table were precisely stacked so that the name of each was underlined by the edge of the one placed on top of it, along with a fat candle that had never been lit and an expensive-looking, bronze statue of a giraffe with a marble base.

Carter must have noticed Radhauser admiring it, or he was trying to deflect attention away from the purpose of the visit.

"I found that giraffe at a little gallery on Main Street. They let me make payments on it until I finally paid it off. The giraffe is my spirit animal." He lifted his chin, his chest thrust forward a little. "It helps me rise above earthly things." There was a calmness about him that seemed practiced.

Radhauser wasn't sure how to respond to Carter's pride, so he said nothing.

A book of Richard Yates short stories lay open and face down on the coffee table. Had Carter been reading when Radhauser knocked? From all appearances, he took good care of his possessions. The kind of man who would polish a sterling silver rattle that had once belonged to his birth mother.

On the wall above the long side of the rust-colored sectional, six 18x30 inch posters hung, matted and framed, at eye level with only an inch or so between the frames. All of them were women in ornate costumes playing starring roles in one of Shakespeare's plays. Their character names and production were written in block letters at the bottom of the poster. Cordelia from *King Lear*, Portia from *The Merchant of Venice*, Lady Macbeth, Ophelia from *Hamlet*, and Desdemona from *Othello*.

It took a moment for Radhauser to realize all of the women in the posters were Blair Bradshaw. He stopped breathing; his heart seemed to freeze in his chest for a moment. When it began to beat again, he took a breath and looked around the room.

A dressmaker's form in the corner featured an Elizabethan costume. His gaze shifted to the posters. This was the costume

Blair had worn when she'd played Cordelia—a floor-length beige dress with cream flowers woven into the richly-textured fabric. It was trimmed in gold along the neck and cuffs of the puffy sleeves. The costume included a short, cream-colored velvet cape, lined in gold satin and clasped in the front with an ornate gold button.

Again, Carter responded before Radhauser had formed his question.

"The Shakespeare Theater often sells costumes they no longer use. I bought it from them." He paused and appeared to ponder something. "I guess about six months ago. Magnificent, isn't it?"

If what Father Joseph had told Radhauser was correct, Carter didn't know Blair was his birth mother six months ago. The man had some pretty eclectic tastes. A Shakespearean costume, a bronze giraffe, and a collection of Richard Yates' short stories. Radhauser had never heard of the writer, but it wasn't as if he knew all that much about literature.

After removing his Stetson, Radhauser took a seat on the sofa. "How long have you been collecting things about her?"

Carter dragged a chair over from the dining room and sat, facing the detective. "About a year now. When I first saw Blair Bradshaw as Ophelia in *Hamlet*, I knew she was someone to watch. I figured if I lived long enough, these things would grow in value."

Radhauser decided to take a chance. "Did you know back then she was your birth mother?"

Carter beamed and couldn't seem to contain the grin that spread across his face. "No, but I was enormously attracted to her from the first time I saw her in a play—not in any weird sexual way, just some deep connection I felt, right here." He paused and put both hands over his heart. "So, I started collecting."

"I guess you're wondering why I'm here," Radhauser said.

Again, his face held no surprise. "I'm pretty sure I know why you're here, Detective."

Radhauser couldn't remember ever having a more cooperative suspect. "I want to talk to you about a case I'm investigating."

He looked Radhauser directly in the eyes, his demeanor perfectly calm. "It's okay to say it. You're here about Blair Bradshaw's murder."

"I understand you were trying to find her."

For a moment, he said nothing. Radhauser could tell Carter was trying to decide just how truthful he wanted to be.

"At first, I was trying to find a woman named Meadow Finney," he finally said. "But that search eventually led to Blair Bradshaw." There was an aura of something odd that came off him. It was in his demeanor, his tone of voice, and his precise words—the matter-of-fact way he delivered them. "Essentially, she didn't want to be found." He paused and shrugged. "I suppose it was a shock, me turning up out of the blue the way I did."

"How did she react?"

He raised his eyebrows, and something in his blue eyes turned dark. "She rejected me."

"Did you leave?"

He hung his head, his gaze on the floor. "Of course."

"And was that the end of it?"

Carter jolted slightly, and he lifted his head to look at Radhauser, his eyebrows raised even higher. "I think you already know it wasn't." He used his feet to inch his chair back—further away from the detective.

Radhauser stood. "I'd like to take you into the station for questioning. In the meantime, some officers have a search warrant for your house and any vehicles you drive."

"I'm happy to go with you and answer any questions I can. I intend to cooperate and provide you with whatever you need, Detective." Carter stumbled to his feet, held his hands out in front of him like he was expecting to be handcuffed. He shook his head back and forth. "I had to."

"Had to what?" Radhauser could feel the electricity in the air.

"You don't understand," Carter said. "How could you?"

"Then tell me."

Carter licked his lips and seemed to study the sky outside the apartment window. "I thought she'd be happy. Proud of me... but when I..." Beads of perspiration broke out on his forehead. "Pleaded. Please...just give me a chance..." He shivered and let out a moan as if he were in pain.

Radhauser reached for his gun. But when he realized Carter was having a flashback, and something that bordered on a panic attack, he eased up.

It happened so fast that Radhauser wasn't certain he'd actually caught it, but he thought he saw the flash of white-hot rage in Carter's eyes, just before he picked up the bronze statue of the giraffe, probably intending to bash Radhauser over the head.

He took a quick step to the left and grabbed Carter's arm. "Put it down. You don't want to add assaulting an officer onto your charges, son."

When he lowered the giraffe back onto the coffee table, Radhauser grabbed Carter's wrists, snapped them behind his back, and cuffed him.

CHAPTER THIRTY-SIX

When Radhauser stepped into the interrogation room, Carter was holding his face in his hands like someone with a toothache. His black hair spilled out between his fingers, and his elbows rested on the table.

He looked up, his face covered with tears. "I'm sorry, Detective Radhauser. I don't know what got into me."

"I'm glad I stopped you before we had to add to your charges. We're placing you under arrest for the murder of Blair Bradshaw. You have the right to remain silent. Anything you do say can and will be held against you in a court of law. You have the right to an attorney. If you can't afford one, the state will provide one for you."

"I don't make a lot of money. I've spent what extra I have on Blair Bradshaw memorabilia." He spit out the name rapidly as if it stung his mouth.

"Are you ready to tell me what happened?"

Carter stared at Radhauser for a long moment, new puddles of tears in his eyes. "It's really hard for me to talk about her. Would it be okay if I wrote it out for you? Like you sometimes see on television."

A written confession was even better than a verbal one. Radhauser slipped a yellow legal pad across the table. "Tap on the door when you're finished."

* * *

Here you sit in police custody. And you can't believe you feel so emotional you can't even speak. But now that you've been apprehended, you must find a way to tell the whole, pitiful story. The last thing you want is to dissolve into another puddle of tears in front of Detective Radhauser. You've had enough humiliation to last a lifetime.

Where do you begin?

Your name is Carter Heartson. You'll be twenty-one years old in August, born in 1980. You weren't what anyone would call a pretty baby with what looked like the entrance to a twisted and disgusting cave beneath your nostrils, separating the two halves of your top lip.

It isn't hard to imagine why no one wanted to adopt you. After being in and out of foster homes most of your early childhood, the Rescue The Children charity finally took you under its wing and provided the surgery needed to correct the unilateral cleft lip and palate. You were eight-years-old when the operation took place, but not before a lot of damage was already done to your self-esteem. All the kids made fun of you. Even some of your foster parents called you freak face. You were never in any one home for more than two years. You could go on and on about the things that happened to you at the hands of your beloved foster fathers and mothers—but it's a common tale, and everyone has heard it all before.

When you were still pretty small, the doctors made some plate-like device to close the opening in the roof of your mouth that allowed food and drink to go up into your nose. But it didn't help that much. You still had trouble eating, speaking, and even breathing. Suffering from constant ear infections, you sometimes couldn't hear the teachers at school—the source of more ridicule.

The other kids mimicked the nasal way you talked, making fun of you constantly. No one ever picked you to be on their baseball or basketball teams. And no one ever walked home from school with you or sat beside you in the cafeteria or on the school bus. You were a social outcast.

Of course, you must be fair. Between the ages of ten and twelve, a bright light shone upon your childhood. An old man, the father of your foster mother, read Shakespeare to you every night—the sonnets, the tragedies, and the comedies. He had a deep and resonating voice, like that actor Morgan Freeman, and when he read, he changed his voice, depending on the part. Bedtime was magical, and your favorite part of the day. When that old man died, that light was extinguished.

But you never lost your love of Shakespeare and classical literature. To this day, there is nothing you'd rather do than disappear into a great book.

As soon as you turned eighteen, you were removed from the foster care system and got a job at the mini mart. You signed up for classes at Rogue Community College where you met a man who owned Custom Decorators, a paint and wallpaper company in Medford. He thought you were smart and creative and offered you a job. You're pretty darn good at what you do now. You can match the most complicated patterns and hang wallpaper with the best of them. You're good at painting too. But why wouldn't you be? In foster care, if you're neat, make your bed, and clean up after yourself, you get more food and fewer beatings. On a paint job, you can cut in around windows and doors without even using tape. Your boss gets a lot of compliments on your work. Some customers ask for you by name now. While you're not a heart surgeon or a lawyer, you take pride in your work.

But being good wasn't enough. What you wanted more than anything, was to find your birth mother. It became a ruling passion, and you couldn't think of anything else. Even though your life was far from easy growing up, you never thought of her as a woman who didn't want you because you were deformed. You created an entire fairy tale. Of course, she didn't want to give you up and cried for days on end.

Abortion had been legalized by 1980, and she could have easily put an end to you before you even began, but she didn't. In your eyes, she was a princess with a very domineering father who insisted she let you go. She loved you and wanted you more than anything, but her parents convinced her she was just a child herself. That she was doing the right thing—giving you a better life with grownups for parents. You know, that bullshit stuff all throwaway kids must tell themselves in order to survive.

But you were different. You had a couple other reasons to think she might have really cared for you. A sterling silver baby rattle, tiny enough to fit into a newborn's fist and engraved with words about a mother's love. That baby rattle somehow followed you from foster home to foster home, and you cherished it, always kept it in a safe place no matter where you were or how horrible your living conditions. For all your life, you planned to show it to your mother—to let her know how much her parting gift had mattered to you.

And you also had a message from her written on a little card and placed in an envelope inside the basket she left you in. The note, you thought, addressed you as Auden. The message said, "O weep, child weep, o weep away the stain…Weep for the lives your wishes never led." So, of course, you grew up believing that she cared. That you were one of those wishes her life never led. Why else would she have left that particular message and called you by that unusual name, Auden? It sounded smart, like a CEO of some big company, the President of the United States, or even the poet who made it famous.

Not that you didn't like your given name, Carter Heartson. You always imagined how much she must have loved you to think of you as the son of her heart—to give you that last name as a constant reminder.

Well, it took you a while, and quite a bit of work, but you finally found her. You didn't have a lot to go on. But from your medical records, you knew you'd been left at Saint Pancras Catholic Church.

So, you began to search. You found out who the priest had been in 1980—some old guy named Father Joseph. And he remembered you. Of course, everyone would remember a baby with a face like yours. He told you that your mother was a fifteen-year-old homeless girl and in no way able to care for herself, let alone a baby with special needs. He said he often worked at a shelter for teens back then, Mission of Hearts. Meadow Finney was a regular on cold evenings.

You were ecstatic. How many Finneys could there be in southern Oregon? Eventually, you found your grandmother—a washed-out, drug-addled hippy—out in the boonies in Wildwood. She admitted she at least suspected her daughter, Meadowlark, had a child in 1980. You have no patience for druggies—too many of your foster parents fell into that category. Sunflower Finney didn't know where her daughter was but thought she'd changed her name to something artsy and married a big-shot lawyer. After that, it wasn't too hard to find Blair Bradshaw.

But imagine your shock when you discovered she was the Blair

Bradshaw, the woman you'd been obsessed with from the moment you'd first saw her on stage in the Elizabethan Theater. What were the chances? You were so excited. You'd been right all along. Your birth mother was a princess.

You made a scrapbook of every photo you had of yourself. Not that you had a lot. And not that many of them were pretty. But you thought she might like to see how you looked at various stages of your life. You included letters you'd written to her as a child and brought along the baby rattle. According to the foster mother who gave it to you when you were eight, the rattle was a love gift from your birth mother. You wanted Blair to know you'd kept it all these years. Before seeing her, you considered calling on the phone to give her some warning, but then decided, screw it. You were confident she'd be happy to see you no matter when you appeared.

By now you had a mustache that mostly covered the scars above your top lip and to most people you looked pretty damn normal. It's really crazy, though. Whenever you look in the mirror, you still see that freak face. You have to squint hard to make yourself believe you finally look like a regular person.

Before going to see her, you saved up your money, visited a stylist to get your hair cut, and even had it blown dry. You bought new slacks and a blue oxford shirt that made your eyes look even bluer. And you bought a new pair of shoes.

You're six feet two inches tall, with black hair and you're in pretty good shape because of the manual labor you do. People say you look like a young Tom Selleck back when he was doing Magnum PI. Personally, you didn't think you'd ever looked as good as you did when you rang the doorbell of her house in Ashland.

The house was huge, and it looked like a mansion to you—stone pillars in the front and two stories high. A little boy answered the door. You figured he must be your baby brother and you were all ready to toss a baseball to him, take him fishing, or on a camping trip into the mountains. He was a cute kid, about ten or eleven, with good manners and a perfect mouth and nose. It's a crazy thing, but your fantasy life with your birth mother always included a little brother or sister.

He said his name was Tommy and he wanted to know how he could help you. So you asked him if his mother was Blair Bradshaw. He said that she was. And you said would it be okay if you spoke to her for a minute. He gave you a big smile—his teeth were straight and white as a movie star—and his hair was the color of sand. But his eyes were as blue as yours. He invited you inside, all trusting and everything, then said sure, he'd go get her.

You could barely contain your excitement. Your mother was about to meet the son of her heart.

Less than a minute later, there she was. At first, you could barely speak. She was even more beautiful in person than in all the posters you'd collected from her starring roles. Blair was tall and slender with long legs and silky blonde hair. A real lady, you thought. You didn't know what you expected. Or maybe you did. Maybe you expected her to react like in those reunion shows on Oprah where the birth mother and her long-lost child sob into each other's arms. But that's not exactly the way it went down.

You said, "My name is Carter Heartson."

Now, of course, you know that name was given to you by Father Joseph from Saint Pancras Church and not your mother. Father had probably felt sorry for the little baby John Doe with the freaky face.

But that day, you waited for Blair's face to register recognition, for her to remember the name she'd given you and throw her arms around you. When recognition didn't come, you tried to help her along and said you thought she was your birth mother. You gave her the date and time of your birth and showed her the rattle.

Instead of lighting up with joy, her face turned gray, and she ushered you out of that house and back onto the front porch so fast you didn't know what happened. Of course, she didn't want her little boy, the perfect one she decided to keep, to know he had a big brother who painted rooms and hung wallpaper in rich people's houses—houses like their own. If Tommy knew about you, he'd know his mother got pregnant at fourteen.

Blair claimed she hadn't agreed to meet with you and that she had privacy rights. No one in her family knew you existed—not her husband and not the little prince who'd opened the door. You said maybe you could move slowly, just have lunch together, meet for coffee now and then, get to know each other a little bit—and then maybe she could tell her husband and your baby brother.

"Look," she said. "I'm happy you had plastic surgery and that you've grown up to be a productive and nice-looking young man, but you have to understand, I was raped, and every time I look at you, I..."

That's what she said, but you knew what she meant. She wanted you out of there. And she didn't want you to ever come back. Since she'd been raped, she probably wasn't surprised you looked like some kind of infant monster. You know she would have had an abortion if she'd had any idea how to go about getting the money. Instead, she'd dumped you at Saint Pancras like the piece of unwanted garbage you were to her.

She all but kicked you off her property. You tried to give her the album and the baby rattle, but she wouldn't take either of them. You understood she didn't want anything to remind her of the little freak face she'd given birth to in 1980.

You asked her to please answer one question and to tell the truth. Did she ever hold you?

She didn't hesitate. The word 'never' rung in your ears for minutes after she uttered it. You left, feeling worse than you'd ever felt in your whole miserable life.

About four weeks later, when you read in the paper about the accident that killed the little prince, you felt so sad. Your baby brother was dead. You were just as upset as you'd been when she rejected you. As hurt and angry as you felt, you didn't want to see her suffer. You thought maybe you could help—or maybe she might reconsider being part of your life now that Tommy was gone. You know it sounds naïve and unrealistic, but you thought you might help fill the void in her life.

On the night of the memorial, you parked your van on a side street and walked through the woods to a place as close as you dared. You stood, out of sight, away from everyone else and watched her sob and fall to her knees in front of a memorial all lit with candles and crammed with flowers and stuffed animals.

After everyone left and the caterers cleaned up the woods around the treehouse—which by the way was nicer than any place you'd ever lived—Blair hung around. She sat on the creek bank behind the treehouse and cried while drinking wine straight from one of the bottles the caterers left. You stood, watching for a moment, while she injected something into her arm. Feeling sorry for her, you approached. When she spotted you, she insisted you leave, threatened to phone the police if you didn't.

You told her you only wanted to help. She shouted at you that nothing could help her now, especially not you. And when she said those words, you heard the chants of the schoolkids again as if you were back on the playground. Freak face. Freak face. Who wants to play with a freak face?

Something inside you snapped. Mothers are supposed to love their children, no matter what. You crept back to your van and got your toolbox and the latex gloves you often wore to keep your hands clean of paint and wallpaper paste. You removed the cutting tool you used for trimming and the little tubes of super glue you resorted to when a stubborn corner wouldn't stick. You slipped a new straight-edge razor blade into place. It needed to be sharp.

Your mother was an easy target—so drunk she was nearly passed out behind the treehouse when you returned. You lifted her skirt and slashed both sides of her groin. You didn't know why—maybe you were trying to get as close as you could to some primal memory of passing through her birth canal. The power of the blood surprised you. Two fountains gushing. You were so angry inside that you wanted there to be a few sexual overtones. After all, if she was telling the truth and you really were the son of a rapist, what would anyone expect?

You told yourself you didn't regret what you'd done, but you weren't completely honest. Mostly because Blair seemed small, childlike, and broken. There was blood all over the place, even on your face. Perhaps it was remorse you felt as you dragged her by the wrists to the memorial. Maybe that's why you arranged her so carefully. Just in case, as some people believe, the soul lingers near its body for a while, you didn't want her to be humiliated or embarrassed when they found her. You tried to make her look decent, pulled her skirt down, ran a comb through her hair, and crossed her arms over her chest. You placed her in the shrine, hoping those mementos left by Tommy's friends would lead her soul to wherever his had gone.

You decided to give her the rattle. But you wanted—no, you needed—it to mean something, so you superglued it to her left breast—right over her heart. You figured Blair could carry that rattle through eternity the way you'd carried it through life. You used the razor to hack off a clump of her hair—even though you were sure she hadn't saved a lock of your infant hair the way so many mothers do.

It was after midnight by the time you got out of there and back to your apartment. You washed your bloody clothes, even your Converse high-tops, in the washing machine in the basement, knowing the laundry room would be empty at 1 a.m. And then, you took a shower and went to bed.

If no one in Blair Bradshaw's world knew you existed, you weren't too worried about the police. You tried to figure out how you felt. You'd just murdered your own mother. But to tell the truth, at that moment, you felt nothing.

* * *

After McBride and Corbin found the wallpaper cutting tool and a pair of Converse sneakers that matched the print on the rock in the creek, McBride took Carter over to Ashland Holding to be booked, then sent to Jackson County Jail. Though he was certain the blood would be a match for Blair Bradshaw, Radhauser sent the shoes and blade to the forensics lab.

Radhauser closed his door and sat alone in his office. He read Carter's account of what happened, then closed his eyes, tried to relax, but felt only a steady tightening of the spring inside his chest. The interrogation was over. Blair Bradshaw's murder solved. Case closed. Then why were the walls of his office closing in on him? Why did it seem harder to draw a breath?

He rose, paced, opened the blinds, and gazed out the window into the Plaza as shoppers darted in and out of the stores and restaurant. After a few moments, he closed the blinds again. In his mind, he saw Blair's body lying in Tommy's memorial and then Carter standing on the steps of the Bradshaw house, begging her to listen, wanting so much for her to care about him. It wasn't hard to imagine the life Carter Heartson had lived. It was impossible not to feel some sympathy for the young man who only wanted to be accepted and loved. It was odd the way he'd written his confession as if he were an outsider watching someone else do the unthinkable.

Radhauser's discontent propelled him down the hallway and out of the building onto the Plaza. Carter's words and the images they painted circled in his mind and before realizing where he was headed, he'd walked up Main Street and stood in front of the Office of Public Defense. He stepped inside.

"Detective Radhauser," Doris, the administrative assistant said. "It's been a while. What can we do for you?"

"I'd like to see Kendra Palmer if she's around." Kendra was a brilliant young public defender, a Harvard graduate, daughter of a world-renowned criminal defense attorney. Unlike her famous father, her main goal in life was to serve, not make a lot of money. She'd helped him free a client he'd been forced to arrest, but knew was innocent.

Doris led him down the familiar hallway.

When she spotted Radhauser, Kendra stood, a big smile spreading over her face. "Hey, cowboy. Long time no see. What have you been up to?"

Kendra looked stunning, her pale skin glowing from the inside. She wore a rust-colored skirt and jacket with a pale-yellow blouse. Her blond hair was cut a little shorter than the last time he'd seen her, falling just above her shoulders.

He gave her a hug and dropped into the metal chair beside her desk and stretched out his legs. "I need a favor." He told her about Carter Heartson.

Her brow furrowed. "But it sounds like you have a confession and a murder weapon. Does he plan to plead guilty?"

"The DA will go for aggravated murder. Life in prison or maybe even the death penalty. I'm hoping you can get the charges reduced to maybe second degree." He told her what he knew about Carter's history, then handed Kendra a copy of the statement Heartson had written.

She studied Radhauser for a moment, her blue eyes darkening. "I see you've got compassion for him, but I suspect the jury will see the murder as premeditated. He may not have gone to the memorial planning to kill her, but he had to return to his van to retrieve the weapon."

"Please. When you read his entire statement, I suspect you'll want to handle the case. Talk to him. Maybe you can get him life or even have the charge reduced. You might even consider extreme emotional disturbance."

She looked him directly in the eyes. "This matters to you, doesn't it?"

He nodded.

"I'll do what I can."

Radhauser smiled. "I can't ask for more than that."

* * *

Three months later

Radhauser arrived at the ten-year-old division Little League championship game late. He zigzagged between lawn chairs holding cheering parents and ran along the fence lines of the recently groomed fields until he found number five.

Holden's team was last up to bat. The score was tied five-all, and it was the final inning.

The bleachers were jammed full of parents wearing red T-shirts and waving banners. Radhauser stood a little left of the catcher's mound, his back against a big leaf maple tree.

Holden was next at bat. He wore his red and white uniform and what looked like a new pair of bright red baseball cleats. He'd grown a few inches during the last few months, and he stood tall and proud as he took a few practice swings in the batter's circle.

Radhauser, who'd played a little baseball himself, was impressed by the boy's stance. His concentration on the ball. There was one out and no one on the bases.

Holden stepped up to the plate and assumed the stance.

"Level swing, Holden," the coach said.

The first pitch was a fastball.

Holden let it go.

The umpire called it a strike, though from Radhauser's angle, the call was questionable.

The second pitch was a curveball, and Holden swung, level and hard. It made that smacking sound that told Radhauser Holden had hit it out of the park.

The crowd went wild. Everyone in the bleachers stood, pumping their fists and shouting, "Go, Holden. Go. Go."

Holden ran the bases like he was being chased by a monster. As he rounded third, he scanned the bleachers until he found Carl Houseman. He was standing next to Sean Patterson, and the two of them had linked hands and lifted them into the air. "That's our boy…that's our boy," they chanted.

Radhauser returned his gaze to Holden. The detective had never seen such a smile. It was like the sun had just come out on that little boy's face. And even though there was no one in the outfield or infield about to throw the ball and make the out, no need for him to do it, Holden Ryan Patterson dropped to his butt and slid the final four yards safely into home.

ABOUT SUSAN CLAYTON-GOLDNER

Susan Clayton-Goldner was born in New Castle, Delaware and grew up with four brothers along the banks of the Delaware River. She is a graduate of the University of Arizona's Creative Writing Program and has been writing most of her life. Her novels have been finalists for The Hemingway Award, the Heeken Foundation Fellowship, the Writers Foundation and the Publishing On-line Contest. Susan won the National Writers' Association Novel Award twice for unpublished novels and her poetry was nominated for a Pushcart Prize.

Her work has appeared in numerous literary journals and anthologies, including Animals as Teachers and Healers, published by Ballantine Books, Our Mothers/Ourselves, by the Greenwood Publishing Group, The Hawaii Pacific Review-Best of a Decade, and New Millennium Writings. A collection of her poems, A Question of Mortality was released in 2014 by Wellstone Press. Prior to writing full time, Susan worked as the Director of Corporate Relations for University Medical Center in Tucson, Arizona.

Susan shares a life in Grants Pass, Oregon with her husband, Andreas, her fictional characters, and more books than one person could count.

FIND SUSAN ONLINE

Website
www.susanclaytongoldner.com

Facebook
www.facebook.com/susan.claytongoldner

Twitter
twitter.com/SusanCGoldner

Blog
susanclaytongoldner.com/my-blog---writing-the-life.html

Tirgearr Publishing
www.tirpub.com/scgoldner

BOOKS BY SUSAN CLAYTON-GOLDNER

WINSTON RADHAUSER SERIES

REDEMPTION LAKE, #1
Released: May 2017
ISBN: 9781370712939

Tucson, Arizona–Detective Winston Radhauser knows eighteen-year-old Matt Garrison is hiding something. When his best friend's mother, Crystal, is murdered, the investigation focuses on Matt's father, but Matt knows he's innocent. Devastated and bent on self-destruction, Matt heads for the lake where his cousin died—the only place he believes can truly free him. Are some secrets better left buried?

WHEN TIME IS A RIVER, #2
Released: September 2017
ISBN: 9781370576975

Someone is stalking 2 year old Emily Michaelson in Lithia Park playground as she plays with her 18 year old half sister, Brandy. Not long after Emily's disappearance, Detective Radhauser finds her rainbow-colored sneakers in Ashland Creek, their laces tied together in double knots. He insists Brandy stay out of the investigation, but she's obsessed with finding her little sister.

A RIVER OF SILENCE
Released: January 2018
ISBN: 9781370326501

The past always finds us—Caleb Bryce frantically gives CPR to 19-month-old Skyler Sterling. Less than an hour later, she's is dead. The ME calls it murder and the entire town of Ashland is outraged. The police captain is anxious to make an arrest. Neither Det. Winston Radhauser nor Bryce's young public defender believe he's guilty. Radhauser will fight for justice, even if it means losing his job.

RIVER OF SHAME
Released: September 2018
ISBN: 9780463177020

Something evil has taken root in Ashland, Oregon. And with it, an uneasy feeling sweeps down on Det. Winston Radhauser. If someone doesn't intervene, that evil will continue to multiply until the unthinkable happens. When a high school kid is branded with a homophobic slur and is hospitalized, Radhauser will do whatever it takes to find the perpetrators and restore his town's sense of safety.

LAKE OF THE DEAD
Release: January 2019

When Parker Collins goes missing, girlfriend, Rishima, files a missing person's report, adamant something is wrong. Radhauser agrees to investigate, soon discovering something doesn't sit right with him. Elderly neighbor, Homer "Sully" Sullivan, finds a body floating in the lake near his cottage. Could it be the missing student? Will this missing person's case become a murder investigation?

ADDITIONAL BOOKS BY SUSAN

A BEND IN THE WILLOW
Released: January 2017
ISBN: 9781370816842

In 1965, Robin Lee Carter sets a fire that kills her rapist, then disappears, reinventing herself as Catherine Henry. In 1985, when her 5-year-old son, Michael, is diagnosed with a chemotherapy-resistant leukemia, she must return to Willowood and seek out the now 19-year-old son she gave up for adoption. Is she willing to risk everything, including her life, to save her dying son?

TORMENTED
Released: May 2018
ISBN: 9781370241750

Fr. Anthony's devotion to God begins to unravel the moment Rita Wittier steps inside his church and struggles to control his feelings. After 60 Minutes' special on the Shepherd Academy, a school for disadvantaged children, Anthony becomes a national hero. But he can't get Rita out of his mind. Just hours after telling her how he feels, she's found dead in her car. Is it suicide, or is it murder?

MISSING PIECES
Released: April 2019

Lillianna Ferguson has spent the last twenty years pretending her father is dead. Her brother, Greg, begs her to come home to care for their father, Calvin Miller, a disabled WWII veteran. When did he ever take care of her? But the surgeon at won't repair the aneurysm without first amputating their father's infected leg. Will she leave her safe life and re-enter the minefield of her childhood?

Manufactured by Amazon.ca
Bolton, ON

20383170R00173